To Africa in Love

A novel by Jim Harries, author of *African Heartbeat and A Vulnerable Fool.*

Jim Harries

WIPF & STOCK · Eugene, Oregon

Wipf and Stock Publishers
199 W 8th Ave, Suite 3
Eugene, OR 97401

To Africa in Love
By Harries, Jim
Copyright©2019 Apostolos
ISBN 13: 978-1-5326-9608-4
Publication date 7/7/2019
Previously published by Apostolos, 2019

Dedicated to my sister, Veronica, and family.

Biography

Jim Harries, the author, tells us a true-to-life story of post-modern commitment and adventure. Jim set out to teach agriculture until his experiences revealed the centrality of the gospel. Born in Newbury, Berkshire, UK, he studied in the West Midlands, London, and Norwich, finishing up with a PhD in theology. Jim has lived in East Africa for thirty years to date.

CONTENTS

CHAPTER 1: A CRUSH

"I want to marry Philo," Mel said.

"But is he going to be interested in you?" Julie replied.

"A man like that needs someone to look after him."

"You are right, of course."

Julie was directing a program of Bible studies for women in Scotland. It was called 'Joseph's wives.' Mel, actually Melanie but people called her Mel, was one of the women who had joined the program. Julie had long blond hair that draped over her shoulders and remained very attractive, although the creases appearing at the corner of her eyes betrayed the fact that she had turned forty. She and her husband had two 'miracle' children: for many years Julie had been unable to give birth. Eventually, the Lord opened her womb. Derek, her husband, was tall, and British by birth. Julie was an American by birth, but had lived in Scotland since they had married. Both of their lives had become increasingly oriented to serving God.

Mel was a younger woman of about thirty. She was sharp, passionate, and unmarried. Julie no doubt realized that she was in part to blame for orienting Mel's passion. Julie spoke much about Philo, and usually in glowing terms. Her life and Philo's life had overlapped in some very significant ways. (That is, of course, not her baby Philo. She had named her baby boy Philo three years earlier, after the man called Philo, who she had first met on her wedding day.) Now Mel's passion had been aroused. The heat of her love seemed to be unquenchable. It was as if God had instructed Mel to chase Philo!

"You'd better tell her some bad things about Philo," her husband Derek advised. He meant well – he was trying to help Julie who was alarmed by Mel's expressed determination to be married to a man who lived far away in Africa, a man she had never even met! Julie, it seemed, couldn't help herself, she kept praising Philo.

For years Mel had worked as a travel agent. How a woman so sharp and so passionate could hold down a routine job like that amazed many, Julie included. Amongst Mel's 'hobbies' was a passion for writing and for journalism. Mel had written a number of short freelance pieces. She was well respected for her journalism by those who knew her. Another passion was philosophy. She had chanced upon Julie through a mutual friend. The friend had had a life-transforming encounter with Jesus which Julie's Bible studies had helped to facilitate. Mel decided to join the same group. The very first day she attended, Julie was also there, and was soon waxing lyrical about Philo. Mel's passions became directed to the sharing of God's word, yet she never forgot what Julie had said that first day. I guess one could say that Mel was not easy to please. Not many men impressed her, which is why she was still single at thirty.

***

While all this was going on in Scotland, Philo himself was far away in the land of Holima, in Africa. Philo was single having never married, despite having topped fifty. That is not to say, however, that Philo was necessarily 'available.' He had adopted twelve children at that time. Add the ones who had at one time been with him and had subsequently left, and the total of his children came to more like twenty-five. These were, of course, orphaned children informally adopted. Philo had so 'adopted' them and lived with them with the help of a Holiman lady who worked as a nursemaid to the children, in his African village home. So, Philo was a single man, who cared for a score of children.

Philo considered his main work in Africa to be Bible teaching, which he did with a variety of churches and fellowships in Holima and always in the Striden and Swahili languages. Philo had been born and raised in the UK, then left for Africa aged twenty-four. He had done much the same work for thirty years. Of medium height, slim, with brown hair, he had started out as a young and enthusiastic agriculturalist. The need he perceived in Africa had re-oriented him to Bible teaching, and it was this commitment to sharing God's word with African people that led to his remaining single. He believed passionately in the importance of what he was doing. Good job too – had he not so believed in it then the storms and valleys of his experiences might have had him leave Africa many years before.

* * *

Before going on, I probably ought to introduce myself. My name is Dave. I am an American from the Seattle area. Like Philo and Mel, I am single, but not so much by choice. I married the love of my life over thirty years ago. Months into our marriage, Cindy's pregnancy aggravated a condition that had not previously been diagnosed. The Lord took her and our unborn child away from me. I still miss her, and all the children we might have had. I am now in my mid-fifties, a tall man with blue eyes and grey hair, usually wearing wrinkled clothes.

Circumstances had me meet up with Philo, about whom Mel was now so passionate. Distraught over my loss of Cindy, I had uprooted myself to make a dramatic career change. I abandoned notions at the time that I should make money in the USA. I met with Christ in my life. I made a new beginning. I began to work in international relations. That is, in evaluating aid packages' delivery in Africa. That is where I met with Philo. One could say it was just a chance meeting. He and I bonded seemingly from the word go. We were in the same vicinity in Zambia. Later, amazingly, I was given an assignment in Holima. Philo had arrived in Holima a few months before me. (Much as he had initially arrived in Zambia a few months before me five years earlier.) Our friendship as a result continued. I was pulled out of Holima before an election in the country that threatened to go violent. At the time, Philo stayed.

I am Julie's brother. I introduced her to Philo, as I invited him to Julie's wedding. Philo was reluctant to part with his books. He was studying at the time. It took a lot of my persuasive powers to convince him to come all the way to Scotland for the wedding. After the wedding, Philo and I had a good time walking in the Scottish Highlands before Philo went back to his research and reading.

It is me, Dave, who will be narrating this story. It is the story of how Mel fared in her quest to marry Philo. Most times, I am close enough to the action to tell you what is going on from memory. Sometimes, as in this instance in the conversation between Mel and Julie, I put my account together from what I heard and what others told me.

* * *

Julie looked at Mel. She was very serious. They were sat at a ladies' coffee morning in the hall of an Anglican church. They were not in Scotland but England. Julie was amazed at the passion in Mel's voice. It was not the first time she had heard her express this passion. It sometimes seemed more of an obsession than a passion! An obsession with a man, a man she had never met! How could Julie, for everybody's sake, quench such madness?

Before Mel and Julie could continue their conversation, a guest speaker was introduced. The speaker had come to tell them of her experiences. "Oh no," Julie thought to herself, as the speaker was introduced. She glanced at Mel. She glanced away again, concerned that Mel might have seen something. She had no mirror immediately available with which to examine herself. Julie imagined, however, that she had gone white. The reason – the speaker had come to tell them of her adventures in Africa! "This might pour oil onto the fire of Mel's passions," Julie thought to herself.

"Let's welcome Veronica with a round of applause," said the chairman to the meeting. As the speaker stood, her pastel pink dress stretched down to her ankles. A wrap, with a delicate soft blue pattern stitched through it, combined with pink colors (or was it red?) hung loosely around her shoulders. It gave her a resemblance to a specific African tribe. Julie had to think about it. Yes! This lady's dress made her look like a Maasai – a tribe found in East Africa. "Even her dress code she picked up from Africa!" Julie thought. She looked at Mel again. This time Mel noticed and glanced back at her. Mel seemed to realize Julie's intention and dilemma. Julie was determined to divert Mel from her Africa madness. Now the speaker they were about to hear was coming to talk about nothing else – but Africa! Mel leaned towards Julie. "This is a prophet sent by God," Mel whispered into Julie's ear. Julie let out a gasp. She felt like grabbing her friend's hands and dragging her towards the exit.

The lady spoke of her adventures in Africa and of her faith in Christ. The two, to this lady Veronica, were intimately connected. "I'm not sure I've ever heard a woman speak who oozed so much faith," my sister Julie told me later. Veronica's account of her adventures was genuinely incredible.

By this time, Veronica told her captivated audience, she was married. While in Africa, she had been single. In Africa, she tasted adventure. Although it seemed to be a job way below her ability, Mel had previously told Julie that she liked working for a travel agent, so that she could share vicariously in the travel-adventures of her clients. Julie tried hard not to look at Mel. When she did look at her, she saw someone transfixed in passionate attention, hanging on to every word of the speaker who, despite being a woman, was dressed like a Maasai warrior.

"Let's talk to her," Mel told Julie, grabbing her hand after the presentation was over. Julie complied quietly and followed her to the front. A few other people had gathered around Veronica. Hardly a crowd. Julie and Mel joined them. A thin lady in a blue cardigan was talking to Veronica.

"My name is Mel," Julie's friend said to Veronica, interrupting. Veronica turned her gaze towards her. "I very much valued what you had to share,"

Mel added. Veronica nodded. Julie looked at Veronica's book. She had written up her story. Her book was entitled *"New Jungle – Same Old Monkeys: My Missionary Meanderings."*

"Do you know someone called Philo?" Mel asked Veronica.

"Wow, slow down a bit Mel," Julie thought at that point. In a sense, it was a fair question. Mel had heard about Philo in Africa. Now here was a lady who had spent years living in Africa, coming to tell her tale. Julie looked at Mel with some shock in her eyes. Mel had whispered to her that Veronica was a prophet sent by God. If now she were to confess knowing Philo, that might be just the confirmation that Mel was looking for to justify her crazy notion about marrying him! They might even know each other? But – Africa is a big continent, so what are the chances that Veronica had ever met up with Philo? The possibility must be slim.

At that point, Veronica answered Mel's question. "I know Philo," she said confidently and clearly while dislodging a lock of hair from in front of her eyes and cocking her head, intrigued by the question. The rest of Mel's animated conversation was to Julie a blur. At that moment, Julie knew she had lost her battle.

* * *

"Dave," Julie told me on the phone, "I've got something to talk to you about."

"Go ahead." It was about 9 p.m. I was at a motorway service station in the UK. Just two more hours driving and I'd be home, but I was feeling peckish. I could talk as I ate. Beside me was a burly looking fellow talking to, I presume, his son aged about ten. I tried to ignore them and to pay attention to Julie. "Do speak up. It's a bit noisy here," I added.

"I've got a story to tell you, and I need some advice," said Julie.

I was holding a piece of chicken in my other hand. "Would it be better to meet up and talk?"

"No, let's talk on the phone." I wondered what was up.

"It's about a friend called Mel," Julie told me.

I, at the time, knew nothing about Mel. "Oh," I said, perplexed, before taking another chunk of chicken into my mouth.

"I tell you what I'm calling you for," Julie added. "Mel wants to marry Philo."

Bits of chicken splatted onto my plate. The burly fellow sitting next to me stopped reprimanding his son for a moment as he looked in my direction, wondering what was happening. I glanced over at him, a little embarrassed as to how I had reacted to Julie on the phone. Julie said that matter-of-factly, as if I should not be in the least surprised by such a revelation. "Say that again," I said.

"Mel wants to marry Philo," she repeated.

"I thought men were meant to marry women. Not the other way around?" That was probably a silly thing to say. In Africa, however, at least in Holiman languages, that was linguistic practice.

"That's what you might have thought," Julie responded, "but she seems determined. She's even had prophetic confirmation."

"What!" The fellow on the next table was still throwing wary glances in my direction. I glanced back with a smile.

"Long story short, I was with her at a ladies' coffee morning. We had no clue who would come to speak. It turned out to be a lady who had lived for years in Africa. Mel took that as a prophetic sign that she should be in Africa. As if that is not bad enough, the lady knew Philo! That to her was like a God-ordained confirmation to a significant prophetic suspicion."

"Who is this Mel?" I stopped chewing, to give Julie my full attention.

"She's a friend of mine in our women's group who works in a travel agent on Tawney Street, she's about thirty. And she's single."

"Well, I am glad she is single if she wants to marry Philo," I exclaimed. I chewed a little.

"What shall I do?"

The answer to that question seemed to me to be straightforward! "Tell her to forget it, Philo isn't about to marry anyone, let alone a girl who works at a travel agent in the UK."

"She's very sharp, and an adventurous sort," Julie added. Julie was relentless!

"Do you think that will make any difference?"

"Look Dave, I've been trying to disavow Mel of this crazy idea for a long time. It's my fault. I told her wonderful things about Philo. Now I can't get her off the thought. She's threatening to buy a ticket to Holima, and to turn up at Philo's door! Then Philo might blame me because I used to tell Mel what a wonderful man he was." Now Julie was feeling guilty. I pictured her having agonized over what to do for ages, maybe weeks or months, before sharing this with me as she was now doing. I managed to get a forkful of peas into my mouth between Julie's talking and my responding to her. "She's very serious Dave! Help me!" Julie added. So the conversation went on.

That ended up quite a long conversation, on a topic that I certainly did not anticipate. It seems Mel was driving Julie crazy on this issue. She thought that I, as Philo's good friend, might be able to help her out. Now – what to do? Julie was telling me that crazy Mel, as I started to think of her, was very serious about buying a ticket and traveling to Holima. "Philo might run amok," I thought to myself. I tried to picture Philo in his African village home, then a feisty thirty-year-old brunette (Julie had described Mel to me) turns up unexpectedly, determined to embrace him and to be whipped off her feet by him. What also intrigued me though was that Julie told me Mel was also a very bright and capable woman, determined to serve God! "How could one bring some good out of this kind of situation?" I thought to myself. It came to my mind that a reluctant Philo might need help. A question did come to mind at the end of our conversation. "Does Mel have any journalistic skills?" I asked Julie.

"Why?"

"Tell me." I was chewing on my peas.

"Yes, she does. She has a lot of interest in journalism, as it happens. She wrote for the university student paper when she was younger, but of course, it's not the way she makes a living now." Had Julie been looking at my eyes, she might have seen them light up!

"You take a day or two to think about this some more. If Mel is as crazy and as determined as you say, then call me again in a couple of days."

A few days later Julie called again. By that time, I had a plan. "Look. Tell Mel I'm a friend of Philo's and tell her I want to meet her," I said to Julie. I needed to get to know Mel better to see if my plan might work.

CHAPTER 2: THE JOURNALISM OPTION

I did not want to give Mel too easy a task. I offered to meet her in southern England. That would require her to travel all the way from Scotland. She accepted. She took a day off work, taking a bus down the previous evening so that we could meet at 11 a.m. the following morning. Mel was short in stature, slim, brown hair down to her shoulders, with a quiet albeit vivacious determined manner about her that I very soon noticed. I was impressed.

We drove to and walked along the Kennet and Avon canal. I asked Mel to tell me about herself. All the while she spoke, I could only think to myself what an incredible woman she was. I had asked Julie to do a bit of research for me. She had already filled me in. Mel had a clean slate. She'd never married, no children, nothing shady.

"You like Philo?" I asked Mel. She didn't answer me straightaway. The gravel of the towpath made a pleasant grating noise under our feet. The path was wide enough for us to walk side by side. Anyone seeing us probably thought I was her sugar-daddy or her father. Mel was somewhat younger than me, or Philo, for that matter. The thought that I might be her father was pleasant. I had no children. I would have loved to have had an attractive adult daughter like Mel. "She's like a daughter," I thought to myself. A pair of coots in the canal were diving periodically, disappearing out of sight, then re-emerging.

"You might think I'm crazy. I have never met Philo. But there's no one else I have ever wanted to marry as much as I now do Philo," Mel said.

"Why?" I asked. I was fascinated as to how a woman could so fall in love. I suspect some of my incredulity carried in my voice.

"I don't know, but something tells me I should go to him."

"Have you had crushes like this before?" I wondered whether Mel was just infantile! She said she hadn't. "Look, Mel. You speak like someone who is crazy. I also want to ask you some crazy questions, if you agree."

"Go on," she said, her voice shaking.

"Do you have any children?"

"No."

"Have you ever been married?"

"No."

"Have you ever been in a relationship. I mean, a serious one?"

"No."

These were likely to be important issues for Philo. Holiness is essential for a missionary, at least from certain African points of view. I felt I was probing a bit too closely. I told her that I had. I had been married, then that my wife died. Mel had not known that. I felt a bit better about myself for asking her all those questions, after having at least answered them for myself.

"So, does Philo want to marry you?"

"I thought you were going to ask that," Mel responded. Her face fell. It was at this point as if I was going to burst her bubble. "Look, we've been walking for an hour. You said you'd take me for lunch. Can we turn back, then we'll have lunch at one o'clock?"

I agreed. We'd just arrived at a lock. It seemed an appropriate point at which to turn around. We headed back the way we'd come. It was drizzling. The trees above our heads were dripping the occasional fat drop of water onto us.

"I don't know whether or not Philo wants to marry me," Mel said. "What do you think? Do you think he will?"

This was amazing! I was being asked to respond on Philo's behalf to a beautiful brunette, and he didn't even know that a wedding was in the offing! Well, what could I do? I just had to say what I thought. "I doubt it. He's pretty committed to what he is doing."

"Will that stop him marrying?" Now Mel was like an eager schoolgirl. She looked at me wide-eyed. I nodded my head a little. "What do you mean?" she said.

"It would be tough to live the way he does with a white wife." These were things I'd discussed with Philo in the past. Mel was still looking at me like a pleading schoolgirl, her eyes agape.

"So, he needs a black wife," she said, feeling a bit attacked.

"No, same applies."

"Why?"

"The way he lives in Africa is incompatible with the expectations of women."

"Maybe I am different?" That wasn't a surprise to me. Everyone is different – in their own eyes, especially when they are in love, or looking for something that is important to them. I appreciated the singing of the birds around me as we walked and talked.

"Maybe," I said, then paused. "Philo may not be as easy to get as you think," I told Mel.

"Then why have you asked me to come here to meet you?" Mel said, this time with her lips curling, not in anger, but as if to question my judgment.

I laughed. "I have hope," I said, despite myself. I found myself looking up when talking of hope. "My hope is in Christ," I thought.

"What hope exactly?" Mel asked, her eyes almost popping out of her head. She could not hide her intense inquisitiveness as to what the nature of this 'hope' might be.

I stopped and turned towards Mel. She stood still. "Look, are you serious?"

"Yes, very." Resolve was oozing out of her.

"You are a Christian?"

"Yes."

"So Jesus is more important for you than is Philo." It was funny, interviewing Mel to see if she was worthy of being Philo's wife!

"Yes." I'm not sure whether there was any hesitation at all in that or not. "Do you realize that if I tell Philo you are coming to visit him, and you want to marry him, he might well say 'tell her not to come.'"

"I had thought of that," was Mel's response, lips pursed, showing some kind of intense determination. We reached the restaurant we were heading for and sat down. We ordered our food.

"Look Mel, you're crazy! Philo is committed to celibacy. Okay – he is not a monk. He hasn't taken any vows. My advice to you though is – forget it! Forget it! Forget it!"

I stood up and went to the bathroom. When I came back to Mel, I started talking with her about politics, the American President's latest antics. She didn't respond. I changed the subject to ladies' fashions. She just looked at me. I asked her whether she'd seen the program about the life of rhinos in the wild. She said she hadn't. I paused.

"Okay. So, you go to Philo. He has no interest at all in marrying you. What do you do?"

"Wait."

"How long?"

"Long as it takes."

"One year?"

"Yes."

"Five years?"

"Yes."

"Ten years?"

"Yes."

"Twenty years?"

"It won't take that long!" Mel exclaimed.

"Could it be that God has put this crazy notion that you should love Philo into your heart?" I added in exasperation.

"Yes," she said again, as resolute as ever.

"Look, let's eat," I said as our food arrived, "then I'll tell you my idea."

* * *

"If I tell Philo you want to visit him, and you want to marry him, chances are he'll run a mile," I said after we had finished eating.

"Hmmm," Mel responded. Both of us remained with a glass of water in front of us, still sitting in that restaurant. I decided it was the time to try my idea out on Mel.

"I gather you like journalism?" I asked her as the waiter came. "We're okay," I told him. Mel nodded. My question perked her up a little. Journalism, it seemed to her, was a very desirable occupation. She liked the thought of being a journalist but had not previously gathered the umph to try to launch herself into a journalistic career. "If you do, and you are seriously interested in Philo, that interest might give you access to him." Mel looked at me, puzzled, while letting out a sigh with a rising pitch.

"Philo has an important message that he wants to share with the West. He is frustrated that no one is listening. If he heard that a journalist wants to come to visit him to do some research, he might be interested. Especially if I tell him that the journalist concerned will listen and pay attention to the end, and not double-cross him, or be bought up by powerful donors. Who knows, he might end up liking you enough to marry you. No guarantees though."

I added another comment, to which Mel took no notice: "By the way, you will never marry Philo. In African language use, a man marries, a woman is married." Mel was thinking intently. It was as if she was about to make the decision that would determine the course of the rest of her life.

"You mean," Mel replied to me in a hushed voice after two minutes or so, "that if I am interested in Philo, then I should make out that I am a journalist? If he hears that a journalist wants to shadow him, he may agree. You say that might be the best, if not the only way of getting close to Philo? You are also saying through your having asked me if I am a Christian and all that, that I should see doing so as being my way of serving God?" I was nodding. "I have always had an interest in journalism," Mel added a little apprehensively.

"Frankly," I answered, "you have to show interest in Philo's cause."

I did not want to take that conversation further that day. We could have discussed aspects of it, but really, I wanted to leave the matter like that at that point. I couldn't tell how Mel had received my suggestion. Was she telling herself, "All I really want is to marry Philo, but I will play along at being a journalist if that is what might get me there?" Or was she seeing my words as opening a means for her to serve God by researching Philo's circumstance? I guess I was happy enough at my progress to date, and wanted to see how Mel would respond after having had time to think and pray about the situation.

Three weeks later, Mel called me. She was a fast worker. She was also naturally good at impressing people with her skills and abilities! By that time, she was a freelance journalist. The *Scottish Evening Standard* had agreed that she could do an investigation on the missionary work of a fellow called Philo, who was living in Holima. I suppose they had nothing to lose – they would only pay her when, and if, and according to the quality of work that she would submit. No salary: it would be payment-on-merit. For her purposes though, she now had credentials as a journalist, working for a top Scottish newspaper.

* * *

The next part of the plan was to let Philo know that a journalist wanted to write about his work. Of course – nothing to be said of the desire of the same journalist to marry Philo! I agreed to engage this process over a chat.

"Hi Philo, what do you say? A journalist in the UK wants to report on your work."

"Hi Dave, you must be joking."

"I'm not joking. *Scottish Evening Standard*, a journalist called Melanie. She wants to come out and write up on what you are doing."

"Tell her she's welcome!"

"Look out – she is serious. Could it work?"

"How serious? Aren't you joking? She wants to come out on to the ground, here in Holima? How long for? What languages does she know?"

"Don't know how long for, but yes, she wants to come on to the ground. She's a very determined lady. I've already talked to her face-to-face. She only knows English."

"What on earth will she learn if she only knows English? Has she been to Africa before? Who is sending her really – is this her own crazy idea or what?"

"The newspaper is sending her. At the same time – you're right also, that it's her idea. She's pretty crazy!"

"Well Dave, you say she's crazy, so's the idea. Tell me though – do you think it could work? I mean – it would certainly be good to get the word further out there. Maybe a crazy journalist lady could fit the bill? Maybe she could do it?"

"That's for us to work out. Mainly for you, I guess. The lady is very serious, it seems to me. We'd need to work out how to do it in practice."

"Dave, tell me, is she a believer? Does she want to do this for the glory of God? You know how it is – secularism seems to be more rampant in the UK than it ever was when we were young. Are you sure she's serious about glorifying God?"

"Yes, very much a believer. Motives are complex things, Philo. I believe she is well intentioned. She has a good track record. We've checked up on her background."

I added the point about the track record there. I hoped that Philo didn't do too much research on Mel. If he did he might find out too much, like that she really worked for a travel agent! Thankfully, Philo didn't trouble himself to research Mel. He accepted that she was a professional journalist, or she wouldn't be working with the *Scottish Evening Standard* (from here on SES).

"Dave. This is a crazy idea. But, just possibly it might work. Will she accept having to do as she is told though? I mean – I wouldn't want a white lady misbehaving in the village and running crazy around the shop."

"You are asking a lot there. Do white women do what they are told? Tell you what – she's a friend of Julie's. Why don't you talk to Julie about her?"

"Friend of Julie's eh? That's interesting. I'll talk to Julie."

* * *

I took the initiative quickly to get in there before Philo. I picked up my phone and called my sister. I was feeling quite chuffed with myself, even if a bit guilty as I was duplicitous. "Look, Julie. Philo may phone you any time. He said he would contact you to find out more about Mel and her plans. If you tell Philo the whole story – he may well pull the plug! Of course – be honest about Mel. Only, I suggest you not tell him that her primary objective is to be his wife!"

"Got it. If Philo calls, I'll talk to him."

Julie had baby Philo on her lap when Philo called about two days later. There were toys strewn around the room. Julie had been involved in a complicated counseling session with a married couple, which was still occupying her heart and mind at the time. "Hi Julie, this is Philo," said a voice.

"Is Philo going to put his neck into this noose and allow a crazy woman to hunt him down?" Julie thought. She knew, better than I, that Philo took advantage of his singleness to live a kind of life that allowed him to achieve things that married people would struggle to do. Part of Julie wanted Philo to have a life partner. Part of her so valued his work, that she was tempted to blow the whistle on Mel. On the other hand, she wanted to follow through with what I had proposed to her, that Mel's romantic intentions should be kept secret from Philo. She still felt a bit bad though. Not that Mel could force herself onto Philo if he didn't want her, but she could give him a headache! She was evidently a brilliant woman.

That is, she could do a good job of sharing the word on what Philo was doing if she put her mind to it. Julie balanced little Philo on her knee. "Hi Philo," she said.

Philo was amazed by what new technology was enabling. There he was thousands of miles away in his African village at his home, yet so easily able to phone Julie, and talk to her at a reasonable price! He was standing under a tree in faraway Holima, watching some women walk by carrying buckets of water on their heads. After some polite conversation, Philo asked: "Julie, what do you know about a girl called Mel?"

"The journalist?"

"Yes."

"She's a high-quality lady with good intentions, and can produce good work."

"You sure about that?"

"Sure as I can be."

"Thanks." The phone call ended there.

CHAPTER 3: SEATTLE IS WORRIED

"Professor Nancy, it's bad news," said Rolly over the phone. "Can I come and see you straightaway?" Rolly's real name was Steve but everyone called him Rolly, except sometimes Nancy herself. That was related to the shape of his body. His whole body struck one as being slightly oval.

Professor Nancy was just then having breakfast at a branch of McDonald's in Seattle. She was sitting with a girlfriend of hers. Nancy was a professor at Western University in the same city and a very prominent person in the community.

"What is it?" Nancy said. She was surprised that Rolly should call her just then. She put her coffee down.

"Philo is getting traction," Rolly told her. He kept his words short. This was just for information. He wanted her to know just enough to realize that what was happening was serious.

"What!"

Nancy's friend, Gertrude, also started at that exclamation. She was Professor Nancy's mother's age. Her face was wrinkled. But yet, to all indications, she was fit and fully in charge of her faculties. She exchanged her smile for a worried expression. Something was up – but she did not know what it was. She peered carefully at Professor Nancy over her spectacles.

"Look, we have a meeting in the King's Boardroom just after 11 a.m. If it's possible, come and join us for that meeting. Then you can enlighten me regarding what you know, and we can discuss what to do," Professor Nancy said to Rolly who grunted, then put the phone down.

"Bad news?" asked Nancy's friend.

The Professor looked at her. She picked up her coffee again, her thoughts twirling in her head, and had a sip. "It's a fellow called Philo," Nancy eventually told her friend, saying one thing while thinking another. "Apparently he is getting traction, whatever that means."

"It seems he's a bad fellow," said Nancy's friend from across the table. Gertrude loved solving other people's complicated social issues.

"Yes," said Professor Nancy, still on remote control.

"What does he do?" Gertrude was twisting her head as she talked.

"He likes African people."

"Well, that is bad ..." Gertrude started saying then stopped herself mid-sentence. She had expected Nancy to say something that this fellow Philo did that was negative. Instead, she said that Philo liked Africans. Well, what is terrible about that?

Professor Nancy gradually arrived back at the scene she was at, across a table from Gertrude, realizing that the latter was not aware of ways in which Philo was promoting vulnerable mission. That is, Philo was suggesting that some Westerners should be engaging with African people using only African languages and African resources. That, to Professor Nancy, was threatening. Professor Nancy was heavily involved in raising funds for projects in Africa, nearly all of which ran using only western resources and western languages.

"I mean he likes them as they are. That is, he doesn't seem to want them to change, or to change them," Professor Nancy told her friend. "Surely Gertrude will side with me on this," Professor Nancy said to herself, while not entirely sure. Her coffee cup hand dropped onto the table.

"That is bad," said Gertrude, thinking that African people must be pretty bad if it is a crime not to change them.

Professor Nancy's conscious thinking was gradually catching up with what she had said. "Look, Mom, I mean Gertrude." (Gertrude resembled Professor Nancy's mom. When she was with her she often ended up calling her Mom.) "When you have to work hard to raise funds to help the poor in Africa, then anyone who is less in favor of outside funding becomes a problem. If our donors were to hear that Philo loved people as they are, and were in the slightest convinced by him, this might threaten our income, and our projects could collapse."

Gertrude had to think about what she'd learned in the previous two minutes. She very much valued and respected Professor Nancy. She was a long-term friend and had been a good friend of Professor Nancy's mother until she died. Now, however, she was puzzled – why was her good friend now so against friendship with Africans? It would be a while before Gertrude could throw more light on this matter and help to alleviate some of the problems that arose from it.

* * *

True to her word, Professor Nancy arrived at the King's Boardroom at 10.57 a.m. Rolly was already in the room. He was very friendly and a very talkative sort – in a good way. The other person in the room was Sam. Sam was a businessman. He was short and stocky, with an impressive mustache on display. Sam was a no-nonsense kind of guy.

Professor Nancy hung her coat onto the back of her chair, then: "Rolly, I was to be meeting with Sam on another issue. After receiving word from you, I told him what you'd said. He agreed that the first part of our meeting should address whatever concerns you have to raise with us. By way of background, I can remind you that Sam is a member of the Senate at Western University. That is to say – he was there when Philo spoke to us a few years ago, even though he was not able to attend the conference held shortly afterward." (What Nancy did not say was that Sam was Gertrude's son!) "I believe I can speak for both of us – that we would be concerned at any rise in Philo's prominence. Hence my shock over what you told me this morning. Rolly – please enlighten us, fill us in."

Sam was no stranger to Rolly. There was little need for formalities between them. Rolly could get straight to the point. The three of them sat around three sides of a longish table.

Rolly began, "One of my roles in the Christian-world, you will know, is to deal with the media." Rolly was clasping his hands, and not looking at his colleagues, as he worked out what to say and how to say it. "I am always on the lookout for issues and perspectives arising from the mainstream media's reporting on issues of foreign mission. To that end, I have various colleagues-in-arms." He looked Professor Nancy in the eye. "You know – we help to alert one another. One such colleague-in-arms is in the UK. He likes to call me, to lament on the disinterest of the UK media in anything to do with sharing the gospel of Jesus. To him, that is close to criminal. That doesn't in itself bring a shift, however. Right at the end of such a conversation, all that he found, he told me, was that a reporter (who he had never heard of) was seeking to do a write up on someone called Philo who was working in Holima. As soon as he'd told me that, he said goodbye, and put the phone down." Rolly glanced at Sam while hitting four of the fingers of his left hand against his other hand.

Nancy was all too aware of what Philo was promoting. What he called 'vulnerable mission.' If Westerners were to engage in ministry using indigenous languages and resources, that could have implications for

Professor Nancy and her colleagues. Primarily, it could undermine the ease with which they might attract donors.

"Go on," said Professor Nancy, after checking that Sam had nothing to say.

Rolly sighed. "Of course, I had more cause to react to that situation than did he – he had never heard of Philo. This all happened late last night. Yes, I think my friend has insomnia. I didn't contact you last night, but I did get up early today to try and carry out some investigations. I discovered that the reporter concerned is called Melanie. She is new and is working with the same newspaper we have been relating to, SES. Her intention seems to be to make a trip to visit Philo in Holima. I don't know when."

Rolly paused. He looked at Professor Nancy and Sam. They had nothing to contribute at that point. He went on. "I felt it was important to make you aware, Professor Nancy, so I phoned you so early this morning on your mobile. You suggested that I come here, so here I am. I am open to suggestions on how to take this matter further."

Sam summarized the issue: "We feel that Philo's message is a threat to mission-convention. Hence our concern that Philo should be getting this kind of attention – yes?" he asked.

Professor Nancy's phone rang. She looked at it, pointed at it to indicate it was an urgent call, and chatted with a man with a Texan accent. Her friends waited for her to finish.

Sam repeated another version of his summary.

"Yes," said Professor Nancy. The small group nodded with her.

Thus encouraged, Sam went on, "Our solution would seem to be – to make sure that Philo gets a bad press!"

As this was being recounted to me, I could only imagine the temper of things in the room. I do not know the tone of people's voices at the time. What they seem to have said sounded slightly sinister. Did they say it in a threatening way? I do not know. Were they laughing and slapping each other on the back after that statement? Was it said with a severe evil tone? I do not know. I am sure that a lot more was discussed than I know or can relate here. At the end of the discussion, a conclusion was reached, something like the following:

"That is your assignment, Rolly," Sam said. "You must try by all means to be Mel's greatest friend. Then, when she makes her trip – you go with her! You have spent years in East Africa. You can be the cultural broker. You know – you are there to help to explain to Mel what is happening! I will talk to the Editor in Chief of SES tomorrow – he is our close mutual friend, it shouldn't be difficult to help him understand what is going on. I will let him know enough of our concerns so that he can also, if need be, put a spanner or two into the works. Your job, though, is to be with Mel. She's a nice girl, I gather. If you convince her that Philo is an ogre. Hey presto!"

"Let me just remind us why we are doing this," said Nancy. "It is for the poor. American and Britain's wealth are not for western people alone. For just one country to get rich and leave the rest of the globe in abject poverty is criminal. We need to provide help to the majority world, but especially Africa. Numerous research initiatives have shown that outside help is very effective at reducing poverty. For the sake of the world and the sake of the poor – we cannot just stand by and let people like this Philo promote his contrary agenda, that threatens to upset aid programs, that suggests that mission efforts should begin by accepting African people as they are! We need to be change-agents, and we should never lose our focus on that important agenda. The wellbeing of millions of people depends on us. We've got to defeat Philo!"

Professor Nancy paused, then added: "I agree with Sam. All you have to do is to convince Mel to dislike Philo. I mean, that shouldn't be difficult. It's not as if she wants to marry him!"

And, apparently, she really did say that.

* * *

Sam had on his agenda to follow up with Rolly on his approach to the UK early the following morning. He did not though, at the time, reckon with a battering that was coming his way!

Sam's wife was away for a week. His regular diet for that week had sunk as low as peanut butter sandwiches. Sam's mom knew he was not very good at looking after himself. As a result, she was optimistic that if she called him for a meal, he would not refuse. She was curious as to whether he could throw any light on the mystifying conversation she had had with Professor Nancy that morning. She didn't tell him that she was curious though. She just invited him to 'come to Mom's for a meal.' Sam accepted her invitation.

Mom and Sam sat at the table. Gertrude delayed raising her issue until it was time for dessert. Then she said, "Sam, I had an exciting time this morning. It's not for me to spread gossip. But I can tell you who I was with this morning. I was with Professor Nancy."

Sam raised his eyebrows. He hoped his mom didn't notice. "What's coming next?" he wondered.

"Tell me what you know about someone called Philo."

"This is not part of the plan," Sam thought to himself! To discuss issues regarding Philo with his mom did not seem a healthy way to go. The issue was supposed to be under wraps, not spreading on the gossip grapevine. "What do you mean, Mom?" Sam asked.

"Look, Sam. You know something about this."

"But Mom ..."

"Don't 'but Mom' me! Did Professor Nancy tell you something?"

It was at that point that Mom's tirade began, and Sam could do nothing to stop it. The version I have here is, of necessity, abbreviated:

"Look, my boy," Gertrude started, in a very combative mom-style. Sam braced himself.

"All you and your cronies seem to care about is money." That was Gertrude's opening sentence. Sam realized that what she was about to tell him was something that she had thought about for some time. "You are determined to save the world with your money. But you forget – Jesus never did that! How many times do we ever read that Jesus raised funds? Zero. How many times did he dig wells, start schools, teach English (or rather Greek), buy bicycles, give micro-loans? Zero, zero, zero, zero, zero! What is it with you? Have you let go of the gospel? Jesus did not give money. He gave himself. You know that. But you act as if you don't. Jesus incarnated amongst sinful creatures like us. You, however, want to help people while staying in your comfortable glass palaces. Donors and donors and donors and donors, that's all you all care about. Donors who think they are clever, as they decide how to portion out their ill-gotten gain. That is – decide who will get their money, to whom are they going to give the most problems." Gertrude paused. She glared at her son. It certainly wasn't a hateful glare. But it was a pleading glare. "Please, my son, listen to Mom." That kind of glare.

"But Mom," Sam started saying as his mom stuck a piece of dessert in her mouth. His dessert, a banana mousse of some sort, was all finished. "We are trying to help people as best we can."

"Yes," Mom said, being careful not to spray too much dessert across the table. Her not having many of her own teeth made spray-control especially difficult. "While you keep your hands cleanly rested on a desk and computer keyboard, and as long as it doesn't threaten you, and as long as you grow fat."

I don't suppose it is every day that an old lady tirades against her grown son. On this occasion though, Gertrude got a goat in her throat. Gertrude was old-school. She believed in people more than she did in money. Of course, so did Sam in his way. His long-armed distant approach to working with African people had often driven her crazy. She believed that one should work with people as people, not as statistics. Sam, in her view, related to the majority world overly through his bank account and his spreadsheets.

"I am not angry with you," Gertrude went on, "I am only imploring you – get people on to the ground to interact with people on the ground. Stop this standoff of putting money up front for everything." At that point, Gertrude thought she had said enough. The volume of her words might not turn her around. But, she had had a go. Their conversation turned to more amicable things. That night Sam's mom did pray for her son, and his cronies, as she had called them. "Give them a heart of flesh," she prayed to God. They say that a mother's prayers are powerful.

CHAPTER 4: BECOMING MEL'S GREATEST FRIEND

"Would you like a coffee?" his wife, Rose, asked Rolly. He was still in Seattle when he made this first call early the following morning. Rolly didn't respond, which in their home-code meant 'yes please.' Minutes later, with coffee in hand, his task was to speak to the Editor-in-Chief of the SES.

"Hello Darren," Rolly greeted him.

"Good afternoon," a voice with a distinctive British accent came back. Darren was in his office overlooking the streets of Edinburgh. Rolly was fortunate to have caught him in and free. He had been running the SES for just over a year. It was, at least as he saw it himself, his make-it-or-break-it job. Except, without a doubt he was going to make it. He had a high expectation of climbing the ladder of media management. Once sufficiently experienced, he aspired to shift into politics, in the British Conservative Party.

After a polite exchange, the two started talking, man-to-man. "You have a journalist working with you. She is called Melanie?" Rolly asked – although what he said came across more as a statement than as a question.

Darren had no cause to deny that. "Right," he said. "They call her Mel," he added. Darren was particularly interested in Mel and her concerns. They had taken her onto the staff as a free-lance journalist not long before. What issue already?

"Look, Darren," Rolly said. Rolly put his face into 'serious' mode, hoping that the contortions of his expression would carry through his voice to the recipient of the phone call. "We are concerned. We gather that Mel is going to write a feature about a fellow called Philo who is in Holima. We know about Philo. Even more – we know him very well. He's a decent chap, but, some of the things he says and writes to be honest (Rolly emphasized *to be honest*), are unhelpful. We do not want Philo's message to get more traction. Were it to do so, it could make life very difficult for fund-raisers like ourselves – he is anti-generosity. That is why I am talking to you now. Try to nip this in the bud if you can. If you cannot, we would appreciate your using your influence to keep a lid on it."

That was the gist of what Rolly told him. Darren was, unknown to Rolly, in a way already a step ahead in the game. Not that Darren knew Philo. He did have a keen mind though. Had he not, he would not have risen so quickly through the ranks to be given a newspaper to manage so soon after graduating from university. Darren had come to realize that the approach of people like Rolly was keeping a lid on many political issues, and importantly, on the gospel itself! Sometimes they did not even realize that their materialist agenda is rooted in secularist advocacy. From what he could grasp of Philo – he was not only threatening donors. He was endangering the whole secular superstructure of society! He was pressuring people to consider first and exclusively faith in Christ. If Philo were to get traction and undermine the lie that the West believed about the adequacy of secularism, the whole of hell could get loose. Darren corrected himself in his mind. The whole of heaven could get loose. If people ceased to believe in secularism, they might develop a much more profound faith in Christ. While nodding (metaphorically speaking) in agreement with Rolly to keep him happy, Darren was plotting his course.

Darren's problem was that he was not quite a convinced Christian believer. But he understood the importance of an approach like that of Philo. He harbored doubts about the definition of 'progress.' Hence, he was not sure whether to fall on the side of Rolly or of Mel and her investigative target, Philo. Darren was sitting on the fence, but his grasp of issues was deep. His phone conversation with Rolly ended congenially.

* * *

Rolly remained with the most difficult part of his assignment. He should meet Mel in person, and generate a friendly relationship with her. His meeting with her had to be somehow profound, impeccable, and consequential in a positive way. If he blew it, he could do irreparable damage to his efforts at blocking her. He had to make sure that Mel got to like him! More than that, he thought to himself, Mel had to love him! He laughed to himself. That wouldn't go down very well. He was a married man. And happily married. But he also understood that many single women lean heavily on male friends. He needed to be that male friend. Mel's confidante! Someone Mel would turn to, and trust. How to get himself into that position? He had to plan for a significant encounter. He could not then have imagined how this significant encounter would occur.

* * *

Rolly went to live in Edinburgh. He was monitoring Mel's movements while continuing with other responsibilities from his bed-sit-cum-office on the third floor overlooking a busy street. One day he took a train to London. Events of that day, however, were to turn out very differently from his expectations. Rolly was unaware that his 'prey,' Mel, was on the same train as was he. He was busy writing on his laptop. Two seats ahead was Mel, with her back to him, talking on her phone.

Everything was normal, until about an hour out of Edinburgh. It was a night train – so it was about 8.40 p.m. Then, entirely unexpectedly and suddenly, in a rural area while passing through trees, the train was plunged into darkness. Before Rolly had time to exclaim "What!" the train shuddered. People started screaming. The train decelerated violently. Rolly found himself flung over a table in front of him, into the seat facing the opposite direction. His laptop flew over the back of the same seat. He hit his knee violently against something metal. The train had not even come to rest when something that sounded very much like machine-gun fire started in front of them.

"A terrorist attack!" Rolly thought to himself.

The train slammed to a halt. The lights blinked on for a fraction of a second, then off again. Then in front of Rolly, the train caught fire! The heat of the blaze burst onto Rolly's face. He turned his face away. There were more gunshots from somewhere beyond the fire nearer the front of the train. Rolly gathered his strength and began to move into the gangway of the carriage, trying to ignore the pain in his knee. As he walked, the light of the fire revealed a female figure lurching onto the ground in front of him. The figure collapsed onto the floor motionless. The heat from the fire was searing. Rolly pictured himself leaping over the body to get away from that terrible heat. Something told him not to do so. (Weeks later, he still didn't know from where he got the strength.) He bent down and thrust his hands under the shoulders of the lady lying under him. Fortunately, she was short and slim, not too heavy. He lifted her by her armpits. Up she came. He pulled her limp form right up to his chest. He grabbed her back, holding her as tightly as he possibly could. Her head bounced on his shoulder. With some superhuman strength, so it seemed, he ran lurching back towards the far end of the carriage away from the fire, with the female body he had picked up, half-carried and half-dragged, in front and under him. He went into the space between the carriages. The outside door was open. Rolly lurched out of the door and down the steep steps while clutching his burden. How he could get down backwards while carrying his load, he did not know. Somehow, he did it. In fact, by that time the grip was mutual – the woman was gripping him desperately as if her life depended on it – as it probably did. There were explosions near the front of the train. Rolly and the other passengers ran helter-skelter into a wood adjoining the railway line. Rolly collapsed, his burden still intact in his arms.

Rolly's wife, Rose, was quick off the mark. She knew her husband was to go to London from Scotland on the train that night. As soon as she saw news of the terrorist attack on TV, she began packing a bag. Rolly was not responding when she tried calling him. She went immediately to the airport in Seattle. When she explained her concern regarding the condition of her husband, she got every help to board the next plane to London, then to Edinburgh. Twenty hours or less after the attack, she was at her husband's bedside in the hospital. (If you wanted to describe her, you could say she was of a similar shape to her husband, Rolly. She had a full figure, a lovely face, and beautiful dark brown hair. In an emergency, she could move quickly.)

When he first woke up, he remembered nothing that happened in the meantime. The memory gradually dawned on him. There was a very relieved Rose. Perhaps not yet entirely aware of what was going on around him and what he was saying, Rolly began relating a confused recollection of his experiences. He had been found unconscious lying in the grass under some trees, holding a woman in his embrace. He was gradually able to state how that came about. A police officer was on hand and recorded what he said.

Meanwhile, in a nearby ward, was a female victim of the same train attack. She had been quicker to regain consciousness. She was told that she had been found in the arms of a man. She remembered him dragging her along some grass under some trees to get away from the burning train. She had located him in an adjoining ward. Checking periodically on his state of consciousness, she finally found him talking with his wife, who by now had a broad grin on her face. She went to Rolly. She held his hand.

"You saved my life," she told Rolly. "You dragged me out of the burning train. I will always be grateful. My name is Melanie, Mel for short. I am a journalist."

After a while, Mel returned to her bed in an adjoining ward. Somehow, although still not clear on what was going on, Rolly did manage to recall that he had been trying to make an acquaintance with someone called Mel. He realized that he appeared to have succeeded – in an incredible way!

The attack on the train was thought to have been perpetrated by ISIS. The bodies of two Syrian gunmen were found. A third Lebanese gunman was arrested but later died of wounds inflicted on him by the police. Ten people died in the attack. Many more were injured.

While saddened and shocked by the general course of events, Rolly was also laughing to himself! Circumstances had expedited his intention more successfully than he could have imagined in his wildest dreams! He had effortlessly, so to speak, achieved an intimate relationship with the very girl he had been targeting!

"You saved my life," Mel said to Rolly for the umpteenth time. Rolly nodded. What could he say? He probably had saved her life. Their seats on the train were subsequently engulfed in flames. If it had not been for him, Mel would almost certainly have died.

"I owe you an enormous amount," Mel added.

"No you do not," Rolly said. "I only did what anyone would have done. You owe me nothing. It was only by God's grace that both of us were saved."

Rolly genuinely believed that to be the case. He was not about to take advantage of a girl because of something, a Christian thing, that he did instinctively. At the same time – like it or not – he had an intimate relationship with Mel!

Rolly thought that the best approach to Mel was to be honest with her. He told Rose the same. Later that day Rose broached the topic with Mel. "Do you realize that Rolly, my husband, who dragged you out of that burning train, was chasing you down?" Rose asked.

Rose enjoyed looking into Mel's eyes as she tried to process that question. Mel was perplexed by Rose's statement. Rolly, in the bed beside them, grinned and grunted in a low voice. Mel looked at Rolly. He opened his eyes more widely to indicate that he was not in disagreement.

"What are you on about?" Mel asked.

"My husband was looking for you," Rose said. "He wanted to build a relationship with you."

"A relationship?" Mel repeated, hardly able to believe that she was looking into Rolly's wife's eyes as she said what she did.

Rose realized that she was being misunderstood. "I mean a professional relationship," Rose clarified. Mel was still looking puzzled. Why on earth did this old man want a relationship with her? "You are a journalist, Mel?" Rose asked.

"Yes," said Mel. Although, even she had to think about that for a while, as to most people she was a travel agent.

"You are working on a feature?" Rose added. "You have made it known that your feature will focus on the work of someone called Philo?" Things were beginning to make sense to Melanie. Soon, a nurse came to attend to Rolly. She left again. "My husband has parallel concerns to yours," Rose added. She paused it seemed for a micro-second, but that micro-second was noticeable to Mel. She wondered what the pause meant. At this point though, Mel was elated. She had found someone who shared her passion for Philo's work! A micro-second later, her elation was deflated. Rose went on, "We are concerned that Philo should be stopped, and his work exposed."

Instantaneously, Mel's heart was thrown into turmoil. Rolly and his wife had an interest in Philo – but they were against Philo! They wanted him stopped, and they wanted him 'exposed.' Whatever that meant, it didn't sound good to Mel. Rolly had saved her life. She felt she owed him everything. Rose was also very good to her. Now both of them were against Philo, but she wanted to marry Philo! Mel's face suddenly twisted into a distorted shape. Rose was alarmed. She ran towards her and, as if she were her mom, enveloped her into her lap.

"What is going on! Why did these people not want Philo?" Mel thought. Mel could not tell them that she wanted to marry Philo! That must remain a secret. It had to be known that she was just a journalist going to investigate Philo to write a feature article about him. Her feature article was going to be glowing. That is what she intended. She hoped by those means that Philo would come to love and appreciate her. She was going to report the wonderful things Philo was doing. But now this?

"What is wrong, dear?" Rose asked.

"I can't tell her that I am crying because I am confused – why do they not like Philo?" Mel questioned herself. "I can't tell them that I want to marry Philo," she added to herself. "I mustn't!" "I am just so happy to find someone who might be able to help me draw up my feature article," Mel lied, as her breathing became irregular in her efforts to keep sobbing at bay.

Unbeknown to Mel, as her eyes were buried in Rose's lap, Rose and Rolly looked at each other. Rolly couldn't believe what was happening! He nodded to his wife. This is precisely what he had been hoping would happen, and those were exactly the words that he hoped he would hear! "Don't you worry, dear. Rolly will go with you wherever you go, to help you out," Rose assured her.

On hearing that, Mel started shaking. Rolly and Rose knew that her shaking was of joy. Mel knew otherwise. To her – that sounded terrible!

* * *

About a month later the same triad, with me besides, was on a flight to East Africa. We had four seats in a row. Mel was sitting between Rolly and his wife, Rose. I was tired and was dozing. But I could still hear the conversation. Well, Mel did not have much to say, which Rolly took as agreement. "We have got to expose Philo," Rolly said. "What he is doing is just too dangerous."

"Quite right, dear," Rose agreed.

"Mmm," I heard from Mel.

"This is our chance to do that," Rolly said emphatically.

My mind went back to the first face-to-face conversation I had with Rolly, together with a Holiman called Ralph, a few years before. I thought that discussion would have convinced Rolly of the error of his ways. Obviously, it did not. I was going to have to do some maneuvering to help Philo survive the new attack. Then – there was Mel – in a kind of terror in case her secret would be exposed, beholden to the man who had saved her life, yet dismayed over what he wanted to do. But then I dozed off and no longer heard what was said.

CHAPTER 5: THE ADVENTURE BEGINS

Visas in hand, we emerged out of arrivals. Mel had been very quiet. I am not surprised! She was about to meet the man she was determined to marry for the very first time. She certainly had some resolve! They say love is a powerful force. The love a woman can conjure up for a man is phenomenal. There we all were in Imbigen. Mel had already created great waves by moving the three of us to join her on this trip, all because of her love for a man she had never met.

Philo walked toward us smiling. Mel was looking at him. Philo's brown hair was short. He had a beard, or was it stubble? His eyes seemed to beam out of his face. It wasn't exactly out of the side of her eye, but she didn't seem to want to look him straight in the eye either. Philo first approached me and hugged me. It was good to see him again. Then he similarly hugged Rolly. Indeed, I remembered they had met around the time Rolly found me in Deja. When it came to Rose, however, Philo merely took her hand. Mel stood pensively alongside Rose. "Perhaps this was the hug she had been looking forward to for months," I thought to myself.

Philo didn't hug her either. He just shook her hand, and said, "You must be Mel. Welcome to Holima."

Philo was very friendly and very welcoming. He was wearing a blue shirt. I guessed it was one with a high spf (sun protection factor) rating. He liked to protect himself from the sun. Both ladies were wearing dresses that reached below their knees. By coincidence rather than design, both Rolly and I were wearing brown trousers and grey and red checkered shirts. When Mel shook Philo's hand, I noticed her blushing. What was she thinking, having met her target in the flesh?

I should explain – the reason Philo was reluctant to hug the ladies was in line with local custom. Not that local tradition held at an airport in a capital city. But Philo had explained to me on another occasion – he was well enough known in Holima – that there could at any point be someone connected to him who might see him. Philo was not looking to spoil his reputation by being spotted hugging a woman – something that would make a member of his community suspicious, wondering whether his celibacy was genuine. Funnily enough, someone approached and greeted Philo as we walked away from our meeting point. He was an ebony black man, presumably a Striden.

"*Philo, itimo nang'o ka,*" were the words which startled Philo.

"*In bende ilal yudori kae,*" Philo responded.

When I asked him to translate what his colleague had said, Philo told me: "Philo, what are you doing here." To which Philo had responded, "You must be lost also to be here." Strange greetings, I thought.

* * *

The next day everyone was rested and cleaned up. We had had breakfast at the church guest house. We were due to spend another day in the city before heading on. This was what Philo called 'orientation time.'

Let me add that I won't write all the comments that might come to mind on the exchanges between Mel and Philo. Frankly, Mel was embarrassed. She knew that I was aware of her deep interest in Philo. Perhaps that is why she was most inclined to avoid my gaze. Rolly and Rose were blissfully ignorant of those dynamics.

"Sorry to hear about that train crash," was Philo's opening line, looking at Mel, and then at Rolly.

"Terrorist attack," Rolly corrected him. Of course, it was both.

"You don't have to be sorry, it wasn't your fault," Mel said.

Her words immediately gave me a *déjà vu* feeling from a previous conversation I had with my sister, Julie, years previously on the way to visit Philo! "Sorry doesn't mean sorry in East Africa," I said to Mel.

Mel looked at me perplexed. I decided to explain that later. (I did. The term 'sorry' is often used in Holima-English, as if one needs to express personal feelings of remorse regarding someone else's misadventure, for which one was not at all responsible.) The look that she gave me made me start though. It reminded me of the way my late wife Cindy used to look at me. Suddenly a thought came to mind. Mel was here in Holima with romantic intentions regarding Philo. He was, at least as far as I was aware, oblivious to this. Mel was a beautiful, passionate but sharp and single girl. "Maybe she is for me?" I thought to myself. Then I pushed the thought aside.

After explaining the train event, it was Rolly's turn to give our conversation some direction: "So Philo, for the next few days we intend to shadow you. You will have to ignore us, just explaining as few things as necessary. We'll participate, of course, in whatever you are doing. Really, though, for the benefit of our journalist friend, Mel, we'll be the wallpaper, making observations."

Rolly evidently thought his statement was a simple declaration of the facts of the matter. That is what he had been thinking over the last month and more while plotting to build a relationship with Mel. Then he kept imagining ways in which he could trip up Philo. All he had to do was find nationals who Philo was working with who had a contrary voice, then hey presto! That would give Mel the ammunition she needed to trash Philo's futile efforts. Why was he so special anyway? I don't think Rolly had a clue that Philo would respond to his suggestion as he did!

"No way," Philo said. Everyone looked at Philo. Philo was a bit taken aback. "No way, I said," he repeated himself.

Rolly found this situation lacking. He decided some anger was justified. "Look, Philo!" he started, his voice raised. "We have come here, four of us, at great expense, taking our time, wanting to be a help and encouragement to you," (when he said that I gulped!) "having traveled for miles on the understanding that you would cooperate with us. Now when we politely tell you that we want to shadow you, that means that at our own expense, using our own means, and taking our own time –, we simply come along to see what you are doing. How dare you say 'no way.'"

As Rolly was talking, I found myself staring at Mel's face. It was first smiling, then as things progressed the smile disappeared, the smile became a frown, then a distressed frown, then ...

"There are things you might not understand ..." Philo started saying.

"Stop that at once," Rolly responded. "I have made many visits to East Africa, probably for longer than you have lived here. Don't tell me that I don't know what I am talking about."

"Look, have you come here to learn, which is what I understood, or to tell me what to do?"

"If you are going to be intransigent, then we've come here for nothing."

"I accepted that you come because it is important, I believe, for the word to get out and for people in the West to understand what is happening in Africa," Philo retorted, "but not to kill the goose."

"Goose!" Rolly exclaimed.

"The goose that lays ..." Philo started saying.

We almost leaped out of our seats as Mel suddenly let out a loud yelp, then burst into tears. Rose put her arm around her as she wept and sobbed uncontrollably. Rolly looked at Philo, and Philo at Rolly, as Mel bawled. "It's okay, dear," said Rose, repeatedly.

Mel had seen herself as meeting a missionary; she had imagined him as a great mythic hero, like the famous Doctor Schweitzer or Livingstone, and she had dreamed of devoting her life to him. Philo appeared to be a very different kind of missionary. She felt upset and confused.

* * *

"What happened?" I asked Mel. It was about an hour later. We had put our gathering on pause. I was sitting with Mel under a tree.

"I came wanting to start a good relationship with Philo. I know that Rolly shouldn't know that. Still – it was hard for me to see them arguing." Mel's voice was still heavily charged with emotion.

"Well, you might be a good person to have around, because from here on they may be reluctant to argue when you are with us!" That was my response to Mel. And it was an honest response. We could hear some lads the other side of the hedge as we talked. They were discussing how to repair a motorbike.

"It is really hard," Mel said, "to keep my love interest for Philo secret." I must have rolled my eyes, as I considered the complicated situation we were in! I hope Mel didn't see my eyes rolling. I think she didn't.

Mel and I talked for a long time. As we did so, I noted other conversations also going on. Philo was standing at the gate to the compound. The gate-man was probably Striden, I guessed, and I later found that I was correct. Philo was chatting with him. Rolly and Rose were also good at making friends. They were sitting in engaged animated conversation with another couple, who I was later to discover were Americans like me.

We re-joined our circle two hours later. We had agreed to have a two-hour break. This time around we began our time together with everyone sharing a thought, and a Scripture that they felt was speaking into our situation. Someone shared from a Psalm. Rolly encouraged us to be of one mind. I shared how Jesus had sent out his disciples with instructions to take nothing for the journey. I felt that was an important challenge for us to consider at that point. Philo talked about the Holy Spirit. Rose shared about ways in which God directs, and that it is vital for us to be open to his leading.

We then had a time of worship. We sang a couple of songs. "I apologize," Rolly said, looking at Philo, after two or three songs. Philo gave him his attention. We had sung English songs. "I mean," Rolly said again, "I apologize for the songs." Mel looked at him quizzically. "I mean, we are singing English songs," Rolly said. Rolly was smiling as he talked, although he didn't look particularly repentant. "That is the way we are accustomed to worshipping in England and America. But I am aware that is not the way that Philo is accustomed to worshipping. He is accustomed to Swahili and Striden songs being sung in an African way. After all his years here, I would very much imagine that those are the songs that speak the most to his heart. English songs will remind him of a foreign place. Yet what to do?" Rolly was being considerate, knowing how deeply Philo was immersed in African ways of life.

"Good insight," Philo said, obviously appreciative of Rolly's consideration. That discussion at least reduced the level of tension.

"Even worshipping God is not a neutral activity," I thought to myself. "Thankfully, though, God is one, or there'd be no unity between people at all!" I was often and much amazed at how God's word and worshipping God together could bring people closer to one another. Eventually, we got back to the business of the day.

Rolly was feeling confident. Philo's prior stand had, after all, brought Mel to tears. He could hardly continue to be as prickly as he had been if the journalist who was coming to do her investigations was going to be continually sobbing on their shoulders. "We need to re-examine just what we are going to do," Rolly said. He paused. "If we were in circles that did that sort of thing, I think we'd agree we have reached a point of no confidence in Philo."

That was a devastating thing to say. Philo opened his mouth as if to protest, then closed it again. When attacked, Philo sometimes just kept quiet. Rolly at that point took advantage of the leverage he had over Mel (so he thought), having saved her life from the train wreck. "Mel, my wife and I agree, that we lack confidence in Philo," Rolly stated. The ensuing silence was pregnant, as everyone digested Rolly's words. "We are going to have a change in direction," Rolly went on. He was sat in his plastic chair facing Philo across a table, with the rest of us between. "Our original plan was that we would be following Philo, to give Mel something to write about. The new plan is that we not do that, at least not yet! Philo seems to be too stubborn for that by far. Instead, what we need to do, at least initially, is to investigate a normal mission context. Then let us see what's next. We go back to Philo if we find it wanting, and if Philo's thoughts seem to make any sense."

"Yes, but ..." Mel started saying. She looked at Philo.

"Sounds a fair plan," said Philo. Philo had a pen in one hand, and his reading glasses in the other hand. Mel didn't know what to make of that comment. Her expression changed from one of imploring him to stand up for himself, to one of confusion.

"A fair plan!" I thought to myself. Philo had a lot of deep insights that Mel wanted to report. But his ideas arose as a result of his in-depth knowledge of existing contexts. Would he be able to comment intelligently about a situation about which he knew little, like another missionary's project?

"The thing we should do is to choose a place at random," Rolly said. "Now here is a suggestion – what is more random than a missionary couple we happen to meet here at the guest house? Rose and I met and had been talking to a couple here at the guest house this morning. They are from America. I suggest they are the random mission project which we should visit to enable Mel's research to take off."

"What!" I thought. That might have been a 'random' meeting of sorts, but Rolly and Rose have already had a good opportunity to sit and discuss with that couple. On the other hand, what of Philo? Then, however, I rethought that a 'random' choice might not be a problem for him. For Philo – mission contexts were wrought with difficulties. He might be very happy for any mission project in the whole of Holima to be investigated. He would be sure that he could easily justify that a vulnerable approach to mission is warranted!

"That's fine by me," Philo said. "I haven't seen this couple, but if you have and they have already invited us, let us take them up on their welcome."

Mel did not have much to say. That might have been wise given her very limited understandings of the contexts about which she was going to write. (Ironic though, I thought, that the one who would, in the end, produce the official feature article, was the one who was also, at the time, the most ignorant!) In due course, Rose left our circle to search for the couple concerned. We had asked her to invite them to our table so that we could get to know them. I accompanied her.

"My friends have agreed that we all come and visit you tomorrow," Rose told the middle-aged white couple who were staying at the guest house. I shook their hands. They were photocopying some papers on the guest-house photocopier. They wanted to finish the stack they were working on, and then they were happy to come with us. They looked like good people. Perhaps Rolly's plan was a good plan after all. We invited them to join our circle. Rolly and Rose had already discussed the possibility of our visit. Now we had all agreed to do just that. Rolly was no doubt sitting smugly in his chair. He had managed to wrap Mel around his little finger and to dominate the planning of the visit. Rose and I brought the couple into view of the table where the others were sitting. From Philo's seating position, he could see us straight away. As soon as we turned the corner, Philo jumped up!

"Robert and Phyllis!" he exclaimed. He ran towards the couple and greeted them extremely warmly. I was a little bowled over by this reaction. Rolly looked on blankly. "I did not even know you were staying at this guest house," Philo exclaimed. The two of them responded in kind.

"Poor old Rolly!" I thought. He'd found a 'typical' American missionary couple, only to discover now that they were old friends to Philo. It transpired that Philo had worked with them for years! Rolly could hardly back out now, as he had suggested the very arrangement. His wife had a defeated look. It turned out to be Philo who did the introductions and not Rolly.

"Meet my new friend, Mel. She is a journalist," Philo said to Robert and Phyllis. "This is a very long-term and good friend, Dave. And Rolly and Rose, with whom you have already sat and talked." Everyone was glad to make acquaintance. Robert was a short, quiet but confident type. His wife was a little more flamboyant. Both originated in Nebraska. They had previously worked in Holima for an extended time. On this occasion they were back for a short visit of just a few months, standing in for what had been their mission responsibility, as principal of a Bible school.

Not that Robert and Phyllis were entirely at ease either though. That evening, they had some serious talking to do, they confided in me later. They were sat next to each other on their bed in the privacy of their room. All was quiet except for some African cicada and a distant roar of traffic. Their conversation went something like this:

"Fancy meeting Philo here," Robert said to his wife. He was apparently looking straight ahead at the wall of their guest house rather than at his wife. The wall was covered with some flowery wallpaper.

"Quite unexpected," was her response. Phyllis was gazing down at her lap.

"He gets around."

"You are worried!" Phyllis emphasized.

"What do you mean 'worried'?" Robert said. He looked into his wife's eyes, and sighed, "Yes, I am worried."

"Hmmm."

Robert reverted his gaze to the wall, vaguely making out the shapes made by the images of the flowers. "We used the wrong version," was Robert's next statement.

"What?" Phyllis retorted, not having understood very well.

"Look, Phyllis. You know what I mean ... (a pause). We should have been more honest with Rolly and, what was his wife called? Jane?"

"Rose."

"Oh yes, Rose." Robert paused, but Phyllis said nothing. "Come on Phyllis. We told version one. We should have told version three."

"Ha, ha," Phyllis chuckled.

"I think you know what I mean?"

"I think I do," Phyllis responded.

"Version one is for potential donors in the USA. Version two is for naive visitors. Version three is what you have to tell when Philo is on the scene – the warts and all account of what is going on!"

"I've warned you about that in the past," Phyllis responded to her husband at that point, having raised her voice a little. She was honest.

"Yes, but it's hard work convincing donors to support your work if you tell the truth. It could take us three times as long to raise funds! Donors don't understand. They think they are so clever, giving you hoops to jump through. The result though – they get told stories to please them."

"Yes, but – what are we going to do now? You, or we, told Rolly and Rose version one. We probably should at least have told them version two. We didn't expect them to take up our invitation. Now they are taking it up – and coming with Philo!" Phyllis responded to Robert, not mincing her words.

"We'll have egg on our face!" Robert exclaimed.

"Worse than that," said Phyllis in response, her voice more on edge than ever.

"What do you mean?"

"Did you take a good look at Mel?"

Robert looked at his wife shaking his head.

"But, you caught what she is?"

"Maybe I missed something," Robert responded.

"A journalist!"

"Really! I missed that. Oh, Phyllis! What are we going to do! I guess we will have to tell things as they are."

CHAPTER 6: CAMERA MISSING

It was early morning on the day of the annual graduation ceremony. We had had a good night's rest. We were all looking forward to the varied events of the day. Already there were many visitors at this college, known as SAT (School of African Theology), although some called it School of American Theology in Africa, SATA. Most people who called it that weren't considered great friends of the school. The reputation was however hard to shift – there was a lot of American influence around.

"Today I am going to be a proper journalist," Mel thought to herself. Accordingly, by 8 a.m., as soon as she'd had a light bite, Mel ventured out into her new world at the Bible college. It was just a few hundred meters from a beautiful blue lake. She could see the reflection of the sun in the ripples caused by the early morning breeze. Various exotic birds occasionally passed over the water. Over the other side of the lake, strictly perhaps a river but an extensive one at that point, the far shore was clearly evident. Mel found herself in a compound where the scattered trees gave minimal shade. Some of the trees were flowering red. Distributed around the periphery of the college compound were houses in various states of obvious disrepair. (Although some of them were not so much in disrepair as unfinished.) She could hear the sounds of children coming from various directions. The whole scene gave Mel a feeling of awe.

Mel started taking pictures from various angles. Every time she took a picture, she already imagined what might be the appropriate caption for it when she did her write-up. 'Beautiful Holima Bible college with a lake in the background' was one possible caption. 'African children playing in the dirt,' she thought might be another. "That didn't sound so appropriate," she thought to herself, but whatever account she was going to produce was going to be honest as well as exotic. She pictured herself receiving some acclaim for her excellent journalism. Then her mind went to Philo. Her thoughts never really left Philo. She was determined to marry him, and support his mission, but softly, softly had to be the way. She had to take advantage of this opportunity to get to know how he lived and the people he lived among. When she looked at the little houses around the compound, she imagined living in one of them with Philo. She shuddered a little. She wondered what it was like on the inside.

Mel was contemplating just how to best include such a house in her picture when she heard footsteps behind her. She looked over her shoulders. A young black man, aged maybe twenty-three to twenty-five she thought, was walking up to her. She imagined him to be one of the students of the college. He addressed her in good English. I mean – Mel wasn't sure what she should expect in terms of people's understanding of English. At least it was easy enough for her to understand what he was saying. She smiled back at him. He seemed as glad as was she to have found a friend. They started chatting. She explained to him how she was trying to take pictures from particular angles. Ross, who was slim and perhaps 5′ 10″ tall, had once taken a course in photography, so could follow her explanation, at least in part. He suggested some shots. He pointed her to a black and white water-bird. "That's called a Sacred Ibis," he told her.

Mel took a perfect photo of it.

A little later two more lads came along. Mel told all three that she was there to meet Philo. She didn't tell them she was a journalist. "No point," she thought. To her joy, all three said they knew Philo very well, and they started singing his praises. When they did that, Mel felt very chuffed indeed. Although – she didn't want to show it too much lest they misunderstood.

"Can I have your camera?" one of the two lads who came later said to her. She later learned that people called him Andrea.

Mel was a bit shocked. Why did he want her camera? She wasn't sure whether or not to give it. She wasn't sure either whether her eyes were revealing her conundrum. The camera was expensive. Should she hand it over to this man, in a strange place, who she had never before met? "People here are poor," she thought to herself. "They need our help." Mel had to make a quick decision. "Would my being generous make me more attractive to Philo?" she asked herself. Mel thought about it: if a Bible student borrows a camera, he surely will give it back, she thought. Not wanting to seem hesitant she handed the camera to Andrea. It was £700 worth of gear.

As they carried on talking, she tried to keep an eye on Andrea, who was carefully examining her camera. That, however, proved impossible. To have done so more would have indicated her concern that he might walk off with it. How could she not trust him? In due course, Andrea, this friend of Philo, disappeared with her camera! It was half an hour later before she had got back to Robert. She thought she had better at least tell Robert that someone had walked off with her camera.

She found Robert talking with another white man. She waited to get his attention. Robert, however, was engrossed in conversation. Her efforts at making eye contact failed. She moved nearer to him in the hope that he would notice her. He didn't! Having moved so close, Mel couldn't help but overhear the conversation that was going on.

"I met with them all two days ago," the other white man was saying to Robert. Robert listened nodding attentively. The other man rather resembled Rolly. He was round. His disposition was entirely different though. He seemed to be flightier! At least that's what Mel thought as she watched him speak. Bill, his name, ignored Mel. He apparently felt that what he had to share was too vital for him to interrupt his flow for the benefit of a girl like Mel.

"They were uncooperative. They seemed to have nothing but complaints."

"Like what?" Robert responded.

"Not enough food, not enough money, not enough help, not enough chairs, not enough room, in fact not enough of everything!"

"You met with all the students together?"

"Yes," Bill said nodding.

"I told you not to." Bill was quiet. Mel wondered why, and was interested by that point over what Robert was going to say next.

"You have not yet realized, Bill, have you," Robert told Bill, "that to local people here we are Father Christmas. They want and want and want all sorts of things. We give and give and give. There seems to be no end to what we can give. Come on Bill – there is no end! If you tell the right sad story in America, you get money. African people around here are not stupid. They know that. They are growing wiser and wiser. Just look at the wide spread of smartphones, accessing data of all sorts from around the globe." Bill was stood there with his head hanging. "Am I right, Bill?" Robert asked him.

"You are," Bill said. Bill had seen missionaries come to his church in the USA. When they told tear-jerking stories, they got lots of money!

"Well?" Bill did not say anything.

"That means," Robert added, "that you and I are the ones putting a limit on what students get. And that limit is set apparently on a whim! So, the students get $2 per hour for working. Well, they know that it is a lot less than they would be paid in America. (Of course, they don't realize that the price of living is much higher in the US than where they were.) They also know that if you and I decided to, we could easily make that $4 per hour. We are their patrons. We provide all that they need. We are also the bottlenecks – saying they shouldn't get more. You and I are the bottlenecks!"

As he said that, Mel thought, "That is sad. What a terrible position to be in – to be a bottleneck!"

Robert got to the point: "Students may appear that they are working with us. They have to fulfill their side of the deal after all. If they weren't students, if we didn't have students, we would struggle to get money. You see – we are making money out of them! We can only make money if they agree to attend our classes. Now that visitors are coming, their bargaining power is on maximum. They know we don't want to be embarrassed before our donors, and we have told the donors we have wonderful cooperative, enthusiastic, committed theological students here. Now they have more leverage over us. But Bill – never expect them to be cooperative in front of their friends. Remember we are the self-appointed bottlenecks!"

Mel was quite shocked at that point by what she overheard. She was beginning to understand though. Donors wanted to be generous. When they saw pictures of that 'poor African,' it pulled at their heartstrings. But the college was not in America. Should students all become much wealthier than everyone else in the community, just because they had enrolled at a Bible college run by Westerners? That would be producing enormous inequality, and dependency. With donors pushing money though – missionaries wanted to be known for being generous and not miserly – it fell to the missionary on the ground to be the bottleneck. "What a terrible job," Mel thought to herself.

"Deal with people in small groups and as individuals, and we can get on well," Robert added, as if to finish the discussion, "but bring them all together ... then it is for God's word. Not matters about foreign money." Bill looked thoroughly reprimanded!

* * *

This time, when Mel coughed, Robert heard her. He turned to find her standing there. How embarrassed he was at having been overheard, I do not know. Bill was leaving.

"Hi, Robert. Look, I was with some men, some of your students, I think," Mel said. "Then ..." She was about to tell Robert about her camera having disappeared. Then her inquisitiveness got the better of her, and she stopped herself. She didn't want to give the impression that she did not trust African people, and why shouldn't Andrea borrow her camera? Doesn't he have as much need for wealth as do the rest of us? "Robert," she said, "you know I am a journalist, and you know I overheard that conversation you had with Bill. I couldn't help it. I was trying to draw your attention, but ... was that all true?"

Robert's mind flashed back to his prior conversation sitting on the edge of the bed with his wife. Then he talked about giving version three of events. Now he had so put his foot in it he may have to give version four! "Look, sit down," he said to Mel. Mel obliged. "You are a journalist. That seems to be fortuitous. Are you ready to put your neck on the line and tell the truth? Or are you scared like everyone else?"

Robert was serious. He wanted an answer. Mel's mind flashed to Philo. "This is my chance," Mel thought. "I stand with Philo," she said.

Robert paused. "Then you want the truth," he said. Robert looked at his watch. "It is a big day today. Yes, it was the truth, can we talk later?"

"Okay."

"So, will you excuse me for now?"

"Well ... there's just one more thing."

"Yes?" Robert said, half stood up to go.

"I gave Andrea my camera."

Robert sat back down again. The walls of his office were a light blue color. It was a very accessible office – there were two doors into it. That struck Mel as unusual. That is why she had been able to walk into the office without Robert's realizing. Otherwise, the office was sparsely furnished. As he sat, Robert had his back to his desk. "Why did you give Andrea, I presume you mean the student we have here called Andrea, your camera?" Robert asked.

"Because he asked me for it." Thereupon, Robert bent forward and rested his head in his hands. "I assume that was okay? I thought he was borrowing it there and then, but he went away," Mel added slightly hesitantly.

"This is an endless comedy," Robert said to himself. Just the evening before his wife Phyllis had warned him, "Tell the visitors not to give people things when they ask for them." He had ignored her advice. He was tired of warning visitors about their students.

Robert walked to the door. He shouted to a student: "Call Andrea." The student ran off. He came back in. "Never give students anything," Robert told Mel.

"But he asked for it," Mel said in response.

"Doesn't matter. It seems you don't understand the culture here. This is not the UK or the USA! Don't think you understand what people are saying."

"But he spoke to me in English."

"Whose English?"

"Well, African English I suppose," said Mel.

"And that is very different from western English. You know Philo says this – and he is correct. We Westerners should stop thinking we understand what African people are telling us because it is in English! In the UK it may be true that people check themselves very carefully before asking for anything. One doesn't just ask without cause. Here though ..."

Robert was saying that when a young man put his head around the door.

"Andrea has gone," he said.

"Where to?" Robert asked.

"Don't know."

"Find out!"

The head disappeared, and we heard the footsteps of someone running away.

"Where was I? Oh yes. People here ask for things on the off-chance that they may be given them. They have a right to ask. To ask is to *taniana*. You wouldn't know that. It is to make jokes. People may ask for something, plead poverty, beg to be given it, but that doesn't mean one ..."

The head came around the door again. "He's gone to town," the man's voice said.

"Wait," said Robert. "… should give," Robert said having turned back to Mel. "Where in town?" he asked the man.

"Probably the Bell."

"Let's go," Robert said to Mel. She ran after him. Fifteen paces on, he opened the door of his Land Cruiser. He indicated to Mel. She got in the passenger door.

"Where are we going?" Mel asked.

"To find Andrea. How much is the camera worth?" he asked Mel.

"£700," she said. "So Andrea's a thief?" Mel asked.

"No," said Robert. The engine burst into life, and the wheels skidded on the ground. "He's not a thief according to this culture, but maybe you acted like a fool."

About ten minutes later they were at the Bell. At least, Mel assumed they were at the Bell, as they got out from the vehicle. Robert's phone rang. It was Philo.

"Where are you?" Philo asked.

"We're at the Bell. Mel gave her camera to Andrea. We're looking for him." Philo cut the phone.

"Now Philo might think I'm a nuisance person, causing trouble for nothing," Mel thought to herself. Mel later discovered it was called the Bell because years before, in colonial days, there had been a bell tower there.

Robert's eyes scanned the scene. He walked towards a group of men. He asked one of them, "Where is Andrea?"

"Uh?"

"Andrea *yu wapi?*"

"*Ameenda shule,*" was the response. (He's gone to school.)

"What are they looking at?" Robert said to the same man. The man looked at him blankly. "*Hawa wanaangalia nini?*" he repeated.

The man shrugged his shoulders. Robert marched over to the group. Sure enough, the men were crowding around a man holding a camera. It was Mel's camera!

"Give me the camera," said Robert. They looked at him. "*Nipe kamera. Ni ya yule*," he said, pointing at Mel. (Give me the camera. It is hers!) The rate of their murmuring increased. "They're going to beat him up," Mel thought.

"*Andrea aliileta,*" (Andrea brought it) said one of the men.

"*Ni yake yule,*" (It is hers, hers.)

"*Msiponipa, nitawaita polis,*" he said. (If you don't give it to me, I'll call the police.)

He was handed the camera. Mel and Robert got back into the car and drove off. "I didn't know white men could still command such a presence," Mel thought to herself, she told me later, as they pulled away.

CHAPTER 7: OBSERVING A GRADUATION CEREMONY

When Robert and Mel got back, it was more than time for the procession to begin the graduation ceremony itself. Robert quickly donned his academic garb. Mel chose not to be a part of the parade, as she wanted to take pictures and carry out some interviews during the occasion.

"People will want to see you up front. You are one of our special visitors," Rolly said to Mel.

"I am a journalist. I am here to do reporting," was Mel's response. He could not convince her to the contrary. In hindsight, her reporting certainly did turn up a lot of interesting things that she might otherwise not have discovered.

Mel was in an excellent position to observe as the procession set out. She was amazed at the dazzling array. While the students wore black robes and mortarboards, many of the faculty had colorful robes that they had inherited from various universities. Whether all that academic-might was justified was something, however, that on that day would be brought into question. In the meantime, though, Mel was able to click away on her recently recovered camera.

Mel was still reflecting, so she told me later, on the loss of her camera earlier that morning. How could such a simple thing cause so many problems? That is, the way people ask for things. The border between borrowing and keeping was very soft. There in Holima, one might beg for something, but that does not mean one expects to get what one is wanting. One might even be shocked, as frankly had been Andrea that morning, on actually being given what he had asked for. There in Holima, it was not considered a crime at all to say, "Give me your camera," to a visitor to whom one ought to show respect. In fact – and I had explained this briefly to Mel – asking someone for something can be exactly a way of showing respect! That is, to ask someone for something is to raise that person to the status of a donor, otherwise known as a patron. It is to lower oneself, as if to say, "I am your child." To ask someone for something, to beg them for it, was a way to show great honor! Mel was still trying to take that in, and still had a lot to learn.

The procession moved to the front of the gathered crowd, although the congregation would continue to swell as the ceremony progressed. Many people, on hearing that a ceremony should begin at 10 a.m. decide to try to arrive at any time between 10 a.m. and noon. This was a very typical

African concept of time. Those in the procession fanned out and took their seats facing the congregation. The opening prayer was given, then the national anthem was sung.

As the ceremony progressed, Mel was struck by an observation: there was something strange about it. For a while, she did not realize what it was. She stood, watching and listening, camera in hand. Then she suddenly realized what it was. The whole ceremony was conducted in English. She had traveled thousands of miles from England. There were only a handful of people there from the UK or America, yet the whole event was conducted in her mother-tongue! She knew that many people's understanding of English was minimal. So why not conduct the ceremony in Swahili which many more people understood? She could only guess at the time – that education sounded English. Education in any other language was to citizens of Holima, it struck her, not education at all. Whereas for people in England (and Scotland) education was a way of learning about yourself, this was not the case in Africa. In Holima, in Africa, education was a means to learn the ways of white people. Even as she thought about that, Mel was amazed.

Various proceedings continued at the front, as Mel's newly-acquired journalist's nose had her meander around. She tried to keep her ears attentive to what was being said. Her ears were certainly attuned to any mention of the name 'Philo.' Thus she heard very clearly one member of a circle of lads sat in one location saying in the course of their conversation that, "Philo is useless." Mel stopped dead in her tracks. She felt bad about having so stopped so suddenly. What saved her from being identified as a snooper, was when one second later the person holding the microphone at the front said, "Let us pray." Mel bowed her head.

The whole ceremony being outdoors meant that close neighbors could benefit from proceedings without leaving their homes. This, Mel later realized, was a version of 'African literacy'! Western people got used to spreading words in written form. At the time of momentous changes in Europe like the sixteenth century Reformation, amplifiers had not been invented. In Holima, the dominant means of sharing a message seemed to be the use of large loudspeakers! That way, Mel thought to herself, the emotional content of the message was carried. It is much more challenging to incorporate emotions into the written word, she realized.

This habit, whereby a circle of lads carried on a conversation simultaneous to the graduation proceedings, seemed to Mel to be a little untoward.

Nevertheless, her inquisitiveness had her take a very bold step at that point. She wanted to know things about Philo! "Why would anyone say that Philo is useless?" she asked herself.

"Can I join you?" Mel asked the circle of lads. They seemed quite chuffed at the prospect of having a pretty white girl join their circle. Mel made sure that her fingers were visible. She wore a wedding ring for protection. "I couldn't help overhearing you talk about the teachers at this Bible college," Mel said, surprising herself with her forthrightness. In the background, dignitaries who were attending the ceremony were being announced. "My name is Mel. I am a journalist," she said.

The lads looked at each other. Mel could only assume that their look meant, "Hey. We are getting heard! It is time to take advantage of this opportunity of getting our issues out there!" It was only then that she realized that the main contributor to the conversation was none other than Andrea! She thought he might have run away given the events of the morning. She wasn't sure though whether he even looked embarrassed. So what if he took her camera to town and tried to sell it a few hours before?

"Welcome, Mel, sit down," Andrea said to her. Mel obliged. "We were talking about the teachers," Andrea said, "here at the Bible school. Some teachers we like more than others. Okay, let's be straight. There is a teacher here we don't like. He is called Philo."

By this point, Mel was bracing herself. If they were about to tell her that they didn't like Philo because he was a womanizer whom they suspected of making girls pregnant, then she was at risk of becoming frustrated and depressed. She hoped her face did not reveal her investment into what was about to be said. For a while, Mel heard nothing of the events that were announced from the podium. Instead, it was as if her ears were stretched intently in Andrea's direction.

Andrea seemed to smile to himself. He had waited for this moment of revenge against Philo! "He doesn't give us a thing," Andrea said.

When Mel heard Andrea say that, and saw the faces of the other lads nodding in agreement, for a moment she was overcome by anger. "How could a missionary be so tight-fisted that he would earn such a reputation?" she thought. "Missionaries should be known for their generosity," she told herself. Had she said it out loud, then it was clear that the circle of lads she was sitting in would have agreed with her. The lads kept on, not only Andrea but also the others, explaining why they didn't like Philo. What it amounted to – was that he was not generous financially.

Looking at Andrea's eyes, Mel was able to make another connection to the event earlier in the day. She glanced at the podium. There was Robert amongst the others, on display to the crowd. All the white people except her were sat up there 'on display' as she now considered it. "People who ask you for things consider themselves to be complimenting you," Mel reminded herself of what she had learned earlier. She looked again at the podium. "Are those white people only valued for their money?" she asked herself. She shuddered at the thought. Now instead of being angry at Philo – she respected him! He had made a stand. He did *not* want to be known for his money even as a missionary. If people hated him as a result, so be it. She was familiar with the kinds of publicity put out in the UK. It was always, it seems, 'Africa needs your money.' "Why does Africa always need our money?" she asked herself. In due course, she excused herself from that group and went on her way.

Before she had got very far, her eyes met the gaze of a friendly woman with distinctly protruding teeth. Mel instinctively smiled back in return. "Heard you, you were talking to those lads," the woman said, obviously struggling to articulate herself in English. Mel found herself looking at her teeth. "I heard them say you are a newspaperist," (for which she presumably meant a journalist), "so I wanted to give you this." She handed Mel an envelope.

"What is ..." Mel started asking.

"It take then you it look," said the woman. Either she did not want to tell about it, or maybe she couldn't – her English was too limited. The woman who had stretched up to engage with her slumped back into her seat.

At that moment a hymn was sung. Mel stood and followed as best she could. It was not easy for her to sing along because the song was in Swahili.

Mel, for some reason, felt it was important to open that envelope straightaway. So once the song was over, she sat on a chair to one side. She had shifted a little further from the podium, but could still hear everything that was said. She tore the envelope to open it. A silly thought flashed through her mind. "Maybe it's an invitation from Philo to something, like a love letter!" It was not. Instead, it was a photocopy of a newspaper cutting. There was nothing written on the back. The woman apparently wanted her to read the content.

Mel explained to me later the content of the cutting as follows: "In it was a report of what a politician connected to a prominent church in Holima had said at a certain meeting. He made a public announcement that his church should not hire any pastors who were graduates from SAT. The reason was because graduates of SAT had become too selfish and spoiled. His experience of these graduates was that when they went into ministry, they had little inclination even to engage with people in their own languages. They wanted to talk to everyone in English. Neither were SAT graduates ever happy with their pay. They always wanted more and more money. That is why he did not want the church to take on any more SAT graduates. He was tired of their griping, lust, and frankly disinterest in actually engaging with people in a pastoral way."

These were some of the issues that Mel brought to me later that evening. Her head was spinning! She had been told that SAT students would ask for things, and that was the expected norm. She had learned that the hard way. She had observed that her fellow white people were sometimes only valued for their money. On that basis – some students did not value Philo at all, because he was not financially generous! Now the very same generosity, resulting in greedy, materialistic students, was ruining their prospects for working in churches for whom they were supposedly being trained. Mel had yet more to learn when it came to the time of hearing the sermon of the day.

***

The size of the crowd attendant at the ceremony had grown considerably after the arrival of the procession. Mel decided she had done enough journalistic interviews for the day so that she could attend to what was happening in the ceremony.

This ceremony was to be a bit different than most. Robert was, it seemed, actually very happy to have Rolly present at the school for the graduation event. So much so, that he decided to give him an opportunity to address the gathered crowd. Rolly, being Rolly, did not hesitate to take advantage of that opening. He was given the first slot to share at the ceremony, following the passing out of certificates and degrees.

Rolly was no stranger to East Africa. He had a reasonable grasp of Swahili and was fluent in what he knew! *"Nimefurahi sana kupewa nafasi hii*

58

kuwatajie maneno machache penye sherehe kuu ya shule ya Biblia," Rolly proclaimed.

You could see the assembled crowd come alive! People shifted and edged forward in their seats, Mel felt. "Wow," she thought, "this is amazing. Use people's own language, and they begin to pay attention." Then Rolly added in English, "For those who couldn't understand, I said a few sentences of introduction to my topic in Swahili. I will continue in English because I do not know how to communicate the rest of what I want to say using Swahili."

By that point, Philo had shifted to sit next to Mel. He obviously intended to translate for her. Mel's knees went a bit wobbly when Philo moved up to her. The point at which Philo reached her, was the very moment at which Rolly switched to English! I saw Philo whispering to Mel, apparently frustrated, "If he can't say it in Swahili, then how does he know they will understand in English?" Then Philo returned to his seat on the podium.

Rolly took eight minutes. The gist of his message, as I understood it, was that he was rejoicing that African people were, as a result of their faith in God, displacing their belief in magic with a reasoned understanding of science, technology, economics, and rationality. Rolly spoke in praise of the diversity of the Bible college curriculum that included anthropology, psychology and psychiatry (counseling) with theology, Christology, and pneumatology.

"Jee," I thought to myself. I knew the main speaker. He was a bishop visiting from Zambia. I didn't manage to catch his eye. He was called Kasabula. When I looked at him, I think I saw him flinching at Rolly's message!

The drama that followed had me in stitches. Not everyone reacted to it in the same way though. Mel seemed not to be impressed by my incessant laughter during the drama. I could hardly help myself. There were just three actors in the scene, a thin boy, a plump boy, and a tall boy. (I don't know their names.)

The tall boy came on to the scene. He was dragging himself along the floor, howling as if in pain. "I'm suffering, I'm suffering, I'm suffering," he said, pointing to his legs he was dragging behind him that were apparently useless. (He was speaking in Swahili – but even non-Swahili speakers ought to have got what he said without much difficulty, from the context!)

Suddenly the thin boy appeared. He was dressed in rather frightening garb and had a type of rattle in his hand. A leopard's skin, or similar, was draped over his shoulder. He began circling the tall boy who was laid on the ground, making sinister noises. As he hopped around him, periodically squatting, his rattle shook violently and continuously. He articulated for the tall boy to stand up. He evidently could not, despite making straining efforts to do so.

Then, once the crazy fellow had disappeared, a fat boy came along. This boy was wearing a smart suit and tie, polished shoes, and he was carrying a Bible. He opened the Bible and made out he was speaking from it. He proceeded to pray, arms stretched up, eyes closed. As he did so, the tall boy began writhing on the ground in front of him! Suddenly the fat boy turned his attention to the tall boy writhing on the ground. He pointed at him and began saying *"toka, kwa jina la Yesu,"* (Leave in the name of Jesus).

I think even the actors were surprised when the whole congregation started saying with the fat boy in unison, *"toka, toka, toka, toka, toka, toka"* (leave, leave, leave). Meanwhile, the anguish left the tall boy's face. He stretched, he tried his legs. They worked! He knelt, then gradually stood. Before long he was jumping around. Then the whole congregation was shouting and clapping in jubilation! I noticed that Mel had taken many pictures to capture those events as they unraveled.

Looking at Robert, I think he was slightly taken aback by the stir caused by the drama. After a congregational song, the preacher was announced. After all the excitement, announcing the preacher seemed rather mundane. Kasabula stood. He was about five feet tall. The podium itself being too tall for him, he stood in front of it, microphone in hand, ready to address the congregants.

I later overhead Philo and Mel discussing that sermon. "Tell me," Mel said to Philo, "I got two things out of that sermon by Kasabula. I wonder if you agree?"

"Tell me what you found," Philo responded.

"One, the preacher seemed to be against education," Mel said. "He was saying *jees* are unhelpful. Presumably, he meant by that, things like anthropology, psychology, and even theology and Christology and pneumatology?"

"I think you are right," Philo replied.

"Why speak at a Bible college graduation, then say the things that are taught at the very college are wrong or unnecessary?" Mel asked him.

"Well, it is good to be honest," was Philo's, I think somewhat cryptic, reply.

"Two," Mel said, "the preacher seemed to think that we, i.e. the graduates, ought to get rich." "Hmm," said Philo.

"How?" Mel replied.

"Through prayer."

"Does prayer make you rich?" Mel asked.

CHAPTER 8: CRISIS MEETING

Proceedings eventually came to an end. There was still to be one exciting event that day – an incident or circumstance that none of us could have anticipated at the time the celebration was still proceeding. It all began with the announcement of the timing of lunch, that Robert decided to make through practicing his Swahili. Lunch for us was to be in the room next to Robert's office.

Amongst others, Robert spoke to Philo. "Make sure you are in the room next to my office, the staffroom, at one o'clock," Robert said. Except he said it in (rather clumsy) Swahili, so what he actually said was *"Uhakika wewe kuwa chumba ndani kando ya ofisi yangu chumba cha walimu, saa moja kamili."* He also tried out his Swahili on the rest of us. I can say though, that Philo heard him differently than did we.

That afternoon, once we'd had lunch, we had a relaxed time hanging around. In fact, for most of us, there was no more program. Mel took the opportunity to search out some people to put together her anticipated account of her time in Africa. The governing board of the school was to have a crisis meeting of some sort at seven o'clock the same evening. As we sat and lounged and chatted, Philo told me he had been invited to attend that meeting. I was a bit surprised – Philo was not a board member, or considered to be in the school administration, so why had he been invited to the board meeting? He also seemed a little puzzled, but it was hardly my issue, so I saw no reason to raise any alarm. It was entirely possible after all that the board might have seen fit to invite him. "Perhaps that indicated a softening of their attitude towards Philo," I thought.

I did have to laugh at an encounter that Mel had with a male student. She was telling Philo and me about some of her discoveries when a student came to talk to us. He had a woman carrying a baby walking alongside him. "This is my wife," he said.

They seemed a happy couple. Both were a lighter color than many of the people in the area. I surmised that their ancestors might have included some different blood. They were themselves, however, born and raised locally. What surprised Mel was a combination of two things. First, the student introduced his wife to us. Then, in the course of the conversation, it transpired that he had not been allowed to graduate.

"I was not allowed to graduate because I am not yet married," he told us, looking especially at Mel. I smiled, mostly to myself, as I saw Mel looking at the man called Dan and his wife, Maisy.

"But you said this was your wife," Mel said.

"Yes, but we are not married," was the response.

"Oh," commented Mel.

"Look, Mel," Philo said to her later, "what you in the UK might call your girlfriend because you are living together but haven't had a wedding, is here nevertheless called your wife."

Seven o'clock arrived. The rest of us were resting and hanging around. Philo set off for the meeting. It was to be in the same room in which we had had lunch – next to the principal's office. Philo told me about it later, so here is my account of what happened.

Philo tells me he arrived at 7.05 p.m. He found no one else there. Then Holiman members of the board began to appear. Philo, looking back, thought they did all have a shocked or surprised expression on their faces when they found him sitting there. Two of them, there were five in all, queried him: "Philo, you've decided to come to our meeting?"

"The principal told me to be here," was his response.

"We are delighted that you are here then. We look forward to drawing on your experience in this meeting," one of them was saying, just when Robert walked in. This was about 7.10 p.m. Robert also looked very surprised to find Philo sitting in the meeting. He was about to say, "Philo, what are you doing here? You are not invited to join this meeting," but before he could say so, one of the Holiman people present had already said, "Robert, good to see you. Excellent idea also to invite Philo along to our meeting. We could learn a lot from his experience." The other Holiman people there appeared to be sufficiently in agreement with him. Robert took his seat.

"Why has Philo come to this meeting?" he thought to himself. He did not by that stage, given the welcome Philo had already received, have the heart to tell him that he was not wanted. "Well, we will have to do the whole thing with Philo here," he concluded instead.

Philo sat intrigued, listening to the proceedings of the meeting. He was not sure why he had been invited, so he intended to say as little as possible unless called upon to speak. It soon became apparent why the meeting had been called. Financial crunch. The meeting had been called immediately after the graduation ceremony while key board members were still in the vicinity.

Philo's report to me commented predominantly on contributions to the meeting of two of the Holiman people present. One was called Olich, the other was called Osuga. Philo already knew the two men quite well. Their positions were quite contrasted. Olich was generally in favor of having theological colleges in Africa funded by Africans. How he managed to survive on the board given that orientation, Philo often wondered. The other, Osuga, was in favor of having outside money fund African theological education programs.

Robert seemed to entirely miss one significant event that helped to set the course of the whole meeting. Philo and the others sat around a large table. Osuga was to Philo's left, and Olich sat to the left of Osuga. Robert was sat opposite the three of them.

"What is the best source of funds for theological education in Africa?" Robert asked.

Olich began speaking in response, "The best source of funds for theological education in Africa is Af..." he was saying. At the time Robert had his nose in his file. Osuga stamped on Olich's foot! So, what Olich said was, "... Af – oooch!"

"What?" asked Robert.

"America," said Osuga on Olich's behalf. Robert did not even notice what was happening!

Osuga had very little hair on his head. He was wearing a heavy pair of glasses. Presumably, his vision would have been very poor without them. Olich perhaps had slightly more hair left than did Osuga. Perhaps most noticeable about Olich was his tendency to say, "uhu," frequently, as if his vocal cords were stuck on 'repeat' mode.

At that point, Osuga glanced at Philo. His problem seemed to be that Philo's Swahili was pretty good. He did not think Philo was aware of his body movements. His shoulders lifted and fell a little. Osuga turned to Olich, and Philo was sure he heard him whisper the following: *"kumbuka pesa tuliokupa na faida tutakapopoteza hawa wageni wakiondoka."* (That Swahili could be translated into English as: "remember the money we gave you and the benefits we will lose should those foreigners leave.")

Olich was not put off so easily, Philo was glad to notice. "There are issues that our people are facing that the American curriculum we are presenting does not touch," said Olich. This time Osuga's foot did not move – he seemed to be fearful about being found out. "We will not be able to address these issues as long as our principal source of funding is overseas. Only local funding will enable the exploration of local concerns," Olich said – I thought rather courageously.

"Oh," Robert responded, a little blurry-eyed.

"I was aware that Robert did not get that argument at all," Philo explained to me. How a source of funding could change the curriculum of a Bible college was a mystery to Robert. In the same way – Robert never could see how the use of a different language could have the same effect. To him, if you used a different language, then that was merely a way of saying precisely the same thing using different sounds.

"The other area of concern is language," Olich added. Philo thought that it was rare indeed for a person in Holima, who was a board member at a theological school, to understand that issue! People who valued African languages became, as far as foreigners were concerned, nobodies. Indeed, English was a language of power and money. How Olich survived on the board given his views, Philo didn't know.

When he said 'language,' Osuga's face tightened, Philo told me. Then Osuga brought out the trump card. "Accreditation," he said, loudly enough to be heard by all. Robert looked at Olich. Olich looked resigned. Olich dropped his objections from thereon. The rest of the meeting, aside from Philo's comments that is, focused on how to secure more money from America.

Philo did not have to explain the accreditation issue to me. Accreditation requirements were killing off what little local relevance might have remained in theological education in Africa. (That which the use of English and foreign funding had not already killed.) Accreditation was needed, so it was supposed, to ensure that the education given was nationally and internationally recognized. Accrediting forced African colleges to teach things the American or British way. Without it, students may not be ready to invest their time – thinking that their certificates might be useless. This left little flexibility in the teaching system. Robert probably wondered why Olich was wasting his time raising issues that were irrelevant given the need for accreditation. Philo and I had discussed the matter before. We thought that Robert probably did not realize that, by ignoring Olich, he was, in terms of local relevance, killing the school.

As the debate went round and round, someone eventually thought to ask Philo for his view, as he was, after all, sitting in their midst. Philo recounted how he talked about the issue to Mel and me later that evening. If he did indeed speak in the way that he later told us, then his speaking was a very bold move indeed. Philo had thought carefully about what to say and how.

"Allow me to draw on experience from being a part of running another theological education program here in Holima for many years," Philo opened. "When I came, and local people began that program around me, I had assumed that they thought I could give them helpful insights into the nature of God. In hindsight, I should have realized that was going to be very difficult using English. That is not the point I want to make now though. Our Bible teaching program ran for eighteen years. From the beginning, I made it clear that I had no finance to invest, and that I intended to invest no outside finance. That did not work! That is to say – the question of my financing the school continued to dominate proceedings for the whole eighteen years. Pretty much every board meeting was about my finance or the lack of it. No, that is an understatement. It was not 'pretty much every board meeting.' It was 'every board meeting!' In hindsight, I have to concede – my appearance was and is such, that every African person involved was convinced from the beginning that I must have lots of money and that my primary responsibility should be to acquire funds from the West. This continued for the whole eighteen years of the operation of the program."

"I am aware that SAT is currently under an American principal. I am also aware that the Americans would like to hand over the school to African management. They would like to do so by gradually withdrawing, as provision for the school comes increasingly from Africa. The difficulty that I faced above is, however, the same difficulty as is faced by SAT today: African people will not be generous in supporting a theological school, as long as white people are involved. That, to them is too crazy. We Westerners help to make it appear crazy! That is – we Westerners often tell African people that we have a lot of money and that we are morally obliged to share it with people in other parts of the world. We believe there should be a kind of equality. Our role as Westerners, as we thus describe it, is to give and give and give. Hence, as long as one Westerner remains in a school like SAT, it will remain tough for African people to be generous."

"The above comes to be a bit like a game of chicken! That is, is the West – or in this case, the missionaries and their sending churches who are supporting this endeavor – ready to drop their prize baby? If not, then how will they ever hand it over? If, in other words, Africans make it clear that withdrawal of funding is likely to result in the collapse of the Bible school, then as long as the Westerners involved would like to see the school continue to run, they are obliged to fund it. They may or may not hand over to a local chief-executive – it really won't make much difference. That is to say – the only way to effectively hand over a school that has been dependent on foreign funds to national management is to withdraw funds. That means – being ready to see the school collapse. It is only when nationals see that the foreigners are sufficiently serious about withdrawing that they will allow a school to collapse, that they may voluntarily invest significant amounts of their own precious resources in it."

Robert listened carefully to what Philo had to say. He had no choice – as he had invited him to join the meeting. At least, so it was said by everyone there, although Robert was unaware that he had done so. "You think rather lowly of us, Philo," Robert said.

What Philo had shared made a lot of sense. Robert was trying to get the initiative back. "You make us seem like compulsive donors – as if we give like a runaway train. As if we have no choice but to give to SAT. I tell you what though – we could stop giving tomorrow if we wanted to. You are wrong. We do not have to pull out before African people will make contributions. Our colleagues will give even as we are giving."

At that point, shouting could be heard in the distance. Robert ignored it and carried on. Philo thought that most Africans present at the meeting raised their eyebrows at that point. I guess that was his interpretation. How he could tell that they did so, I do not know. To Philo that meant – they were not going to say it, but no way would they or their people give to a project run by a white man! "What you do not seem to realize, Philo, is that the running of SAT is a partnership. We have agreed ..."

By this time the people who had been shouting were clearly nearer. Robert looked aside, concerned, before completing his sentence: "... agreed on how we are going to work and that is what we will do, and everyone will pull their weight. We are not going to allow any school (at that point there was a violent knock on the door) to drop."

"Come in," Robert seemed to shout. As soon as he had done so, the door was pushed open, and in no time, three students were standing in the boardroom. One of them was Andrea. "Principal, help us," Andrea said, looking straight at Robert.

"What?" Robert responded.

"My dad has fallen. He is badly injured. He was startled by a dog. You know (he mentioned the name of a neighbor to the school who kept a dog). My dad has cracked his head. Even worse, we can't feel a heartbeat."

By the time he had said that, a group of about five women had come to the door. They certainly made sure we knew they were coming. They were wailing loudly. They started talking in the Lile language, talking to Robert as if he might understand them. One thing they were saying for sure was *"Baba wa Andrea."* That is, they were shouting "The father of Andrea."

That was more than Robert could bear. He sprang up. "Take me there," he commanded.

"Let's pray," said Philo, but Robert was already out of the door. It would typically have taken ten minutes to reach Andrea's dad's location. That night, Robert, with a crowd sprawled behind him, got there in half the time. There was Andrea's dad sprawled out on his back. Unlike his son, who was quite skinny, Andrea's dad was a stout fellow. All around him was an enormous din – women, but also some men, wailing noisily. Robert rushed through the crowd and knelt at Andrea's dad's side. He felt his pulse. There was a pulse, he discovered!

"Dad is liable to get heart attacks," Andrea said. At that moment, Andrea's dad convulsed. Froth came out of the left side of his mouth. His clothing was soiled from his left shoulder to his waist. Seeing him convulse, and realizing that he was alive, some of those who were wailing changed their mournful wailing into noisy prayers.

"Tell Pilot to bring the vehicle," Robert snapped to one of the Holiman board members. The latter sent a child running. "He's going to hospital straight away," Robert said.

"We don't have money ..." Andrea jumped in.

Robert looked at him. "I'll pay!" he said. Five minutes later the principal's 4x4 turned up. "Take him to Deja," Robert said to the driver.

"They're on strike," Andrea reminded him.

Robert had forgotten. "Where should he go then?" Robert asked Andrea. Andrea mentioned the most expensive hospital in the area, and that was four hours away! "Take him," Robert said.

Then Robert paused. He knew what he had to say next. "I'll cover it," Robert said. Robert explained his reasoning to me later. The word was almost certainly going to get out, that the father of one of the students had a crisis as he left school on graduation day. He was hardly Robert's responsibility. But – Robert had to think about how that would be understood in America. Americans, without doubt, would want him, as principal of the school, to be generous in such a circumstance. The thought of him not helping and the man dying was unthinkable.

Andrea's dad died four days later. Robert paid $3,000 for the hospital bill, then another $500 for the mortuary bill. Well – Robert had to prove to his donors that he cared for the students, and by implication for their families. Of course, the money that paid the bill wasn't his – it was raised (and was easily raised for such a medical emergency) from generous foreign donors.

At that point, as Pilot drove Robert's 4x4 the four hours to the hospital that was not on strike, the meeting reconvened. "Where were we?" Robert asked after they'd sat down.

"You were telling us that you were sure that you didn't give compulsively," Philo said.

"I am not sure if I was laughing or crying under my breath as I said that," Philo confided in me later, "given the way that Robert had just single-handedly committed to covering any medical expenses arising for Andrea's dad!"

"Ah, yes," said Robert. He was quiet for a while. He was tired. "Look," he said, "given the emergency we have just had, I will raise the money in the West to cover the deficit. Next time, though, it will be a joint affair, including African contributions." The latter came across almost as a threat.

As Philo finished relating his story, Mel and I were sat in a small ring of chairs, outside, alongside the scene that had been the graduation event. The cool of the evening was beautiful. It was getting late, so the flurry of activity of the day was finally passed. "I'll report that," said Mel.

69

"Wait, don't," said Philo.

"Why?" Mel asked.

"You never report things that are embarrassing to Westerners," Philo said.

"Like what?" Mel asked.

"Like that Robert had to go back on his word and raise all the funds himself," Philo said.

"Oh no. I won't report that," Mel said. "What I will report is that the foreign principal agreed to cover all the expenses for the sick man, including a contribution to the funeral."

"Okay," Philo said. "Yes, I guess you have to report that. Make Robert feel good! And – make it more difficult for him to be convincing next time he tells the Africans that they should contribute money to the school because it is becoming hard to raise funds in the USA."

"Hmmpf," Mel and I said in unison.

"One question is still troubling me," said Philo. We looked at him. "Why did Robert invite me to the meeting in the first place?" I laughed, rather too loudly.

"He didn't," I said.

"Yes he did," said Philo. "He said to me clearly that I should be there at 7 p.m."

Mel also looked at me inquisitively. "How can you say Robert didn't invite Philo?" she seemed to ask without opening her mouth.

"You don't know, do you?" I laughed again. Both Philo and Mel were training their eyes on me like I was mad! "The meeting was at 7," I said. "Don't you see! Lunch was in the same room at one o'clock. Robert was practicing his Swahili." I think Philo got it then, but Mel still didn't. "Robert invited Philo for lunch," I said, "not for the board meeting!" Mel was still puzzled. "Swahili time is six hours out from English time," I explained. "Robert forgot that. He invited Philo at one o'clock. That is "*saa moja*," yet "'*saa moja*' is seven o'clock! Philo should never have been at the board meeting!"

CHAPTER 9: LOVE POTION

It had been a long day, and we were overdue for some rest. But, I was to discover, the day was not over. It was about 11 p.m. when we finished the above conversation. We were walking bed-wards. As we walked, Mel pulled on my sleeve.

"I want to talk to you. Philo is not to know," she whispered.

My mind began racing – "What is that about?" I thought. "I'll come," I whispered back.

Philo had retired to his room when I went back to the house where Mel was staying. The moon was almost full. The cicadas were making an enormous din. Otherwise, the night was quiet. I could see the reflection of the moon glinting on the water. The sandy soil made a slight scraping noise under my feet. There was Mel, sitting alone outside of her house; I guess I should add – looking incredibly beautiful! She was resting her chin in one hand. One leg was raised higher, the other lower down, her dress covering both. When I got closer, I also realized that she did not seem to be entirely at peace. I sat beside her. We were quiet for a while, looking out towards the lake – a breathtaking scene.

"Thanks for coming," Mel said to me. "I am troubled. I needed someone to talk to. Otherwise, I might not be able to sleep at all tonight."

"I'm here," I said. Her presence, the proximity of her body, was taking me captive. "Can I get a chair?" I asked. She nodded. I relocated myself, a little further away, this time sitting in a chair and not on the steps right alongside Mel.

"While Philo was in the meeting," Mel began to recount, "I sat here on this veranda. I was quietly working on my laptop. I never noticed a woman come up, till she was right here beside me. She was about fifty. I don't know who she was. Medium build. Attractive figure."

I was intrigued. "What on earth happened to Mel while Philo was in the meeting?" I asked myself.

"The woman startled me when she started talking to me," Mel said. "I looked around. She was very close. You wouldn't believe what she said," Mel added.

"Go on."

"I can see that you love Philo!" she said.

"Ooh!" I exclaimed, quietly.

"I couldn't believe what she was saying," Mel added.

"Hmm," I said.

"What was I supposed to say in response? How on earth did she know? Well, she answered my question. 'I saw it in your eyes,' she told me. To be honest, at that point I was a bit scared," Mel added. "I could not deny it, which of course amounted to a confession."

I had that temptation that I guess always comes to me when I talk to a beautiful woman on the verge of tears, to go and pick Mel up and hug her. I resisted it.

"'We can help you,' the woman went on, in broken English," Mel said. "What do you mean 'we can help you'? I asked. 'Come along and I'll tell you,' she told me. I surprised myself by the way I just followed her. We walked about 200 yards, I guess it was, to her house. She invited me in. I hesitated. She came and took my hand. This house had no electricity. It was lit by a smoldering wick in a little metal tin. I sat down. I was mesmerized. I sat at her table, next to an attractive African girl, maybe twenty years old. She didn't say anything the whole time. I guess she was another customer."

"Then the woman put a small bottle in front of me." Mel carried on. "Alongside it, she put a small packet. In the packet, of transparent plastic, was something like salt. The bottle seemed to contain the same thing. 'Put this into his food, and he will love you,' the lady told me. 'Look. The bottle is expensive. You can have it if you want. But – I can give you a sample for free. Take this packet. Put it in his food! Then he will love you. When it starts to work, then come back and get some more,' she told me. 'My number is on that paper,' she added. There was a piece of paper in the packet. She took the package and pressed it into my hand. I didn't check what was on it at the time. Then she took my other hand, and led me back to where I had been sitting," said Mel. "Look, in the beginning, I thought I shouldn't tell anyone. But then I thought I should tell you."

"Where is the packet?" I asked. Mel pulled a small packet out of her breast pocket. She held it out to me for me to see, then put it back into her pocket. "Are you going to use it?" I asked.

She just looked at me, not answering. "Look. I've told you, pray for me," she said after a while. I did. Right there and then. "I'm hoping, now that I've told you, that I will be able to sleep," Mel added.

"Thanks for telling me," I said. I took her hand. I shook it, in a way that I hope was affectionate – like I was a trusted mentor. Then I walked back to my room. Thoughts of what might have been, had I still been a married man with a wife beside me every day, were filling my mind with sadness. I went to bed and eventually sleep took me.

CHAPTER 10: CLASH

Rolly had been a keen observer of what had gone on in that graduation. He had also laughed at Robert's error – when he discovered how Philo had inadvertently got invited to the crisis board meeting. Both he and Rose knew about the incident with Mel's camera. Whether they knew all about the other revelations that Mel made, I do not know, but I doubt it. The morning after graduation we were to have breakfast together.

"I'm looking forward to learning more about your work," Mel said to Philo over breakfast. I guess she was doing her best to make it clear that she was there as a journalist.

"Yes," Philo responded. "If you want to know more, other than what I can explain to you, you had better learn Swahili," he added.

I don't know if he knew that such an answer would rankle Rolly. I for one was not surprised when Rolly responded angrily. "Who do you think you are, Philo, telling us that without Swahili we cannot understand what is going on in Holima? I have been in and out of Holima all the years you have been here and more. I don't think you can claim that because I do not know Swahili, I am ignorant." Swahili was the straw that broke the camel's back.

Philo looked at Rolly. "Oh no!" I thought.

"Look, you said you would help us to understand what is going on around here," Rolly went on, "but now you are refusing even to have us go with you. Mel here has gone to a lot of expense and trouble to come out here to do research that should be in your interest as well, so why don't you cooperate?"

"Who are you going to listen to," Philo asked at that point, " the African people or me?"

Rose came in then. "We will listen to you, and we will listen to the African people," she said.

"Yes, but who gets the priority?" Philo added.

"What do you mean?" Rose asked in return.

"If we disagree, that is, if I disagree with what African people are saying, or they disagree with what I am saying, then who do you believe?"

Philo was here getting to the nub of a crucial issue. I could see what he was saying. I am not sure, though, that the others could. That would soon be revealed as the conversation progressed. It was a critically important question for Philo. He was probably pretty sure what their answer would be. They would say that at the end of the day they would listen to the African in preference to him. Then he would say that they had better talk to Holiman people rather than to him. But if they weren't going to listen to him, then what was the point of their being there with him?

"You seem to have a problem with pride," said Rolly at that point, looking at Philo.

I thought that was a bit below the belt.

"What do you mean?" Philo responded, biting his lip.

Rolly answered. "You seem to think that you are the only legitimate authority around here, that others have no right to make up their own minds."

I could see tears well up in Mel's eyes as he said that. She could not take harsh discussions between Christians very well. It was upsetting, and in her judgment, Philo was reacting with pride rather than gentleness. At the same time, she also wanted to come out in Philo's defense – but she did not know how to. It seemed to her that Rolly was right. Why should Philo be insisting as he was, that he should be the authority over and above Africans!

Philo glanced at Mel. "Can you answer my question please?" Philo said. "Who are you going to listen to if our accounts do not tally, the African or me?"

The spread laid on the table was terrific. It was one of those breakfasts when one had to be very careful or one would have no appetite for lunch. What or when lunch would be anyway though, I didn't know. Maybe it was appropriate to eat a big breakfast? Philo reached for the milk, and then he poured himself a cup of tea. The Americans were drinking coffee. I was drinking water and orange juice. I had had a couple of pieces of toast, an egg, a banana, and some yogurt – so I thought I had probably had enough to keep me going for a few hours.

"Are you worried that no one will listen to you, Philo?" Rolly said, one could almost say mockingly. "Do you have to establish your superiority before we begin? You are, of course, cleverer than all the Africans around here."

By this time, he was openly mocking Philo. This was, to me, such a classic situation! They were the visitors – even though Rolly had visited Holima many times, he had never lived there. The visitors were outnumbering Philo (if I count myself) four to one. Rolly, with his wife, of course, backing him, and Mel too poorly informed to comment, seemed to acquiesce. Why was I not supporting Philo? Well, I would in due course, but I wanted him to present his case himself. I was also very aware, and I am sure so was Philo, that almost everyone in the UK and America was likely to be backing Rolly. How could Philo know more about Africa than Africans? He would all too easily be condemned as a colonialist!

Mel said slowly: "I am here to write a report, not to agree with anybody."

At that instant, I saw tears welling up in Philo's eyes.

"I think it's time you learned to listen," said Rolly, putting Philo squarely in his place.

"It would be helpful to me if you would answer my question," Philo asked again.

"I think they have answered it," I said.

I had to pity him – if that is the right term to use, for the times when he found himself having to stand up alone to the masses. Philo had learned three African languages. Two he used pretty much daily. He had lived in Africa for thirty years by this time, twenty-five of those years in the same village, in Holima. He was a devoted student of pretty much everything, dedicated, single. Then everyone coming from Europe or America seemed to disagree with him, few understood him.

"Then go and talk to them," Philo said at that point. (Just about then a girl (of the Lile tribe) came to check that we were okay. We said we were fine.) "And leave me alone."

Rolly leaned back in his chair. "Look, Philo. It is not that we do not want to listen to you."

"Right," Philo agreed. "It is though – that you do not want me ever to contradict what Holima's citizens are saying. And, if I do so, then you will simply consider me to be wrong. Have you ever wondered why not many people want to serve in mission for a long time these days? Well, it seems you have your answer."

"You mean they are all egoists like you who need to have everyone listening to them?" Rolly answered.

"Not exactly," Philo said.

"What then?"

"Do you encourage new long-term workers to learn local languages?" asked Philo.

"Yes, very much so," Rolly replied. That was an essential concern to Rolly.

"Why?" asked Philo.

"To help them in their ministry."

"So, someone who has learned and used a local language may have acquired some wisdom?" Philo asked.

"Yes," said Rolly.

"If they have acquired such wisdom and understanding, then why override them?" Philo asked.

"It's not me who will override them," Rolly said, "it is the African people, because they live here and know things the best."

"And what language do you listen to them in, those African people," Philo asked Rolly.

"In English, of course."

"Well, if you and people like you can get all the insights you need through listening to Holiman people when they talk to you in English, then why should I, or anyone else for that matter, learn to talk any African language(s)?"

"Well, you needn't," Rolly said quickly in breathless haste, only realizing too late that he had contradicted himself.

"Look, the bottom line in this issue," Philo said, "is this – you, as it seems most Europeans, will take the side of the African you don't know rather than a fellow Westerner you do know. Fair enough. I don't have to tell you which side to take. You are free to choose. But then – why should I want you to keep me company when I am engaged in sensitive ministry? Just so that you can condemn me and what I am doing, by citing Africans?"

"It seems to me you are just tying yourself in knots," Rolly retorted.

Quick to support her husband on this occasion, Rose added, "I'm not sure I want to follow Philo anyway. I would rather go to Imbigen and spend some time with my friends."

Before long, Rolly and Rose got up and left. Perhaps they walked off. It seemed a bit like they marched off!

We had been sitting for a long time, so I suggested to Mel and Philo that we go for a stroll. We had not yet had the opportunity to walk to the lake shore. We set off in that direction. By the time we did so, the sun was climbing in the sky. It was getting hot. That was something one had to get used to. The cool of the morning didn't last very long. "Walking places in Africa is always interesting," I reflected as we went. In Africa, the mark of human habitation is everywhere – children, chickens, out-houses, houses, maize plots, goats, women fetching water, people about their business. African places always seemed to be alive with humanity.

"In some ways, when you were talking just now," Mel said to Philo, "you sounded proud." "Hmm," said Philo. "I guess I might have. I am tired of seeing so many prejudices get accepted without analysis," he added.

"Philo did not finish explaining himself," I told Mel. She looked at me, then turned to look at Philo who was two paces behind us. We eventually got to the lake edge. We sat on a tree-trunk, looking out across the lake, Mel in the middle, me on the left of Mel, Philo to the right.

"Dave said you hadn't finished explaining," Mel said, turning to Philo.

"Rolly is right that African people have a much better understanding of what is going on than I do," Philo said. "What he did not think to consider though was – whether they can communicate that back into English."

"Or – how they communicate that back into English," I added. "It is possible that Philo knows less than they do. But he may also be able to explain things more accurately in English, his mother-tongue, to mother-tongue speakers, than will African people who have learned English in school. Or, let alone accurately. Philo, who knows where we are coming from, can explain things in a way that makes sense to us."

"Okay," Mel said. "So then the reason a missionary needs to learn and use the indigenous language is not only so that they learn how to engage with people here, but also so that they can communicate what is happening here more effectively to people back home!"

"Rolly feels threatened," I said, after a pause.

"Yes, I understand that much," Mel said. As she talked, Mel was casting her eyes around the lake, admiring the scene. "If you are right, then you are implying that Rolly's using English in Holima, and other places, is far from adequate. In fact, besides, you are even implying that Africans may be deceiving him!"

Philo laughed lightly at that point. "You may be right, Mel," he said. "I noticed something in the board meeting I was privileged, whether legitimately or otherwise, to attend."

"Oh," I said, encouraging Philo to spill the beans.

"When one of the Holiman people started explaining things to Robert, another stepped on his foot, under the table, to stop him," Philo added.

"So, you think he was trying to be honest about something?" I asked.

"I don't think so, I know so!" Philo assured them.

"Philo, this is complicated," said Mel. She looked into her lap, then looked up again. She paused, obviously thinking about things. "You are either an angel or a devil," she said.

"Well observed," Philo said.

Ironically, that comment seemed to dispel some of the negative vibes from our engagement. The mood improved. The profundity of that remark struck me. It showed that Mel was beginning to understand. She never mentioned the third option – that Philo might be 'neutral' and merely agreeing with what Holiman people are doing. I was sure that the topic would come up again. It is something that secular people rarely consider, but that every Christian should consider. Many African people did not even know about Christ until one hundred or 150 years ago. Since then they have poured into churches, and they have formed churches. The influence of the West has, however, contributed to some of those churches being very oriented towards collecting money. The point being – there may be lots of residues of paganism, lots of demons not dealt with, in more African parlance. Then how could Philo agree with Africans?

Before long, Philo spoke up again. "There was a missionary looking for someone to take on, to help in the administration of a school in Africa. I was with him when the person, a Holiman himself, basically warned that he should not be employed. The reason – he admitted that he was used to operating in a corrupt environment. He would not be able to help himself – he would continue to be a corrupt and a divisive influence. The missionary took him on anyway! In many ways, he didn't have much choice. There wasn't a queue of reasonable alternatives standing at the door. Anyway, he took him on, and as the Holiman had predicted, he came to be a divisive and destructive impact on the school."

That was Philo's brief account.

CHAPTER 11: RETREAT

"Rose is upset with you. She wants to go back to Imbigen. She doesn't want to carry on because of the things you have been saying, Philo." Those were the words of Rolly a couple of hours later. Philo had been talking to Rose about the beauty of the lake. It seems Rose had not been able to hear him. We were all sat under a tree. Although the log we sat on under the tree was quite comfortable, Rolly and Rose had a spectacular view. We were facing the other way, towards them, away from the lake. "Now your stubbornness is destroying plans others have made with the intent to help you out and make your work better known," Rolly added.

"I said you were welcome to visit, not to shadow me," Philo emphasized.

Philo stuck to his guns, but he was distraught! I had seen him like that before. One occasion was in front of the Senate of Western University in Seattle. Then he had pretty much collapsed. Philo's problem was that he stood in the way of idealistic people's visions of how they were going to help Africa. Rolly was trying to force Philo to comply by putting him into a guilt-trap.

Rolly, usually a peaceful and amicable person, had decided that he was not going to allow Philo's folly, as he perceived it, to get in the way of things. "You agreed that we come here. You are now not going to dictate what we do and how," Rolly said. As he said it, he was pointing his finger right into Philo's face. Rolly was rather short. I get the impression that at the time he would have liked to have stood on a chair so that he could be looking down at Philo. "You are a proud idiot," he added with his voice raised.

"We need another time of fellowship around the Word," I thought. Now – I could very well see Rolly's point, and Philo was being stubborn, but did that warrant Rolly shouting at him with his finger almost going up Philo's nose?

"Steady up, Rolly," I said. My words were to little avail.

"You think you are clever and the only person who understands Africans," Rolly said, with venom dripping from his tongue.

"It seems to be I am the only one who concedes that I don't always understand them," Philo said in response. How Philo managed to keep his cool sometimes amazed me. Not that he wasn't churned up inside.

"Look, my wife is in tears because of you," Rolly said. Indeed, there was Rose, carrying suitcases towards the car, with her head bowed, crying. Rolly stormed off in the direction of his wife.

"Dave, the cat is amongst the pigeons or something," Philo said to me. I nodded. "I think you had better go."

"You mean you think I should go with them?" I asked.

"They need your support right now," Philo added. "Especially Mel."

Mel sat on a chair about ten yards away. She could hardly believe what was happening. She certainly didn't feel able to stand up to Rolly. How closely that was related to his having saved her life on the train that day, I couldn't know. He was older than her. He was a senior married man. She was a single gal. She would have liked, I imagined, to pull alongside Philo, hug him, and tell him "I will never leave you." But whatever efforts she might have been making to communicate her love to Philo, that had as yet been to no avail, were about to be terminally terminated. Meanwhile, Philo might have been shocked out of his boots to realize Mel's actual intentions on this trip!

The sun was by that time high in the sky. It was the hottest time of the day. The dry earth must have been hot to the touch. I waved to Mel to follow me. "Better pack your bags," I said. Philo was, presumably, looking at my back as I said that. Mel went to Philo to shake his hand.

"I'll see if I can come back to do more research when the circumstances are better," I heard her say. I thought that was an interesting comment. I didn't believe in 'interviews.' Mel seemed to be on the same page as me. "What she was able to learn in the push, shove and helter-skelter of life beat a pile of interviews hands down," I thought to myself.

I went to my room to pack my bags. When I looked behind, I saw Philo walking towards his room. I thought about Philo as I arranged my clothes. His determination to be *vulnerable* left him right out on a limb. There were we, his friends from far away. His fellow white people, about to walk out on him and abandon him to his African fate! We would have each other to talk to. He would be left with the African people he had chosen. Philo hung on in there with them, no matter what happened!

I thought Rolly wasn't going to be up to praying together before we left. He was sitting upright, lips pursed, in the passenger seat. Behind him was Rose, looking extremely distraught, with Mel beside her trying to console her. I walked over to Philo. Standing alongside him, I prayed for all of us. "Vulnerability is costly" were my parting words to Philo, as I walked towards the car. I got in and started the engine. We pulled away. Before long we were on the tarmac road heading for Imbigen.

Philo later told me what happened after we had left. Philo packed his bags, or rather a bag, attached it to his bicycle and set off for home. When he got to the junction, there was Olich. Olich waved to him to stop.

"*Osiepeni gisedhi,*" he said to Philo. (Your friends have gone, indeed.)

"*Ee,*" Philo responded.

"*Imakoriga kodwa!*" Olich added. (You hang on to us!)

Philo was not in an emotional state to do much talking. He was too choked up. He just nodded back to Olich. An English translation of what Olich went on to say is something like the following. "You really do hang on to us Philo. At all costs! Do you know the trouble with white people? Even when we tell them we are corrupt, and only interested in their money, taking advantage of them, they don't believe us!"

"Well, that is true," Philo said to me later. "And wonderful in its way. Although in the end, unfortunately, when one says goodbye to the truth, it is also not wonderful."

What Philo meant was that it is beautiful to think of people as not-sinners. That is – to see them as being forgiven, and as having repented (turned around) in their lives as a result of becoming Christians. The problem, though, is that Westerners think that when one becomes a Christian, one becomes a Westerner! Once someone has become a Christian, everybody thinks that we are all the same. That, though, does not work, because cultures and habits are so different. As to Philo – well yes, it was as if the Striden were his people – it was their children he was rearing!

* * *

No one said anything for a long time, as we were headed back to Imbigen. I was concentrating on passing trucks on the highway. That doesn't mean that our minds weren't active though. Mine certainly was.

We got onto a quiet piece of road. Much of the land on both sides of the road was cropped. Then, somehow extraordinarily, alongside a cropped stretch of road, there would be a piece of bush-land. That is, land that looked as if it had never been cultivated, that had nothing but scrawny grass for the occasional cow! It was Rolly who broke the silence.

"Philo's attitude makes me angry," he said.

"Humph," I responded.

"He seems so proud – as if he is the only one who knows what he is doing."

"Perhaps he is," I said.

"What do you mean by that?" Mel piped up from the back.

I explained – that I certainly knew of no one else who lived in an African-way as Philo did. Every other white Westerner seemed to build his relationships (or hers for that matter) on western superiority. That is – on the fact that they know English (for example, English teachers). Or, the fact that they could access money – so could run projects. Philo ran no projects. The way he lived was also incredible – riding a bicycle, even though in his mid-fifties by that time, living in a house without conveniences, relating closely to churches that were very indigenous, and so on.

Once I had explained all that, Mel asked, "Well, if he has all that, then why doesn't he want us to see it; to be with him in it?"

"Because that doesn't work," I said.

A herd of cows crossed the road in front of us. Fortunately, they were off the road by the time we arrived, so I only had to slow down a little.

"Philo does seem much too perfect," Mel commented at that point. "Does he not make mistakes?"

After she said that, I heard Rolly grunting in agreement, and then mumbling something under his breath. Something, I guess, like "stuck up he is!"

I didn't know just how to answer Mel and Rolly on that one. Philo got where he was by making mistakes. I'd known him for years, and he had confided in me some of his mistakes in the past. But now, it was like Philo was out-of-sight. He was making his mistakes doing things that we could not understand in the first place.

"How does a farmer explain to a hunter-gatherer what he is doing wrong?" I asked. No one answered. I could almost hear the cogs turning over in Rolly's mind!

"You're talking in riddles," he said.

"Have you ever seen a chicken fighting with a pigeon?" I asked again.

"You do say some daft things ..." Mel responded.

"Answer me then," I said.

"No," said Mel.

"So, why not?" No answer.

"Have you seen a pigeon fighting a pigeon? Much more likely!" I said.

"Okay, so like-fights-with-like," said Rolly.

"That's it," I said. "A pigeon doesn't understand the issues that arise between chickens, and vice versa. Well, could it not be that we Westerners don't understand all the issues that arise between African people? Those are the mistakes Philo is making, and the issues he is engaging. He doesn't tell us about them, because we wouldn't understand them in the first place."

There were no more responses. I guess my colleagues understood me. Or at least, that they understood something! I changed down a gear, then another. The hill we were climbing was steep.

"He just sounds selfish to me," Rolly said. He was still determined to trash Philo.

"I know you are used to something different," I replied. "I know of many missionaries, and you probably know more than I do. They respond differently . That is, when they expect visitors, then they make provision for them. They buy vehicles, put up guest houses, set up western-like facilities et cetera, then they give their visitors 'short-term mission' experiences. The visitors are happy because they get exposed to some African life in the raw. They go back home to think about it, reflect on it, and show their pictures. Philo doesn't do that."

"You can say that again!" Rolly exclaimed.

"I like him the way he is," said Mel.

I think Mel regretted saying that as soon as the words left her mouth. Rolly glanced over his shoulder – puzzled, I suppose! We had to stop for some more cattle crossing the road. At least it was cool in the vehicle, thanks to the air-conditioning.

"Does the fact that Philo does it different make him wrong?" I asked Rolly.

"Does Philo help anyone?" asked Rose.

"He teaches the Bible," I said.

"Well, yes, but does he help anyone?" she reiterated.

"Not that tired old argument of gospel versus social action," I thought. I was not going to go there. "That depends on whether you consider the Bible to be God's word," I said. Rose shut up.

"He doesn't want us to go with him," Rolly declared.

"So, are you ready to walk, ride a bicycle and sleep in any old village hut you end up at?" I asked him.

"No," he said after a while.

"Even less so Rose and Mel," I said.

"So?" questioned Rolly.

"Your presence would transform what Philo does and how. To Philo how he does ministry is as important as that he does ministry," I said. That seemed to make sense. When I looked into the mirror, Rose was asleep.

"But why does he have to be so proud with it?" Rolly asked.

"He is not proud," I said. "You take him as being proud because he does not bend to what you tell him."

"Or to African people," Rolly responded. "A number of them have said that they don't like the way Philo lives – instead of imitating how African people live, he should be showing them how to live better! African people tell me that."

"Yes, a better way of life, i.e., more money. Why should African people care about how Philo lives?" I asked. "Except that is – they might be fearful; if other foreigners who came to them lived like that, they'd get less money."

"So why don't you live that way, Dave?" Rolly asked me.

"I was going to ask that," Mel chipped in.

"Not sure I could," I said. "But that doesn't mean I condemn Philo for the way he has chosen to live. I respect him for it!"

"Even when he keeps you at arm's length?" Rolly asked. I nodded.

We made the rest of the trip in silence. By this time traffic had slowed down a lot. We were nearing the center of the city. I was occasionally coming to a complete stop.

"You have hit on something important," I said to Rolly. "Other people don't like the way that Philo does things – because they don't want to have to do things that way. That's the reason. It is not because it is wrong. Not at all. But – it is difficult, they don't want it, and Philo shows them up! Africans also realize that. They know that if they make life easy for incoming foreigners, they get more visitors; these visitors bring more money, and on it goes. It's about money."

As we drove, a bird sat on the road in front of us. The bird took off but misjudged our speed. We heard a slight thud as it clipped the mirror of the car. We later found spots of blood on the front of the mirror.

"But does that mean I would have understood him had he used Swahili?" Mel asked.

"How long does it take to learn a language?" I asked.

"I don't know," she said.

"Okay, let's say it takes a year," I said.

"Okay," she said. I glanced into the mirror. I saw Mel leaning against Rose.

"So, if you learned the language while living with the people, do you think you might learn what 'give me your camera,' i.e., *'nipe kamera yako'* would mean, in a year?"

"Well, yes, if I spent all that time and people kept asking me for things," Mel said.

"Well, there you are," I said.

"But that isn't about the language. It is about the culture behind the language," Rolly said.

"Which is why Philo doesn't trust you to talk to the Holiman people in English," I replied.

Because Rolly was concerned about his wife, he insisted that we find a quality hotel. He didn't want to be messed about, and for Rose to freak out. We pulled up to a hotel in the city. Our bags were carried into the reception. It was an extremely smart place. "Look, let's get cleaned up, then meet for supper at 10.30," Rolly said. We agreed. I went to my room. Mel went to hers. It had been a long day! By suppertime, everyone ate quickly, wanting to get to bed.

* * *

The next morning over breakfast, it was the ladies' turn to butt heads! We met at a table in the corner of the dining room. Rolly said grace for us before we all set off on the breakfast-hunting expedition. It seemed that way anyway – as the choice was massive. We gathered back together with our diverse versions of 'how breakfast ought to be.'

"I am so glad that we are back in Imbigen," said Rose. "I have been in touch with my friend. We are all welcome there for lunch. They are not far from here. And they have a swimming pool. She is an excellent cook. There are all sorts of entertainment there – from table tennis to a large-screen video. In fact, I propose that we spend the next two days in Holima with my friend. She has a flat on her property that will easily accommodate the four of us. It has four bedrooms. She will let us have the whole flat for just $50 per night. We can stay there. We can swim. We can eat. Then, also – all the city's entertainments are available to us; game-park, restaurants, you name it! Now I am really beginning to enjoy this holiday."

As she spoke, Rolly made appreciative noises. He seemed ready to ditch the whole idea of trying to work out what Philo was up to. It was about then that I discovered a feistier side of Mel.

"If we do that, we will be making Philo's words come true. We will be proving him right, and not wrong," Mel said. Her feistiness took us all aback. Well – maybe I less so, as I was aware of her marriage intentions.

Then, however, Rose started to cry. "Look, my dear. We have had enough of Philo and his antics," she said.

Mel had begun saying, "Therefore I think we should ..." before she stopped in her tracks.

"Don't talk any more about Philo. You will only upset my wife if you do!" said Rolly. I was shocked. Mel looked shocked.

"Remember why we came here?" Mel said. "I came here to do some journalism. You agreed to support me in it. We need to do what we set out to do, and that is about Philo." When she said the word "Philo," Rose screwed her face into a shocking shape!

"Is this emotional blackmail or what?" I wondered. I beckoned Rolly. We walked off and left the two ladies sitting there.

"I don't think this is very appropriate behavior," I said to Rolly, once we were out of earshot. "If Rose is upset, fair enough. But – I don't think we need to declare Philo a taboo topic of conversation. He is, after all, the reason why we are here."

Rolly acknowledged that what I said was right. He went back to the table. He took his wife by the hand. They went, for twenty minutes or so. When they came back, Rose appeared more composed. Thinking that Mel may be afraid to do so at that point, I took the conversational initiative. I mentioned something that I had been thinking about.

"We seem to have done to Philo what everyone else does to Philo," I said. "That is, we have left him in the hands of the African people! It is not that Philo doesn't want our friendship though. It is just that he considers that there is a need for a bridge, that is for cultural adjustment, if one is going to relate with the people of Holima as he does. Because we are not willing to make the needed adjustments, we are not helping his work. He is being honest with us. Unlike some other people – he is not prioritizing us white people just because we have money. He is not telling African folks to put on a show for us. He is protecting his African network from the damage that would be done by short-term missionaries like us."

When I said that, something seemed to register in Rolly's mind – I guess it was realizing that he was a short-term missionary. Rolly looked at Rose. "Rose seemed set on having ten days in Imbigen between the swimming pool and the restaurant," I thought.

"Look," Rolly said, "Philo has ditched us. He's basically told us to get lost. Let's do that, as far as he is concerned. He does not want us."

Then Mel came in. "But does that mean that we don't need him?" Mel was following another tack. "We are all aware how, in recent decades, interest in and commitment to Christian mission has seriously declined in the West. This should be of concern to us! More and more so-called mission is only short term, and that short term is getting shorter and shorter term. Then we have Philo – with thirty years of missionary experience under his belt and going strong. That is – he is neither discouraged, disoriented, or disillusioned. He seems to be very content. In his own way, he is reaching many people. Should we write him off and ignore him because he doesn't do things the way we want him to? Maybe some of the things we don't like about him are the very foundations for the ongoing sustainability of what he is doing?" Mel paused. She seemed to want to know if we were tracking with her or not. No one added anything, so she assumed we were and carried on. "Could it not be that Philo's reluctance to embrace the kinds of short-term-mission things we want to do, is the very key to his success? After all – come on – we are all too familiar with the problems caused by western domination over Africa today. That rewards English knowledge, generates and perpetuates corruption, encourages lies and deception, and not only that, it dummifies western academia."

"What do you mean by the latter?" Rolly asked.

"I could try and explain that in many ways," Mel went on, "but let me say this; when short-term visitors to Africa claim to be knowledgeable and morally upright, then if or when they conclude that Africa needs money, they do not allow much criticism of their position. When simplified statements are made as if they are simply statements of ultimate truth by do-gooders who are sure they are right – that becomes hard for academia to stand up to."

"I am sure Philo could add many other reasons for contemporary academia being blinkered," I added.

"You are convincing me, somewhat, I concede," Rolly said. "But – a big problem remains, that is, how can we shadow or investigate and find out more about what Philo is doing if he does not want us to? That is– if he insists that we first learn Swahili, and probably Striden, and don't shadow him?" The discussion turned again to languages. "So then tell me this," Rolly said. "Why does Philo want to insist that everyone learn Swahili or an African language before they engage in ministry? Even before they start listening to Africans!"

I glanced over at Rolly. He was serious. I glanced at Mel. She was attentive. "Because otherwise you just misunderstand too much," I said.

"But people know English!" Mel said emphatically.

"But do they know your English?" I asked. "Someone, Andrea, asked you for your camera. Which language did he use?"

"English," Mel said.

"Did you understand him correctly?" I asked.

"Well, no," she said.

"Well?"

"You've made your point," Mel added, after a pause.

CHAPTER 12: HUNTING AND SPYING

There was silence for a while. It seems everyone was conceding that we could not accomplish our objective. We were defeated! Mel could be forced to return home, not having done her job. We would have to turn back disappointed. Then, strangely, almost eerily, Rolly started laughing.

"Hey folks, I have just had an idea," Rolly said. "You won't believe it ..."

"We cannot either believe it or not believe it unless you tell us what it is," Mel said. She spoke warily – perhaps expecting another attack on Philo.

Rolly laughed some more. "I can't believe it myself," he said.

"What?" I asked.

"Look, dear, it's not fair on us if you laugh at an idea and you don't share it with us." Rose had, I suspect, been very happy to discover that we were defeated and did not know how to find out more about Philo's work.

"Come along, dear," he said. "Excuse us a minute," he told the rest of us. Rolly took his wife's hand. He sat with her out of earshot. We saw him appearing to scold Rose, presumably for wanting the high life in Imbigen when we were supposed to be helping Mel do her research. Then he told Rose something else. After that, he had to comfort her, obviously distraught again! The two of them came back to our table. "Sorry, folks, but I wanted to share my idea with my wife before sharing it with the rest of you," Rolly said.

We looked at Rose. Whatever it was that made Rolly laugh, seemed to have made Rose distraught. Perhaps, I thought, and it turns out I was correct, he had come up with a way of exploring Philo's life, and that had disappointed Rose who wanted to stay in Imbigen for a bit of fun.

"Okay," Rolly said, "here's what I was thinking; why do we need Philo's permission to explore his work, when this is a free country? I say we should shadow him without his permission, and even without his knowledge!" I could see why Rolly had laughed.

"That's crazy," I said.

"But is it?" he replied. "We could paint ourselves black, then follow him everywhere and he wouldn't know it was us!" Rolly laughed to himself. "Just joking," he added, "but – what do you say? Look – we don't have to paint ourselves black. We just have to remain incognito and follow him around from a distance."

"You're crazy," I said. "Don't you realize that Philo rides a bicycle. Can you see the four of us riding bicycles after Philo and staying incognito?"

Suddenly, at that point, Mel burst out laughing. She couldn't help herself. Her head went up and back as she let it out. People on neighboring tables looked at her. She glanced around noticing, so toned down her volume. "That is so-o-o funny," she said. "I've been picturing the four of us on bicycles trying to keep up with Philo and him ignoring that we were there!"

"How on earth will we even know where he's going?" I asked.

"You have forgotten one important thing though," Rolly said. "Philo is ..."

All at once, we heard a gunshot! Everyone in that dining room froze. It seemed to be very close. The next moment there were four shots in succession, also close. Some people laid on the ground. It wouldn't be the first terrorist attack in Imbigen. Someone shouted "*laleni chini.*" We joined those who were laid flat on the ground.

We were down for about one minute when an announcement came over the hotel loudspeaker system: "Ladies and gentlemen, we apologize for the gunshots. There is no cause for further alarm. Please continue with your breakfasts. The thief has been found and killed."

We sat back on to our chairs, dusting ourselves off. "Pheww, I thought we were going to heaven on the fast lane," Rose exclaimed.

"Why kill a thief, why not just catch him?" Mel exclaimed. I felt I knew where she was coming from. Could I explain?

"If a thief is caught, massive expense and inconvenience follow for everyone, not least the police. If he finds a wealthy benefactor, the chances are he'll end up released through payment of a bribe. When courts are corrupt, instant justice at times has to prevail."

Mel's eyes revealed that she was not impressed with that explanation. I wasn't myself, to be honest. I didn't like the system of instant justice either.

When our conversation on how the fate of the said thief most likely came about had abated, we went back to planning our holiday!

"What were you saying again?" I asked Rolly.

"Philo is about to go on a trip," he said. "He won't be taking his bicycle. But – he has publicized to his supporters where he will be every day. That's the trip on which we wanted to accompany him. 'Trip,' that is 'safari,'" Rolly stated for some reason. (The meaning of safari in Swahili is not 'looking at animals in the African bush,' as it is in English. It is simply a 'journey.') "We can follow him simply by going to the places where he said he would be," Rolly emphasized.

Now I had to laugh! All kinds of images popped into my head. One was of the four of us wearing camouflage gear lying on the ground as if we were crack troops! Another was of me standing on the top of a truck with binoculars, spotting Philo walking somewhere. Another was of the vehicle that we would use – that it would have blackened windows. Then I saw, in my mind's eye, Mel wearing a balaclava as she wielded her camera. Then I pictured myself sitting in an African cafe, wearing a wig with my back to Philo, hoping that he wouldn't recognize me! "Maybe, though, we have a workable plan," I thought. This was going to be the *safari* of a lifetime – hunting Philo!

* * *

The next day, four intrepid hunters set out in search of a missionary. We started early as there was a long drive ahead of us. We were heading for Swaro, in Philo's home area. According to the information he had put out, Philo was to begin his trip the following day.

It did not take long for our adventures to begin. We were not to go right to Philo's home. Instead, we stopped about two miles away. It was a rest stop before we started searching for a secret place to stay overnight. Secret, that is, from Philo! We intended to shadow him for as long as we could from as close as we could without him realizing.

We had rented a twelve-seater bus. I was sitting behind the wheel. We thought that would be as incognito as is practical. It looked much the same as did the regular buses that were constantly plying their business of taking people hither and thither for money. We had thought about trying to get one with tinted windows but decided against it. A regular bus but with tinted windows might raise too much suspicion, and stand out too much, we thought. At that point, parked in Swaro, Rolly and I were sitting in the front seat of the bus, as the ladies were heading to some shops.

* * *

We were parked on a hillside, facing up. We were just off the tarmac, and the shops were thirty or so yards from us, away from the road. Then as we were looking around while sitting in the vehicle, someone with the appearance of a mad-man ran up to the ladies. I was a bit concerned! This was an African man, clad in a long robe colored red and white plus a hat of the same color scheme. I looked at Rolly thinking that we ought to run and defend the women from this marauder. Rolly did not seem too alarmed, so I shelved the thought. There were lots of people around. The ladies weren't far from us. The man was a member of a *Roho* church. I had previously visited such a church with Philo. Rolly, and presumably also Rose, knew something of these kinds of churches. Many churches were led by or followed the example of churches in the West. *Roho* churches very much did their own thing. In some ways, they seemed to want to combine communication with ancestors and the worship of God.

The man ran up to the ladies, but he did not grab them or run into them as I had feared he might. Instead, he merely accompanied them, his robes flowing out in multiple directions. Let's say, the ladies seemed to be alarmed, but not petrified. The marauder looked as if he was talking to them. He stopped short of the shops. Then when they re-emerged from their shopping continued behaving, accompanying them, in the same way. Mel later said that what he was telling her was that he could help her to draw Philo's attention! The man, I then discovered was named Ode, continued to make a fantastic spectacle as he danced alongside the ladies as they came back to the vehicle. His behavior was evidence, of course, we realized in due course, that he took us to be friends of Philo (the only resident white man around). So, I guess, he felt free to be familiar with us.

When the small group of three, the ladies and the marauder, reached our vehicle, the man came to my window. "Welcome to a fellowship this evening," he told us. Well, that seemed pretty unlikely. We didn't even know where we were going to be staying. "I assume you are staying at the Swaro Guest House?" he added.

"Where is that?" I asked. He pointed to a sign maybe just 200 yards away.

"Our fellowship will be right next to that guest house," he said, "starting at 8 p.m."

"You are a friend of Philo's?" I asked Ode. He nodded. I glanced at Rolly, who lifted his eyebrows and shrugged his shoulders as if to say "anything is possible."

Meanwhile, I was wondering what on earth would this involve. It seemed though, that if we were going to be exploring Philo's activities and looking at his ministry, and if this man and Philo were friends, then if they were going to have a fellowship that evening, joining them could be a very apt way to begin things. We might even find the opportunity to ask them some probing questions about Philo and his work! The man pointed to a shack made of iron sheets, then he left. The "shack" (as it appeared to us) was right alongside the guest house.

The guest house concerned was not far from the main road. It seemed clean and decent. We sat and enjoyed a cold drink, glad to be away from the tiresome and all-too-often-potholed road. "Interesting fellow who accompanied you on your shopping trip," I said to the ladies.

"Not half!" said Mel.

"I presume from his outfit that he is a member of a *Roho* church," said Rose. "It was on that basis, that even when he began his antics, I thought, well, I had nothing to fear. He was most likely waiting to prophesy to us, or maybe wanting some money," she added. Rose knew about *Roho* churches. They were quite common around Philo's home. Members of those churches tended to wear white robes, often with red crosses stitched onto them. They emphasized beating drums, dancing, and hearing from what some considered ancestral spirits, which others like to know as being the Holy Spirit.

"Ahmm," Rolly said, not sure that the fellow was entirely as innocent as Rose made him out to be.

Looking around the room we were in, we had indeed come down a grade or two from the Imbigen hotel. Things were generally a bit rough for someone used to living in the UK, and especially America. They had simple plastic seats and a wobbly plastic table for our fizzy drinks. The ladies had already inspected the bedrooms, which seemed to be "satisfactory." There was no running water in the en-suite bathrooms, but the lady there had assured us that they would provide hot water if we needed it for washing. One of the rooms had a sit-on flush toilet plus some water in a barrel beside it to flush with. The other had a ceramic toilet at ground level, and also water available for flushing. We decided, so as not to leave the singles alone, for Rose to share with Mel, and Rolly and I to share the other room. At least the whole place was relatively quiet, being a few hundred yards from the main road. Also, there weren't many customers. There were a couple of men, tall men, I thought, lean, not fat, sitting drinking something, as we had our first drinks. The men were engaged in a serious, quiet conversation. After that, there was just a spattering of occasional visitors to the guest house. Some rooms seemed to remain free.

I was not very surprised when the ladies opted out of joining the evening fellowship. They were worn out from all the traveling. We agreed together to have something to eat quickly so that us men would be free by eight o'clock. We all ordered chips, except for Rolly. I think those of us who ordered chips later regretted having done so. The cooking of the potato chips seemed to leave something to be desired. My stomach felt heavy for the rest of the evening, and on to the following morning. Rolly probably did the wise thing by ordering a local dish. The local dish may have been strange to his taste buds, and may not even have tasted good, but at least if one orders something people habitually cook, one can be relatively sure that it is cooked well.

Leaving with Rolly for the evening fellowship reminded me very much of a previous occasion on which Philo, Richard, and I had attended a similar event near Philo's home. That time the event was part of a funeral. (Richard was at the time on a short visit from the UK.) This time it was simply a prayer time. That had been an amazing evening, actually night, so I was in hopeful anticipation as to what we would be experiencing on this occasion. I told Rolly a little about that previous visit to a *Roho* church. He was himself not entirely unfamiliar with what we were about to experience. He had also already heard reports of that earlier visit.

This occasion was in some ways quite different from our previous experience. We entered a small mud building, about 12 feet by 15 feet, with a corrugated tin roof. It was lit by one small smoky flame that emerged from a metal can about the size of a tea-cup. I was surprised that they had not innovated to provide some solar-powered LED lighting, as had many people by this time, almost twenty years into the twenty-first century. The flame flickered on the table at the front of the building. The man who had invited us, in due course, came and sat at the front facing three women who sat, legs together stretched out in front of them, on grass mats laid on the floor looking towards him. Rolly and I were given our seats between them, facing sideways. The platform at the front, the *sinagogi* as people were inclined to call it, was slightly raised. Our time there together, perhaps a total of about one-and-a-half hours, included periods of singing and prayer, much of it while standing, occasionally on our knees. What was striking to me was the message.

The man, Ode that is, seemed to be in his element. The dancing shadows of the flickering light emphasized the varied motley colors of his long robes. Rolly and I had already shared briefly using our faltering Swahili before he stood up to give the closing message. He had introduced us to the ladies present as "friends of Philo." Well, at least we seemed to be on target in our assumption as to why we were getting such a warm welcome from people we had never met. He told us that he was a very great and long-term friend of Philo. (He was speaking his best Holiman English, with some Striden terms inevitably getting mixed in.) His short message, after he had finished praising Philo, was aimed at us.

"We are different from you," he said. I don't suppose he had two white men appear in his service every evening. He was taking this opportunity to make a point he felt to be important. "You have your ways of solving problems," he said, "we have ours. You build hospitals. We do not need hospitals. That is because we have medicines already. I can treat lots of different illnesses without ever studying at a university," he said. "You want to employ people for a monthly wage," he said. "We don't do that. We help each other. Someone works for me to help me out. Then if they are in trouble, they can come to me and I will give them something. We don't pay wages. We help each other," he emphasized. He went on to talk about insurance. "We don't need insurance because we have each other," he added.

So he went on, pointing to myriad ways in which he saw weaknesses in the white man's culture that was being introduced to Holima, and benefits in what he considered to have been the indigenous people's original way of life. He thought himself to be Elisha, following in the steps of a man of God. He believed white people like us to be like Gehazi – who wanted the money that Elisha had refused to take because the healing he had done was by God's strength. We, the white people, always went after the money, he said, thus ignoring the essential things of life. At the end of our time he did, however, encourage us to contribute to the offering!

By the time we were finished, it was about 9.30. Rolly and I walked the thirty seconds back to the guest house. There was no sign of the ladies, so we went to our room. By the time we had each retreated to our sheets at opposite ends of the room, I felt like I was a small boy again, sharing a bedroom with my sister, Julie, many years before! Then sometimes we used to talk late into the night. Now Rolly and I spoke.

CHAPTER 13: TO THE LIGHT OF A CANDLE

"What did you think of tonight's message?" I asked Rolly. I wasn't sure I would get a response. I thought he might want to sleep! Our lights were already out, but I didn't hear any snoring.

"Hrumphmuphibum," I heard a sound.

I did not realize then how long an animated conversation we would have that night, each laying on our backs in our single-beds, looking into the darkness. Well – it was not complete darkness. A few fireflies were hovering around the room above our heads, outside our mosquito nets.

I was surprised when Rolly grunted. "The kind of thing you hear all the time," he said. "The way people talk you'd have thought they already had their country sorted out. They don't need to pay wages as we do in the big-bad-West. They don't need insurance. They don't need, you name it. They have got everything worked out. Drives me crazy!" After a while, he added, "Do you think Philo would just have agreed with that man then?"

"I think that Philo would have said – the problem there is English. That is, Ode was explaining how they, the Striden people, do life, but using English. He knew terms like insurance and salary. He considered that they, local Striden people, have equivalents. Hence they don't need those things. To say instead of 'salary,' we have 'help each other,' sounds so good doesn't it?"

"Yes, not half," said Rolly.

"But I'm not sure that Ode is aware of, or perceiving at all, how our western conception of wages and insurance enables our economy to do things that their economy never can."

"Yes, it is striking," Rolly responded, "that Ode should say what he did with such confidence. If he represents Holima, then he is at the same time constantly extending a begging bowl to the West. That's it, Dave," Rolly added. "Part of you wants to say 'don't be stupid, shut up, and listen,' but it is like they can't. They are convinced by what they have. That is who they are, we could say! Okay, so fair enough, but then they also keep receiving aid from the West!"

"What Philo would say there," I added, "is that we need to engage with people in their own language! When Ode says 'salaries' we hear him as if he is saying something in the English world. It doesn't make sense – how can 'helping each other,' given human selfishness and numerous other problems, substitute for salaries? Because we hear Ode speaking to us in English, we cannot understand the logic of what he is saying! He seems to be destroying our logic."

"So then Philo, who can understand their language, can make sense of their logic?" Rolly asked.

"Yes, well, I guess he can begin to," I replied.

"'Beginning to' isn't going to help him or anyone else very much," Rolly said.

"Yes, but who is even helping him in his endeavors?" I asked. "It is almost like no one. All the Westerners with power who are controlling Holima are effectively investing in English, not in African languages."

"You mean," Rolly was laughing to himself at this point, "that all the aid that is pouring into Holima, is destroying sense!"

It was one of those moments at which I felt ashamed about what our people were doing. I'm not sure whether Rolly's laughing indicated shame, agreement, or bemusement.

"There is another major issue lurking there though," Rolly said. He apparently wasn't *so* tired yet!

"Oh?" I exclaimed. "We are in the West determined to treat black people as if they are the same as us," Rolly said. "But today we met a Holiman who insisted that they are different."

"Go on," I said.

Rolly had had enough of lying on his back. He got up and emerged from his mosquito net. He turned on the light. "Why don't we talk while we can see each other?" he asked me.

"Mosquitoes," I said.

"Ah! Darned nuisance," he said. He went back under his net. Now, though, with the light on. It was a bright strip light. Now he had identified a problem. Stay in bed lying down, and it may be less conducive to conversation. Get up and emerge from your net, however, and mosquitoes have a field day. Turn on the light, and more insects come into the room. What we needed was a chair and table to sit around, all covered in a mosquito net! Sitting in bed is uncomfortable, as there is no back-rest. Rolly propped himself up on one elbow. That didn't look very comfortable. "Darned mosquitoes," he repeated. Of course, we could have sprayed the room, but then we would have had that unpleasant spray odor in our nostrils! "Well, are they the same as us or not?" Rolly asked.

"Tell me!" I answered.

"If they are not, then why do we treat them as if they are back at home?" Rolly said in a beleaguered voice!

Rolly was referring to the practice in the West whereby all people were to be considered 'equal' and should have equal opportunity regarding what they can contribute to society, and what they should be able to get out of life. For many in the West, this translated into 'we need to treat other people as if they are the same as us.' When Westerners assume people in Africa to be 'the same as them,' that means that any problems in African development cannot be due to the people. They must all be about lack of infrastructure, an untoward climate, and so on. This also means that when the West is more and more dominant globally, even African people are no longer able to or allowed to know themselves as they are. Hence they cannot compensate for 'who they are,' in the ways that they live, even if doing so might have brought them socio-economic development. I wished Philo had been there. "He would have enjoyed this conversation," I thought. "Go on," I said again.

"It is crazy, Dave," Rolly said. "We in the West say, no *insist,* that they are not different. You come to Holima, and someone says, 'look, we are different.' They want to have their cake and eat it!"

I laughed a little. "It is not 'they' who want to have their cake and eat it," I said. "It is us, Westerners, Americans, Brits, who want to give them a cake, to have and to eat."

A motorbike went by outside. Then another.

"Meaning?" Rolly asked.

"It is not them saying that they are the same as us. It is us saying that they are the same as us," I said.

Rolly collapsed back onto his back. That left the light in his eyes. "Look, let's turn the light off again," he said.

I jumped out of bed and did so. I lit a candle that was there on the table in case of power cuts. I thought that might be conducive to conversation. "When the candle burns out, then we sleep," I suggested.

"So, is it all a big lie?" Rolly asked. "Is it a pretense – are we in the West just pretending that Blacks are not different from Whites?"

"You know the problem with treating black people as if they are just the same as us Europeans," I said.

"Tell me," Rolly said.

"We in the West might insist that Blacks are not different from Whites, for the benefit of our western society. Maybe that helps us. But – the same becomes globalized."

"Hmph." That was Rolly.

"Yes – I mean – then because of globalization, Holima has to treat its people as if they are Americans or Brits. As if they are white. Even if they are not! Condemning recognition and identification of the differences between people like between Westerners and Africans is done on the basis of an assumed norm. It is also true for Asia. We impose a norm that is western. So, saying 'they are not different,' is saying that everyone is a Westerner, or is like a Westerner!"

Halfway through my sentence, a moth dive-bombed the candle and extinguished it! Moths have a self-destruct instinct. I got up and lit it again.

"The horror of making out that everyone is a Westerner," Rolly said, "is what?" (That was a rhetorical question.) "It is that, when western ways of life are supposedly globalized, even people in countries like Holima have to be treated as if they are Westerners, and can't express their real self anymore. Governments, even, in the developing world, are strait-jacketed. They are rendered inflexible in what they can do in their own countries. If there's any policy they want to introduce or anything they want to do in their interests or that of their people, and if that is something that Westerners would not like to have done to them, then they can't do it!"

The tower of Babel came to mind. In that biblical account, all the people in the world endeavored to come together, forcing all into one language and understanding. God came down and dispersed them! God, it seems, from that and other accounts, is happy for, or even in favor of, peoples living differently according to their traditions.

"You've got it!" I told Rolly.

"But that is crazy!" Rolly said. "Why aren't people aware of this?"

"Defeats me," I said. "But there is more," I added.

"Oh, no," Rolly responded. I looked at the candle. It had a good inch left.

"Okay. Two things in brief." I said. The half-dead moth was still flopping around the base of the candle. At that moment it fell onto the floor. "I guess we will come back to this conversation again in the future," I said, "but I see at least two more things. One, many of the peculiarities of western culture arise from our Christian history."

Rolly seemed to latch on to that one. "You can say that again!" he said emphatically.

"If we assume Africans, say, to be already Westerners, that means in effect that we are assuming them to have much of Christian character. That means that it has become almost illegal to point out reasons for the need for African people to become Christian."

"Do you think Professor Nancy has ever heard all this stuff?" Rolly responded at that point. Professor Nancy was his boss back in America.

"I don't know."

"She will be amazed!"

"Okay," I said. "You see how the agenda that condemns any acknowledgment of difference is concealing the work of the gospel?"

"Dave, this is incredible. Then Christians shouldn't be against the open recognition of differences between people in diverse parts of the world. Yet, because the West is so much against racism, many people in the West, including Christians, prefer to play safe and just try their best to treat everyone the same!"

"Hmm."

"But that all has massive implications," Rolly said.

"I think so too. Better tell Professor Nancy!"

"However, ..." said Rolly. He did not finish his sentence.

There was less than a half inch of candle left. It could go out at any time.

"That was number one. What is number two?" Rolly finally asked. "You'd better explain briefly – I'm getting tired and the candle is nearly out."

I looked at my watch. It was half eleven. "Number two is that as a result of the assumption that African people must never be treated differently from western people, African leaders of all sorts are forced, yes, really forced, to conceal the truth."

"What!"

"To be sensible, and treat their people in sensible ways, they have to go contrary to advice from the West. But, to go contrary to advice from the West is to have their funding questioned. So, to keep their funding, and remember most of them are dependent on western funding, they have to bend the truth. They must make out they are doing one thing, responding to their people as if they are Westerners when they are actively doing another."

"You are saying," Rolly came in then, "that policies in the West that condemn compensating for the difference between African and western people are generating corruption in Africa."

I was nodding, in so far as one can with one's head on one's pillow. Rolly could not have seen that, so I grunted. "Uhumm."

Another moth dive-bombed the candle. The room went dark. "The candle is out, but it's not finished," I said. "Should I light it so that we get the benefit of the last few minutes?" The injured moth was fluttering furiously. "How cruel to light a candle!"

"Bring light in the wrong way and others die," said Rolly. He got that. "However, ..." he said again.

"What?"

"Well, we are both Christians, we can talk about differences and we know what we mean. Christ's love is universal, even if people are different. But you have to realize that much of the time when people talk about differences, it is with a racist agenda."

"Maybe, but ... It is important to be clear on the danger of our position." We were walking a narrow path. Certain types of racism are undoubtedly bad. The Bible does, however, talk of nations. Right back in Genesis 10 and 11, God is clearly in favor of languages separating people and presumably cultures. It is not 'wrong,' it is merely natural for there to be differences between ethnicities or nations. The problem has come in recent times – when certain ethnicities, notably white Europeans, have managed to become incredibly wealthy and powerful. This has enabled them to lord it over others. This is what Philo was against, in what he was promoting as vulnerable mission when it came to mission work. As far as serving God is concerned, Philo was saying, and I agreed with him that inter-ethnic relationships should not always be built on the material and linguistic superiority of one side.

"Don't bother. Let's pray. Dear Lord," Rolly prayed, "we thank you for a good day, lots of good experiences and even for a good late-night conversation. We pray for Rose and Mel and Philo. We pray for wisdom to know how to be discerning regarding the things we are learning. It seems, Lord Jesus, that you are teaching us some important things about how your ministry should be done here in Africa, here in Holima, and probably many other places. May your name be glorified. Amen."

I repeated, "Amen."

"*Nind maber*," Rolly said.

"*In bende,*" I responded in the Striden language. (Sleep well. You too.) Sleep gradually took me, as I listened to the two moths swiveling around in circles on the floor, injured by the light.

CHAPTER 14: ROMANCE REVEALED?

While we men were having an interesting time in our own way, we were later to discover that the ladies, while we were in church, had adventures of their own – of a more feminine variety.

Rose had been with Mel when Ode startled both of them as they went to the shop from the car. She became aware, thus, of the possibility that there may be more going on in terms of Mel's relationship with Philo than met the eye. Rose was wise to be careful about how to broach such a subject. She was no spring chicken on these issues. That evening though, Rose would, through circumstances, end up taking the blunt approach.

After the men had left to attend the night-fellowship, the two ladies sat for a while in silence in the dining room. Then suddenly Mel started sobbing and shaking in front of Rose. Rose, who had been thinking about how to broach the subject of Mel's relationship with Philo, became alarmed. What was going on?

"I can't cope," Mel said (or rather screamed – not loudly, but to say she only spoke would be an understatement). Mel's scream startled Rose.

"You can't cope with what?" Rose said. Her tone was more alarmed than she had intended. "Everything!" Mel screamed (quietly).

One would have thought Rose, as a mother-kind-of figure could (and should) at that time have used a soothing voice. She didn't. She was more stressed than she cared to admit. What bubbled out of her was what was in her head at the time. "You are worried about Philo!"

Without apparently processing her words through her frontal lobe, Mel replied, "I want to be closer to Philo, help him, maybe marry him if he was willing. Where is he? Why can't we be with him? Why don't you like him? What have you got against him? Why does he reject us like this?" Those and more questions shot out of Mel's mouth in a scattergun motion – they seemed to bounce off the furniture and reverberate around the room.

At about that point, it seemed, the girl serving in the restaurant, noticing the commotion, thought it would be helpful to call the manager. He was not far away, so about a minute later arrived on the scene. The manager of the guest house was the pastor of a church within Swaro. He knew Philo very well. He immediately assumed the white people who had come to his guest house to be friends of Philo, so at this point was concerned for them on Philo's behalf. The best thing he could think to do for the ladies

106

who were panicking in the restaurant was to pray for them. When they didn't immediately respond to his verbal approach to them, that was what he did. Many Holima Christians do not know how to pray quietly, and thus the manager's prayers were noisy. His loud praying proceeded to intermingle with the sounds of the quiet screaming of Mel, and the rather alarmed distressed consternations being uttered by Rose. Eventually the manager, a reasonably stout man, perhaps a little above average height, who everyone there just called *'manaja,'* withdrew and left the ladies to sort themselves out.

Rose went up to Mel and hugged her. That did make Mel feel better. They apologized to each other for getting upset. That's not to say that Rose was entirely at ease with her discovery. So – Mel the journalist, was Mel the wanna-be lover!

"Was that a wolf in sheep's clothing, or a sheep in wolf's clothing, or what!" presumably Rose was asking herself. Later, back in their room, Rose tackled Mel in more detail. "So, Mel, what is your relationship with Philo?"

Mel was startled by the question she did not want to hear, mainly because she didn't know where it was leading. "I am a journalist, and I have been assigned to investigate Philo and his work," she said. "It was not intended to be an undercover investigation," she added, "but it is Philo's elusiveness that is making it that way."

"Do you like Philo?" Rose enquired.

That, Mel told me later, was the question she had been dreading and that she hoped no one would ask her. Mel did not like telling lies, she assured me. Given the general stress of the situation already, Mel at that time, metaphorically speaking, collapsed. Her response to Rose was, "How did you know?"

"So, we really are on a wild goose chase," Rose blurted out.

"Please don't tell anyone!" Mel pleaded. Her hope of a relationship with Philo was not supposed to be known. At least not by the likes of Rose.

"So, you have dragged us on this trip, supposedly of journalistic endeavor, just so that you can, you hope, convince Philo to fall in love with you!"

The only thing Mel could think to reply is what she had already answered. "Please don't tell anyone."

"And we thought you were a serious journalist."

"Please don't tell anyone."

"And now you have us running around like headless chickens helping to chase down your romantic utopia in the name of the church."

"Please don't tell anyone."

Rose was not very happy with her revelation on Mel's status. She was also tired. So also, she thought, must Mel be, after the long drive from Imbigen. She had been surprised that the men had found the energy to go to the fellowship. She looked at Mel and took pity on her.

"Look," Rose said, "I will not say anything right now. Okay?" Mel nodded, feeling at least encouraged. "I think we are both tired. Let's go to bed. We can talk more another time." They headed for their beds in the Swaro guest house, and before long they were both asleep, exhausted by the emotions of the day.

CHAPTER 15: SITTING UP FRONT

The next morning cocks started crowing three hours before dawn! I heard them, but they did not disturb me overmuch. Mel told me later that she could not say the same. She heard them and couldn't get back to sleep properly. In fact – many things were stressing Mel. It was only the problem of getting woken up at 3.00 a.m. that she explicitly told me about. That was enough to have me concerned for her.

We each had egg and bread alongside a cup of tea for breakfast. There were other options available for those who wanted to partake. Bananas were available a few hundred yards away. They were small bananas. Much smaller than those that people in the UK are used to eating. Mel had said she'd never seen such small bananas. There just does not seem to be a market for them in Europe. European people are often pleasantly surprised by the variety of bananas when they came to Africa! There were also fizzy drinks available. An alternative to bread would have been *mandazi*. That is – drop scones. They are made of wheat flour mixed with water, typically some sugar, some oil, and baking powder. A lump of dough is dropped into boiling oil. A few minutes later *mandazi* emerge; their flesh is a little like that of a doughnut. No fresh *mandazi* or *chapati* were available there that particular morning, so we opted for the sliced white bread. (*Chapati* are like unleavened savory pancakes, but heavier than pancakes.)

Rolly seemed, as usual, to be the dominant voice at breakfast time. He had noticed a lot of the details of that worship time that I did not notice at all. He was busy telling the ladies. He told them of the dirt floor of the church, that had been decorated while there was a thin layer of mud, into swirly patterns, making it resemble a carpet (with some stretch of the imagination). He explained that we left our shoes in the doorway, and that there was a different doorway for men and women entering the building. He was explaining that feature of doorways when a big man walked into our dining area with his much smaller wife. I saw them enter out of the corner of my eye. Instead of finding a place at which to sit, they made a beeline for us. Rolly stopped his account to give them his attention.

"Hi," said the man. He was wearing a suit and carrying a motorcycle helmet in one hand. He did not seem to hesitate to use English. He and his wife both wore large smiles. His wife also greeted us using the same relaxed English. We gave them our attention. "The manager told us you were here. Can we join you?" asked the man. We made agreeable noises.

As a result, he pulled up a chair on one side, and his wife on the opposite side. There was not much room around our small wobbly breakfast table, but they got in there somehow. The man turned out to be the pastor, called Dan, of a local Pentecostal church. His wife introduced herself as Sue. These were more friends of Philo. "Philo has abandoned you here," suggested the man, not unpleasantly. Well, that was an interesting take on things!

"No. Not exactly. We are just here," I said. I was glad not to have to explain why we were indeed 'friends of Philo,' but Philo wasn't looking after us!

"My church is very close to here. Welcome to join us for the morning service," said Dan.

We had not yet thought about where we might go to church that day. We were still enjoying a relaxed breakfast. Pastor Dan explained how to find his church building. He was on the way right there already. In fact, he pointed out that the music that we could hear playing over a loudspeaker was coming from his church. He and his wife were both very friendly and suggested that we get to the church at ten, just about forty-five minutes later. After they had left, we all thought that would be a good idea, so prepared ourselves, then set off following his directions, with ten minutes to spare.

The church was easy enough to find. The music was still being broadcast. There was already much activity in the church; people coming and going. We received a few warm welcomes, then filed into the building. Rose led us as we filled up a row of chairs about a third of the way from the front of the building. We settled, locating our bags and Bibles strategically, anticipating whatever was going to happen next. Then we were surprised, although it was mainly Mel who was surprised, to be ushered to sit at the front facing the congregation.

"Why are we put to sit at the front facing the congregation," I saw and heard Mel whispering to Rolly.

"This always happens," he responded.

"What do you mean?" Mel whispered back.

"When white people attend an African church, they are very likely to be asked to sit at a prominent place – if not actually on the platform facing the congregation."

Mel was one of those souls who preferred, when at church, to match with the wallpaper. She certainly had not expected to be given such prominence. "Why on earth have they asked us to sit here?" Mel asked Rolly again with an added urgency. She did not want to be 'on display.'

As Mel and Rolly whispered back and forth, things were beginning to move for the church service. The recorded music had ended, and some young people were singing into microphones. Their voices were now being broadcast to all and sundry in the vicinity.

"We are white people. That's why," Rolly said. Mel kept looking at him. "White people are in some African churches considered very special."

"What?" Mel responded.

"In the old days, white missionaries used to be in charge," Rolly explained. "Nowadays, though, the reason is very much to do with the ongoing importance of white people."

"How come? What 'ongoing importance'?" I heard Mel whisper back.

"Nearly all successful churches are dependent on white people," Rolly said. He looked at me. It was harder for me to whisper to Mel without everyone else in the church hearing. This time it was his call to answer the questions. We were asked to stand up and sing. Mel was determined to get answers. After the song, she nudged Rolly to continue.

"Pastors in much of Africa vie for white 'friends,'" Rolly explained. Mel seemed to be horrified! She had thought the days of racial discrimination were over, only now to be told how white people specifically were in heavy demand.

"Why?" she reiterated, apparently dumbfounded.

"For money. It is hard to find other people who are as generous and have as much money as white people. Hence church leaders desire white friends to help their churches to prosper. Getting a white person is like getting a prize catch. Then they put us at the front, to give us authority. You or I could, if we wanted to, start dictating things to the church. They would give us all their ears."

"You mean they'd just do what we told them?" Mel asked incredulously.

"Not necessarily," Rolly said, "but they might give us the impression that they will."

"You mean to encourage us to be more generous?"

111

"Yes!"

"But, but ... why, why, why?"

"Look, Mel. You've been born and raised in the UK. To you, British people might be just 'normal.' On a global scale, however, they are far from 'normal.' British people's long history as Christian believers, perhaps especially Protestants, has given them a singular attitude to generosity. Then, of course, Britain had an enormous empire. African people are very aware of British generosity just as they are aware of British exploitation. Then, the industrial revolution gave white people a lot of wealth to be generous with. Having wealth does not, of course, in itself necessarily result in 'being generous,' but it makes it easier."

"Why are we more generous?"

"Look at how the Bible tells us to be generous," Rolly explained. "Imagine that being meditated on and then explained and emphasized over generations and generations." That gave Mel food for thought, I am sure! Poor Mel was feeling a little embarrassed at being on display to the gathering congregation.

As is typical in African churches in these parts, a 'start-time' for a service is a little arbitrary, because people often arrive at church at a pretty steady rate throughout perhaps an hour-and-a-half.

The singing was incredible and noteworthy. Perhaps Mel had never before experienced such heartfelt singing? She was moved. Many visitors to Africa are amazed by the quality of singing – by comparison, especially to half-hearted murmurings that some western congregations are accustomed to call singing. Mel got caught up in the moment – even though many of the songs were probably entirely new to her. That part of the service I felt, and she said as much later, she enjoyed!

After the singing came a time of testimonies. Now I wanted to tell Mel to stop her whispered exchange with Rolly while the service was progressing. This could be distracting to the whole congregation. I was reminded of Jesus' saying as he entered Jerusalem, that if he told his disciples to be quiet, the very stones would cry out in praise. I thought that if I intervened to ask Mel to shut up, she might just burst at the seams!

A woman stood up and told us that God had healed her son's leg within a week of her telling the congregation that he had been injured.

"Was that a miracle?" Mel whispered to Rolly. This time Rolly indicated that he and I should switch places. I obliged. Now Mel repeated to me "Was that a miracle?"

"What do you mean?" I said.

"Do miracles happen here that do not happen in the West? How come?" By that point, the boy was there rolling up his trouser leg revealing healthy skin on a healthy leg.

"What do you mean by a miracle?" I asked. This was a favorite topic of Philo's he had often talked to me of. I noticed Rolly also straining his ears to catch my response. Perhaps that was a question that was still puzzling him – hence the reason he had switched seats with me! "Well, aren't there miracles in the Bible?" Mel asked.

"Miracle is an English word," I said to Mel. I tried to speak so that Rolly could also overhear, but without being distracting to the congregation in front of us. That was no easy task.

"So?" Mel responded. "I can only read the Bible in English."

"The English term miracle may not mean what the original biblical term meant," I said. "In fact, the term miracle in English generally translates two Greek terms, *dunamis* and *semeion*."

"What do they mean?"

"Well, power and sign."

"Then why are they translated as miracles?"

"Because they are amazing," I said.

"But isn't a miracle something that goes contrary to the laws of nature?"

"Were there 'laws of nature' in New Testament times?"

"Presumably."

"No."

"Come on ... are you telling me that in those days there was no nature?" Mel asked with her eyes wide.

I heard Rolly laugh under his breath!

"People did not know or recognize the category of 'nature' that we know today. The first 'laws of nature' were put together in the last three or four hundred years," I explained.

Rolly then said, in a rather loud whisper: "Pull the other one, it's got bells on."

"No. Ask Philo," I added. "That means, that in Jesus' time, a miracle was not, and could not have been understood as something contrary to or super-to nature, as a miracle is often defined in English today." I don't know what Rolly thought about that. Mel went quiet.

Then Mel said: "Okay. I think this is what you are saying. You are not saying either that Jesus' healings were miraculous, or that they were not miraculous, in the way 'miracle' is understood today – as being something contrary to the laws of nature. So, you are not a liberal. But you are questioning – how can we be sure that a 'miracle' is something 'supernatural' when in New Testament times there was no distinction between 'natural' and 'supernatural' in the first place. So then, was the way this boy was healed a miracle or not?"

By the time she said that, another lady had stood up to give her testimony. Her story was quite different. She had just gone to Imbigen and back by bus. On her way, she had observed another bus having an accident. She was thanking God for having protected her from having a similar accident.

I wished at that point that Philo had been there to answer some of Mel's questions. I guess Mel wished the same! She had come all this way to see Philo, and now she had to make do with the likes of Rolly and me. Mel's answer to my explanation, of course, indicated that she had not understood it. I was at a bit of a loss as to what to say.

"We'll talk about it later," I suggested. "Remind me!"

After the lady who talked about her bus journey, an old man stood up. He, like the others, stood between us and the congregation, so had his back to us. The choir was sitting to one side. The gathering was growing. By that time, there might have been sixty adults in the congregation. The man told us about the sickness of his wife. She was his second wife, as the first wife had died, so the second wife was about twenty years his junior. One could only imagine – that having acquired a devoted partner twenty years junior to him, the old man thought he had found someone to look after him into his old age. But, unfortunately for him, his twenty-years-younger-wife got sick. Doctors diagnosed her with cancer of the esophagus. At least that is what I understood from the man translating for us into English.

The old man then seemed to get very emotional and angry. He started talking more quickly. From the little I picked up from the Striden and the English translation, he was talking about a certain widow. The same widow had been looking after him, helping him with food, after he was bereaved. Then he married the twenty-years-younger-lady who at the time was not sick. Before long, I noticed the pastor signaling to the translator. The man kept talking without translation. He looked around a little shocked. His translator looked back at him blankly but did not translate. I don't suppose Rose or Mel had a clue what was going on. Rolly might have done. Mel touched my arm.

"What?" she whispered.

"The pastor has stopped the translation because the man is accusing a neighboring widow of killing his wife ... through witchcraft," I added. Mel looked stricken. "He should not be doing so. Especially not in church. That is why the pastor has stopped the translation."

Just then, the pastor stood up. He stepped forward and stood alongside the man who was testifying. He put his hand onto the man's shoulder. The man kept going, presumably explaining how he knew that his wife's illness was being caused by his neighbor who was, according to him, a witch. The pastor nodded to the boy at the mixer-desk. He turned off the microphone the man was using. Pastor Dan drew the old man back towards the congregation. The man sat down, all the while protesting, not too quietly, presumably about having been forced to stop telling what to him was a plain and vital truth. There followed a time of worship.

As we worshipped, Mel whispered, "That man was accusing a witch of trying to kill his wife?" I nodded. "But he said the wife had cancer?" she added, in the form of a question. I did not try to answer her during that song. She would have to bring up the topic again later if she wanted me to try to continue to explain things.

All in all, there was a lot during that church service that shocked Mel. She kept on whispering to me throughout most of the rest of the service. I felt I would be over-extending my license with Pastor Dan, even though he was a patient man, if I kept whispering away to Mel. He might start to think that Mel and I were in love or something! To Pastor Dan, I don't think there was anything out of the ordinary happening in church that morning.

CHAPTER 16: CELEBRATION AT CHURCH

We were fortunate to have attended that church on a day when they were having a celebration. What exactly they were celebrating we for some reason never quite discovered. It meant, however, that it was a special day, and there was food available after the service! After leaving the church, we noticed that people were eating rice and beans. To me, rice and beans make a delicious combination. I am not sure Mel, Rolly or Rose felt the same.

A few minutes after the service ended, and as people began to eat their rice and beans, we were called to follow a certain lady. She, as many African women, had large swaggering hips. Her bright blue dress almost reached her ankles. The beauty of being in 'conservative' Christian circles – as a man, I did not have to constantly be distracted by a view of bare female legs and thighs. Her hips, however, swayed vigorously from side to side as she led the way. She ushered us through a door. There was a set of comfortable chairs around a smart-looking wooden table. There was even a bookshelf with some books on it. I didn't get to see what they were. I rather suspect that they were testimonies to success written by American prosperity preachers and by Nigerians. Such were, in my experience, common fare in African pastors' bookshelves.

We need not have been concerned about what we might be given to eat or drink. Things in the pastor's office were entirely different than they were out in the church building and in front of the church (where other people were eating). There, in the pastor's office, beef, chicken, and fish had all been prepared. To accompany them there were *chapatis* and rice. Fruit available included oranges, mangoes (already cut up), and bananas. Cold fizzy drinks were lined up, about five varieties and two sizes for us to choose between. Tea was also available on tap.

Now Mel was upset! "Pastor, we can't eat all this good food while everyone else is just eating beans and rice," Mel said. Now I do not know if the pastor understood her words.

"Let me call my wife!" he said. He sent the girl who had led us into his office to fetch his wife. (I guess he had not understood Mel's concern. In the West, we think churches are places where everyone, regardless of age, gender, origins, and ethnicity, are treated the same. Here, we and the pastor and now apparently his wife were to be getting super special treatment!) "We have put this on so that you know we really appreciate visitors," added the pastor.

"Another reason Philo doesn't like to have us shadow him," I whispered to Mel, making sure I was well outside the pastor's earshot, "is so that he does not have to be an extra special visitor wherever he goes!"

"Do we have to enjoy all this sumptuous food while here in Africa where so many people are hungry?" Mel asked.

"Yes, they are trying to honor us," I responded. The pastor and his wife in due course left us to finish our drinks and biscuits by ourselves. He said he had a few people to see and issues to attend to.

While he was gone, Mel said, "Why all this?"

"You tell her Rolly," I said.

"No, you!" Rolly responded. I think Rolly was getting wary about losing arguments.

"Rose?" I said, trying to pass the buck.

"You," she replied.

"Look, you are potentially a big donor," I said to Mel. "Besides, this is the way people do things here. Visitors, especially foreign ones, plus pastors, are given special treatment. They are considered set-apart, after all. Africa works on the patron-client system. That system thrives on having a few people who are different/special/well off, while many depend on them, praise them, look up to them, and benefit from what drops from the lavish spread of their tables."

"Yes, but the others are just eating rice and beans. The pastor is eating chicken and drinking coke!" Mel said, really just repeating herself. No one responded.

CHAPTER 17: JUDGING PASTORS

"One thing that puzzled me," said Mel later, back at the guest house, "is why did the preacher preach in English?" We were sitting on those plastic chairs again.

Rolly was the first to respond to Mel: "He is an educated man, so why shouldn't he use English? English, I think you know this, is the government-recognized language in Holima. Children spend many years in school learning English. I imagine that the policy of the government is to keep on encouraging the use of English until one day they allow tribal languages to die. Then Holima will become like a European country. It will be counted along with Australia, the USA, and the UK and so on, as a native-English-speaking country. That will help Holima enormously, as then they will no longer have issues like that of tribalism, and things like witchcraft will disappear because everyone will be educated."

It was at that point that we began to see some of the stuff that Mel was made of! "Hang on," Mel said, "but how can the Striden people being addressed understand their pastor if he speaks to them in English?" Mel looked, could I say 'daringly,' at Rolly.

"I have just explained that everyone goes to school. Everyone learns English. Everyone knows English then ..."

Mel interrupted. "You are missing my point, Rolly. The people are not living their lives using English but using Striden. That means that they are familiar with the issues of Striden and endeavor to address their issues using Striden solutions. What has English got to do with that?"

Rolly asked Mel to explain. "Look, Rolly," she said. "I appreciate that you are older than me and have been doing this job for a long time," (at that point I swallowed) "but surely you are not serious?"

Rose hadn't been paying attention. But now she seemed to start to listen in. "What was this spring-chicken of a single girl going to teach her experienced husband, who had once rescued her from a train wreck?" I guess she was asking herself. I stayed quiet. I wanted to hear what Mel was going to say.

"Okay. Let me take a simple example," said Mel, "the case of the accusation of witchcraft that we heard this morning."

"Okay," said Rolly. I nodded. Rose was also paying attention.

"I have never heard of anything like that in any churches in the UK," Mel said. "Fancy accusing a widow of murdering your wife without ever touching her or doing anything to her, just because the widow concerned had hoped she might be the wife!"

"Hmm," said Rolly. He scratched his ear. He was also bouncing one leg that he had folded on the knee of his other leg, perhaps indicating that he was thinking carefully about what was said.

"Have you ever heard of that happening in a British church?" Mel asked, looking at Rose.

"No," said Rose, while shaking her head.

Soon after, two boys ran into the guest house. They were pushing used motorbike tires using sticks. That was a favorite game for children in that part of Africa. When they saw us, they grabbed their tires, turned around, and pushed them back out of the compound.

"So, it seems to me this is a problem that is peculiar to this context or maybe to Africa." We were quiet. "Rolly tells me that we want people to use English. What happens when someone uses English to articulate a very serious (for them) problem that involves the identification of a witch?"

None of us had an answer for Mel. "The microphone gets switched off!" she said. "The issue is hidden, concealed, ignored, not resolved."

"That was a profound observation," I thought. "In fact," I mused, "if Mel can come up with that kind of profundity, then one day Philo might agree to marry her!"

"That means," Mel went on, "that if Striden people use English, they are thereby rendered incompetent at resolving their problems."

"Wait a minute," said Rose.

"Hang on first," said Rolly – both of them speaking simultaneously! Rolly went on (preventing Rose from speaking. The significance of his actions did not seem to occur to him though!) "You forget that English also has a term, witch. English is perfectly capable of translating, or engaging, a conversation about witchcraft."

"Really?" said Mel. "You are sitting on a train in London, in the UK. You hear someone say they have been bewitched. What do you think of them – you, as a Brit, an American, I mean?"

120

"They are crazy, deceived, and unenlightened to believe in witchcraft," Rolly said.

Mel probably hadn't expected Rolly to walk right into her trap, just like that! There he was though – marched right into it! "Yes. Witchcraft is something you, as a Westerner, don't *believe* in. You (as a Westerner) consider it primitive. Someone who thinks they have been bewitched is, to you, unenlightened." Rolly was nodding, still not sure where this was heading. "So, why was the translator stopped, and the microphone turned off, today?" Mel asked.

"Because the things the man was saying weren't helpful," said Rolly.

"So, if we had not been there, would it still have got turned off?"

"Of course."

"How do you know?" Mel asked Rolly.

I chuckled as I thought of Rolly's dilemma. How could he know what might have happened if he was not there, because he had never been there when he was not there!

"Well, I don't know for certain," Rolly admitted.

"So, it is possible," Mel said, still on her streak of brilliance, "that had we not been in the church, things might have been handled quite differently?"

"Okay, I admit it is possible."

"What to them, quite possibly is very normal, a routine problem to be solved in a routine way – someone is being killed by witchcraft – is to us English speakers something abominable. Was the issue resolved?"

"In the church, you mean?"

"Yes."

"No," said Rolly.

"There you are!" said Mel. By that point, Mel was leaning forward with her hand holding her chin.

"Look, Mel. Clarify," I said. "If people discuss their own issues using their own languages without translation," she said, "they are free to discuss them however they want to. Now here's a key point – but I will state it only briefly; if you learn their language, not least if you learn it properly, you will in the course of doing so also learn how people conceive of their issues. But, and this is the big thing, if you expect them to be able to freely discuss their issues using your language (English) you have deceived yourself! Because they know that native-English speakers despise such things, they will not want to talk of cases of bewitchment. They will be silent on them. They will, instead of addressing them, ignore such issues! That is why African people using English will render them incompetent."

"But what ah ..." said Rose.

"Don't think that English is 'African,'" Mel added, interrupting Rose. "Yes, Africans may know English. But it is not their language. And – there is a big danger when using English that we (Westerners) might be overhearing! Especially now that globalization is going on in leaps and bounds."

"But what about the ..." Rose said again.

Mel cut her off again. Now she had a point to make, in defense of her 'lover'! "I can now quite understand why Philo doesn't want us to shadow him."

Rose gawped. She remembered their previous evening's engagement. No way had she expected Mel to say she understood why she had to be separate from Philo!

"Why?" Rolly asked.

"You say." Mel looked at me. I was trying to keep out of the heat, but now Mel was flinging me into the frying pan of western mission discussion!

"Okay," I said. "One, Philo has learned the language. That is how he has learned 'how people conceive of their issues' as Mel has already mentioned. That itself is a biggie," I emphasized. "Plus, Philo does not have money to spend ..."

Before I could continue, Rolly snapped; "What has that got to do with it?"

"It means he doesn't condemn people," Mel jumped in.

"I don't condemn people," said Rolly straightaway.

"Hang on, Dave," Mel said to me. "Let me just explain this to Rolly; then you can carry on." I nodded. "You help pastors?" Mel asked Rolly.

"Yes," said Rolly.

He seemed, so I thought, to enjoy answering that question, because Mel had not asked me that question, and seemed to imply that Philo did not help pastors. Yet unfortunately for him, Rolly was digging himself into another hole!

"Sometimes you help them with money?" Mel asked.

"Yes," said Rolly, putting his neck further into the noose.

"Sometimes you help them with big money?"

"Yes."

"There are two pastors, A and B. A says he does not believe in or have witchcraft in his church. B talks much of fear of being bewitched. Who do you help with your big money?"

"A," said Rolly with little hesitation.

"You judge!" said Mel. We paused to let the penny drop. "You condemn people," Mel added. The penny dropped again.

After a pause, I picked up where I had left off. "Philo doesn't condemn people because he does not have money," I said. This time, when I looked at Rolly, he stayed quiet. "That means people can be honest when Philo is around." Rolly now actually looked sheepish. "Thirdly, Philo has maintained his stand over many years." Rolly had been in and out of East Africa endlessly. But rarely for long, and his primary investment was clearly with American missions. He could not have the kinds of relationships and reputation for consistency that Philo had.

"Thanks, Dave. Well put," said Mel. "I quite understand, if only for these reasons, but I am guessing there are others, why Philo doesn't want us with him. Our presence spoils what goes on! Our presence has people be super-careful of what they say. Our presence has people shut up about their real issues. Our presence, we could even say, forces people to tell lies."

"No. There you are going too far," Rolly said. "They won't tell lies!"

"No?" asked Mel rhetorically. "Do you believe you have been bewitched? No! Do you ever consult the witch doctor? No. Do you believe in the same doctrine as does our home church (in America)? Yes ... Are those not lies?" Mel asked Rolly, who was looking sheepish again.

Our conversation ended there. We could no longer blame Philo for not wanting us to be with him. One consideration for me, though, was that perhaps he might not mind too much if, or when, he discovered that we were tracking him without his permission! "That was okay – at least within reason," I thought. As long as to Philo we are 'they,' things could still be okay for him. Our tracking Philo would not result in his condemning people or judging people, as long as we did not make judgments according to who Philo's friends were. And Philo had often made it clear to me, and I could easily enough explain that to Rolly and to others – Philo made friendships with bad people as well as good people. My mind had to come to Jesus' own words there; "I have not come for the healthy, but for the sick," Jesus said, whereas modern-donor-missionary types like Rolly definitely try to give to the healthy and not to the sick (for example, misguided heretics, deceivers, and so on).

We had not answered the question as to why the preacher used English. We had only discussed the problematic use of English. We would have to come back to why he chose to use English as his preaching language. That would be a few days later.

CHAPTER 18: BIRDS FALL FROM THE SKY

Late in the afternoon, it seemed to make sense to take advantage of the remaining daylight to take a walk. The cool of the late afternoon makes for a beautiful time in many parts of Africa that can get very hot in the middle of the day. I suggested that we go for a stroll. Rose and Mel had emerged from their siesta. They agreed. Rolly told us he just wanted to stay around the guest house, so only the three of us went.

We set off. We did not walk too quickly. It was still relatively hot when we set out. "Shall we walk down towards the river?" I suggested. The ladies agreed. As we walked we were far from alone. People were crisscrossing paths with us. Motorbikes were also going up and down. We eventually got onto a track where there were fewer motorbikes, so we had less dust thrown up into our faces. We continued to reflect on the day's events. I took the opportunity to explain the cancer situation of the man Mel had asked about.

"Mel. You had asked about the man who said his wife had cancer, then that she was killed by witchcraft?"

"Yes!" Mel exclaimed, remembering.

"So, what was your issue?"

"Well, according to the old man, did she have cancer, or was she killed by witchcraft?"

I didn't answer straight away. Mel was coming at this from a particular angle. To her, it was either cancer or witchcraft. She did not seem to think it could be both. "Both," I suggested. I had to raise my voice, as she was two steps ahead of me.

"How, hmmm?"

"Biomedical explanations do not undo people's rationalizations related to witchcraft," I explained. "Couldn't, for example, the witch have attacked the wife in such a way as to make her sick with cancer?"

Just then, a woman walking in the other direction to us suddenly stopped and exclaimed; "Philo's friends!"

"*Kamano*," (indeed), I replied.

"Hold the baby," she said to Mel. Mel had to be quick, or the baby might have dropped, so keen and quick was this lady to give Mel her offspring. "Philo paid for this picture months ago. I haven't seen him since," she added after she'd pulled an envelope out of a bag. I took it, at which point the lady, who was rather short and slim, abruptly grabbed her baby and marched on again! One upshot of all that was that Mel's thinking had moved on from the outstanding issues with the man whose wife had died of cancer, and went on to another question she wanted to ask regarding that church service.

"Another thing I noticed in the service today," Mel said, "was that people in the church were very interested in making money."

"Isn't that different from churches in the West!" Rose commented. "In the West, we are concerned about, and often discussing, how best to *give* money. Here the concern is on how to *get* money."

"We have to get money to give it," I added.

"Well, yes," Mel said.

"But – what you say is correct," I agreed. "It is like Rose said; here people expect God to give them money."

"What is wrong with people here?" Mel asked. "Why do they think money comes from God? I mean – they are right. In the end, everything comes from God. But God doesn't just make money fall from the sky!"

"Funny you should say that," I commented at that point. We had just come to a corner. There were a few people crouched on the ground selling their wares. I pointed the ladies to an old man among them. In front of him on the ground were some brown objects. Beside him was a woman in front of a large cooking pot that was sitting on three stones under which she had lit a fire. The man had very grey hair. He was smiling. The woman seemed to be preoccupied with something as she was waiting for the water in her pot to boil.

"Here's something that ..." I started saying when Mel interrupted me.

"They are birds!" Mel exclaimed suddenly. We walked a bit closer. Sitting in front of the old man were about fifteen little brown birds!

"I was saying," I went on, "here's something that falls from the sky! Funny that you said that Mel, that money doesn't fall from the sky. These birds do fall from the sky!"

"How do they fall from the sky?" Rose said. She was also intrigued by the discovery we had just made.

"They are quail," I said, "not identical to the quail we get in the UK, but related."

"Okay," said Mel. She had questions written all over her face as she screwed her eyes up in disbelief over what she was seeing.

"Quail like the sound of fellow quail. When they hear other quail crying – they want to be there. So, people have realized a way of catching quail."

"Of making quail fall out of the sky?" Mel asked.

"Yes!" I said, enjoying the way I had stretched Mel way beyond her usual 'radar screen.'

"I'd like to hear about that," she added. "You mean a nice fat quail is flying overhead, then suddenly it decides to land just where someone wants it to land, and then it agrees to get caught?"

"Yes!" I said.

"Hmmph! Not sure I believe you this time," Rose said.

"Let me explain," I said. I needed time to articulate this in more detail. I looked at the eyes of the ladies. They indicated that they'd be ready to allow me to speak. "What you have to do is somehow is catch the first quail. Then, people make a special little basket called a *sigol*. They put the quail into the *sigol*, so that it can't get out. They then cut a long pole. They attach the basket to one end of the pole, and then they stand the pole upright. As a result, the quail is suspended high up in the air in the *sigol*. Now, what does the quail do? It calls out to its friends. When its friends hear its voice, they come. Quail know, however, that a quail lives on the ground. They don't think that their friend might be at the top of a pole in the sky. They land and look for their friend. They run around like crazy, searching for their friend whose voice they are hearing. Knowing this is how quail behave, the man hunting the quail sets up some wire nooses on the ground. He makes some pathways through the undergrowth, then strategically positions a noose. When the quail runs around frantically, it runs into a noose. As it does so, the noose tightens around its neck. Now it is stuck – it can't go backward or forward. The man comes, picks it up, opens the noose and puts the quail into its own basket. Now he has two quail to attach to the pole."

"Why aren't the quail flying away?" Mel asked at that point, pointing to the fifteen birds sitting in front of the old man. The old man realized what I was explaining, and was laughing watching the ladies' faces.

"Wait and I'll explain. As I was saying, by doing what I have described, an African man can make meat fall out of the sky. That is not so different from money falling out of the sky is it – so why shouldn't money fall out of the sky?" Neither of the ladies answered me. I think they were just amazed at how people catch quail.

"So, you mean, people today still follow the kinds of thinking that says food, even money, can fall out of the sky?" Mel said.

"Well," I said, "you asked why those birds aren't flying away? Come a bit closer." We all drew closer.

"Are you friends of Philo?" asked the old man.

"Yes," I said. I think Mel was happy – at least she could be identified as a friend of Philo's! "Mel here asked why the quail on the ground in front of you do not fly away," I translated to the old man, then I addressed the same question to the women. The old man decided to give us a demonstration. He reached into a basket beside him. He pulled out a quail, being careful that the others in that basket not escape.

"$0.50," he said, holding out the bird.

"What, to eat?" asked Mel.

"Indeed," he said. That is when he did his live demonstration. He held the bird in one hand, took hold of one of its wings in the other hand, then he bent the wing up and broke it! He turned the quail around. He proceeded to do the same with the other wing: snap! Then he grabbed one leg. He broke its leg. He took hold of the other leg: snap. He put the bird on the ground with the others. No wonder the birds weren't going anywhere – they had all had their legs and wings broken!

Mel's eyes were nearly popping out of her head. "How cruel!" I know she was thinking. "How cruel," she whispered to me. But that was not the end.

"How do you cook them?" Mel asked. The old man spoke to the woman next to him. "*Nyise kaka itedogi*," he said to her (show her how you cook them). The woman grunted. She picked one of the birds from the ground. She started plucking it!

"She is plucking it and it is still alive," said Mel. This time she didn't even say it quietly. She said it loudly! The woman must have understood something. She laughed as she carried on pulling feathers off the bird. She pulled off all the feathers – head, back, stomach ... all! The poor bird was sitting in her hands, naked! Not only naked but with broken wings and broken legs. All it could do was to pheep and, not surprisingly, appear extremely alarmed and frightened. Then the woman tossed the bird into the water that she was heating in the pot, that was presumably close to boiling, so that the bird would start cooking. I think that neither Rose nor Mel were very impressed.

Having had that demonstration, we walked on. Now the ladies were full of questions! Especially Mel.

"So," she said, "we have seen how indeed people here might believe that money might fall from the sky as do quail." She paused. "But, birds are physical things. What I wonder – is how they can believe that money can fall from the sky – of spiritual origin. I mean, it is clear to anyone, that money is physical, but prayers are spiritual. How can the spiritual – a prayer, for example – make either money or quail fall from the sky?" Mel was certainly apt to ask deep questions!

"You are made of spirit?" I asked Mel.

"Well, yes – my soul is," she said.

"How does your spirit make your body move?" I asked her.

"I just move it," she said.

"But – don't you see – that is a miracle. Because Newton's laws of physics say that nothing happens without a force having caused it to happen. How does your spirit that is presumably not physical, manage to move your body that is physical?" Neither Mel nor Rose had a response to that.

"We Westerners have been raised on the basis of certain philosophies," I said. "We take them as if they are written in stone. But they are not. They are mere thoughts of men that have become mainstream. But they are only mainstream in certain parts of the world. They are not mainstream in Africa. People in Africa think very differently to ways in which we think in Europe."

"Such that to them, wealth arising from prayers isn't a 'mystery' at all," said Rose. I am not sure if she was stating or asking.

"Absolutely," I said.

"So, what you are saying is that although for so-called rational Westerners it may seem silly that we should pray for money, to African people it is not silly at all. So also, while for many Christians in the West it is wrong to expect that becoming a Christian should result in one's being wealthy, that need not be the case in Africa."

"That's right," I responded. "It is tough to understand African people, we could say. They are to me, and I also guess to Philo, a mystery."

"The things that quail have taught us!" Mel exclaimed at that point. "Is there anything else we should learn from quail?" she asked.

"Yes," I said, "but I want to keep you in suspense until we find a place where we can have a drink. It has been a hot day. I think we've walked enough. Let's go back to the guest house first, then talk some more." The ladies agreed.

We went back to the guest house, each absorbed in their thoughts, where we found Rolly waiting. "Come and join us for a drink," we invited Rolly. He was happy to oblige.

"Would you believe it, I've been on the phone," Rolly told us.

"So, what have you been doing?" No one thought to ask him who he had been on the phone to.

"Dave has been showing us how to prepare quail for eating," Rose said. "It is quite a procedure!" After sitting down we discussed such with Rolly, and enlightened him about our walk and especially about the quail.

"Dave says that was also teaching us about Africa," Rose said. "We want him to elaborate now."

"Okay," Rolly said, wondering what on earth was coming next! He seemed to be worried about something. But the issue of the quail appeared to be the most pressing, so I went on.

"Okay," I said. "The point I made while with the ladies was that for African people, money can fall out of the sky. (I explained that a little to Rolly.) I want to draw further teaching from that, by the way the quail we saw were treated. We have four things that happened that decapacitated the quail."

"Being?" asked Rolly. "Break wing one, break wing two, break leg one, break leg two." "Okay," he said. Rolly had come across quail-hunting and its associated practices before.

"Four things have similarly incapacitated African people!" I went on. "One, break wing one – they do not use their languages. They are ruled therefore by use of a language the categories of which they do not understand. Two, break wing two. They have been told that their history is nothing but a plethora of evil. African people are not supposed to live out their history. They are supposed to reject their history. They are supposed to act as if their history is the history of the white man. Three, one leg broken. One is not supposed to treat African people differently from Europeans. One should treat them the same as Europeans. Whatever there is about them that is different must not be acknowledged. To acknowledge it, to treat someone like an African, is illegal by international law. (Although strictly racism might be not to value someone just because they are of another race, in practice it is often to have not to treat someone differently even though they are different. Then it is to treat someone as if they are who they are not.) Four, second leg broken. African people are told, by dominant western people and culture, not to believe in values, or in God, but to believe in money. That is – education is secular. Governments should run on a secular basis. The very powerful dominant secular world tells people whose life traditionally has been all about prayer (in a manner of speaking), that prayer is nothing! Finally, African people are plucked bare – their types of houses, their types of clothing, their pride in themselves, their ways of disciplining their children, their polygamous institutions, you name it – all are trashed! They are to live just like white people."

It was as if, while I said all the above, the women were holding their breath! Then, when I had finished, that finally gave them the chance to say "pheeeeeeeeee-ewwwwwwww-wwww!"

Suddenly, as I paused from my monologue, Mel started crying. First, she sobbed a little, then more, then tears started pouring from her eyes, then she cried and cried and cried. Emotions didn't overcome the rest of us as they had Mel. But we could, well, and I think I speak accurately on behalf of Rose and Rolly too, appreciate the depths from which her tears were emerging. In fact, Rose did also shed some tears. It seemed my account had been just too graphic. For the ladies who had been there, the image of those quail sitting pretty, yet entirely dependent and helpless, was too recent. To think that such were African people was just too dehumanizing to deal with.

"But why don't people realize that?" Rose asked.

"Why do they keep on? Why does the West keep its light so much under a bushel? Western nations were reared on faith in Christ. It is that faith that made them who they are. Why do they now present secularism to

Africa? Why do they so often conceal the living source of so much that has made them who they are today?" I added.

CHAPTER 19: MESSAGE FROM AMERICA

"Look, I am going to be honest with you," Rolly said.

The ladies had gone. Rolly and I were left alone. It would have been nice if we had been sitting together in a quiet spot. That evening though, it wasn't quite so peaceful. Instead, not more than a few yards away was a rowdy mob of about twelve local people, ten men, and two women. It seemed rather excessively boisterous for a church council meeting! They looked at times to be much enjoying themselves. At other times, they were equally noisily arguing and at each other's throats. It was all in a good spirit, however. One thing at least struck me – this was yet another demonstration that the church was fundamental to people, and that the church was dealing with issues that were very important to people!

"Okay," I said to Rolly, ready to listen to what he had to say to me.

"I would appreciate it if you do not share this with the ladies. I think it won't help anything if they were to discover it. It is about my conversation this afternoon."

"Conversation?" I asked. I knew we had left Rolly alone. So now – I was interested – who had engaged him in conversation?

"With America," he said. I realized he was referring to the phone conversation he had mentioned previously.

"America is a big place to be talking to," I responded.

"My boss," he said.

"Nancy," I thought. "This could be serious!" "What, Professor Nancy?" I asked.

"None other. She called:

'You are calling me on a Sunday?' I objected straightaway.

'Apologies, Rolly. Found a cheap means of calling you Sunday morning only! How are you doing?'

'I'm fine,' I said.

'What's your time?'

'16.51' I said.

'I thought it would be good to talk rather than email.'

'Sounds good to me.'

'I received your recent report. You are encouraged?'

'Yes,' was my response.

'What Philo is doing is making sense,' I said to Professor Nancy. 'You are with Philo?'

'No.'

'Why not?'

'He's avoiding us.'

'Why?'

'We're finding out gradually.'

'What do you mean?'

'Philo told us he couldn't allow us to shadow him. We'd cramp his style!'

'Ha, ha, ha (a bit of a nasty laugh by Professor Nancy). Is he cracking up?'

'I think he isn't.'

'Then what is happening?'

'Look, Professor Nancy, I am not sure how to say this. Philo is right.'

'Right about what?'

'He is right. The impact on his ministry of having a gang of white people like us tail him would be negative.'

'He is so special, is he?'

'No. I mean, yes. Look, let me explain.'

'The words of a mad man.'

'Professor Nancy, Philo is right. His sheer vulnerability is paying him dividends. We are seeing that – even though we are far from him …'

'So, he's converted you, Steve?'

'He has a …'"

As Rolly was telling me all this, a child brought me a letter. It must have been a child of the guest house manager, which seemed strange. I thought Rolly was also surprised, so he stopped his staccato-style explanation. It was a letter from Mel, addressed to me! I read it through quickly. It was not meant to be confidential.

"Would you believe – Mel has written me a letter!" I said to Rolly. "It's a fascinating letter. Let me read it to you," I added. I read it to him. Here is what was written:

....

Dear Dave,

Our time in Holima is proving to be amazing, even though we hardly see Philo. I could come and tell you what I now want to write, but I thought I should write it. We've been doing a lot of talking. Hence, I'm resting my tongue a little.

I want to emphasize, that I am increasingly profoundly convinced by the things I am seeing and by what I am hearing. What you are telling us. Many of those things that you have learned from Philo are mind-boggling! I think they are very valid. They are also very, very challenging. I feel a lot more people should hear this message.

Primarily, I want to come back to the four points that you mentioned on our walk. The two wings breaking and the two legs breaking. I felt what you said was very important. I hope you will have further opportunity to expand on that.

Yours,

Mel

....

"That's quite a letter," Rolly said. "In fact, after you're telling me about Mel's letter, I'm not sure that I can continue relating my phone call with Professor Nancy!"

"She's right, that I left those points unexpanded upon," I said. "It would take a long time to explain them thoroughly. To explain everything in one walk – might just have been too much! I wondered what to do. Now Mel has clearly indicated – she wants to know more!"

I told Rolly to wait for a while so that I could go to the bathroom, before continuing his account. By the time I came back, he was ready to carry on.

"Okay, let me carry on, I was saying," Rolly went on:

"So he has converted you, Steve?" Professor Nancy said to me.

135

"He has."

"What did I say?" (Rolly tried to make sure he recounted their conversation as accurately as he could. He seemed to be processing what he was saying as he talked.) "He has made and is living an amazing case. A compelling case."

"I am amazed to hear you speak like this," Professor Nancy said.

"You are not here."

"Do you think that because I am not there with you, I am stupid? Does one have to be in Africa and with Philo to learn about Africa?"

"No, but you are missing the context."

"Context. My hat!"

"Really!"

"Is context so important?"

"You know," Dave told the ladies, Mel and Ro (Rolly referred to his wife as Ro to some of their good friends) "that what we are doing to Africa is comparable to what people here do to quail." (Rose had called Rolly and told him the quail story even before we got back!)

Thereupon Nancy asked: "What do they do to quail?"

"Break one wing. Break the other wing. Break one leg. Break the other leg. Pluck it when it is still alive. Throw it naked into boiling water."

For a while, Rolly told me he heard Professor Nancy breathing, but she did not say anything. Then:

"Are you crazy?" she asked. This time, Rolly explained, he did not answer.

"I fear you might have flipped your lid, along with Philo. Look, Steve, I need to tell you straight. I wanted you to be there in Africa to show Philo up. You have all the experience. Point out where he has been misled for goodness sake. What to do now – send someone else? Come myself? Pull you out? You do not seem to understand, Rolly. There are millions of people employed in the aid industry whose livelihood you are threatening. We are in the process of negotiating massive donations to help other millions, or is it billions of people (pause) I want to know – have you jumped ship, or can we still rely on you to put Philo right? Steve – your position here is at stake. I'll give you till tomorrow morning (which

136

of course for Rolly is afternoon) to give me a clear response." (She had put the phone down).

"Dave," Rolly said. "If I lose this job, the chance that my income would continue at the same level if I get another would be meager indeed. Mission is what I do, and what I am paid to do. But I don't do it in the Philo way! Look – I am too old to retrain now. Much is at stake. Yet I have costs to meet – I have a house and I'm paying the mortgage. You know also, I think I've already told you, that my sister got sick, and I'm committed to paying her medical bill. She was never insured. She ran up an enormous bill before she died."

Rolly's comments warrant further reflection. What we were saying and doing was threatening to make heads roll! Should I, should Philo, now do a 180-degree turn, so that Rolly and people like him not lose their jobs and fall flat on their face? If someone like Rolly lost his job, and were he to end up in dire economic circumstances, that somehow seemed a lot more serious than having just more Africans drop below the poverty line. Rolly, after all, was 'one of us'!

There are other ways of looking at this issue. One other way is to consider if the Christian West had not gone heavy-handedly into Africa, someone else much worse might have done so. Someone else might have tried to annihilate African people, as for example many colonialists at one time tried to do to native people in parts of South America. I don't deny such truths. Yet, as a Christian in current contexts, we need to deal with the morality of where-we-are-at. Should we be here to empower African people, and enable them, or to add our contribution to that of others, such as Professor Nancy, who despite best intentions want to make them forever dependent on the West?

CHAPTER 20: THE CHASE

Our ships collided! Mine was a merchant ship, taking produce to Europe. The other was a pirate ship. The pirates were lined up standing on the edge of their vessel ready to leap. We were only trying to make honest trade, but now we were under attack. "Hoist the sails," came a command. I rushed towards the folded sail. Our only chance – was to get the sail hoisted, so that the wind might carry us far from those pirates. Then the crash happened. "Crash, crash, crash," as their ship rammed ours. For some reason, the pirates never leaped over onto our ship. Then it happened again "crash, crash, crash," noisy, uncouth, interrupting ... For a moment, perhaps just a fraction of a second, I was in both worlds. "What is going on ...?" I asked myself. Someone was bashing on our door. I opened my eyes. It was still dark.

"Who is it?" I said.

"It's Mel. Wake up. We want to go early."

My dream quickly rescinded as I became aware of myself, and recalled I was in a room in a guest house in Swaro. In the other bed in the same place was Rolly.

"What time is it?" I asked.

"5.30 a.m.," Mel replied. "We've got to go now!"

I got up. I turned on the light. Nothing. We obviously had a power cut. "Rolly," I said.

He grunted. "What does Mel want?" he asked.

"That we should get up. Philo is leaving early. We've got to get to Deja before him." Mel said through the door.

"Okay," I said. "We'll set off in five minutes."

"You settled the bill yesterday, yes?" Mel came back.

"Yes."

"Okay."

"Hey Rolly, five minutes and we are leaving," I said. Rolly had his phone in his hand by that point. I found mine. That gave us the light we needed. By the time we stumbled outside our door with our bags packed, Rose and Mel were standing by the vehicle ready to go.

"What's the urgency?" Rolly asked.

"Philo is going to Deja early. We've got to get there before him." Mel declared.

"Why?" Rolly asked. Mel ignored his question.

"Am I allowed to visit the bathroom before we set out?" I asked. It was a rhetorical question – I don't know what I would have done if Mel had said no! Then I checked. The keys were in my pocket. Five-forty a.m.! I got into the driver's seat. I turned the key. The engine roared to life.

Something had got into Mel. Now she was in charge, and she was an investigative journalist working with James Bond! "Go, James," I thought I heard her say. Once all were aboard and the door was shut, I played the part. Our wheels skidded, gravel shot in all directions. By the time we reached the exit to the guest house, I might have been doing twenty miles an hour. A left turn, up the hill. Fortunately, there weren't many pedestrians around at that time of day. There was the main road.

"Deja full speed," I shouted. I glanced at Rolly. He looked a bit nonplussed. "Full speed?" I asked. No one answered. I went at a moderate speed. A bit later, "What happened, Mel?" I asked.

"Someone phoned. Told me Philo is leaving early, so I thought we'd better get to Deja before him."

"Who phoned?" Rolly asked.

"Don't know," said Mel.

It was, frankly, an enjoyable time of day to be on the road. The first tinges of dawn were visible to our East. The street was quiet. It was cool. We made good headway. I saw Mel's excited face in the mirror behind me. Rose, beside her, had shut her eyes. Gradually the scene around us got lighter. There seemed to be more vehicles on the road. Of course, that tends to happen when one approaches a city. In due course, there was the view of Deja city in front of us. Still distant, shrouded in mist, beautiful in its own way.

Mel had remained silent. As we approached the city I asked, "What is the plan, Mel?"

"Find Philo," she said. Okay, I thought – that was not very helpful.

"How, where?"

"We need to be there to intercept his bus," she said. I pictured us standing on the side of the road wearing our handkerchiefs over our noses, wielding sticks as if they were guns, holding up every bus that came into Deja and searching it, till we found Philo.

"Better go to the bus station then," I suggested. No response. "What do you think, Rolly?" Perhaps Rolly was wondering whether it was such a good idea having a journalist as a tour-guide.

"Why not," said Rolly. The bus station was not easy to get to. That is – once we got close to it, there were jams in all directions. We entered a jam. All around us were buses! (Because we chose our vehicle to resemble a bus, we did not look too out of place.) People were staring at us – presumably looking for a number on our window, so that they could know whether or not to wave us down and board us for their particular destination.

"Park here," said Mel.

"You are not allowed to park here," I said.

"He's parked," Mel said. She pointed out a motorized rickshaw, otherwise known as a *bajaji*. "Yes, but he is not a bus," I said.

"Is he for hire?" Mel asked.

"Yes," I replied.

"Look, you go and park. Rose and I will wait in the *bajaji*." Mel elbowed Rose. "Get out." Rose started into life. She looked around bewildered, then did what she was told. They slammed the door. I started laughing.

"That lady's got some pluck!" said Rolly. I was laughing. Rolly was mainly incredulous. I pictured Rose and Mel in the *bajaji*, telling the driver just to sit there and pretend everything was normal. Mel, with a broad-brimmed hat, peering out with a pair of binoculars.

Parking in Deja is not so easy. One had to make sure there was security. Without security, one might come back and find one's vehicle gone, or smashed, or wheels missing – or at least so it is said. I gave a security guard a dollar and parked in a hotel parking space. We started walking back towards the bus station.

Then Mel called, "Don't come or Philo might see you." She cut the phone.

"Mel said don't come," I told Rolly.

"Where should we go then?"

"Wait until further orders," I said.

"How about breakfast?"

"Yes, right," I said. "As long as, that is," I said laughing, "we be ready to drop everything at a moment's notice should we get a call from Miss Boss."

While Rolly and I had breakfast, the action was happening somewhere else. The *bajaji* driver didn't mind sitting tight once he'd been assured he'd get some money. Rose and Mel waited for about an hour. They ate *mandazi* and drank a coke for breakfast, purchased from local traders. "There he is!" Mel then said excitedly to Rose. Rose looked very carefully. There was a white man, in the crowded bus stage, carrying a bag. It did look like Philo. "Let's go," said Mel.

Rose grabbed Mel's hand. "But he'll see you," she said. "Then he'll know we are tracking him." All Mel wanted to do was to run up to Philo. "Don't, he'll see you," Rose said again. Mel slumped back into her seat. She looked at Rose. She hadn't thought of that. But then – had they not wasted their time? Now they couldn't go and meet Philo after all. "There he goes, he's walking towards town," said Rose. Rose decided she'd better get excited with Mel. If you can't beat them, join them! "If you want to find out things about Philo, we can't do it. We'll have to send someone."

"What do you mean?" Mel asked.

"We need a spy!" said Rose.

"Who will spy?" Mel asked.

"We need to find someone."

"Where?"

CHAPTER 21: PRIVATE INVESTIGATOR

"Where do you hire an intelligent capable person for a day?" thought Rose. "At a lawyer's office," she said, answering her own question.

"Let's go!" said Mel, feeling by that point more and more like a journalist.

"We need a lawyer's office," Rose said to the *bajaji* driver. He obliged. Ten minutes later they alighted at a sign saying, 'Commissioner for Oaths.' They paid the *bajaji* driver, and were left on the side of the road. It was about 9 a.m. They went into the office.

There was a receptionist. "The lawyer is coming right now," she said, "just a minute." The ladies sat and waited for two hours. Every time they asked the receptionist she said, "He'll be here in just a minute." One time she called the lawyer. "He said he's just parking his car outside," she said. They waited for another one-and-a-half hours. At least this gave Mel time to plot her strategy.

By the time the three hours plus were over, we had gone to join the ladies. So we sat together, waiting for the lawyer. Most of me didn't want to ask Mel what she had in mind. I was quite enjoying the excitement that arose from having her direct the program. I looked around at our waiting room. Other people would occasionally come in and talk to the receptionist. No one else joined us in waiting.

"What have you got in mind?" I did eventually ask Mel.

"Investigative journalism," she said. That is all that Mel said. The receptionist, who wore long artificial hair, was keeping an eye on us over the top of her laptop. I guessed she was twenty-five. Very dark skin. Not unattractive. We waited.

A greying man with a suit eventually walked in. We all sat up straight in expectation. He opened another door and entered an office. "That him?" Rolly asked the receptionist, who we had discovered was born in Silo (hence people called her NyaSilo).

"No," she said. Five minutes later another man came in. He was also greying, and also wore a suit plus a set of heavy spectacles. "That must be him!" I thought. The daughter of Silo talked to him.

"Welcome," he said, ushering us into his office. We went in and sat down.

Mel was rather blunt and to the point. Locally, long introductions would have been an appropriate prerequisite to business. Mel, however, was not so familiar with such customs. "Look," Mel said, "I am a journalist. We are checking up on someone. We need your help."

"Okay," said the lawyer, called Frank. For a lawyer's office, his surroundings seemed surprisingly bare. There was a rubber stamp and a few documents on his otherwise empty desk.

"We want someone who can go to someone called Philo, he's in town, and ask him questions. Philo is not to know that we have sent the person concerned. Can you do that?" Mel was sitting on the edge of her seat. I guess she was concerned that we might have been waiting there for all that time for nothing.

Frank looked at her. "How are we going to find Philo?" he asked.

"Call him," Mel said. She had thought through that one.

"Then once we've called him, what next?"

"Tell him you are an old friend, and that you want to meet him."

"You are paying?" Frank asked Mel.

"Yes," she said without hesitation.

"$50 per hour," said Frank.

Mel thought about it. "Yes," she agreed.

Frank got up. He opened the door to talk to the daughter of Silo. "Send Jamie," he said. He came back to sit down. "Jamie will do this," he said.

Two minutes later a very tall, slim man, also very black, perhaps in his late thirties, came in. "This is Jamie," said Frank. "He is used to dealing with these kinds of cases." Jamie had a soft voice. It was at that point that I realized what Frank thought was going on. Frank, no doubt, had lots of clients wanting him to check upon their spouses. He assumed Philo to be the husband, and Mel the jealous or suspicious wife! This time, for a change, he was to investigate white people. But – why not? If Mel was paying. Jamie then was his 'stuntman,' prepared to get embroiled in love triangles to make a living. Jamie had a strange scar under his chin. I wondered what kind of scuffle with a jaded lover had at some point or other earned him that. "The clock starts now," said Frank. "Plus a $30 consultation fee payable to me."

Jamie led us to his office. The layout and color scheme of his office was similar to that of Frank's office, but it was smaller. There was a stack of papers in one corner. There were three smart-phones laid on the desk. We sat on one side of a desk. Jamie sat on the other side.

* * *

"I am a journalist from the UK, investigating the life and work of a British missionary called Philo," said Mel.

Jamie was listening intently. Let us say more accurately, he was interpreting intently. This was not Jamie's first customer. Of course, he was not used to dealing with white people so much. At least one supposed not so. Presumably, most of his clients were Striden. He himself was a Striden. He was used to dealing with Striden people's complicated love-tangles. What happens when a non-Striden person comes along? Well – he takes them as if they are also Striden. Now – Striden people don't usually talk straight. They talk in riddles, indirectly. Especially so when it comes to wanting help determining whether one's husband is going astray! One doesn't tell the investigator 'my husband is going astray.' No; one is indirect.

"I want you to find out about this man ..." Mel was at risk that her whole agenda could be re-interpreted, misinterpreted! I was not sure that she realized. It became clear later that she did not. Mel imagined herself to be in the UK, or in some imaginary country where facts were facts and people told the truth.

This circumstance did have me reflect more widely. When Westerners make proposals, related to projects, funding, or development to Africans, they think they are communicating straightforwardly and directly. But – is that how they are received? How can it be, if the people they are communicating to do so by intuiting, and dancing around an issue in circles? "The process by which Mel will learn about African communication might be interesting," I thought to myself.

Mel filled in the details – including of the newspaper she was working for. We were all three of us, I think, very impressed by the articulate way in which she communicated to Jamie precisely what she wanted.

"Call him. Have your phone on speaker," said Mel. Jamie did so. Mel had her pen and paper out.

"Isn't this snooping?" Rolly whispered to me at that point.

"Perhaps. That's what journalists do, isn't it?" I responded, also in a hushed tone so as not to throw Mel off course.

"Hello, Philo," said Jamie in a loud clear voice. I guess Mel was excited at the prospect of hearing Philo's voice, even if she wasn't the one talking with him, and even though the theme wasn't marriage! We were all excited to hear how this great venture of Mel's would work out, although not sure we should be snooping!

"Nadi. In ng'a?" came the response. Oh no! Philo was not going to speak English. Mel tilted her pen forwards, not knowing what she ought to write. Her face was blank, so it seemed to me, perhaps thinking 'oh no, why is nothing simple?'

"This is your friend Jamie," said our private investigator.

"Jamie. *Ok apar nyingno,*" came Philo's voice.

Jamie put his phone at arm's length and whispered to Mel, "You said he is a white man. This is a Striden."

"No. That's him. He is a white man," Mel stressed.

"Don't you recall our meeting?" said Jamie to Philo – part of his undercover-agent strategy no doubt!

"*Akia,*" (I don't know), Philo responded.

"Look," said Jamie, "I gather you are in town. Where can I find you?"

"*Antie e Posto sa ni. Kidwaro yuda bi e ot mikayi bang' nus sa.*"

"I begin in English but he is speaking only Striden!" Jamie said to us, with his phone at arm's length.

"*Kare,*" said Jamie. End of conversation.

"The best plans of mice and men," I said to myself, laughing.

"Why does he not speak English?" Mel asked. Not sure if she was angry or just frustrated! "He doesn't with Holimans, Mel," I said.

"Even though Jamie made it clear repeatedly that he wanted to speak in English – Philo refused!" Rolly exclaimed.

"That's how he is," I said.

"Why didn't you tell us?" Mel asked.

"You didn't ask," I said.

"But why?" said Mel. "So that other people don't understand?"

"No, so that other people do understand," I said.

145

"Hmmm?" Mel asked.

This needed more explaining. I realized, again, how many people think that people speaking the same language are bound to understand one another. "Striden people," I said. "So you think everyone in the world should speak English, Mel?" No answer. "There are many reasons Philo avoids English. English is a problem. You discovered that? ... Tell you later," I added. That was, at the time, too much for Mel to take on board.

Before long, it was 'later'! It was for us now to wait for Jamie to come back and give us a report. We had spent an hour walking around town exploring. We had bought some lunch.

"Dave," Mel said, "you said I discovered that English was a problem. What did you mean?"

Before answering her I glanced at Rolly. I was aware of his predicament concerning Professor Nancy. That afternoon she was going to call him back. His job was on the line! If he believed what he was now seeing and hearing he would be out of a job, and he was at risk of financial calamity. If only people took the time to get to know Africa at depth, they would become wise to so much that bosses in the West were ignorant about. Yet, those things might put their jobs on the line. Now we were discussing yet another of those things. "Poor Rolly," I thought.

"You talked to Jamie," I said to Mel, "telling him how to investigate Philo. Yes?" I spoke in a low tone.

"Yes," she said, copying my style.

"Did he hear you?" I asked.

"His English is excellent," said Mel.

"I am not sure he heard a word," I added.

Mel hadn't got it. "How come?" Mel was looking back and fore to Rose and Rolly to support her.

"You wanted Jamie to investigate Philo the missionary, yes?"

"Yes!" said Mel.

"He is investigating Philo the unfaithful husband."

"I don't have a husband ..." Mel started saying, then she realized what was going on! She was quiet for a while. Her eyes kept going back and fore between the rest of us. "So, what you are saying, Dave, is that while Jamie

146

understood every word I said, he did not understand anything at all?" I nodded. Rolly looked depressed. Rose's eyes started going back and fore between us. "But then," said Mel "what should I have done? How should I have talked, so that Jamie understood?" We sat quietly for a full minute. "There is no way is there?"

We remained quiet for a while longer. Then, "There's something we have missed here," said Rolly. We looked at him. We were by this time sitting around a table. We had ordered drinks. Not because we wanted to drink sweet, fizzy stuff but because it would have been wrong to sit at that table and not order anything. Rolly commented, "I follow what you are saying. But you also claim, or Philo claims, that you can be better understood if you use the indigenous language. I don't see how, now, though. Even if Mel had been able to speak to Jamie using Striden, he would still have been misunderstanding her."

Rose tended to be quiet. Now she came into the conversation. "One thing, dear," she said, "is that had Mel known Striden, she would have been more capable of articulating herself precisely. Although Jamie's English is good, I think he was nervous talking to white people. English isn't his first language. He does not know British/American English. He does not know the clues that we use, perhaps very subtle clues, to indicate whether we are serious or truthful." She paused, then went on. "That could include body-language clues! Like the look in your eye, a slight raising or dropping of the voice, and all that."

"Had you been a Striden lady," I said to Mel, "then even if you used English with Jamie, you could have incorporated the right clues so that Jamie might have understood you, were not looking for investigation of a lover! The problems of English are accentuated when Holiman people use English with us Westerners."

"Ah! But doesn't that mean that there are also problems for them when we use Holiman languages with them?" Mel said.

"Yes," I said, "but an important consideration is – how has one learned the language? Learn Striden, if you are a Westerner, from a book (as Holiman people learn English), and you will miss the clues. Learn it from Striden people as they use it, and you might get the clues!"

* * *

"Philo is very friendly, and a man of God," said Jamie, an hour later. "Our conversation was entirely in Striden. You can't get Philo to talk English," he added. "Here's what happened." Jamie gave us an oral account of his conversation with Philo and promised to send a written version later for an additional $40, to which Mel agreed. Here's what Jamie related:

J. You don't remember me. But I remember you.

P. (silence)

J. How's the woman? (Mel groaned when she heard this. Dave was correct. Jamie understood her as checking on whether Philo was faithful to her, his presumed wife!)

P. Which woman?

J. You know ...

P. Fine.

J. The government subsidizing secondary schooling means more money in people's pockets. That is an opportunity for some to turn to drink and adultery. (This was apparently a strategy by Jamie, to ask Philo an open-ended question, to encourage him to comment on his affairs or his love-life.)

P. Good point.

J. Many women here carry STDs and AIDS.

P. We need to pray, there are many Christians in Holima. But many of them do not know how to avoid falling into sexual immorality.

J. Has me worried!

P. Why? You do not need to worry if both yourself and your wife remain faithful. (Now Philo was counseling Jamie!)

And so it went on.

"Look. Write it out. Send it to me," Mel interrupted Jamie. Mel's undercover investigative reporting seemed to have hit a brick wall. Jamie had not done what she had asked him at all! Mel paid him some of his money there and then. "Send me the report, and I'll send you the rest," said Mel. "By the way, where did Philo say he's going next?"

"He's gone," Jamie said.

"Where?"

"Hongera," Jamie responded.

148

As soon as we parted ways with Jamie, Mel went back into overdrive! "Hey. Philo has gone! He's headed to Hongera. We must go!" she said to us. I enjoyed the lively version of Mel, so I played along.

Just then, as Mel was accelerating us back to our vehicle, Rolly's phone rang.

"Sorry, no time to talk," said Rolly.

I guessed that must have been Professor Nancy.

"Are you serious?" said Professor Nancy (presumably).

"We're being rushed!"

"In Africa?" said an incredulous voice.

"By a crazy British woman," said Rolly.

"But I am going to be tied up for a week," said Professor Nancy.

I saw a smile break out on Rolly's face. Then on Rose's face. It was a funny thing about Rose. Things happening to Rolly that would affect their whole future, often didn't seem to faze her in the slightest. "Sad to hear that," said Rolly, "must go!" Then he cut Professor Nancy off.

"Let's move as fast as we can," said Rolly, entering into the spirit of the occasion, rejoicing that Professor Nancy was off his back for a week.

Have you ever seen a group of excited school kids? If you have – that gives you an idea of what we were like just then!

"Which bus did Philo board?" Rose asked, also catching up with the pace of things.

"Don't know!" said Mel eagerly. That unknown had become a source of adventure; there was something important that we had to find out, but for a moment no one knew how.

Before long, we were on our way. The four of us had got back into our minibus. The ladies were sat behind, men in front. Mel was in the back on the left. Soon we were cruising down a long, quite straight, flat road. On both sides of the road were homes and farms. Motorcyclists, a few cyclists, pedestrians and others (for example, cattle, dogs) were on the same road. Roads in Holima had their particular hazards.

"There's a bus!" Mel shouted. I almost jumped out of my skin. Sure enough, still some distance ahead of us was an African bus. "He might be in there," Mel shouted, bouncing on her seat like a ten-year-old who is telling her dad that she has seen an ice-cream van.

"Wow!" I thought. "We are on a roller coaster." We caught up with the bus.

"Overtake slowly!" Mel commanded. As we overtook, she craned her neck. "Can't see him," she said, slumping back into her seat, disappointed. Rose gave her sidelong looks! Then there was another bus. "Another bus!" Mel shouted.

"It certainly wasn't always easy for a girl to hide it when she was in love," I thought, "but Mel doesn't even really know Philo. What will Philo make of it if he finds out a love-crazed woman is chasing him like this?"

This bus-checking procedure was repeated about four times. Then, on the fifth occasion, "There he is!"

"Shhh! If you make such a noise he might notice us," Rose said to Mel. Rose, of course, knew of Mel's underlying motivation, but was committed to not making it known that she knew.

Not having to stop periodically as did Philo's bus to allow people to board and alight, we got into Hongera way ahead of Philo. Mel had noted the name of the bus. We asked in town where that bus would come to rest. It was near a multi-story guesthouse. We made our way to that hotel.

"Let's book a room now," said Mel. We made sure to book a room (we booked two rooms – as that was to be our overnight stay) overlooking the bus station. Our rooms were on the third floor (American – fourth floor). We got to the window just in time to see Philo's bus pull in. Camera and binoculars in hand, we intrepid spies observed an unsuspecting Philo for half an hour meandering around eating peanuts, as the bus sat looking for additional passengers.

We were aware that it was not Philo's final stop. Once his bus had set off again, we clambered down the stairs and into our vehicle for the final chase. Then, about five miles out of town, before we had caught up with the bus, Rose spotted Philo as we sped by. "He's in that village!" she pretty much shouted.

No one else had seen him. We turned and drove back slowly. A child waved at us furiously as we passed back, relatively slowly past the same village. Four or five men were sitting in a little hut along the side of the road. I imagined that the hut was probably used at certain times of the day for a woman to cook *chapatis*. No white person emerged from any of the huts.

"So that must be where Philo is staying," Rolly said. "Here are we anticipating keeping each other company in a run of the mill guest house in town," Rolly added. "Philo, meanwhile, is an honored guest at an African village. Hosting five of us, most of us unfamiliar with what's going on around us, would have been a very different kettle of fish. Philo alone, who's used to living in an African village anyway, is easy. I can understand again why Philo refused to let us shadow him. We would have cramped his style no end! With us, he would have been forced to keep our company, act like us, and be a visitor representing a foreign country. Alone, he can be vulnerable. He can get to be with the people. Had we been there, everything would have had to have been in English. That is – simple selected conversations. Now Philo can engage at depth. I now understand why he wants to be vulnerable!"

CHAPTER 22: FOOD AND BEVERAGE

Later that night, we later learned, Philo was 'victim' to a slap-up meal! The following night, however, things were to turn very nasty indeed, and being 'alone' was not to be so pleasant for him. Being alone and exposed, as was Philo, had a smooth side and a rough side.

We had one more lesson to learn that evening. Well – one more important, significant, intriguing lesson, that is.

The dining room, or restaurant, we sat in that evening was populous. If I recall rightly, what we all ate was chapati with green-grams, popularly called *dengu*. I felt we stood out somewhat. That was normal, of course: just four white people in a sea of black.

"The investigative undercover reporting didn't work too well, despite the money we had to pay," Mel conceded.

"I'm glad you have perceived that, …" I said.

Then she added, "... because we went about it the wrong way."

"What would have been the right way?" Rolly asked. Rolly did seem to be a troubled man. He'd evaded Professor Nancy that day, but for how long? Even if it was for a week – the day of reckoning would inevitably have to come. He would have to, for the sake of honesty, confess that he was no longer opposed to Philo, so could not fulfill his purpose of being with us!

"The mistake we made, sorry, I made, was to go for a pro," said Mel. "We should be asking local pastors about Philo. Then we'll find out the truth – is his vulnerable way of working using local languages and resources worth imitating or not?"

"Hmmm," Rolly said. "But, his friends will praise him. That is part of the patronage system. You praise people for a reward."

"You mean," Mel said, "you can never trust what people will say about someone if it's good, as it might be praise for the sake of praise? Then what …"

"I heard you mention the name of Philo?" There was a very bald African man speaking to us. He had inadvertently cut off Mel in mid-sentence. He was short, slight, and wore a cap. "I know Philo. That is – if you mean Philo from Swaro. He is a wonderful man."

"We are friends of his," Rose said.

"He is a great friend of mine," the bald man replied.

"Okay," Mel thought, I suppose, "Let us say something negative about Philo, and see how he responds." "Philo is very miserly," said Mel. "I am surprised to hear you say that you like him."

That was quite something for Mel, of all people, to say! A younger African man also came alongside the bald man.

"He's wonderful!" said the bald man. "I have a church here in town," the bald man added. "I need a vehicle to get around in. Reaching sick parishioners is getting very difficult. As you are friends of Philo, I know you will help me."

Mel wrinkled her nose. "How do you want us to help you?" she asked.

"$1000 will do," he said.

"But we don't even know you and ..." I touched Mel's hand. She shut up.

Then the young man spoke up. "I am also a very good friend of Philo." The young fellow had a goatee beard. "Look, I understood what you said errr ...?" he asked.

"Mel," Mel said.

"Mel. Philo is outstanding. He is not like other missionaries. He spends time with people. He knows our language. More missionaries should do what he does. I need a motorbike. Can you buy me a motorbike, so that I can serve people?"

"Sorry," I said.

We turned our eyes into our own circle, ignoring what had become a crowd of three or four. I knew – that if we gave them our attention, they would not leave us, but they would want money. Eventually, they left us alone.

"There's an answer to Mel about asking local pastors about Philo," I thought. Although I am not sure Mel got it in depth.

The ladies in due course retired to their room. I had an issue troubling me that I wanted to talk over with Rolly.

"Rolly," I asked. We had ordered another cup of tea. There were fewer people in the restaurant by then. "Why have Whites in Africa remained so distinct from local people? Why do they not mix with people? Why do they not become, it seems, ever, a part of African ways of life? Why are they (we!) always better? Always telling other people what to do and how. But – never as insiders except to our own communities? Why don't we mix in?" I noticed Rolly's eyes were closing. I woke him up to drink his tea. My questions would have to await their answers another day.

* * *

Rolly went on his way, leaving me still drinking tea by myself in the dining room, when somehow, unexpectedly and out of the blue, my phone rang. It was none other than Philo!

"Dave, *nadi?*" (Dave, how are you?) Philo asked.

"*Ber,*" (fine) I responded. "How're the others?"

"They're okay. I was with them. They've now gone to bed."

"I feel horrible," Philo said, "about seeming to have abandoned you. I mean, I haven't abandoned you. I've just taken leave of absence. I think you know what I mean? You all came, wanting to spend time with me. Well – that I would have agreed with. But – you wanted to come with me as I did ministry. But that can't work. Now I do feel rotten. You are in Imbigen, here I am miles away, yet you came out to visit me. Sorry about all that."

As Philo spoke, torrents of thoughts went through my own head about our current situation. Immediately – do I tell him we are not in Imbigen, but just five miles from where he is? "Silence is not a lie," I thought, but I was not so sure. But then – should he feel bad? Shouldn't visitors always be welcome when it comes to Christian ministry? Do we welcome visitors back at home, or in the UK, I thought? Of course, a big difference is that should visitors join our homes, fellowships or churches back in the West, they are not people on whom we are also dependent. Entertaining them is something we do willingly and freely, not to pay off implicit debts or obligations to donors.

Africa's dependence on the West means that when western visitors come, it is as if one is obliged to look after them. Then also – required to be dishonest to them! That is – to conceal things from them that they may not like to hear or see that could affect the flow of funds. Add to that language. When English is used, then it is a snob's game. So, I guess I respected Philo for making a stand. For being honest! For being courageous enough to tell people from his donor-country, 'No. You are not the number one priority in my life. You have, indeed, sent me here to do a job. For me to do the job properly, you can't be with me all the time.'

"Philo, don't worry about it," I said.

"Is Rolly very upset?" Philo asked.

"Not really. He seems impressed!" I added. I wanted to encourage Philo. Rolly might indeed be impressed. He had visited vast numbers of missionaries. I don't suppose he has got the cold shoulder like this very often.

There was something different about Philo.

"So how are you doing, Philo?" I was aware that Philo was visiting the home of one of the boys who once lived with him. This boy had lived with Philo for ten years. Now he was back with his family, (that is, his siblings, as his parents were long dead).

"I'm doing great," Philo responded. "I have had a very warm welcome here by all of the family. In fact, it seems, all of the whole village. I have drunk tea, eaten bread, *mandazi, chapati*, peanuts, bananas, then *ugali*, rice beef, chicken, fish, cabbage – I've been welcomed here like a greatly honored guest!"

"While here we are in a guest house, not welcomed by anyone – except a few people who wanted our money," I thought to myself.

"You had a good trip?" I asked.

"Yes. A strange thing happened though in Deja."

"Oh?"

"Yes, a friend of mine came. At least he said he was a friend of mine. He looked me up, called me, then we sat and talked. Then he said that a white lady wanted to know if I was sexually immoral – if I'd had African girlfriends and that kind of thing! He could not tell me who she was. He said that for $100 he would give her a glowing report. What did I care about some white lady? Of course, I didn't give him the money. But – it looks like someone is after me, Dave."

"Lucky you!"

"Not sure it is 'lucky me,' Dave. Who is that person? What does she want? Why doesn't she come and talk to me face-to-face?"

I wanted to tell Philo that perhaps the reason she didn't talk to him face-to-face was because he avoided white people! I did not say it. I decided to muddy the waters: "Who knows what the guy wanted?" I asked.

"Anyway, I am fine, Dave. I just thought I ought to call. It's great to hear your voice. Do greet the others and tell them I am fine."

"Will do, Philo."

"Cheerio."

"Bye for now." (Philo put the phone down.)

What was happening was strange. Here were we, Philo's good friends, avoiding him while secretly following him! I guess that was Mel's doing. Mel wouldn't take 'no' for an answer! What this was about in another way, was short-term mission. No end of so-called missionaries ('so-called' because they barely have time to reach the people they should be reaching) are nowadays swamped by short-term visitors. The mission calendar revolves around the arrival of, then entertainment of, groups from overseas. That ends up the apparent *raison d'être* of mission! The missionary is there on the field, to provide a base for people to go and have holiday experiences, or locations for an internship from their university course. "Why not?" you might ask. Well, yes – but how is the missionary supposed to be serious in relating to people he is supposed to be reaching with the gospel when his principal identity is holiday-camp manager for wealthy patrons and their children from far-off lands? Add to that – those wealthy visitors might have a bloated sense of self-importance and be determined to spend their short visit being in charge and changing things.

Of course, we wouldn't be chasing Philo but for some crazy woman! "If Mel or someone else were ever to write about our adventures, it would make a great read for people doing a short-term mission," I said to myself.

CHAPTER 23: RACE

"Look, Dave," Mel said to me the following morning. "There is something you said, I think it was the day before yesterday. You said, when you were explaining about the bird having all its legs and wings broken, something about not treating people differently. You said that not wanting to treat people differently was breaking the leg of an African! What did you mean by that? I mean – I understand that people in the West want to value others in the world, and this would seem to be good for Africans. You are saying that treating African people as if they are Westerners is not actually in Africa's interests at all. How come?"

While it was still early, the streets of Hongera were already busy. Mel was keen to see the fishing boats. Early in the morning, they'd come in from a night's fishing. Market-women and others would then go up to the boats to strike a deal with the fishermen, ready to carry their catch away on their heads. Hongera was a confusing place to walk around. It would have been easy to get lost if one wasn't careful. Philo had once told me that his father had got lost in this very town. He'd been walking around alone, failed to identify the landmarks he needed to get back to where he and Philo were staying, so had to go to the police station to be reunited with his son. Philo was thrilled that his dad had come from the UK to visit him. Philo had appreciated his dad's willingness to share in some local life.

On that morning, we didn't get lost. Watching the fishermen gave one a Galilean feeling. One could imagine Jesus walking along the shores of the lake, speaking to his disciples amongst the hustle and bustle of fishing and related activities. We talked as we walked.

"Are African people competent as they are?" I asked.

"Well, yes," said Mel.

"Are they the same as us?"

"Well no, not exactly."

"So then they are, or even let's say they might be, different, but that is okay?"

"Yes."

"If being different is okay, then why should we have to treat them as if they are the same as us?" I asked.

After I had asked that question, some men came along and hassled us. That was to be a recurring experience as we walked. Everybody was everybody's business in this part of the world. The local people weren't afraid to ask us what we were doing on their lakeshore. Many wanted us to buy fish. Many, I imagine, were trying to work out – was Mel my wife or my daughter?

"Well, because ..." Mel started. Then she hesitated. "Because different implies inferior," she added.

"Is it necessarily true? Does different need to imply inferior?"

"Well, no."

"So why does it imply inferior?"

Mel was quiet. The fishermen around us were less quiet. Some talked, others shouted. Various birds, resembling seagulls, were flying noisily over our heads.

"One reason, because of evolutionary theory. A lot of evolutionary theories put African people as 'less evolved' than western people," I said.

"I guess you're right," Mel responded.

"That seems a bit rotten I think; 'you are less evolved than me!'"

"Yes, that does seem rotten," Mel agreed. I smiled. I wondered whether we used that term 'rotten' because of a smell of rotten fish hanging over us? I liked eating fish. But I could understand people who were reluctant to do so given the stench around us.

"But what if the difference is not inferiority? It is just different, and that is okay? Well, saying one should not be racist is not allowing that option – is it? It is saying 'to be different is not okay; hence I will ignore what is different about you and treat you the same as me.'" It had taken me a while to work that out. There's an enigma regarding racism: to be against racism, can be to be racist, especially if in one's effort not to be racist, one is drawing attention to race. In theory, not being racist is valuing people who are different equally despite their differences. In practice, it is often trying to ignore difference so as to treat people in the same way.

As I looked around, I was observing Holiman people doing things that one rarely saw happening these days in the UK. The fishing-culture in the UK was very commercialized. Here it was about individuals eking out a living, each trying to get a competitive edge. Again I thought about

158

Galilee. "But," I thought, "that 'different behavior' clearly isn't of genetic origin. It is a cultural response to the need to make a living in a particular context."

"Oh, I see," said Mel. "So not to treat people differently from yourself is a claim to be superior. That is – to claim that one is the norm! Wow. You mean …" That seemed to cause Mel to think. She repeated, thoughtfully, "To try not to treat people differently from yourself can be a claim to be superior!"

"Are you going to Imbigen?" a lad asked us at that point. He was looking for customers to fill his bus! We looked like we ought to be travelers. We politely disavowed him of such intention on our part. The lad was about seventeen, I thought. He was wearing a peculiar red cap.

Then Mel added: "That means to be not-racist is to value your own people more than you value other people."

The lad with the red cap followed us for a while before he gave up on us.

"Another way to look at that," I said, "is to look at the possibility of different nations having different norms."

"What do you mean by that?" Mel replied, with a puzzled look on her face.

"Okay, so perhaps we should not treat others as different." Mel was nodding. "Well, then, if an outsider comes to America, we should treat him as if he is American?"

"Yes," said Mel in agreement. All around us people wore surprised expressions, wondering why these white people were wandering around in their midst.

"Then what about if someone visits Holima? How should they be treated?"

A boy stretched his hand out to Mel. His only word was "Money." Mel ignored him and carried on walking. "Well, according to what you say, as if they are Holiman," she said.

"Right," I said, "and are visitors to Holima treated that way?"

"Well, no, not at all," Mel said.

"Dave, Mel!" Rolly called at that point. He'd seen us from a distance and decided to join us. It would have been hard for him to hear everything we were saying. But he began to follow our discussion when he walked with us.

"Explain," I suggested.

"Well, what I am thinking is this. When western people go to Holima, they do not expect to be treated as Holiman people. They think they are better than Holimans."

"That's right," I responded.

"Now, if Westerners who go to Holima don't expect to be considered the same as Holimans, then why should Holimans in the West be assumed to be the same as Westerners?"

"Well," Mel said, "to be honest, because Westerners consider themselves to be better than other people. Then their superiority embarrasses them!"

A heavily pregnant lady walked past us at that point. Looking at her, I guess she was in her early twenties. That is, much younger than Mel. I wondered whether she considered herself inferior? In a sense, white folks like ourselves are considered very superior. On the other hand, that lady was fulfilling her womanhood in a way that Mel was not. Had Mel been living in that part of the world, I thought, she would be determined to get married, otherwise women and even men would have looked down on her for being still single, and not yet having had a child.

"Right. If the West was merely saying, 'don't treat others differently to us when they visit us,' then there ought to be a variety of standards regarding how people ought to be treated in different countries. Instead though, the rules are globalized, and Whites who are on top are considered to be the norm which everyone else ought to follow," I said, "and that applies wherever you are in the world."

"So, was that pregnant girl living a norm that meant that Mel fell short?" I asked myself? "Probably. Mel, though, had access to a lot more money than did that heavily pregnant girl. Who was better off?" I did not have a good answer to my question.

"So, are Whites superior?" Mel asked me. As she did, a woman removed a basket from her head and laid it before Mel. Mel had to walk around it.

"Buy fish," said the woman. Many other people were walking around there. She did not put her wares on display in that way to others, but only to Mel, the white woman.

"Well, I'm glad you've asked that question. It tends to be a taboo question," was my response. I noticed that Rolly was pricking his ears, tuning in to our conversation.

"Yes," said Mel, apparently thinking about the implications of what she had said.

"Firstly, let me say that is a theological question." I did love to point people to the reach and impact of theology on diverse aspects of human living.

"What do you mean, Dave?" Mel asked. The woman with a basket of fish was following her. I turned around and used my broken Striden to discourage her from doing so, explaining on Mel's behalf, that she was not about to purchase any fish.

"Ultimately, the only person who can judge if someone is superior is God. Otherwise, superiority is always contingent," I said to Mel a few paces on.

"How do you mean?"

"Let's take an example. Three people are running away from a lion. One would expect that the one who can run the fastest will be most likely to escape, yes?" … "Hey, look at that kingfisher!" I added pointing. There was not only one kingfisher. There were many, 'hunting' while hovering over the water of the lake. That one, though, was particularly close and seemed particularly beautiful in the light of the early-morning sun.

Mel turned to look at the kingfisher, as did Rolly. Then, in response to our conversation, she said, "Yes," while still looking quite puzzled.

"So – running fast is a superior ability?" I suggested.

"Yes," Mel replied.

"Now imagine the lion is chasing people towards another lion. Then the person moving the fastest is most likely to fall into the trap."

"Okay, so now a slower mover seems to be superior," Rolly said. Rolly had evidently come to the point at which he could follow us.

"Absolutely!" said Mel.

"We are doing some good thinking!" Rolly exclaimed.

"So then, I hope you see what I mean?" I added, "that only God can be the final judge."

"I'll give you another example," Rolly said, "which is a very contemporary one." We turned our ears to him. "Some people may be so clever that they know about atomic particles, so they can invent nuclear bombs. Let's say people A. Another people, people B, are 'primitive' so they don't invent nuclear power. People A have a civil war, and a nuclear explosion kills them all. Which people were superior, A or B?"

"Well, B," said Mel.

"Yet, up to the start of the civil war, everyone might well have thought that people A were the cleverer."

"I see," said Mel.

"Let's sit here," I suggested moments later. There was a concrete platform of some sort next to us. I didn't know what it was for. It looked clean enough, and gave us a great view over the lake. We sat, Mel between Rolly and me. "Only God can judge in the end, because only God knows the end of things," I said. I paused to let that truth go home. Neither Mel nor Rolly responded immediately. Probably they were enjoying the view over the lake, despite the wafting smell of rotting fish! "Okay," I added, while admiring the view over the lake. "So let us put aside the religious thing for a moment. Let us assume we know that people A are 'superior' to people B."

"Okay," said Mel, turning towards me.

"Well, the question then arises, presumably, of how to help people B catch up with people A."

"Good point," said Mel. Fortunately, the woman who had been following Mel put her basket back onto her head at this point, and strolled off.

"Let's take Rolly's nuclear example. Let us assume that having nuclear knowledge is good. How should people A best help people B?"

"I think they should ..." Mel started saying.

"Uhuummm," I interrupted her. "Let me give you options." I looked at Rolly. He seemed to be happy for me to carry on. Funnily enough, at that moment one of the birds flying overhead released a deposit that landed on Mel's shoe! Mel shrieked, then wiped her shoe clean. I was glad it hadn't landed on one of our heads. So, I think were my colleagues! "Either, acknowledge B's ignorance, so that one can teach them how to do better *or* assume that people B already know."

"There's no point in assuming people B already know if they don't," said Mel, "because that assumption will not help them to learn."

"You've got it, Mel," Rolly said. Mel swiveled her head to look at him. "To assume that all groups of people, nations or races are the same and are the same as the 'superior' race, if there is such, is not to help them. It might keep them in their ignorance. For example, if people A all know something anyway, then it may not be taught in their schools – there'd be no point because they already know! If people B don't know that thing, then treating everyone the same by insisting that everyone has the same curriculum in school is holding people B back by keeping them ignorant."

"What you're saying is, for example, that giving African people an educational system or process that is the same as a western one, is a way of keeping them in ignorance?" said Mel. Rolly and I both nodded. "So that's it," Mel said. She was feeling a bit overwhelmed. I wasn't surprised.

We seemed to be ready for a change in tack. "Philo teaches people the Bible. Why?" I asked. Mel turned her head back in my direction. Rolly was apparently doing his best to take in what I said. Ahead of us, two or three small sail-boats were passing from left to right across the lake. I imagined that was the kind of scene that Jesus used to see on the shores of Galilee.

"Because we believe it is God's word," Mel said.

"Right! You see how important that is. Anything less than God's word, and one risks all one's great wisdom being assessed, in the final analysis, as folly. Everything then hinges on just what is inspired by God."

"Mmmm," said Mel, unconvincingly.

After I had said that, Rolly piped up "Look over there." We followed his eyes. There was an old man in a boat castigating a young man. "I just thought it was funny," Rolly explained. "As you were talking about 'folly,' to see that man castigating his son. He's probably saying; 'son, you don't know how to fish'!" Both of us nodded. It was fun being there while so much life was happening around us.

"I want to raise another issue about the gospel though," I went on. "Look. This is an important question: what is it that has enabled the West to have its current superiority, if it is superiority? That's a bit of a rhetorical question. I want to suggest an answer."

"Go on then," Mel said by lifting the palms of her two hands.

"It is the gospel."

"How do you know?" Mel said.

"Many things. For example, look at all of today's prosperous western nations. Well, aren't they all Christian?"

"Yes," said Mel, "but there's the chicken and the egg."

"Look, you are right that nowadays in the West not everyone believes in the gospel. That is because of people's efforts at not being racist. I mean, it is good to be not-racist. But, other agendas that piggy-back onto opposition to racism may be less helpful. People who don't want to recognize the differences between European and African people are concealing the impact of the gospel. This happens when opposition to racism takes the Christian (or post-Christian) West as the norm. It pretends that everyone else is the same. Why? That results in concealing the impact of faith in Jesus on people's lives."

"That is very new to me!" said Mel. "I'll have to think about it." Rolly's face was screwed up into a hyper-thoughtful expression.

"Notice, that such opposition to the recognition of difference applies especially to *values*. No one is saying that one must think black people are white. So, it's not about physical things. It's not even about running fast. No, it is about values, like working hard, or having love."

"I get that," Mel said.

I went on: "Well, if we choose to ignore differences between people, then we end up anti-gospel. We end up making out that everyone in the world is already Christian! Therefore, there's no need for evangelism, conversion, the gospel. Why encourage people to become Christian, if they already have everything that Christians strive for?"

Mel was beginning to understand my point of view, that concealing the difference between people was a ploy by secularists, under cover of a pretense that they are against racism, to disguise the role of God in people's lives. I hoped it helped her to understand Philo's role in life better, why he did what he did.

"Philo, having seen through this screen of secular deception, saw no other moral pathway but to commit his life to sharing the gospel with people in Africa. Even as he did so, many western people were laughing at him! Because the anti-racist rhetoric had deceived them, they could not see the point of what he is doing. This also meant that the so-called secular West was not secular at all in the way that western people think they are. The West is deeply theological. Only – they have little awareness of their theology, which presumably means that instead of actively engaging in their theology they simply presuppose it. As a result of their own self-imposed lack of self-understanding, the West is poorly equipped to help others."

The trouble with a conversation such as this was that it might have been further raising the status of Philo in Mel's eyes! If I were not careful, I would be helping Mel not only to stay in love with Philo, but to sink into hero-worshipping him!

At that point we got up and walked back to our guest house, talking about other things. We found Rose expecting us, and sat down at a table waiting for breakfast. This time we weren't in the restaurant, but outside, behind it. I wondered what Rose was thinking about our choice of location for breakfast?

"Is this okay for you, Ro?" Rolly asked her, apparently reading my mind. We were hardly in a 'pleasant' spot, as there were buildings all around us and various interesting fishy smells, but at least there was more fresh air than had we been inside. Rose grunted. She wandered off. I think she was hoping for a nicer spot.

* * *

"So what is a typical breakfast for people around here?" Mel asked as we sat around that table.

"Good question," Rolly said. "*Ichamoga nang'o gi chai gokinyi?*" he said to someone walking by.

"*Rabwon,*" the man responded.

"Sweet potatoes – according to him," Rolly translated.

Just then Rose came back. She pulled out the fourth chair at our breakfast table and sat down. It seems she'd failed to find a better spot.

"That would presumably be with black tea, with or without sugar?" Mel added.

"Of course, it would vary," Rolly said.

We ordered our breakfast. Most of us had a big (well, biggish) donut and tea. As we sat, I shared my surprise news: "Philo called me last night."

"Really!" the others said in unison, causing me to laugh.

"It was quite funny. He thought I was in Imbigen!"

"Did you tell him?" Rose asked.

"No, I just said nothing on that."

"How is he?" Mel asked.

"Okay," I said. "He seemed to do much better than us last night on the food front. He got a hero's welcome."

"Where did he sleep?" Rolly asked.

"Right there, in someone's bed. He didn't know whose bed of course," I filled him in. "You know what he told me?" I added. "Some white woman sent a spy after him! The very person who was sent, well, actually Philo wasn't sure that he wasn't an old friend he had met at some point, made Philo an offer. He said that if Philo would give him $100, then he would tell the white woman who sent him that Philo was faithful, and paint a very positive picture of him. 'Did you give him the money?' I asked Philo. 'For what ...' he replied, then started laughing."

"So much for sending an investigator, if he can be so easily bought!" Rolly said. Mel looked embarrassed. I was happy that she didn't descend into depression at that point.

"So, what was the $100 for?" Rose asked. She obviously wasn't fully awake yet. We didn't even answer her question.

"Then later, when we asked local people about Philo, we got a grossly exaggerated hagiography," Rolly added.

"So how do you find out the truth of what is happening in an unfamiliar foreign culture?" Mel asked.

"It has something to do with $100," Rose said. We guessed by that comment that she was now more awake and aware of the issues we had in mind.

"Really, though?" Mel asked to emphasize the critical point to our discussion. This was no small matter to Mel. She spoke hurriedly, with a donut in her mouth, wanting to make sure she got her question in quickly, so not having had a chance to swallow.

"That will depend on the truth you want," I said, "and the truth they think you want."

"And the truth that pays," Rolly said.

"The most!" I added.

The previous day, Mel had been the leading light and a ball of energy. Now, however, she was becoming discouraged. I was not surprised. Many people come to Africa from the West with high ideals as to what they want to do. Typically, they know just how they are going to achieve it. Then it falls flat! That includes, it seems, even endeavoring to find out what a missionary is really doing, and how well he is doing it!

"How on earth am I going to do the research I want to do with any accuracy at all?" Mel asked rhetorically.

CHAPTER 24: DAVE RUNS AWAY

"Hi there," a voice came at that moment, as we were still finishing our breakfasts. The voice had, it seemed, a mixture between a German and an Australian accent. I turned. A short, plump white woman was standing behind me.

"Fancy meeting you all here. Thought I'd come and say hello. I saw you on the road. I was surprised to find you eating in a place like this."

"Oh," said Rose, not quite sure how to respond to that (presumably a little embarrassed to be eating at 'a place like this'!).

"My name is Gail," she said. "I'm here with my husband. We live in Michiki."

"We are just passing through," Rose responded.

"Please pay me a visit if you can," said the woman. A lock of hair fell over her eyes as she spoke. She pushed it back.

"Where is Michiki?"

"It's about forty miles from here, East."

"Not sure if we'll get there," said Rose.

"You could almost read the longing in Rose's eyes, having found a white female friend, she wanted to spend time with her to have a natter," I thought. Well, today it seemed that Rose was in luck!

"Well, Rose, today's plan – is to go to Michiki!" I announced. Rose broke into a smile. She then exchanged phone numbers with her already very-special new friend!

We got our bill paid, and in due course set out for Michiki.

* * *

The dynamics in our vehicle seemed entirely different from what they had been the day before. Rolly was thinking about what on earth he would say to Professor Nancy should she get him on the phone again. Mel was not her yesterday's usual self at all. As we drove along the same road that Philo would undoubtedly have to travel, she didn't bother inspecting any of the buses we passed in case Philo was to be found in them. While Rolly's dilemma was also Rose's dilemma, and she stood with her husband, she seemed quite emotionally detached from the prospect of having no money and an unemployed husband when back in the USA. As for me, well I

168

guess I was wondering "What on earth is coming next?" on this crazy adventure of ours. One good thing, perhaps, was that we were due to stay in Michiki for three nights – a bit more opportunity to settle and even rest than we had had in Hongera.

Michiki was a crazy town. Crazy – hectic – busy, people walking in all directions on busy streets, particularly one busy main street, plus a constant flow of motorcycles both ways up and down it. Other vehicles were also there *en masse* – trucks, private cars, 4x4s, buses, *bajajis,* and so on. While people from some of today's mega bustling cities might have found Michiki to be a quiet rural enclave, to the likes of us it was a crazy urban center. (Although, we were to visit many perhaps just-as-crazy large cities before our time in Holima was over.)

We sat outside a café on the main street. We had ordered and eaten things from inside. We remained sat there, talking. We needed to find a place to stay. 'Where to start?' was the question. Rose then had a great idea – 'Why not ask her friend?'

After we had discussed various options, I walked off to some shops looking for a few bits and pieces. What happened next is probably best first described from the point of view of the three people left behind! Rose was on the phone: "Yes, dear, we'd love to, that would be great. If that is what you would advise that is certainly what we will do ..."

Mel was slumped on a chair beside her. Rose, Mel, and Rolly remained outside the café on the side of the crazy-busy main street. In the heat of the day, and all, tea didn't seem the right thing, so they were drinking fizzy drinks (in Rolly's case, water). Rolly was looking pensive. Evidently, Mel was lazily following my movements, looking depressed.

"Hii hii hoo hoo, la di da di daaa," went Rose, chattering away on the phone.

Suddenly Mel sat bolt upright in her chair. "Look!" she said. Rolly looked. Rose was rather too absorbed by her phone conversation to take much notice. Rolly couldn't see what Mel was looking at.

"It's Dave!" Mel said. "He's running away!"

Indeed, I was. On skinning his eyes, Rolly saw occasional glimpses of a white figure through the crowds, vehicles, stands and general chaos, running away from them, apparently as fast as he could! He also sat bolt upright. I had only gone to buy a few things in a shop, so why was I now running like crazy? Rolly couldn't see anyone following me. I didn't seem to be being chased.

"Follow him!" Mel exclaimed, anxiously.

"What!" Rolly responded. Rolly did, though – he started running after me. Well, he could hardly run as I could, but he started out in the same direction, presumably hoping he might keep me within his field of vision. Meanwhile, Mel called my phone. As I ran, I heard my phone ring, but I didn't have the opportunity to answer it. Rose put her hand over the mouthpiece of her phone. Being simultaneously engaged in another conversation, she wasn't really following what was going on.

"Where are you going, deareeee?" Rose screamed at Rolly, who was running away from her as fast as he could! Everyone within thirty yards turned to look at Rose, then at Rolly.

A man with an alarmed expression on his face ran up to Rose. "Has he taken something?" he asked her. For a Holiman, he looked strange, as he had a large hooked nose. Mel looked at his feet as well, to find he was wearing trainers. Hence, she thought, had he wanted to, he wouldn't have had trouble catching up with Rolly. Good job Rose said 'no,' as the normal procedure if someone is running away was that he was a thief. Had she said 'yes,' or if someone were to shout 'thief,' the crowd might have sprung into action, grabbed Rolly, and beaten him to death.

Mel by this time was standing and straining to see Rolly's progress. Rolly stopped. Even Mel, from where she was standing with Rose, could see that he was puffing and panting. Rolly in the meantime was watching me run to and jump onto a moving motorcycle that then took me way beyond his field of vision. Rolly staggered (well, the sudden sprint had taken it out of him) back to the ladies.

"Saw him jump onto a motorbike, and he was gone," Rolly told them.

"Who's got the keys to the car?" Mel asked them. Rolly and Rose looked at each other blankly. Wherever I had gone, they were now stuck for transport until I came back.

"Yes, dear. Yes, yes. Looking forward to that. We hope to see you soon, love." Rose called off.

Rose was mentally back with us after her ten-minute animated 'female' phone call with her friend, to find Rolly sitting and panting, Mel looking worried, and me gone, apparently with the car keys. "What's happened?" Rose asked.

"Dave has run away," Mel said, her voice still in panic mode.

"I always knew he would!" Rose said.

"What do you mean 'you knew he would'?" Rolly asked Rose.

She looked a little bewildered. "Men can't be trusted," Rose said. Rolly laughed. Mel tried calling me again. The phone rang in my pocket as I was on the back of the motorbike. I let it ring. I was concentrating on the chase!

While the others were wondering what was going on as above, well, here is my account: I emerged out of a shop, then glancing to my left, saw what I was sure was a white man. "That's Philo!" I thought immediately. I strained my eyes. He was far away (a few hundred yards). "We'd found our prey!" I thought. I glanced back towards the others. I didn't have time to go and explain or Philo would be gone. I started running towards Philo. I was aware, of course, that the idea was that I not be seen, so I tried to dodge behind obstacles to keep out of sight from him. I was gaining ground. Then I realized that he was talking to a motorcyclist. Moments later he was sitting on the back of a motorbike and he was on his way! I hailed a motorcycle that was coming past me. He slowed down for me, then I did the most amazing thing that I can't, with hindsight, believe that I did, but I did. That is, I ran up and jumped onto the back of the moving motorbike!

"That way, *Ngwech*!" I shouted to the rider (*ngwech* = quickly). I was soon able to point out the bike with Philo on it. "Follow him, but not too close. I don't want him to see me," I said. "If he stops, we must stop. Don't get close!"

Fortunately, my motorcyclist was big, tall, fat, and wore a large floppy coat. That is, as a result, it would be difficult for Philo to identify me or even for his rider to realize that a white man was following them, should they look behind. I relaxed a little. My phone rang. I ignored it.

We seemed to go on forever, round endless corners, up and down hills, dust flying everywhere. I guess it was a ride of about forty-five minutes. We probably weren't going particularly fast – although it seemed fast to me, as I was not used to being pillion on a motorbike. We passed low bushes, just a few taller trees. There were houses in homesteads, not sure whether to say periodically or frequently. The landscape was undulating. We eventually saw Philo's motorbike leave the main track.

"Where does that path go?" I asked my rider.

"Don't know," he said. To be safe we stayed on the main track. Fortunately, otherwise, I might have lost Philo at the last minute, I saw the home at which Philo alighted. Fortuitously again, I saw that another home was not far from it. All being well, by following another route, I reckoned, we could reach that home while remaining out of sight (behind my big rider) to the people in Philo's homestead, and to Philo in particular. We went around a slightly longer route. I ducked as did my rider, or we might have got hung up on some low branches. Of course, I didn't know whose home it was we were pulling up to. The main house itself blocked our view of where Philo was, but we were not far away at all. I quickly took the motorcyclist's phone number and gave him his due, before attending in more detail to my immediate context, and location. "Today, I am really spying!" I thought.

"*Hodi!*" I said, standing near the door to the house. A grey-haired woman, aged I guess about sixty, came and stood in the doorway. She looked at me puzzled.

"*Mos kuom buogi mama,*" I said in Striden that must have been very rusty. (Sorry to startle you.) With true Holima hospitality, however, she immediately invited me in. I prayed, then sat. As the lady of the house went into the kitchen, I stood up and peeked through the window. A perfect view of the homestead Philo was in was staring me in the face! There was a large *kraal* in the middle of the homestead. There were no cattle in it at the time – presumably, they were out being grazed somewhere, I surmised. Then I counted – one, two, three larger houses. It seems the man of the home had three wives. There were a good number of additional houses that must have been the sons' houses. The man of the home was at least in his forties, maybe in his fifties or older, I thought, – to have so many sons who'd built their own houses, with their wives. I should say the man was a farmer – there was little evidence that he might be someone who worked far away, such as in Imbigen, and only came home to build a house. Many of the roofs were thatched. When I saw the small gathered crowd of which Philo was a part, I noticed from the layout of the homestead that they were outside the house of a son, not a wife. I could not therefore know – was the head of the homestead a member of the church, or only his son, or only (possibly) a wife to his son? Anyway, there was Philo chatting to people.

I sat down. I didn't want the lady of the house to know that I was a spy. I quickly sent an SMS, "chasing Philo," to Rolly. The lady came back in.

* * *

Rose's friend called back. "Hello, Rose."

"Hello, Gail."

"Look, I've talked to my husband. We welcome you all to stay at our home. We have a guest-flat. It has two bedrooms, a sitting room, a small kitchen, but just one shower and bathroom. Will that be okay for you?"

Rose had turned her phone on to the speaker setting so that Mel and Rolly could also overhear. Rose looked at her colleagues. Both nodded back at her.

"That will be great," she said. "Look, please come early. Be here by three-thirty. Then at four o'clock, we will have high tea. Then supper will be at 6 p.m.," said the female voice, with the strange mixture of a German and Australian accent.

"Certainly," said Rose. "We will be there by three-thirty. Goodbye, dearie."

"Goodbye."

("Wow, was Rose good at making friends!" I reflected later. Women do have giftings in areas in which they beat men hands down – like spontaneously making instant good-friends in strange places!)

"Let's make sure we are on time," Rose said.

"Dave has the car key, and he's chasing Philo," Rolly reminded her.

Rose's face fell.

* * *

My hostess seemed very glad to have had a visitor unexpectedly appear! She welcomed me like a long-lost cousin. She didn't seem to have any questions about why I might be there. She paraded four children in front of me. In each case, she did say, "This child is at school, and needs school-fees." (There may have been more to her hospitality than met the eye!) Once she had introduced her children, she sent one of them to buy some bread and another one to bring some sugar. I assumed she had her own cow, and hence that she already had the milk with which to make the tea.

After a while, left alone again, I glanced out of the window. No one was visible, except one of the wives of the home, outside her house washing dishes. The other people had entered the house of the meeting, I assumed, ready to start. A woman came, went to the house, and also entered. I sat back down. Before long, I heard a loud prayer. Then I heard people beginning to clap and sing. I wondered just what I was to do with the information I was gathering? I had run after Philo without a plan, only on an emotional impulse. "Give it to Mel!" I supposed. I tried to imagine how Mel might end up writing up her visit to Holima. To be honest, I was a bit defeated to know how. But – all I saw myself doing at that point was collecting information for her.

The lady of the house came back. With her was her oldest granddaughter. The lady wore a long black dress. Her granddaughter, we might say in the UK, was dressed in rags. I guess the granddaughter was about twelve. She had not yet reached puberty, but she looked like it wouldn't be long before her body shape changed. They together served me white tea with sugar and bread and ground nuts.

"Well, I am a stranger, and a spy at that, who is being well looked after!" I thought.

The lady began telling me her story, as I drank tea. Her oldest son was called Leonard, she told me. She seemed glad to have someone to talk to. I guessed she was a widow. Perhaps I would find out why it looked like her grandchildren were left in her care. "Perhaps her daughter was dead?" I postulated.

"An bende dadhi e chokruok," (I would also have gone to the meeting), the lady said. She spoke a lot of Striden, with bits of Swahili and English mixed in, which is widely known as 'code-switching.' I am not sure Philo was over-impressed whenever people added liberal amounts of English to what they were saying, although that was a common practice. It helped me, with my minimal Striden, and of late, severe lack of practice, as I had not been living in Holima. The woman began telling me her story.

At that moment, the loud singing and clapping became all the more audible. "That must have been a praise session," I thought.

Just then an SMS came on the phone, "you have the car keys," from Rolly. I checked my pockets. "Yes, sorry," I wrote back. I imagined my colleagues there, fretting about not being able to go anywhere till I got back. "Back as soon as possible," I continued, knowing that it wouldn't happen quickly, drinking tea as I was, and not wanting to leave until everything was finished in the neighboring homestead.

The woman told me that she used to belong to a particular indigenous Christian denomination. That is where she went to worship with her husband when he was alive. She no longer felt bound to that denomination once her husband had died. Meanwhile her neighbors – not the ones worshipping, she was at pains to point out – wanted to take some of her land. She knew that because her children were struggling. One was getting a poor grade in school. Another was sickly. Then her oldest daughter could not get a stable husband. The oldest daughter eventually died, killed by some curse, resulting in her taking on the rearing of her four children by herself. The death of her daughter threw her. She had no money left to give to any witch doctors. She could not see how she could rear four kids on thin air. It was then that a neighbor of hers came to tell her about Jesus. Of course, she knew about Jesus, but she had not known that Jesus could save someone, could heal them, and could fill them with the Holy Spirit. She agreed to be prayed for by members of the church – that is the one Philo was with. That required her to kneel with her arms stretched up, while the pastor and others put their hands on her head and prayed noisily. At the time, she recounted, she shrieked and fell down convulsing violently. They kept praying for her until all the demons had left her. So, she was born again. Ever since then, she has had a new beginning. She has trusted God and not her abilities. She has been amazed that she always seemed to have enough food on the table, and her children (grandchildren) had been able to keep going to school.

This was such a typical Striden testimony! I wished that my colleagues could have been with me to hear it. But then – without the skeletal Striden that I knew, they would not have been able to understand it. Also – the very frequency of this kind of testimony made it problematic when Westerners heard it. It was like it was of a 'testimony genre.' It was the kind of thing people say of witch doctors who have helped them, Jesus, who has helped them, donors who have supported them! That is not to say at all that it is not valuable. But – such testimony needed to be understood in context. It is the kind of testimony African people tell about what Jesus has done in their lives that can appear, if transferred to western thinking, that they are more devoted Christians than anyone in the UK or America! Of course, it is possible that they are. But – to understand such a testimony correctly, one had to be able to understand it in relation to things that were said more generally, to acquire patrons, not in isolation.

As I was contemplating the above, I was hearing people in the house where Philo was, talking. "That must have been testimony time," I thought. That is the time given over in many Christian gatherings for people to tell of what God has done in their lives. I think that is right and good. But if Westerners believe that God, therefore, does miracles in Africa that he doesn't do in the West, or that Africans have enormous faith, they will have heard only half of the story. To take what people say out of context is to misunderstand it! What not all western people realize is that African people live according to what in the West is known as the patron-client system. In that system, the patron provides for the client, and the client praises the patron. This means that if you appear to be wealthy or powerful, then you will get praise. That praise need not be related to truth, except tangentially. Accept the praise, and you are expected to give something. Give something, and then you should expect praise.

My task right now was to keep my hostess talking. "Leonard's mom, what do you mean by so-and-so!" I asked. To say 'Leonard's mom,' sounds clumsy. In Striden, though, it is very common to call a lady after the name of her child. Then it would be '*Min Leonard*,' which is not clumsy at all. I had to try to make sure that Min Leonard did not go to the meeting, where she was bound to reveal my presence. I also had to extend my stay, if possible, until Philo's meeting was completely over. As Leonard's mom talked, I heard phrases being used in testimonies in the hut where Philo was, like: "We should not be poor," and "God healed me," and "I used to have AIDS" and "You must be filled with the Spirit." Eventually, after a few more songs, it came to the time for Philo to preach. Unfortunately, I don't know what he said! Min Leonard noticed I was getting tired. Indeed, I was. Trying to listen to what was happening in Philo's fellowship, while also paying attention to Min Leonard, was proving too taxing! Min Leonard left me alone. I put my head back and must have slept there in my chair for half an hour.

* * *

While I was chatting to Min Leonard and dozing, back in Michiki, Rose was pulling her hair out! She desperately wanted to impress her new friend. Her friend had said we should all be there by three-thirty. Now it was after five o'clock, and no sign of me back in town, yet I had the car keys in my pocket!

Eventually, I think about six o'clock I got an SMS; "We've gone by taxi to the home of Gail. Call for directions and follow us by vehicle when you are ready."

* * *

I woke up to hear enormous noise emerging from the house where Philo was. All the people in the house were screaming at the tops of their voices! For a nanosecond, as I came to, I was concerned, thinking; "why are all these people screaming?" You would have thought there was a gunman in the house, or the ladies were being raped and robbed! The screaming that people engaged in during prayer was little different from someone screaming in agony. Occasionally, one heard stories of women being attacked in a prayer meeting. No one would take any notice of their screaming, because all the women were screaming anyway. On one occasion I heard reported that a pastor murdered his wife. He did so in a house where people, including women, often visited him for prayer. Because those visitors would often scream as they were delivered from demons, no one walking by took any notice of the wife's screams for help, even when her husband set about attacking her with a machete!

The screaming was of course directed at the demons that were troubling people. I have to say that 'demons' is not a good translation of what it is. It is the best word available in English, but they are not actual demons as western people think of them. People in that house were people with problems. Well – aren't we all! This was their opportunity, a window of time, designated for them to get very serious with their problems. This could be screaming at the problems to go away. It could also be crying to God to help them. Eventually, the screaming died down.

Suddenly I thought, "Where is Min Leonard?" I was concerned that she might have gone to attend the meeting. When the noise died down, however, I could hear her snoring in the other room of the hut.

When I looked out of the window again, the meeting was over. Some people, actually the women, had spilled out of the house. They were sitting, scattered around. The men presumably received their 'snack' sitting in the house. As they sat, they were drinking tea, and they were eating. From what I could see, what they had with their tea was something called *nyoyo*. *Nyoyo* is a mixture of maize and beans. The maize (American English – corn) and beans are boiled together in water. Sometimes tomatoes, onions, and other things can be added, sometimes not. If not, then the maize and beans are eaten 'just like that,' typically with a good amount of salt.

As I watched the people eat, I remembered something that Philo told me years previously, and that I have also subsequently found to be true. That is – that many conversation topics that we regularly engage in the West are taboo in Africa. In the West, people talk about the most rational way of doing something. Perhaps, for example – which is the best route to a given destination. Generally speaking, African people do not discuss such things in those ways. For them, it seems, there is no rationality without witchcraft. Hence, if one is not careful, one can quickly be suspected of being a witch.

For example, should I ask you, "How are your children?" If I show too much interest in your children, the suspicion arises that I am comparing their performance in life with that of my children. Then if I find that your children outstrip mine, I may bewitch yours. If your children subsequently get problems, you might blame me! Why else should I express intense interest in your children after all? Mind you, in the West, we also have taboo topics, like differences between black and white races that are related to values, and all the personal questions that make British people say: "Keep conversation to the weather!"

Eventually, people dispersed, and Philo with them. He remained, at least as far as I could tell, totally unaware that I was there! Philo was being carried on the back of someone's motorbike. No point in my following him now. I would tell Mel what had happened. That would suffice for one day. I raised my voice a little, Leonard's mom woke up. I thanked her for her warm accommodating hospitality. She offered me a place for the night. That is a standard offer. I turned down her offer.

Soon I was walking back in the direction of Michiki. My motorcycle taxi told me he was on his way. He picked me up. By the time I got back to the vehicle, it was after seven o'clock. No sign of the others. But then, I had not expected to see them. Rolly gave me directions over the phone, and I joined them at our new accommodation – a very comfortable two-bedroom cottage in the compound of an expansive missionary house!

CHAPTER 25: YOU HAVE TO TRUST THEM

Gail had set aside a plate for me. By the time I had washed and brushed, it was eight o'clock. I sat with the others. There was Gail, her husband Gary, and the four of us. We sat on comfortable reclining chairs in their living room. Gary was short, quite thick set, with a surprisingly bountiful head of hair for his age. He spoke with a clear American accent. I should say Texan. There was, I soon discovered, quite a lively discussion already going on.

"I trust them," said Gary. "So why should I need to travel to our projects or learn the local language?" For Gary, one either trusted someone or one did not. It was for him a simple decision. How could he work with Christian brothers and sister, albeit Africans, unless he simply trusted them? "If there is a decision, they make it. Isn't that right, dear?" he said, turning his head to where Gail was sitting. Gail returned his look nodding. "They are good people," Gary added.

"We've been telling Gary and Gail that I am writing a paper about Philo's mission," Mel said. "Tell me, Dave, do you think Philo trusts the Africans? I mean – would he allow them to run a project without supervision?" I thought I had better play for time, and try to learn the lie of the land before answering, even though I had a pretty good idea of what my answer would be.

"Can you explain what you mean?" I asked. By that point, things that Philo had told me about trust had come to mind.

"The problem of some missionaries is that they do not trust the Africans," Gary said, leaning back in his easy chair. I sensed a condemning tone. This was a verbal game of one-upmanship. If you say, 'I don't trust Africans,' then the question is why? In explaining why you 'do not trust the Africans,' it is like you have to drag them through the mud. That comes to be like a divorce court – in which couples have to convince the court how bad their partner is to get a divorce, in the process of which their relationship is ruined! This time, though, I had a rejoinder to give, in this game of cut and thrust.

"I think the problem is not with the trustworthiness of the Africans but of the missionaries," I said, cutting to the chase.

"Well, I can assure you that I am consistent and use great integrity in my work," said Gary in a loud, clear voice. At the same time, I noticed him moving his fingers in a way that suggested to me that he was not quite as confident in himself as he seemed. If Gary had a confidence problem, could he deal with my challenging him? I would have to find out. I thought though that my point was valid.

"Yes, I accept that, I don't doubt that, from a western point of view," I said.

"What do you mean 'from a western point of view,' Dave. Are you a relativist?"

"Wow," I thought, "this sounds like the civil war has begun!" I tried to find a way of talking that was less threatening.

"What I mean, Gary, is that what we in America or Britain consider integrity may not be what African people consider integrity. This is because our integrity tends to be with respect to our lifestyle and values. African 'integrity' though has to be with respect to their lifestyle and values." I wondered at that point whether we were shortly going to be asked to leave.

"Nonsense!"

"Give him a chance to explain himself," (I wondered whether I only get one chance!) Gail said.

I could feel myself sweating. I tried to avoid Mel's gaze. She was lowering her eyebrows to intensify the glare she was sending in my direction. Suddenly I burst out laughing. I couldn't help myself. "Sorry, folks," I said. "I'm just overcome by the seriousness of all this." Gary managed a smile. "We missionaries come under pressure in certain ways. Our donors, for example, and our visitors, expect certain things from us. We act with integrity by fulfilling what they and our supporters, in general, expect us to do. Local people around here, though, come under different pressures. They are under pressure from their families, churches, clans, tribes, cultures, ancestors, to do certain things in certain ways and to relate to people in certain ways. That parallels the ways our people call us to account. Their absent ancestors parallel our absent donors. They are being set different criteria for accountability than are we."

"Sounds like bunkum to me," said Gary.

Well, I had dug a hole for myself by this point, and I had little choice but to continue, although I realized that I might no longer be Gary's favorite visitor. "No, Gary – African people are answerable to their communities. That puts them under pressure to comply with dictates by their communities, to do things a certain way, to respond in certain ways and so on. You and I are largely unfamiliar with the worlds of those communities, which they are responding to ..."

"Bunkum," repeated Gary. "Isn't it, dear?" he said, turning to his wife.

I wasn't sure how to read Gail's expression. "Well," I thought, "here I am knocking my own nails into my own coffin! Then again," I thought, "perhaps the fact that Gary deferred to his wife meant he was not 100% sure that my words were bunkum!"

"African people often cannot trust us foreign missionaries," I said, "because we do not understand, or even know, the pressures they are under to do what they do. Hence, from their point of view, because we ignore the demands that they are under, we say and do stupid things."

"Humph!" said Gary.

I half-expected him to say, 'look here young man, remember you are my visitor ...' but fortunately he didn't go that far! "Hence," I continued, "African people are forced not into integrity, but into *bitegrity*."

"*Bitegrity*," Gary said, laughing.

"Yes, they are required to fill their own norms by their own people, then we come along and give them a different set of standards and expect them to fill those as well."

By that point, Mel had her head down. If I read him correctly, Rolly was indicating to me that I should shut up. Rose was turning pink. Gail, however, fanned the flames. Perhaps she was glad that her husband finally had someone answer his over-confident posture. I could not know.

"Come on, Dave, give us an African example," she said. I looked at my colleagues who continued to cower.

"There are many examples I could give," I said, "but you may not appreciate them."

"Try us," Gail said.

"When we think there is urgent critical work to be done, African people will take a day off with no notice, for a funeral, regardless. There's an example."

"There you are, dear," said Gary to Gail. "That troubles us a lot. People make commitments to do things, then they drop their commitments when they receive notice about a death. That's what I mean when I say they lack integrity."

His response threw me. He had previously said he 'trusted' Africans. I was now discovering that he might not have trusted them 'that much' after all! Telling us that he 'trusted them,' was perhaps a strategy he used habitually for donors and other foreigners.

"Gary," I said, "don't you see that impromptu attendance at a funeral is a way for an African man to demonstrate integrity – everyone is expected to be there, and he is there! For us, it can be seen as a lack of integrity as he has reneged on his commitment to us. That is what I mean by *bitegrity*."

Gary nodded, slightly, but said nothing.

"Another classic then, 'abuse of funds.' Don't you see that 'abuse of funds' from one angle is 'good use of funds' from another?" I paused, then carried on. I found myself articulating with my arms as I spoke. By this time I was no longer leaning back in my chair, but leaning forwards, towards Gary, empathetically. "So, money comes from overseas that is perhaps intended to feed orphans. The African realizes, however, that feeding orphans but upsetting the dead is a bad combination, because later the dead who are upset will haunt the orphans. Therefore, money can be diverted from feeding orphans to pleasing the dead, for example having a good funeral, and to do that is integrous, given the relevance and activity of the dead."

"But the dead are not visible, and don't do things," Gary said. He was still leaning back in his chair, but I felt that his heart and soul were leaning forward!

"That's what you think," I said. "Foreign donors are just as invisible, by the way, to people in Africa, yet we respond to things that they do, might do, think, all the time. There's a parallel there when it comes to African people's responses to their dead. Look, I am only explaining what seems to happen," I added. There was a pause. I suddenly realized that things had changed for Mel. By now, her head was still bowed, but she was smiling. I had been hoping she would not burst into tears. Now I needed to be concerned that she did not burst out laughing! That was a relief. No one had a response for me. Perhaps they had got my point? Rose and Rolly raised their eyes a little.

"Classically, it concerns money. Western missionaries cannot be trusted, especially because they have money," I added.

"We use money to help the people," said Gary.

Gail waved her hand at him. "Carry on," she said to me. I seem to have struck on a raw nerve with her; I was connecting with something she had experienced.

"Come on," I said, "we keep ultimate control of the purse strings. We keep the prerogative of deciding just when a lot of money might suddenly *have to* be used. We can at any time pull a wad of money (given to us for the purpose by our donors) out of our pocket, so as to generously 'solve' a perceived predicament. We decide when, where, how much, to whom, so, we cannot be trusted! We force African people to adopt *bitegrity*, to please us. We ourselves, in our own *integrity*, in terms of our relationships with donors, render ourselves not to be trusted by African people."

"I have never heard such nonsense. What do you think, Gail?" asked Gary. (It now seemed I had been wrong to think that Gary had turned around! I wasn't sure just where I was standing with Gary. He was referring to his wife again.) As Gary spoke, I noticed Mel fumbling intensely with something on her lap.

"So, how to resolve this?" Gail asked.

"Use people's own languages to learn about the constraints they are under, and don't use outside money," I said. Gary started laughing. It was not a terrible, terrible laugh, but it was not a good laugh either.

Then Mel put her hand to her ear. She started standing up. "Philo is on the phone!" she announced to everyone. That seemed to be a ploy to change the topic! Anyway, it worked. She had turned the phone on to speaker setting.

"How are you, Philo?" she said.

"I am fine," he said. We were all listening. Then we were all shocked to hear Philo talk in a thin trailing voice.

"We are wanting to greet you," Mel said, her pleasurable tone probably not yet having registered with the alarming sound of Philo's voice. She was soon to register!

"Thanks, it is good ..."

That is as far as Philo got, then came an enormous din: "**Uuaaaggg-hhhHH-HHH**," over the phone. We heard the sound of Philo's vomit hitting the contents of a basin or bucket, splashing into liquid. Philo then, evidently, dropped the phone. There was a clattering noise. We could still hear clearly what was going on. Philo vomited and retched for another full minute, us hearing every sound. Then it seemed that Philo collapsed! Moments later, we heard voices of a man and woman, speaking Striden, running up to Philo. Philo by this point was silent.

* * *

"Is he unconscious?" I thought. I knew Philo fainted easily. What were my colleagues thinking? "Perhaps that he was … I hope he is not dead … too bad," I thought. I looked at Gail. She was as white as a sheet. Gary appeared to be in crisis. Rose and Rolly's eyes were wide. Mel looked as if she was about to scream. The couple, whom we assumed were with Philo, started praying noisily in Striden. We were unknown but captive listeners. Mel waited for a little, then she hit the 'cancel' button.

Silence.

"He's sick," I said.

"Or dead!" Rolly said. Mel's eyes were moist, but she did not cry. Rose and Gail were both shaking. I was majorly stressed. I am sure my other colleagues the same. It was like Philo's funeral.

"Look, he might not be dead!" I exclaimed loudly. I grabbed the phone from Mel. I called. Engaged tone.

"Where is he?" Gary asked.

"I don't know," I said.

"Who is he with?" Rolly asked.

"I don't know them," I said.

"Who knows them?" It was Rolly again.

I shrugged. "I don't know." I was trying to think. I fell back into my chair. "What do you want to do?" I asked Rolly, but really everyone. "Should we find an ambulance to rescue him?" An obvious silence fell over the room. "What can we do?"

"What should we do?" Gail said.

I did not give her an answer. We didn't know where Philo was. "It is probably malaria," I finally said. "It can turn bad. I'll just keep calling."

This was a mega testing moment; nothing we could do or should do! How to do nothing when your good friend has just collapsed? You are maybe ten miles from him, but you don't know where he is. Other friends are thousands of miles away. Of course, Philo thought that we were hundreds of miles away. The people he was with probably had no clue about our existence. I kept trying the phone. Thankfully Rose broke out into song, a worship song. We joined in. Phone still engaged. I prayed. We sang. Rolly prayed. So we went on for about two hours, intermittently discussing whether there was something more that could be done by us, but concluding that there wasn't.

"Dave, is there nothing we can do?" Mel said in one break between our singing.

"Philo has made a decision," I said. "That is, he has rendered himself vulnerable to the African people. He did not have to go and stay in that village. He could have stayed in England. In England, there is the NHS (National Health Service), and there is no malaria. Philo has come to where there is no NHS and where there is malaria. He has decided to identify with Striden people in this way. The Striden people do not get modern medicine. They know to counter witchcraft by prayer. That is the treatment Philo will be getting. His choice! If we knew where he was, we ought to rescue him. But we don't even know!"

Eventually, we sat mostly silently. The first person went to bed at 1 a.m. I was trying to think – how are we going to explain this? I imagined my report: "Philo died that night in a home he was visiting. We were just a few miles away, but we could do nothing to help him."

* * *

The next day at eight o'clock, Philo called. He found Rolly and myself were up already, both sitting silently in our chairs in our bedroom.

"Sorry to frighten you," he said. "I vomited, I have malaria. I lost consciousness. I'm still very sick. But I'll be okay. Please do pray for me! I'm on my way to see a doctor now." His voice was weak. He called off. We breathed sighs of relief. Rolly went to tell the ladies, then to tell our hosts.

* * *

That morning Gail had invited us to join Gary and her for breakfast. Because we had been up late, she had told us that breakfast would be at nine o'clock and not at eight o'clock as had been initially planned. When we met at nine, there was still a subdued feeling around the breakfast table. Not that we were sad. It is just that no one was jovial. People were thoughtful. The air was thick with contemplation.

"Morning, Gary," I said.

"Morning, Dave. I hope you had a good night's sleep," Gary responded.

"Very good," I said. "Good morning, Gail."

"Good morning, Dave. Good to see you today. I hope you feel rested."

"Yes, I do."

"Hi there, Rose. How's the morning?"

"I'm doing fine, Dave. Trust you had a good night's sleep?"

"Yes, I did," I said, "even though it seems to have been short."

"Good morning, ladies," Gary said to Mel and Rose when they emerged.

"How are you doing, Rolly?" Gail asked him.

"Fine," he said.

Gary and Gail had the habit of having a devotional at breakfast every morning. They followed a year's program that had a thought for every day. When we were sat, the smell of coffee and fresh buns filling our noses, Gary put us on to spiritual-pause. The passage Gary read for the day was from Luke chapter 10. Here's my version of verses 3–4: "Go (all of you), I am sending you like sheep amongst wolves. Do not carry a bag of money or a bag or shoes and do not greet anyone on your way." Gary read the blurb that went with the passage.

The blurb was okay. Of course – the writer of the blurb did not have 'mission in Africa' in mind. His thoughts related to a suburban American context. We heard it. At the same time, I think all of us were thinking – what does this passage say for us here, as we are? Gary prayed for us, then we launched into the generous and varied spread that had been put out by Gail.

After a minute or two of silence, Mel was the first to speak about what I think we were all thinking. I was stirring some yogurt into some cornflakes as she spoke. "Philo should not be alone," she said.

Well, that comment had more depth than Gary and Gail might have realized. It reflected a deep longing in Mel's heart. I thought of Gary as against Philo. Gary was not alone! Neither was he hungry – at least he had no reason to be hungry that morning. His house was extensive and well equipped with modern technology. Two 4x4s were sitting in front of the house – one his, the other his wife's. He had Gail on-tap whenever he might need her. Gail did not have a job. She had already told us that her job was looking after Gary. So then – Mel aspired to turn Philo into a Gary. I was not sure that Philo felt lonely. I certainly often did.

"The Bible tells us that God made a companion for man," Rolly said. Rose was holding his hand. She squeezed it. I don't suppose Rolly went hungry too often.

"You know that people tend not to be at ease with single men," Rose said. "Put a single man somewhere, and no one will visit him."

"Except a buxom female who has an agenda," I added. It came out like that, then I regretted it, and looked at Mel sheepishly. She just smiled and winked at me. I'll never understand women.

"A single man in so many ways is in a difficult position," Rolly acknowledged, although not from experience.

"A single man may well not be respected by a community," Rose added. "People think there is something wrong. People also like to relate to a woman. Or at least to know that there is a woman around when they visit a man. Who will visit a man when there is no woman around?"

"I also believe that a single man without a woman around is trouble," said Rolly. Mel had made no further contribution to the conversation that she had opened up. Her eyes, though, were carefully scanning the face of everyone who contributed, as they spoke. I, being single since the death of my beloved Cindy, felt uncomfortable.

"Although," I added, "men in the Bible always seem to act like single men. Well, not always, I guess. But frequently or typically. Does the Bible ever mention Isaiah's wife? Peter had a wife – but we don't know what she ever said. Women like Sarah and Rebecca are depicted for their negative influence. Then what about the wife to Job! Hosea's wife fills a negative role. David had many wives, but when he was thirsty it wasn't a woman who brought him water, but men. There were many women in the New Testament church, but none of them wrote anything that came to be included in the New Testament canon. Eve, of course, drew Adam into sin. Elijah and Elisha, the great prophets, always seemed to live as if they had no wives, even if they were married."

"So why is that do you think, Dave?" Rolly asked.

"I'm not sure I dare speak," I responded. I looked at Rose and at Gail. Were they at that point embarrassed? I do not know. Biblically, women tended to have very passive roles. Contemporary western women did not always seem happy with such role models. Women like to be with their men, it seemed. Biblically, however, often they were not.

"Women want men so that the men can make them happy," said Rolly. "That is not only them, but also the children that they have, might have, and let us say are designed to have. Just look at how differently single women can live from single men. Single men camp, single women build nests. In fact – evidence has shown that a woman's life expectancy is unaffected should she be widowed. A man's life expectancy, statistically speaking, is much shortened by the death of his wife."

"What you seem to be saying, Rolly," I responded to him, "is that women are strong, but a man is weak."

"Yes – each is strong in their own way," Rolly added. "A man is strong if he has a woman standing behind him. Without her, he can fall apart. A woman can be very strong without a man ..."

"One thing we can add," I said, "is that without a woman, a man is vulnerable. That vulnerability emerges in many ways. Fundamentally, we can say that a man alone needs help! He needs someone to cook for him, to wash, to clean, to keep him company ..."

"Right," said Rolly. "A woman does not need all those things in the same way. What she needs is money. Once she has money to buy the food she needs, she can do all the rest herself."

"A big issue though is sexual temptation," I said. "Or sexual compromise."

"How do you mean that?" Rolly asked.

"Because the active partner in sexual relations is a man, if he can control his desires, then he is 'safe.' A woman, however, is much more vulnerable to advances by a man. Being passive can save a man. Being passive won't save a woman sexually, because sexual acts are done to her."

"So, what does that imply?" Rolly asked.

"Single women are strong in that they do not need help to thrive. But they are very vulnerable to sexual advances by men. Single men at least can be strong to resist sexual advances, but they need help to live."

"Where this all started," Rolly said, "was when Mel said that Philo should not be alone. As women like Mel take pity on Philo, they might look after him. They may be much less inclined to look after a fellow woman. His needing people to help him can render a man a part of a community. He just needs to control himself sexually. A woman can be independent of a community, but what the community wants from her (that is, the men), they will pressurize her for. If a woman missionary has a man, he will protect her from her sexual vulnerability. If a male missionary has a woman, she will protect him from his vulnerability to a community."

"So then," I added, "a single man is vulnerable to a community's advances, but a single woman, at least a youngish one, is vulnerable to sexual advances." I don't think we had finished that matter. We had shared a few thoughts. Perhaps that is the best that one can do.

CHAPTER 26: THE FINANCIAL CONTROLLER

There was no point in chasing Philo that day – as he was going to be at his temporary home, resting and recovering, we all hoped, from his malaria episode.

"Come along with me, and let's leave the ladies here alone for the day," Gary suggested to Rolly and me. "There's something I want to tell you," he added, a little ominously. In due course, we got into his 4x4. Gary turned on the air-conditioning. "Look, gentlemen. You really have me thinking," Gary said. We pulled up to the large iron gate of the compound. The security man on duty took no time to come and open the gate. With a respectful salute, he sent us on our way.

"I am amazed by your stand-offishness to Philo, even when he is sick," Gary added.

The dust poured off the wheels of our vehicle as we motored along the road. I don't know if Gary was thinking the same as me. I was pitying the pedestrians! Ahead of us, all was clean and good. Behind were massive clouds of billowing dust. Yet there were many pedestrians with us on that road. I could only guess that they did not much appreciate Gary charging past them, as it gave them dust all over their clothes, never mind in their lungs.

"What you are saying, in effect," Gary added "is that we need to look after our own people less." Dust continued billowing out behind us. Gary drove on unthinkingly – it was a route that he followed every day. I was very interested in Gary's comments and wondering where he was heading. I decided to say nothing, at least for a while. It seems Rolly felt the same.

"We have short-term people come here often," Gary said. "The money we spend to entertain them and keep them is phenomenal. If one of them gets sick, we pull out all stops. On one occasion we arranged for transport to Imbigen by airplane. It cost us $2,000. When he got there, they gave him malaria medicines that we could have bought here for $1. But knowing who the lads' parents were – we felt we had no real choice but get him to the top hospital in the capital city as fast as possible."

Before long, we were on tarmac. The billowing dust ended. Later we were back on a dusty road again. We pulled up to a gate. Gary beeped his horn. A security man came and let us in. He was wearing the same uniform as was Gary's home security. Obviously, the same company. We pulled in. Gary turned to the right. We were in a compound surrounded by a high wall. The buildings in the compound were simple but functional. I had the impression that they were made to an American design. They were certainly not local style. I wondered if all the building materials were imported from the USA. I did not share that thought.

"Wash the car, boss?" said a lad as we stepped out.

"Yes," said Gary. "Come with me," he told us.

We followed him. His office was on the first floor. In it was state of the art computer equipment. An attractively-dressed sharp-looking African lady sat in the adjoining office. "Good morning, Mr. Simons," she said in polished English (thus we learned Gary's surname).

"New work?" Gary asked.

"In your inbox," said the secretary.

We went into Gary's office and sat facing him across his desk. "This is my Africa," said Gary. He hit the bell on the desk. "Rita," he said to his secretary. Rita's skirt fell rather short of reaching her knees – that somehow surprised me. "Urgent cases only today, as I have visitors."

Rita withdrew. Then the phone rang. "Morning boss," said the voice. "Authorization for a cheque, $15,000, children's items, project number 3466."

"Items to be delivered when?"

There was a pause. "Seventeen days," came the answer.

"Agreed," said Gary. He made a note in a notepad.

"You are hard-hearted to neglect your colleagues like that," said Gary. "Darn it, I do not mean that in a bad way," he added. There was a knock on the door. "Come in," said Gary. A fellow, wearing a blue suit with a pink tie walked in. He nodded to us, acknowledging our presence. He placed a paper in front of Gary.

"Your signature needed," said the man. Gary spent a minute looking up and down the paper. He signed. The man left.

"But how do you do it?" Gary added. He looked perplexed and strained. "How on earth do you do it?" he added. We did not answer his question.

Gary proceeded to explain something of the project to us. They were taking care of the sponsorship of about 475 children. Technically, they were orphans. They were scattered throughout the area. To get the job, he had responded to an advertisement. They needed someone to help orphans. Gary and his wife thought that it would be an excellent opportunity to serve. They managed to jump through all the hoops. They came out a few years back. Gary had had visions of building deep relationships with a few deprived African children. He had pictured himself being moved to tears with gratefulness, when children would come to him and say, "Thank you for helping us, Mr. Simons." He had imagined the joy of finding a family so that he could reunite a child with a tearful mother. When Gary got to Holima, things were somewhat different.

It was then I interrupted Gary. "Look, Gary, Mel is here. She is a journalist. The kinds of things we are learning here might be of great interest to her." Gary agreed. We called Mel and explained. Mel was very willing to come. Gary instructed his secretary. His car was sent to his home to pick her up. A little later Mel joined us.

Before Mel arrived, one person had come to have a building design agreed to by Gary. Another came and told him of a rise in the price of maize. Should they go ahead and buy at the new price or should they negotiate was the question presented to Gary.

"The people tell me," Gary explained once he'd left, "that they need me in the office. Donors trust me because I am an American. Local people trust me more than they do each other. The most useful thing I can do for people here is to keep the money flowing. Then they also add, and quite rightly so, that I do not understand either the local language or the local culture. How, then, can I effectively engage in complex issues regarding choice of children to take on, dealing with relatives, or even negotiating with difficult government officials? I should leave those roles to them. I should confine myself to bringing in money and making sure that things look good in the West so that donors remain happy. Other things I should leave to them."

At that moment, the secretary knocked again. This time it was to tell us that Mel had arrived. Mel came in, sat down, and joined us. We brought her up to speed. Then Gary continued.

"I mean, I agree with them. Certainly, they know their own people better than do I."

Just then, someone else came in. "Service of Land Cruiser at the local garage. Completed yesterday. Bill $1,345. Your approval, please." Gary signed.

"But I hate it!" Gary said. "My fulfilling this role does not help to bring any change to a 'white man's role' here in Holima. It confirms to local people that white men are super-men. Not approachable except to have cheques signed. Not familiar with any local languages or issues. Not sociable. Not even caring – except caring that there be enough money. It is like – I am here to be a machine." Gary paused, then added. "Let alone corruption! I know that fake receipts are being issued. When a car goes to get fuel, a $30 receipt is issued for $20 of fuel. The person buying the fuel puts $10 into their pocket. This is going on all around me. But what on earth can I do about it? How can I check on it – if everyone is in cahoots? Sometimes I question things. But then – I get a smoke screen. I could put someone in prison. But – is that why I am here, to put people into prison?"

We sat quietly, appreciating Gary's honesty in sharing openly with us. Gary's mentioning putting someone into prison reminded me of the experiences I had in my very early days in Africa, in Zambia.

"I am like a fat cow with a big udder," Gary added.

"What do you mean, you are like a fat cow?" Mel asked. Mel was jotting things down in her notebook.

Instead of answering, Gary looked at me and said, "You tell her."

We could hear people talking in one or two nearby offices. The view out of Gary's window was of a dirt road. It was not very busy. Fortunately for us, the dust seemed to blow the other way. We could see trees, rather than the ground, through Gary's window – that was, of course, a reflection of the fact that we were on the first floor (in the UK, second in the US).

I coughed to clear my throat. "A fat cow with a big udder is one that can produce a lot of milk," I suggested. "A farmer who has a cow like that goes to great expense to keep the cow happy. Food is always available. Fresh water is always available. Grass is carried to the cow – the cow does not have to go foraging or it might be attacked by a tick, be chased by a dog, scratch its leg, or something terrible like that. The farmer will provide everything that the cow needs. The farmer's interest is in the udder. He will milk that cow I don't know how many times a day. The more often the better. One day, if the cow is no longer capable of producing milk, it will be slaughtered. Matter ended."

"That's it! You said it better than I could. I see that you understand, Dave." said Gary. "Even worse than the cow – I make my own money. The farmer, as just explained in your story, goes to great trouble to keep the cow. He builds a stall, he sweats as he carries in the grass, he stays up late if the cow is sick. Here though, people do not need to do that. Their part is just to enable me to cow-tow to donors. They know I need statistics and photographs. Occasionally, donors come from America. I entertain them. People here do what they are told, behave well, and say nice things when the donors are around. They promise not to complain to them. Should they complain to the donors, then they know that I could be 'in for it.' That's the deal. I bring in the money. They are confident in that sense, to keep donors happy. When donors are here – everyone smiles. When they are gone, back to normal."

"Let's put it this way," Gary went on. "Donors put in accountability structures to prove that their money is being well used for its intended purpose. These requirements are very carefully designed – by blind men! They are blind. I mean – they can't see what is going on. If their stipulations are fulfilled, they are happy. I have to fulfill those. Giving my previous example, they want to know, that fuel is being purchased and used for transporting the people and inputs necessary for our project. Now, I know that fake receipts are the order of the day. What would happen if I blew the whistle? Well – everyone here would hate me for blowing the whistle on them. So also, everyone 'there,' i.e., amongst the donors, could hate me for making life complicated. Then they would accuse me of not liking African people because I was accusing black African new Christians of being corrupt! If I close my eyes, it's like I am a money launderer! I'm the white face that engenders trust, where trust is unwarranted. Like I said yesterday – I have to trust people, then let them sort things out amongst themselves. I think you know that the people have their own boundaries as to what are appropriate levels of corruption. If someone takes too much corruption money, for example, then they have means of blowing the whistle on each other. That is why ..." Gary started saying.

Then Rita walked in. "You are wanted for buying cooking oil," she said.

"Not available," Gary said.

"Are you sure ...?" Rita added.

"Quite sure," Gary said.

"May I ask," Mel interrupted, once Rita had left, "what Rita meant by saying that 'you are wanted for buying cooking oil'?"

"You may ask," Gary said, "but should I give you my answer? Okay, I will. There is always a long queue where we buy cooking oil. If an African goes to buy it he can take three hours before he gets the oil. Hence, we have a deal – that I go with them to buy oil. When the sellers see a white man, they let him go to the front of the queue. Hence, I agree to go with them, to reduce their shopping trip from three hours to fifteen minutes. It's a favor I am used to doing."

"Oh," said Mel, writing in her notepad.

"That is why" Gary started again, "I was so amazed by and impressed by your account of Philo, that you gave me yesterday. Even when Philo gets sick, he gets no special treatment."

"Hang on," Rolly said, "I am sure he got A1 treatment at the clinic he went to because he had money in his pocket with which to pay the bill. Someone without the money might not have got treated at all."

"Okay, okay," said Gary. "So Philo still sticks out like a sore thumb. But not like an aching, cut, injured, blasted, hammered, sore thumb, like I do!"

At that point, we all laughed.

"You realize," Gary went on, "that I am treated like God. And I hate it. I don't know the language. How could I learn it, when my vital place is in this office? I hate being God, but that is the role that people see me fitting into. How has Philo avoided that 'God' role?"

CHAPTER 27: AT THE BANK

"Look," Gary said at that point, "it's time for me to go to the bank. There are some negotiations and procedures I need to do there. I would be pleased to take one person, but the bank would be overwhelmed by the three of you. I suggest that you, Dave, and Mel have a tour of this place. Let Rolly accompany me to the bank. I can find you a Striden man to give you a tour. When you are tired out, we have a small mobile canteen where you can rest. If you need anything else, ask Rita." We agreed. "Rita!" Gary called. Rita came. "Please find Dave and Mel someone who can give them a tour around here. Show them where the café is so that they can rest when they want to. I will go with Rolly to the bank. We will be back within two hours."

I want to report what went on between Gary and Rolly, while Mel and I had our tour. That's according to the explanation I got from Rolly. As to why Gary preferred to take Rolly to the bank, he explained that to Rolly straightaway. I seemed to know the most about Philo, and Mel the least, but he got the impression that if anyone retained any skepticism, then it was Rolly.

The bank was not far away. It took them just about five minutes to drive there. Rolly and Gary's conversation occurred during pauses. Gary knew that between his various negotiations at the bank, there would be 'blank' periods of time.

"So, Rolly, you seem to be the most skeptical about Philo. Why?" Gary launched into conversation as they were still driving towards the bank. Gary, of course, did not at the time know about Rolly's dilemma regarding Philo!

"Same reason as you," said Rolly. "Let's be honest. I need to keep my job and my paycheck, and it is not being paid by people who like the kind of thing that Philo does. Or who support the kind of thing that Philo does. My boss is on my back. She sent me here to put Philo straight. She thinks his influence may be very damaging. But perhaps a bit like you, the more I associate with Philo and his work, the more convinced I become."

"Ha!" said Gary, as they pulled into the bank. The bank building was smart. It seemed almost 'solitary,' surrounded by some green. There were half a dozen parking places outside it. Gary was a regular customer in the bank. Together with Rolly, he was immediately shown into a private back room. Gary naturally brought the bank a lot of business.

"Make out you are a donor or potential donor. That way we will get the best treatment," Gary said, winking. (Rolly wasn't sure he was winking, but he guessed he probably was!)

"So how does Philo do it?" Gary asked.

"Quite simple," Rolly responded. "Well – but in another sense though, very complex! He says he tries to keep to two rules. One, use local people's language in engagement with them, and two, in key ministry relationships do not use foreign money."

"But those are the two things people want us for!" Gary exclaimed. "How can we do anything without them?"

"Now your exclamation has pointed to the sheer relevance of Philo's message," Rolly commented. "Yes, those are the things people want us for. Yet, we say, we are here for the gospel. The gospel of what – of money?"

"Ha! So, how can you survive here if you don't have foreign money and languages?"

"Philo would love you because you keep falling into his trap," Rolly said. "That is an excellent question, as I understand Philo, and a fundamental question. If we have nothing more to contribute than money and the use of the English language, what does that mean? Are we a different species to Africans, like ships passing in the night – no connection? Or more likely, is our agenda, of always advocating better languages and better resources, what is damaging our ability to contribute in other more helpful ways that might instead be happening? How do we define our mission, our link to Christianity?"

"Excuse me," Gary said, as he attended to a bank employee.

"Tea, coffee or soft drink?" the smartly-dressed employee asked Rolly. Rolly opted for tea.

"So then, according to that theory, it is our rush to 'help' people using money, which is always of dubious value before God, and foreign languages, that stops us doing God's work!"

"Yes," Rolly replied. "What Philo is advocating is also a little subtler than that though. He doesn't say that all foreigners in Africa should work in that way, which he refers to as vulnerable, but that some should."

"And by saying that some should, he is implying that too few are. Probably correctly," said Gary.

"Yes," Rolly answered.

"So then, he is one of those 'some'?"

"Yes."

"Sugar?"

"No, thanks."

"I trust you did want milk?" Gary added.

"Yes, I'm learning to like milk in tea over here."

"So then, what exactly is your relationship with Philo? Are you with him or are you not? You don't seem to be?"

"Yes, we'll see the manager," Gary added to the bank employee talking to him. Gary seemed to feel very at home in the bank.

"Mel wanted to research Philo. We are accompanying her to do that. We expected to shadow Philo. You know – like short-term missionaries shadow missionaries. Philo to explain things and show us the ropes, and so on. Well, Philo refused."

"Refused! And you had come all the way here to do that!"

"Yes."

"Why did he refuse?" Gary asked.

"Actually, now having understood better – I can quite see why Philo refused. Our presence with him would transform what he could do, and how he could do it. How could we acquire an understanding of how Philo functions if our presence, at the same time, makes it impossible for him to do what he normally does?"

"Well, though, many missionaries have short-term visitors come to them. One could even add – many missionaries seem to be pretty much fully occupied by short-term visitors!"

"And that," Rolly responded to Gary, "Philo would argue with some justification, is exactly the problem. Missionaries then have to do things in a short-term way. Short-termers come to recognize that way (using English and paying your way into everything) as the only way, i.e., the 'real' way, because that is even what long-termers are doing. Then when they fault that way – as you did today – they give up before they start."

"What do you mean, they give up before they start?"

"They don't take on long-term mission assignments. It has become very rare."

"So, Philo is carrying the flag for God, but the rest of us are not," Gary added.

"As you suggested earlier – the rest of us are, instead, trying to be God," Rolly emphasized. "Ha, ha, ha!" Gary laughed. It was a bitter laugh of acknowledgment, not of derision.

(More bank business.)

Rolly added: "As I said – my job rests on my disagreement with Philo."

"And if it didn't?"

"Then I'd have to agree, as it all makes sense, but ..."

"But what?"

"Whether Philo will get any recruits to do mission in his vulnerable way is another question."

"And if he doesn't?"

"You mean if we just carry on as we are? You tell me, Gary. Holiman people go to school in English for years. From what you know of them as they help you run the orphan program, can they do what you do?"

"Of course not," said Gary. Rolly had expected that answer, but was still a little taken aback by the simple bluntness of Gary's response to his question. "They have their own way which is not my way," Gary added.

"That is exactly what Philo might say!" Rolly responded.

Gary carried on: "I'm not saying my way is superior. I am just saying it is different. Can they do it my way? No."

"If they can't do it 'our way' then why are we saying they should do it our way?" Rolly asked.

"Ha, ha, ha. Because the thought that maybe they can't is too terrible to think about," said Gary.

They left off that topic that was taking place between banking business in that smart little bank. Gary and Rolly went on to talk about the weather and other things. Later, when we were all back together in his office again, Gary picked up where the two of them had left off.

"I was talking with Rolly," Gary said, "and we concluded that African people cannot do what we Westerners do. What do you think?"

"You are a racist," said Mel.

"That's a conclusion many might draw," I agreed. "That conclusion is too unpalatable for people in the West. That is why, even though it is unavoidable, they try to ignore it." "Unavoidable?" Mel asked.

"Look, it won't be easy to convince anyone of this, because it goes at 180 degrees against what the West wants everyone to believe. It raises too many issues. One question often raised, which I think is a distraction, is that of whether African people are therefore less intelligent than are Westerners," I said.

"Why is that a distraction?" Mel rejoined.

"It assumes that intelligence is a product of evolution. Then, to imply that Africans are less intelligent is like saying they are behind Westerners in evolution. That is to assume mechanisms like natural selection and survival of the fittest, according to which then, African people should now all die!" I was a bit surprised at myself for having been so bold.

"But then, how can you say that they cannot do what we can do, without implying that they are less intelligent?" Mel asked.

"Oh, come on," I said. "Someone is better at one thing. Someone else is better at another. What's new? Do you think that a musician is less smart than a man who builds his own home, or less smart than an electrician or a mathematician? A math professor may not be able to open a can of food to save his life: he lives in a math cloud. We are all different. That's point one. Second, doesn't African life require intelligence? Yes, of course it does, but different kinds of intelligence than required in the industrial and technical West. Thirdly, the way people think changes over time. Especially because of things they are told and believe about God. The reason the secular world is terrified about this issue is that they might have to acknowledge a role for God, or for what they call 'religion,' in human advancement. Fourth, it is for God to say that one person is more intelligent than someone else!"

"So then, is vulnerable mission, that Philo is advocating some Westerners should adopt, good or bad?" Gary asked.

"I think that depends on who you are," said Rolly. "If you are a Westerner, maybe bad, as it sounds like hard work. If you are a wealthy prosperous African, maybe bad, because it could upset your means of access to wealth. If you are an African who is not particularly wealthy or prosperous, then definitely it is good. Vulnerable mission is 'how to help someone to help themselves.' Other varieties of mission or development intervention are 'how to render people dependent on western largesse'!"

"Oh, come on," Gary said. "Aren't you too quick in drawing such a conclusion?"

"No," replied Rolly. "That's something I've been thinking about for a long time. I've only just realized that vulnerable mission is the means to that which I have been advocating."

"Okay, explain," Gary said.

"Intelligence designed in the West works in western context. When you say something that sounds intelligent in the West, it may not-at-all be received as intelligence in Africa. Not because Africans are stupid, but because they are intelligent! The foolish ones are those who forget that thinking, like intelligence, is contextual. In their own context, an African is as intelligent to his context as a Westerner is to his. An African in Europe might seem stupid. A European in Africa the same – to Africans. Is the ability to make money in a capitalist system the ultimate measure of intelligence? No. Someone who may be very good at making money on the New York stock exchange may be totally useless at thriving in an African cultural context. To rear chickens in the light of African culture requires a contextual knowledge different to that of operating in the stock exchange in western culture. That is why, then, education in Africa should be evolved starting in the African context, and communicated in an African language, so that it be mindful of African culture," Rolly responded. Well, Rolly finally got it. I wondered for how long before he bowed under pressure from Nancy.

"I'll tell you something Philo told me once," I added. "Philo was born and raised in the UK. In that UK context, whenever Africa or Asian people came to a UK church, they seemed backward or behind. They did not seem to get what was going on. To Philo, that was because those people were not very bright. Now, fast-forward, and Philo has been in Africa for thirty years. Even after all those years and having learned all those languages, Philo finds himself in a parallel position in Africa as did Africans in his previous experience in the UK! He often does not get what is going on! As we in the UK might think Africans are not very smart, so they can think that of us! The difference is – that the West makes money."

CHAPTER 28: 'YOU ARE FIRED!'

Later we were back at Gary's place. It certainly was a nice quiet place. We explored their garden. Their gardener did a good job of making the area look nice. There was a set of chairs and a table under the dense shade of a mango tree. We sat.

We had yet another invitation for supper from Gary and his wife, and we were not in a hurry to decline. We were also trying to think about what to do on Sunday. That Sunday (the following day) Philo would still be in the area, so we decided to stay put. That way we kept Mel happy. The next question was – where were we going to worship?

"Which is your church?" we asked Gary, in a pause after he'd been pointing out some of the flowers in his garden.

At that point, Gary looked at Gail. Then he looked at us a little sheepishly. "Sorry. Don't go to church," he replied.

I tried not to sound too shocked. "You don't go to church?" I said.

"No," he conceded. Gary had a flower in his hand as he spoke.

"Now, I mean, I don't want to be judgmental here, Gary, but I thought you were missionaries, and surely a missionary at least goes to attend church on a Sunday?"

Gary was on his back foot. "It's not that we don't want to," Gail said. A lock of her hair fell over her eyes.

"That seems to happen when she's unsure of herself," I thought.

"We used to. It did not work out!" Gary added.

I turned my head slightly sideways as a way of encouraging him to explain. "Probably to do with money," I thought.

"It has to do with money," Gary said. "Look, have a drink," he added. It was not long till suppertime. But we were ready for something to drink. Gary tossed the flower over his shoulder behind him, as we walked and followed him into the house.

"Okay," Gary added a few minutes later. "Yes. It is to do with money. They always wanted money from us. It became very, very difficult. We thought that the only way to resolve the tension that was building up was to leave. To find another church. But – we haven't found another church. If we were to attend another church, then the same issue would likely arise. We would be expected to provide a great deal of money." We were quiet for a moment. "Look, sit down," Gary said, pointing to some chairs.

"So, where should we go to church tomorrow then?" I asked.

"There are lots of churches around we could take you to," said Gary.

"It will work – they won't cause you problems, wanting your money?" I asked.

I noticed Gary stealing a glance at Gail, presumably checking that she was still on board with him. Gail was standing beside him. I guess her glance in his direction acted as confirmation to him.

"We can find somewhere to go," he said as he folded his legs.

"I have a suggestion," Mel piped up at that point. She had been listening intently enough. There was plenty of fodder for any writing she was going to do later. Mel was no doubt committing things to memory. She leaned forward, touching the fingers of her two hands together. She wanted to understand local churches better. "Gary finds us an appropriate church. That's where we'll go. What I propose, though, is – that we then call Philo. We could tell him about our experiences, and he could explain things to us."

"Sounds fair enough," I thought.

"Good idea," said Rolly.

"Well, look, why don't we call Philo now and ask him about where to worship?" Mel said.

"But Philo believes we're in Imbigen," I said.

"Really!" Gary exclaimed.

"Yes, we haven't told him that we are following him."

"What! That is so funny!" Gary responded. Gary was looking open-mouthed at Gail. "We've certainly found an odd set of friends," I guessed was the meaning of that gesture.

"There are lots of churches in Imbigen," Mel said. "The fact that we are going to go to a church doesn't mean that we are not in Imbigen."

"Let's do that anyway, let's call him," Rolly agreed.

Before we called Philo, Gary had some questions. He was looking at the faces of the three of us in turn. He was dreamily wiping the condensed water off his glass at the same time. "You were a little shocked when you discovered that Gail and I do not go to church. You know – now I am a little shocked at the way you are deceiving Philo." Gail's eyes were also full of questions.

"So perhaps we should tell him where we are?" Mel said. She kept bumping the fingers of her opposite hands together as she spoke. She thought, I suspected, that if he knew we were in the vicinity, he might come and spend time with us.

"Ideally Philo shouldn't know," I said. "As soon as he finds out that we are here, then he gets a problem of divided loyalties. Hence, it's better he thinks we are in Imbigen. Just for the sake of his ministry and his relating to the people he is with. If they get wind of our presence, four of Philo's good friends stacked up in a guest house a few miles away, then they will feel that we are also their guests, and that will majorly upset the way Philo can relate to people. At the same time, I agree with you, Gary. We shouldn't be underhand. If Philo were to ask, 'where are you actually?' I mean, I would tell him, but he hasn't asked."

"Perhaps he doesn't want to ask?" Mel suggested.

"It seems wrong," Rolly said. "But," he added, then he paused, "being here on the ground opens our eyes to things, especially to how Whites are received and treated. You are a case in point, Gary. It might be a question of – which is the greater evil! Frankly, though, we don't have to be near Philo. We might almost as well be in Imbigen. Although, I think it is helpful to be in the vicinity, so as to be experiencing the same cultural context as is Philo," Rolly added.

"So then spying is morally justified," said Gary, laughingly.

"No," I said, "it is morally mandated!"

"What do ..." Gary started asking, but I interrupted.

"I mean that the West should listen. They are controlling things in Africa. Yet they are blind. They are blind because they are not here. They are further blinded because they are determined not to be accused of treating people differently according to their ethnicity. The way they seem to avoid being accused of racially-based bias is to pretend that African people are just the same as are western people. That is folly. That is immoral."

We had got ourselves into another impromptu discussion.

"Does one immoral act, blind control of Africa, justify another, spying on Africans by people like Philo?" Gary asked.

I did not answer straight away. As we were spying on Philo, was he in another sense spying on African people? I knew I had little choice in what to answer. "He is not spying. He's only relating in a way that taboos in the West otherwise render impossible. The situation, of vast ignorance of the West about Africa, and we could even say also 'vice versa,' does not justify it, it mandates it. And we can add, it needs guts to do it. It needs someone like Philo, who has committed himself as he has. These days, you've probably noticed, the western media doesn't even like sending white journalists into black Africa. They want to rely on black journalists. But – that is also folly. How can Westerners understand what an African is reporting? They can't! The West is scared, as I said before, if they get too close that they will find themselves, on their own evaluation, to be superior to African people. Yet, as we've already mentioned, if the whole comparison between the West and Africa comes to be re-evaluated, that will raise many questions about the positive role that the gospel played in the history of the West, questions that the secular West does not like!"

"Can we call Philo now, and ask him about church tomorrow?" Mel said. "After all, mostly he calls us. Wouldn't it show our appreciation for him if we called him?"

"Let me talk to him too," Gary said.

"I hope you won't spill our beans," I said to Gary, who grinned.

Mel called Philo. "Hello, Philo," she said, in a way that startled all of us. She added a pot of honey to every syllable! "How are you doing?"

"Not great, but okay," said Philo. "I had multiple injections. Last dose tomorrow. I am sure I will be fine. Thanks for your prayers."

"We have a question," said Mel.

"Go ahead," Philo responded.

"We want to attend an African church tomorrow morning. After that," more lashings of honey in her words! "we'd like to call you with our questions so that you can help explain what we experience, if you are not too tired. Will that be okay?"

"Please do. Any time after, er, four o'clock should be fine," Philo replied.

"Yes, dear," Mel responded.

"Dear!" I thought.

"Give me the phone," Gary said. "Hi, Philo. I am Gary."

"Nice to talk to you, Gary."

"I've been with your friends. They tell me you are currently staying in a village home?" "That's right."

"Tell me what it's like. I mean – is it just a normal home? Do you have electric? Is there running water? Flush toilet?"

"None of those," Philo replied.

"Okay, that's what I wanted to know," Gary said.

"Where are you from Gary?" Philo asked.

"I live near Michiki."

"Wow, I am near Michiki!" Philo said. "That's quite amazing."

"Of course, so are, what, ... Hmm," Gary said awkwardly, "looking forward to hearing more from you tomorrow after church," he added, realizing he nearly let the cat out of the bag! Brrrrrrrr went the phone. He put it down.

We never did ask for any advice from Philo on which church to attend! We didn't call him back.

Supper was ready. We sat at the table. The veranda to the house in which we sat had mosquito screening all down one side. Through the screening, one could see the carefully pruned ornamental trees in Gary's garden (or yard, as Americans would say). It was a beautiful time of day as it was cooling down. It was wonderful to be able to sit at such a bountifully-adorned table at such a place and during such a time of day with such amicable company.

We had barely sat, people were half-way through loading their plates when Rolly's phone rang.

"Rolly. This is Professor Nancy," said a female voice with an American accent, clear as a bell for all to hear.

Rolly started rising. "Saturday evening, Nancy!" he exclaimed.

"No, Saturday morning," she responded.

We did not hear much more, as by that point Rolly was walking away. There had been, however, no friendly 'how are you doing?' from Professor Nancy to Rolly.

"Rolly has met his D-day," I thought.

Ten minutes later, Rolly came back. We stopped talking. Rolly's shoulders were slumped. His face was ashen. He sat back in his chair. He reached for a piece of lettuce. "No job," he muttered.

"Saturday evening," Gary said, "and you have been fired!"

"Yep," said Rolly.

I looked at Rose. Their relationship was amazing. There was no doubt she stood by her husband in all things. At the same time, she seemed unperturbed. "How'd it happen?" I asked.

"Board met yesterday, made the decision. It's not only my 'rebellious nature,'" Rolly added. "It is also because donor funding is becoming harder to come by. Yes – in our circles, Philo does get attributed blame for some of that. They can't afford to pay me. I'm too old anyway. I am nearing retirement age," Rolly explained.

"And you told me, Rolly, that if you lose your job, you could be in deep financial trouble," I said.

"That's right," he responded.

"How long have you worked with Professor Nancy?" Mel asked.

"Over thirty years," Rolly responded.

For a few minutes, none of us said anything as we thought about Rolly's plight. Rolly filled his plate, but I don't think his mind was on his food. The rest of us slowed our eating-pace, rather as if we were on a slow march in empathy with Rolly.

"You are counting the cost of being a disciple," Gary explained.

I was surprised to hear that kind of talk from Gary. I think so was Rolly!

"You have decided to stand with Jesus, over and above the donors," Gary said. "That has a cost. You are paying the cost. But believe you me, Rolly, the rewards are greater than the costs."

I was well and truly taken aback by that kind of input from Gary!

"Thanks, Gary," Rolly said. I had that 'warm feeling.' The feeling, that is, that we were coming together as a group, and appreciating one another.

After a while, Gary left the table. He called Gail with his voice, eyes, and hand. Gail went with Gary into another room. They were gone for ten minutes. They came back.

"I have a phone call to make to the US," Gary said. He made the call right there and then. He made it still sitting at the table. "Hello, is Larry in?" Gary asked over the phone, leaning on one elbow.

We didn't have a clue who Larry was, but it seemed that Gary wanted us to overhear his phone conversation with whoever it was.

"Not today, it's Saturday," he was told.

"I was working. I was at the bank here in Holima today, in spite of it being Saturday," Gary said in response to a female voice. It might have been Larry's wife or his secretary. "Tell Larry I am resigning," Gary went on. "He'll get my letter on Monday. I am sorry for telling you on a Saturday. There is a particular reason I wanted to tell you now." When Gary said, 'resigning,' we heard the girl gasp on the other end of the phone. "I will do my three months, of course, while you look for a replacement. Greetings to Larry." Gary cut the phone.

"Solidarity," said Gary, simply. Rolly looked moved. He was lost for words.

All that was a lot to take in during one meal. We did not say much until we finished eating. After coffee, tea and After Eights, reclining in the easy chairs, Gary said some more: "Thank you all for coming to Michiki. You have given me hope. Gail and I were in despair over our role here. We were so set apart from the people! We had no local friends, apart from our house employees."

At that point, Gail started crying. The tensions of months of discussion they had had on this issue were proving too great. The fact that her husband had finally made the decision he had, one that he had apparently been contemplating for a long time, was overwhelming for Gail. Mel went over to her and put her arm around her. Rose also went on her other side and took her hand. Once Gail had stopped sobbing, all three women continued to sit in contemplative silence. All three men stood. We walked out into the garden in the dark. That just seemed to be the right thing to do. The cool night air was pleasant.

Monumental decisions had just been made and communicated in the lives of four of us. Had a visitor walked in at that moment, they would have been amazed at how somber was the occasion! Although, as Gary had explained, Gail and he got no visitors, unless foreign folks like ourselves. If a local person came to visit Gary he spoiled his reputation in the community, as everyone would assume he was coming just for money. The house-help had gone home. The six of us mourned alone.

"Sing," I said to Mel half an hour later. Mel had a pleasant voice. She led us in some songs.

"Anyone can pray," I said after that. Everyone did.

Then I read the passage from Scripture. "No one begins building a tower unless they have first counted the cost." I commented on that passage. The West was trying to build a tower in Africa. It was only counting the financial cost. Not wanting to be accused of being racist had become a big excuse. Through fear of being accused of being racist, people were pretending that western and African people were not different. The work to be done in Africa was being concealed, I explained. So much work in Africa is based on economic principles – that African people themselves do not understand. It is based on western superiority – to save Westerners from getting their feet wet or hands dirty. Jesus' work was not done in a finance office. Paul did not do his mission work by handing out drachmas to Gentiles, so why were we Westerners doing ours by handing out dollars to Africans? There was much need for repentance.

Before long, I felt that Mel and I, the singles, should leave the couples alone. Mel and I went to sit on the veranda. From there we could relish the cool and beautiful sounds of the African evening. The two couples needed husband-wife time, I felt. Mel and I were too emotionally drained to do much except sit and listen to the sounds of the night. When I went to bed, about half-past nine, Rolly was already in the room and fast asleep.

"Perhaps his having been sacked has given him a certain peace," I thought.

CHAPTER 29: BACKLASH

I pretty much anticipated what happened the following morning. A backlash!

We were sat at breakfast. Things were quite subdued. Then Gail said something. "I've been thinking. Generosity can't be wrong," she said. She had waited for meal time, and we were sat around her breakfast table. Gail seemed to be breathing heavily.

Then to my dismay, all four others agreed with her. I say 'to my dismay' as I didn't like it when suddenly everyone else had a position, and it was like I was alone voting for the opposition. I wished that Philo had been there! But he wasn't. He had an injection, then he was on the bus to his next destination, we discovered later.

My heart went out to Gary and to Rolly. They must have been going through a tough time. On this occasion, I was tempted to leave this topic aside. My initial response to Gail was "let's talk about this another day." Fortunately or otherwise, though, everyone in the group spurred me on to talk about it there and then! They may have had a hard time. They wanted to know that their 'hard time' was justified. If Gail was right, and generosity just can't be 'wrong,' they should do a very quick U-turn.

"Come on, tell us what you think," Rolly said, insisting that I respond to Gail.

There are many ways I could have answered the implicit question I had been presented with. It was only contemporary capitalism, coupled with modern technology (industrial revolution, nowadays, computerization,) that enabled the West to produce massive current levels of wealth. How could we expect Scripture to address a context that was not extant when it was written? There was no big capitalist America in Jesus' time. Admonitions to generosity were intended and interpreted differently then. Alternatively, I could have questioned whether missionaries like Gary were really 'generous' in the classic sense at all. Someone who is generous in the classical sense is someone who gives out of their lack. Paul once said this of the Macedonians in the Bible – he appreciated what they gave him, especially because they gave out of their own poverty. Gary's work was being a conduit for other people to use. Gary was not 'generous.' He facilitated, perhaps, other people's generosity. Donors in the West needed middlemen like Gary to fund and account for the finances they gave. Why? I decided to try to tackle the latter question as that seemed the most productive way to go forward.

"Why is Gary needed to do the job he does?" I asked in response to Gail's question. "Yes, more tea please," I said to Gail, who was offering. I waited for an answer. I found myself fidgeting with my pen. I tried not to.

"Okay. Bottom line. It is very hard to find an African to do that job," said Gary. "In fact, I hear of cases where an African is so used. They end up corrupt and corrupting."

"Meaning?" I asked.

"I'd heard of similar things in other child-sponsorship programs. Auditors come in, and everyone is sacked," said Gary, who sounded stressed.

"Thanks," I said to Gary. "Going contrary to what you said to us the other day then; Africans can't be trusted?" I suggested.

"Guess you are right," he responded.

Those comments by Gary just the other day, by now seemed to have been made in a different era entirely, if not in a different world! "We had certainly moved on from that discussion we had on the first day we sat with Gary and Gail!" I thought to myself.

"Okay. Why can they not be trusted?" I asked. This time no one answered. No one dared answer (through fear of it being thought, as a result of their response, that they might be racist?) or knew how to answer. I said nothing for a while. "Million-dollar question. Epistemological error. Let me explain," I said.

"Wait, let me go to the bathroom," Mel said. Others followed suit. That gave me more time to think and prepare what I was going to say.

"Look, I'm going to come at this in a bit of a roundabout way," I said. "It might sound ridiculous, but please bear with me." All were quiet. "There were two countries, one called Africa that played tennis, another called Europe that played soccer. Which is the better game?"

"You can't say which is better," Rose responded (perhaps thinking she'd caught me out!).

"Right, Rose," I responded. "Yet, in history, Europeans thought Africans should be playing soccer. When they didn't seem to be, they wrote back home; 'Africans play soccer with a ball just three inches wide,. they don't know how to kick the ball ... they don't want the ball to go into the net ...

212

they wield a big stick ...' Europeans thought 'that is all wrong.' (All they knew was soccer, and for a soccer player, that all sounds very wrong!) So Europeans started raising funds (note that, I emphasize, raising funds!) to correct the soccer that people were playing there in Africa. Get the error?"

"Yes," said Mel. "Africans weren't playing soccer in the first place. They were playing tennis."

"Correct," I said to Mel. I let that sink in for a while. "Africans, who played tennis, were now being paid, generously (I emphasized the word 'generously'!) to learn how to play soccer. How could they refuse that? They accepted the lessons. In fact, they were being paid very handsomely to play soccer."

I asked Gary the annual turnover of the child-sponsorship program he worked for divided by the number of children being sponsored. He gave us a figure. I can't recall what it was. But – it was more money than a laborer in Holima could earn for a year working full-time. "Because they were used to the patron-client system, they were full of praise for the people teaching them to play soccer. Meanwhile, the people teaching them to play soccer, who got all the praise in return, thought they must be doing a grand job! Meanwhile, teaching soccer in Africa has become a massive industry with millions employed, like Rolly and Gary here until yesterday, earning decent salaries."

Neither Rolly nor Gary made any immediate comments in response to that, although I left a pause. Rolly sneezed at that point. A mosquito flew past Gail's ear. She swiped it. Then she got up and offered us all some insect repellent to put onto our skin. As we did so, no one spoke, as (I think) we were hanging on to the point we had reached in our discussion, as if it were a beautiful flower that, if we had changed the topic, might have wilted.

"Soccer and tennis are like metaphors," Gary said. "Soccer stands for western ways of life. Tennis stands for African ways of life."

"Correct," I said.

"But there's nothing wrong with soccer!" he added.

"Ever seen soccer being played during a tennis match on a tennis court?" I asked.

"Okay. Got your point," Gary said.

"You got it?" I asked the others. In my mind's eye was a tennis tournament at Wimbledon in London, and someone running amok with a football on the court as the competition went on. Not pleasant!

"Ah," said Gail. "So you are not saying that generosity is wrong as such. In these latest examples, or metaphors as Gary said, you are saying that western generosity is misdirected. It should be helping people to improve their tennis but instead, it is teaching tennis players soccer!"

"In terms of this example, correct," I said. "Look," I added. I noticed myself putting my finger onto my nose. "I don't think I will try and expound on everything that the scenario I have presented teaches us. That would take a long time. We can keep discussing in the days ahead. There is just one more important point that I want to draw from it, though, that pertains to Philo."

"Okay," was the response from the others.

"What happens when a tennis player (African) reports back to soccer players (Europeans) on how their soccer is progressing?" I let the question hang. It was a critical question. No one else said anything, so I answered the question myself: "Two things: One. The soccer they know is that played while dodging tennis racquets and balls on the tennis court. That to them is soccer. If a European asks them 'how is your soccer playing going?', of course, it is going very well. But if the European would come and evaluate African soccer with his own eyes, he would find it to be terribly confusing. Two. Remember that it is always in the interests of Africans to say 'please help us to play better soccer,' as the latter makes the money." Again I paused. I hoped that someone was getting me! Rolly sneezed again. Everyone's eyes indicated that they were still very alert. "It follows that for Europeans to know how soccer or tennis or anything else for that matter is being played in Africa, requires a European reporter to be in Africa, to communicate what is happening in Africa.' It is not that Africans cannot be *trusted* in that sense. It is that they cannot be understood. Hence Philo's role, as a European in Africa, is so important."

"Does the corollary apply?" Gary asked, his hankie still in his hand.

"Explain," I said. I could see where he was coming from, and that he had an important point to make.

"If African people are ill-equipped to explain themselves to western people, does that not also imply that European people are ill-equipped to explain themselves to African people?"

Gary paused, then when he found we were quiet and listening intently, but not answering his question, he carried on. "That questions an enormous amount! That brings the whole of the western educational system in Africa into question! That implies that the West may not be so clever concerning Africa as they think they are."

"That which we have legitimately to communicate interculturally is the gospel," Rolly added.

CHAPTER 30: AFRICAN CHURCH EXPERIENCE

Our discussion threatened to delay our preparation for church. By ten o'clock, however, we were ready to go. Gary had selected a particular church. He did not know much about it. He had seen people gathered there as he drove past. There was enough space to park a car there. We agreed to go with him.

"Let's give it a go," we responded to his suggestion.

Our ladies were suitably decked out for church. Both Gail and Rose donned hats. Mel did not. All of us men dressed casually, Gary with a striking red sports-shirt adorned by an image of a snazzy car.

"Just maybe, they won't know who I am," Gary said, envisioning how his reputation as a donor might skew everything that happened in church that day!

As soon as we pulled up outside the church, we realized we had already made an error. The church was not far from the road. Around it were just low bushes, grass, and other vegetation, but no tall trees – there was nothing that might conceal a vehicle from view. Gary's vehicle was a beacon, informing all and sundry just where he was and where we were that day, whether they actually saw him in person or not. We should at least have walked to church, or ridden motorbikes, rather than going in Gary's car.

The church building, though it wasn't unusually large, that day came to be packed. Perhaps that is because Gary's 4x4, visible from the road and frankly from all directions, could be seen parked outside the building? Where wealthy people, especially white people, especially in a nice big 4x4, turned up at a church, there would typically be extra crowds on their way because of handouts to be had.

We walked into the back of the church building and sat down. We separated, men on the right and women on the left, as was the local custom. We waited. As we waited, the leaders at the front were whispering to one another. Then they got six plastic chairs lined up at the front of the church, facing the congregation. One of the men came to us, greeted us, then told us to go and occupy those seats. The ladies especially tried to resist. They did not want to be there on display. But our hosts persevered, till there we were perched up at the front, on display like wares for sale! Actually, more accurately, as a sure sign (so people hoped) that we were there to make some financial donations.

The service leader asked for a couple of songs. Then I heard him say (and I told the others later) that that day they would sing only English songs in honor of their visitors. He then sought a translator. The translator translated the next few sentences. "Today we are going to change the planned order of our service. Many visitors have honored us. We want to hear from them. All three men will teach us. The women also, if they have a message for us."

Then, not translated: "We will not have our traditional dancing, drumming, prayers for the sick or other activities today, as our visitors may not understand. We will have a short service, giving them ample time to teach us. We need four ladies to come now and help us prepare food. The money we raised last week to install a metal door into the church will be used to feed the visitors."

"Tell them to do what they normally do," Rolly whispered to me loudly.

"I'm not going to tell them what to do," I responded. I am not sure that any of us were prepared, but we proceeded, all three of us, to preach. The translator, unfortunately, made mincemeat of what we said. I was not sure people would get my accent or understand me if I translated, so I did not.

Before the service ended, we received a special appeal for funding for three departments. The choir needed $700 for choir vestments. The youth were raising funds for a PA system and needed $1,200. The pastor had a desperate need for a vehicle to enable him to visit his parishioners – for which he needed at least $3,000. Then there was a general collection for widows in the community, before the usual freewill offering. Ninety percent of the service, it seemed clear to me, was done in a singular way just for the visitors. Most likely, if we hadn't been there, the only offering might have been the regular freewill offering.

After the service, the six of us were filed into a small house next to the church. We were given cold drinks and a good lunch, paid for by the money that had been raised for the church door! Then the pastor came to tell us, in very Holiman-English, that he was glad for our coming, we should come again, and his grandma's hospital bill was so high that he did not know how he would ever manage to pay it without help. We expressed our thanks for everything, then went home.

"Was that a typical African church service?" asked Mel, the member of our group who had little reason to know better, with a crooked smile.

"No!" we, all the rest of us, said in unison. Mel was a bit taken aback by the strength of our response.

* * *

"Afraid we didn't have such an exciting church service," Rolly said to Philo.

We were all listening in to the phone, set on speaker.

"What happened?" Philo asked.

"Everything was severely anglicized and the main objective seemed to be getting money from us."

I think Mel was learning many things from this conversation. She had clearly been aware that we were somehow disappointed with that morning's service. She had also been amazed by the pressure we seemed to be put under in numerous ways, to contribute financially. She could though, of course, not know what good things she was missing. That is because she had minimal experience of how exciting African churches can be when people are not desperate to impress white people. Mel was learning as we went along.

"How did you get on, Philo?" Mel asked.

"I traveled miles on the back of the pastor's motorbike," Philo said. "And yes, thanks for your prayers. I am feeling well again! When we arrived at the small but packed church, it was already in full swing. The PA system was on full volume. Young people especially were packed into the church. It went on for hours – boiling hot! Lots of people healed and a good number of people saved."

"So where are you now?" Mel asked.

"I'm at the home of the bishop. It is quite funny. I've been talking with him about this and that. He has been showing me his farm. He is very innovative in what he is growing. His sons are now helping him out. I have told him that I am expecting a phone call, so he has released me, and here I am sitting under a tree talking to you."

"So, what's funny?" Mel asked.

"Well, it is not really 'funny,'" Philo said, "but – I think the bishop is wondering when I am going to leave, yet I have nowhere to go. That is – he's used to having white visitors who retreat to a hotel or guest house for the night. I don't blame them for doing that kind of thing. But I have no such plans. I reckon that staying with people in their homes overnight gives one much more by way of learning opportunities."

"So what do you expect to learn?" Mel asked.

"The point is usually that I don't know what I don't know, so I don't know what I have to learn," Philo responded. "Ask me tomorrow," he added.

"Look, Philo," I moved closer to the phone so that he could hear me clearly. "I have to agree – that a group of white people using English struggle to get close to people and what they are doing. You are right – if we had gone with you on your trip, we would have transformed your kind of experience into our kind of experience."

"I still feel bad about having had to refuse you," Philo said, "but I am glad you understand as to why I did so."

We nodded.

"We just all nodded when you said that," I told Philo. He laughed! "We are on second best," I told him. "We have not been very successful at experiencing the 'real Africa,' but still want to ask you questions about it."

"Well ... er ... hmm ... go ahead," said Philo.

We looked at each other. "Now what?" I guess we were thinking.

"Okay. Here are our questions. One. People go to church expecting to get healed. What do they mean by that? Really – does God heal supernaturally? Two. People expect their prayers to bring them prosperity. How will that happen? Three. People's time-keeping never seems to be at all accurate. How can we help them with that? Why are they so poor at time-keeping? Four. People around here believe in magic. Why?"

Philo paused for a while. "Look, give me time to think about how to respond to you," Philo said. "Can I call you back in maybe half an hour?"

"Okay," I said.

When I looked around at the others, they were a bit shocked. – "Why was Philo so hesitant – him who knew all the answers?"

Then unexpectedly, certainly for me, Gary came forward. He had been sitting a bit further back. Now he moved closer to the microphone.

"Philo, this is Gary," he said.

"Hello, Gary," responded Philo.

"I want to tell you that I have resigned," Gary said.

"Resigned from what?" Philo asked.

"Resigned from my being in charge of child sponsorship."

"Oh," said Philo. I guess that Gary was expecting more encouragement than that. Philo said nothing more. Then, "Why?" Philo asked.

"When I heard about how you work, I realized that there is another way," Gary said.

"The work was difficult?" Philo asked.

"I am only wanted for my money. But I wanted to share Jesus," Gary said.

"I'm impressed, Gary," Philo said. We were glad that he had some encouragement for Gary! "And everyone who has left houses, or brothers or sisters or father or mother or children or fields for my sake will receive a hundred times as much and will inherit eternal life." We were quiet. Philo was quoting Scripture.

Rolly leaned forward. "I've been fired, Philo," he said.

"Fired!" Philo exclaimed.

Rolly didn't respond. He was too overwhelmed.

"Does that mean you don't have a job?" Philo asked.

"Yes, it does."

"Then you are due to get a hundred times as much," Philo retorted, still citing Scripture.

I didn't know that Philo was aware of Rolly's predicament. It seems Philo had already turned his ear to Rolly on that issue at some point. Presumably, that was when Rolly was still more feisty in opposition to him. We all realized that Jesus' words, that Philo had just quoted, spoke right into Rolly's situation, as they did into Gary's.

It was quiet. A little while later Philo said, "It was because of me you were fired, wasn't it?"

Now that would sound bad, but Rolly had little choice but to concede as much.

220

"Yes, more what you represent than your person," he said. "They see you as a menace."

"Look, this is a lot to cope with in one go," Philo said. "Let me call you back in a half hour." He was gone.

We were all stunned and shell-shocked. Somehow, that brief conversation with Philo had been a massive strain. It had brought home the reality of what was going on. It was like our known world was crumbling around us. It was like God's Spirit was wanting to blow in a fresh way.

"You know," Rolly said, "Philo just asked if it was because of him that I had been fired? That was Philo speaking. Yet that was not Philo speaking. Philo was not talking about himself at all. He was talking about Jesus. Jesus said, 'all men will hate you because of me.' I am getting some of that. You will get some of that too, Gary."

Gary nodded, as if in slow motion.

"You know what's been going on?" Rolly said. "We've been serving Mammon."

Rose and Gail were kind enough to think of our stomachs. They went to prepare some drinks. Mel volunteered to help them, but they turned her down. We enjoyed some drinks.

About forty minutes later, Philo called us back. "It's me," he said. "I've been wracking my brain over the questions you asked me." A pause. "I don't know how to answer. You want to know about healing and time-keeping, and the prosperity gospel, and magic. Those are huge questions. Maybe I will come up with an answer later. For now though – I don't know good answers I can give you in English. About healing, let me just say, remember that there is no supernatural. About the prosperity gospel – let me leave you with a question, how does one get to prosper, except through prayer? As for time-keeping and magic? Magic is an English term, taken presumably from the Greek, as isn't it the Greek language that talks of the *Magi* coming to the baby Jesus? Maybe I'll have better answers another day. I hope you don't mind if I say goodbye for now so that I can talk to the bishop."

"That's fine," I said.

"God be with you," said Philo.

"What does Philo mean, there is no supernatural," Gary asked at that point. Gary cupped his chin in his hands. He evidently thought that God is the supernatural. On that basis, if there is no supernatural then there is no God! How could Philo not believe in God?

"Supernatural is a man-made term," I said. "That seems crazy!" I thought Gary might be thinking. "How can supernatural be man-made? That does sound like the biggest nonsense out there!" I found myself imitating Gary's pose, with my hand supporting my chin. Looking at Gary, I thought we must look like a bunch of philosophers!

"To have the category 'supernatural,' someone has to say 'this is natural, that is not,'" I explained. I wanted to respond carefully. I was aware that there was much confusion on this issue. "At some point, someone said 'this happens by itself,' i.e., 'God is not involved.'"

"That is very sensible," said Gary. "Like an apple falling from a tree." He had thought of Isaac Newton.

"That was nonsense," I said. Gary gave me a strange look. "No one knows how the brain works. Something as simple as the brain. We all carry our brain around with us wherever we go. I can even say: we are what it is! But no one knows how it works!"

"Ahmm," said Gary.

"Without your brain, you can't even perceive an apple is falling from a tree. A person is an amazing thing. We can't comprehend him. No. We might say everything is 'natural.' But then, what does it mean to say the most incomprehensible thing, like the human mind is natural? It means that nature is one big mystery. Or, we could say everything is supernatural. I couldn't even lift up this cup without the life inside me, that comes from God, that is in natural terms, according to known science, inexplicable. To say that there is a natural and a supernatural, and then to say that the supernatural does not exist, is a big fraud."

"You know what I think Philo is trying to say?" Rolly came in at that point: "We Westerners won't be able to understand Africa unless we re-understand ourselves, and so far, we have got ourselves wrong."

CHAPTER 31: HIT THE ROAD

"If we can, we will join you when you reach Kosompa," Gary and Gail said as they stood at the window to our vehicle. It was around 9 a.m. We thanked them abundantly. We tried to encourage and reassure them. We had come as guests, we left as very close friends.

It was Monday. According to Philo's schedule, he had a bit of a trip ahead of him. We were going to make the same trip. Still incognito of course! This time around we did not bother checking in which bus Philo was traveling. Having spent three nights at the same location, however, we were excited to be moving on! Rolly offered to drive on this leg of the trip. I was happy to let him do so. We had been discussing how a large vehicle racing along a dirt road kicks piles of dust into the nostrils of pedestrians. I guess that is why Rolly drove that first part of the journey excruciatingly slowly! But – try as he might, he could not make the road dust-free. To do that I guess we'd have to go slower than walking pace. Sometimes extravagant means of doing things (using a vehicle like ours, instead of traveling by foot or motorbike) was unavoidably offensive! Once we were away from Gary's home and on the tarmac, however, it was to be tar road all the rest of the way.

"Was I surprised when Gary resigned that day," Rose said.

"So was I!" Mel added. "He must have been incredibly frustrated for a long time."

"And," Rose added, "he has been unable to see another way out. That is, no solution is available! Unless he was to abandon operations to corruption, as Westerners call it using English, the only other way was for him to have been the bottleneck man for everything. Saturday afternoon at the bank doing business. Can you believe it?"

Mel reminded us of the time we had been at the Bible school, and how Robert had talked about himself being a 'bottleneck.'

"I wonder what Gary will do next, once his three months are over?" Mel asked.

"I don't know about Rolly here," I said, "but I can tell you what usually happens in such a case, in my experience."

"Huh?" said Rolly.

"He'll go home to the USA and be off the scene. Whether it will be because he doesn't care, gets caught up in life in America, or just because he will not see any way of making a further meaningful contribution here in Africa, he will abandon missionary work."

"Gary was very inspired though," Mel said in his defense.

"He might be the exception," Rolly said, "but I agree with Dave – once someone leaves the field, forget them! In other words – don't believe the promises people make as they are about to leave the field, because they won't keep them!"

"Maybe we will hear more in Gary's case," I thought.

"Something that I found significant," Rolly said, "was the confidence they oozed at the beginning."

"I was going to say something about that," Mel said. "But explain what you mean, Rolly."

"I've seen it before, of course: I trust the Africans, we have a great project, we are very successful, we are making a great impact ... and of course we are living apart from them, in a comfortable idyllic home ..."

"There was quite a smokescreen," I said.

"Yes!" Rolly said, "Everything is hunky-dory. Everything is wonderful – the pitch to the donors!"

"Then, then, then," I started interrupting Rolly before he'd even finished his sentence, "Gary resigns on the basis of one vulnerable fool: Philo!"

"Fool?!" said Mel in a voice that sounded like a mixture between a woman telling off a cat that had jumped onto a table, and one of a woman who had just discovered her husband dead on the floor.

"Wait, wait, wait," I said. "Let me explain." I glanced at Mel. She seemed to be ready at least to give me a chance to explain myself. "Philo wouldn't deny being a fool," I said.

"You so sure?" said Rose, doubting my credibility.

"Yes!" I said. "You have to be a fool to get on in mission."

"What do you mean?" Rose retorted.

"Didn't Paul say 'I am a fool for Christ'?" I asked. Surely that would make the ladies happier, if I put Philo on a par with the apostle Paul, I thought!

224

"I mean, I mean lots of things. One thought is that God's way can seem to be folly to people. There are ways in which we would evidently see that mission should be done. Then there is God's way of doing mission. God's way of doing mission is likely to have people say that you are a fool." I hope I had by that point redeemed myself. "One example," I added. "It makes sense if you are going to engage in mission in inhospitable territory in a far land, that you make sure you have a lot of resources to draw on. It may not make sense to God though. It is helpful for people to see how you cope with the kinds of difficulties that they have. 'Only a fool would go to Africa to do mission without a lot of financial backing,' someone might say. Yet the best way to do mission is like that fool."

"I hear you," said Rolly. "I have always advocated for well-resourced mission, as you describe it. Now, though, I hear what you are saying."

Mel had let off attacking me, so she asked Rose, "Rose, now that you have been fired what will you do?"

"According to what Dave just said, we should be fools, eh dear?"

"Funnily enough," Rolly responded, "we discussed this last night; how to be wise-fools if you like, although last night we didn't use the term 'fools.' We do want to finish this trip with you if that is okay."

"Hmm," I said.

"Hmm," said Mel, also in acknowledgment.

"Of course, you both should do what you need to do, and tell us if we can help in any way," I added.

"Then, well, what next? Dave has said, once someone leaves, in a way you can forget them. I also agree with him, that the prominence of short-term service is in these days, well, sickening. Supposedly, it is because the African church now needs the kind of help that short-term workers can adequately provide. Actually, it is more often what we have just experienced – people resign."

"So, what will you do?" Mel pressed her point.

"We don't know yet," said Rolly.

We had climbed a long hill. The road, though, was smooth – it was a good road. We descended again, then crossed a large river. We were not too far from our destination. We were about 1200 or 1300 meters above sea level. That meant that it wasn't as oppressively hot as it would have been at a lower elevation. I was dozing as we traveled, as it seems in due course was everyone else except, of course, our driver.

The best advice we could find was that we should make the local Catholic guest house the base for our operations at our next stop. From there we could make *spying-trips* and implement other strategies that Mel might devise for keeping an eye on Philo. The Catholic guest house was fairly central to a small town called Kisiwa. Lake seemed to be on three sides of the town. Also noticeable was the presence of large birds, marabou storks, foraging for scraps of anything, everywhere. They were obviously not edible, or they wouldn't have survived living so close to hungry people.

After unloading our bags, and ensuring our vehicle was at a safe location, we sat to eat some hot *chapati* with some cold drinks. That was not the most nutritious diet we had ever had, but it helped to fill a space. I was thinking in my mind that later in the day we should search for a more decent place to eat. I'm not sure that Rose would approve though. Pretentiously nice hotels had, according to Rose (and I am not saying I disagree), the most-dodgy food.

There were not so many people in that eating area. A TV was on one wall. Fortunately, the volume was turned down low. Otherwise, the room struck me as being pretty dull. All the more surprising then, somehow, when two slim and attractive looking ladies, possibly in their mid-twenties, walked in. The girls made a beeline to where we were sitting and introduced themselves. One said she was called Adongo, the other Adhis.

"Where are you from?" they asked. They were standing beside us, gently leaning on each other, while laughing amicably. They seemed to ooze confidence. Well, it was nice to have some lively young female company. We encouraged them to pull up some extra chairs at our table. We did not realize at the time where this welcome would soon be leading us.

* * *

"Interesting that you have come from Michiki," said Adongo. "We were just with a British fellow who has come from Michiki."

At this, Mel nearly jumped out of her chair. Well, she controlled herself. She did not want these girls to realize that it so happened she was madly in love with that British guy. I guess at that point, she was probably envious that these two beauties had just been keeping Philo company. We were now also in grave danger that our cover might be blown. What if Philo discovered that we were not in Imbigen after all, but just a half a mile away from him in Kisiwa? All these ladies had to say was "Let's call Philo," and the cat would be galivanting way beyond the bag!

The two girls were, it transpired, working as teaching assistants in local secondary schools. That was with a view to eventually become teachers. They were closely connected to a church in town that oriented them to doing evangelism, including in the schools they were at. They would attend Christian gatherings in the schools, and encourage students in their Christian walk, they told us. I was beginning to wonder if all this was an elaborate fund-raising plan, and whether they were about to ask us to help them out financially. That didn't transpire.

Our two new African lady friends had a decent grasp of English. As we sat and chatted with them and noted that they were not about to call Philo, we noticed a transformation in Mel. The rest of us were somewhat older than Mel. It appears she had adjusted her own pace so as to fit with ours. The presence of these two energetic twenty-somethings was changing that. From behaving beyond her age, Mel was transforming into someone younger! She revealed a side of herself of which we had been mostly unaware. Instead of having two girls visit a group of four 'older' people, we now had three girls attending with a group of three older people!

"We're going for a night in the town," said the two girls.

Mel seemed to forget that she was white and those were black girls. "I'm coming with you," she said. When she said that, the two girls looked a little shocked. But they soon regained their stride. The town they referred to, it transpired, was four hours away by bus. It was, as it happened, our destination for the following day. Well, Mel was determined to leave us oldies behind for a while, and make the trip ahead of us with the two beauties.

The two girls left. They said they'd be back in half an hour to collect their new friend and take her to the bus. Shortly after the girls had gone, Philo rang.

"Hi, all. Trust you are well. I have moved on. I am at a lakeside town called Kisiwa," Philo said.

"Oh," I said as if otherwise I wouldn't have had a clue. "What will Philo think when he discovers that we are shadowing him, albeit at a distance!" I asked myself yet again. If he found out, we might have to stop following him. Then I thought – perhaps that was Mel's ploy! She did not want Philo to find out that we were with him. The two girls might have given him a report on their finding us. Her way of getting the girls away from Philo was to join them on a trip to town. If she occupied them there, they would be less likely to phone or visit Philo and tell him who they had bumped into!

"Remember that I told you yesterday that I wasn't sure what would happen," Philo said.

"Yes," I said. I put the phone onto the speaker. "We're all listening," I added.

"I think the bishop and his wife were a little shocked that I did not leave," Philo said. "They said they'd had various white visitors over many years, but they'd all made bookings in a hotel. I just stayed on! It was a bit of a classic. I displaced the bishop's wife from her place in her husband's bed! She slept on the floor in the sitting room, and I in her bed. Anyway, that was okay by me, and hopefully also by them. Unfortunately, I didn't sleep much anyway. So tell me – how are you doing?"

"We're doing fine," I said. "Mel's getting ready for a night in the town. We're enjoying sitting and chatting."

"Well, good to hear. Greetings to all," said Philo, before calling off.

"Are you sure you are wise going with those girls for a night out in town like that?" Rolly asked Mel.

"It will be in town. Towns are the same everywhere," said Mel. "I'm looking forward to being on familiar territory. It feels like I've been in rural Africa for too long!"

We went on to talk about other things. I mean, Mel was hardly a teenager, and we weren't her parents.

"Does she know what she is letting herself in for?" Rolly said after Mel had left. "Probably not. We'll hear more of her story later," I responded.

"Those girls are Christians. I guess she thinks she'll be okay as she is going with Christians," Rose said.

"Let's hope you are right," Rolly added.

The girls did not come back. Fortunately, one of them had given Mel her phone number. "Where are you?" Mel asked over the phone. The only way to make sure she ended up going with them, it seemed to Mel, was to wait for them at the bus station. She told them she would be waiting there.

CHAPTER 32: DRAMA AT THE GUEST HOUSE

Meanwhile, the three of us were left in the guest house in Kisiwa. Rolly, presumably, was wondering what on earth he would do with the rest of his life. The problem with Philo's mission style, which Rolly was now valuing, is that it just is not easy! It is not something one can easily just step in to in one's fifties or sixties. Especially not if one has a wife. Rolly could see, no doubt, why many Westerners weren't too pleased with Philo. He was challenging the functionality of what was easy, yet what he was proposing was much more difficult. For Westerners that is. It was not more difficult for Africans. For them, it was getting encouragement really for what they were doing already. No wonder, though, that African people often seemed to fall short, when to 'succeed' as western projects envisaged, they had first to be Westerners. So crazy is the system.

We had been shown to our rooms. The vote was that at that point we would go to rest. Then at seven o'clock, we would gather again for something to eat at some nearby place. Rolly suggested that we then have a time of fellowship at eight o'clock. When we agreed, he said he would look into the management of the premises, if they could give us a room to use as a chapel, or if we should just go ahead and use one of our sleeping rooms.

I was impressed to discover that the guest house management had a room available in which we could meet. We were rather a small group. We did not think that would matter to God, so why should it matter for us? Rose led us in some singing, after which every person was given an opportunity to share something particular that they had learned. Rose kicked off. She reminded us again of Luke 10:4, a verse in which Jesus told his disciples not to carry provisions when they set out on evangelistic journeys. "Many western people these days ignore that message," Rose told us. "But they ..."

Suddenly the door to the small hall we were in flew open with a crash! Rose stopped in mid-sentence, obviously startled. In the same moment, a noisy crowd of African children charged through the door! They carried on in the same noisy mode, oblivious to us until one of them saw us. I am not sure who was then the more shocked, we or they. The eyes of a boy of about eleven went wide on seeing us. "Look, be quiet, look, visitors," I imagined him saying when he noticed our presence.

Within seconds there were about twenty children in the room. Again, I could only imagine that this was their room that they regularly used for their meetings. To us, the children had intruded on our small fellowship. To them, we were strangers who had imposed on their fun, whatever form it was going to take. I was aware that East African children were very respectful of adults. We saw that demonstrated when, on having realized that we were in their room, they sat on the floor lining two sides of the room with their back to the walls of the room.

Soon, my phone rang. It was Mel. "You wouldn't believe the places I am walking through here in the dark," she said to me.

I was glad that Mel had phoned. It showed that she appreciated us, as we appreciated her. I was very fond of her.

"Anyway, I've arrived safely, as it goes. Trust you are well?"

"Yes," I said. "We've just been invaded by children."

"What?"

"Look, tell you later."

"Okay. Goodbye." We finished our conversation.

Having said that children are respectful, I guess the exception is when they see white people outside on the street and other areas that they consider to be their playgrounds. Then they shout at them and run up to them. On this occasion, however, there was no such behavior. The children sat quietly, as if waiting to be told what to do next.

Rose, not surprisingly, was not sure what to do next. She was still standing there, her Bible open in front of her, now looking at the children, twenty-odd of whom were looking at her. Roughly speaking, half were boys and half were girls. They were dressed as if they had been to church – that is, not smartly dressed, but decently dressed, although none of them were wearing shoes. Their ages I estimated as being between ten and twelve. They sat there continuing to look at us. We, in turn, sat looking at them, except for Rose who was standing.

She knew enough Swahili to use to greet people, which she did proceed to do. "*Habari zenu*," she asked the children. Before the children could complete their responses, we heard the voice of a woman coming through the doorway. She seemed to be scolding the children. Presumably, she was saying, "why have you all gone in to sit down quietly when I told you to ... do something else?"

I was only guessing. I could not understand what she was saying, at speed and with vigor. A lady, about twenty-five years old, burst into the open door of the room we were in rather as the children had done, boldly and without a thought that someone else might be there. She started looking around at the children, castigating them without noticing our presence. Seconds later her eyes fell on to us, and her tone instantly changed.

I guess seeing that we were Whites, she said, "Sorry, sorry, me not I you see."

We smiled back. Whoever had told us we could use that room had obviously not realized that this group of children had already booked it for the same time!

The lady who was with the children bore a generous mop of braided hair. That was not unusual for young women in these parts. They attached long streams of artificial hair to tufts of their own, a laborious process that they seemed to much enjoy. As a result, that gave them a semblance of European women with a long flowing crown to their head. In my eyes, it certainly made her appear very beautiful, accentuating her large brown eyes and her undulating figure. She looked at us in shock, but I should say, not untowardly so. That is, she was surprised to find us there on 'her territory' with the children, but at the same time, she was evidently a confident woman.

It was evident to us that we should leave the room to the children. Rolly and I stood as if to leave, and Rose also made moves towards the door.

"You not go," said the woman.

"*Kwani?*" I responded, "*Wewe ubaki na watoto,*" (you stay with the children).

"Please stay," she said, "please you them see children they as do drama."

There was a little to-ing and fro-ing. I must admit as soon as I heard that the children were going to do some drama, and that we had an invitation to stay, I was in favor of staying. I looked at Rose and Rolly.

"Let's stay if they want us," Rolly said.

"We'll stay, *tutabaki, ili tuione drama,*" (we'll stay to see the drama), I said to the lady, who by that point had introduced herself as Angeline. We sat down at one end of the hall. Angeline, however, preferred us on the side, so we relocated our chairs to be along one of the side walls.

It transpired that the children were practicing for a biblical drama competition that was to be held a few days later. The actual competition was to be held in Entio, the town we were due to travel to on the following day. Anyway, having put thoughts of our little fellowship aside by this point, we were looking forward to enjoying and learning from whatever the children had in store for us. I only hoped that Angeline saw our presence as an asset, as we gave her children a real live audience to perform to!

Angeline organized the children. One sat with a drum between his legs. They started their performance with a song, standing where we had been sitting, singing enthusiastically and vigorously. Then followed the first drama. I tried, as inconspicuously as possible, to maneuver my phone to capture the scene by video. Lighting was poor. Unfortunately, in my efforts at being inconspicuous, I forgot to press the record button.

I wished Mel had been there. She would have been amazed; no stage fright! These kids had no trouble at all displaying themselves.

"Why are children back in the West so reluctant to play-act like this?" I asked myself.

We didn't know how long or how often the children had practiced, but there was something awe-inspiring about the drama that was performed. Certainly, Angeline was no professional drama coach. As far as we could see, she was merely a local volunteer.

"Wha! – Abel was dead. The sheep that he had brought (another of the children) was now running amok, bleating crazily after the death of his master. The sheep didn't seem to have realized that it, too, was headed for slaughter," so the drama, a re-enactment of the story of Cain and Abel, went on.

The next drama was from Acts chapter 12. It was hard to follow the drama, given how little we knew the language. Real shame.

"Bet you are wishing you had put more effort into learning Swahili, so that you could understand all they are saying," I whispered to Rolly.

"Not half!" he said. He was straining his ears, but still much was passing him by.

The actions made it clear that Peter had been released from prison. There he was walking along the road. That must be the people in the home of Mary, John Mark's mom, I thought. Something didn't seem right though.

"Why are the people in Mary's house shouting?" Rolly asked me. "From my understanding of the biblical account, they should be at prayer?"

The child acting as Peter went and knocked at the door.

"No wonder the others couldn't hear Peter knocking with that noise!" I said to Rolly.

"Amazing," he answered.

The drama had reached the point where Peter raised his hands so that the people there be quiet. Up to that point, all the people had started making a din again.

"I never imagined so much noise when people were praying," Rolly said.

"Nor had I," I conceded.

Then Rose joined in our whispered conversation. "You know, it has always puzzled me, why Peter had to raise his hands for people to be quiet. In my mind's eye, I never perceived the people as making a noise. According to these children though, those people were very noisy, which explains Peter's actions – they were probably so noisy, that even if he had shouted for them to shut up, they might not have heard. He had to raise his hands to get them to respond!"

"So these children, or their teacher Angeline, have given us a hermeneutical key to unlocking this Scripture," I said.

Moments later the drama was over. We applauded. The children did seem happy to have had an audience.

"We now need period small to us to prepare for sharing the last," Angeline said to us.

"When we read the Bible, and discover that people are praying, don't we always imagine them sitting or standing really silently, with perhaps one person speaking," Rolly said.

"Yes," I responded.

"But on what basis?" Rolly asked. "Does the Bible say that when people pray, they should not make a noise?"

"Well, yes it does," I responded. "Remember Jesus saying that when we pray, we need not make a noise like the heathen do."

"Oh yes! It does," said Rolly.

"Now, I guess Jesus must have said that for a reason. He wouldn't condemn people for praying noisily, if they were not praying noisily," I suggested.

"Right," said Rolly.

"Jesus didn't say 'your prayers must never be noisy,'" I added.

"No," said Rolly. "You know," he added, "prayer and meetings would be rather more exciting places if everyone would be speaking out loudly at the same time! Fewer people would fall asleep and it would reduce mind-wandering."

"The main point for me here though," I said, "is that these children, even without our understanding the language they are using, have, whether they are right or wrong, opened up a new hermeneutical horizon for us."

"What do you think then ..." Rolly started asking. As he was talking we could see that the children were about ready for their next drama. It was strange, talking as they prepared. It was as if the whole thing was to be done on our behalf. Rolly continued, "... about the Jesus film?"

"The what?" I said. I hadn't heard him very well given the noise the children were making.

"The Jesus film," he repeated.

"What about it?" I asked. This is a film produced in the USA that exactly follows Luke's Gospel.

"Well, prayer is always depicted in it as being by one person, and it is never a din."

I had to think about that one. As I thought, my eyes continued to follow what the children were doing in front of us.

"You mean," I said, "that even though the Jesus film takes Jesus' words exactly as in the Gospel of Luke, it may still be corrupting the biblical text if it misrepresents people's behaviors?"

"Not so much even that it misrepresents them," Rolly said, "but that it represents them according to only one cultural tradition – ours."

"I think you ..." I started saying. But it was time for us to pay attention to the third and last drama.

The next drama was from *Matendo kumi na saba*. "Acts 17," I whispered to Rolly and Rose, in case they hadn't already got it.

Acts 17 was harder to follow. Then, however, we saw the children acting as if everyone was reading his own Bible.

"They've got that one wrong," Rolly whispered to me. "Literacy rates were low in those days, and without the printing press, copies of the Bible were scarce and hard to come by. They had to be copied by hand remember."

I didn't argue with him on that one. I think many readers get that wrong. Readers in the West probably imagine everyone in Acts with their own Bible. "Even their own Bible on their phone," I thought to myself.

Then, however, again came a noise. A group of our child actors rose on their knees, hands stretched upwards, crying out loudly! "What's that?" I asked under my breath. I wished my Swahili had been good enough to go and ask Angeline to explain. "If only Philo had been with us," I thought.

"It looks like for those children, becoming a Christian means crying on your knees with your arms stretched up," said Rolly.

It clicked in my head! "Yes, that is it," I said.

In my mind's eye, I could picture people telling new converts, or potential converts, "If you want to become a Christian, kneel down, lift your hands above your head and cry out loudly to God," as people do, say, in some Holima churches. We watched to the end of that drama. We gave the children another round of hearty applause.

"Thank you very much. Now, children, they are leaving," said Angeline.

"*Swali moja*," I said (one question). "*Kanisa lenu ni gani?*" (What church are you with?)

"Pentecost," she said.

"Aha," I thought. That explains it. Or – it explained a lot. These weren't Catholic children as we thought, as we were in the Catholic guest house. "Good for the Catholics to allow other churches to use their premises," I said.

Rolly and Rose nodded. "You were saying before the final drama?" Rolly said to me, as we were back to enjoying the quiet of our own company in that small hall.

"Oh yes," I said. "We were discussing the Jesus film. What I was saying, I think, was that the Jesus film is deeply culturally loaded."

"Is that bad do you think?" Rolly said.

"Hmm, I don't know," I said, "but it is certainly adding to the text."

"But so is a preacher every time he preaches." We moved our chairs. We had ample space now, and no reason not to be in a circle.

"Right," I replied, "but how powerful are those visual representations? I don't know just how powerful they are to people here, but I guess they could be very powerful."

"Like, that's gospel," Rolly said, emphasizing the irony in what he was saying.

"Yes," I said.

"It would be nice to know how the Jesus film would have appeared had it been put on by African people," Rolly asked.

"Too late," I said.

"No, it is not," Rolly responded. "It could still be done."

"But, don't you see," I said, "there is now a standard with which it will have to either equate or differ?" I had often thought about that.

"Yes, you're right," Rolly said.

"Still," I added, "I think it's a good exercise to try to dramatize the Scriptures."

"What do those dramas also tell us about evangelism and discipleship in Africa?" I asked Rolly.

"What do you mean there?"

"Presumably, people should be encouraged to become Christians in the way that makes sense to them. That seems to preclude foreigners, especially Westerners, from being evangelists."

"Oh, I see what you mean. I agree with you, to some extent."

"Fair enough," I responded.

"Just think though," Rolly said.

"Yes?"

"How much we have been challenged and been given food for thought from those few minutes of drama, and we hardly understood anything that the children were saying."

"Yes," I responded.

"Well, think about someone like Philo, who is in a sense seeing dramas like that all day every day, for years on end. No wonder he might find the efforts of Westerners who come 'fresh' to Africa to be lacking."

"It would have been good to have had Philo here," I said. "Rose, you were talking when the children came in," I continued.

"Oh, yes," she said. "What I was trying to say is that what Jesus is advocating in Luke 10:4 when he says not to carry anything with you when you go to evangelize, is even more important now than it was then, because of the terrible reputation western people like us have, always using our money to force what we want to happen."

"Well put," I said. "Rolly, what do you say, in brief?" I went on.

"I have realized," he said, "that when the Bible talks about giving, i.e., generosity, tithing, et cetera, it also always talks about losing. That is – the person who gives remains with less as a result of giving. When it says 'give to the poor' for example."

"What do you mean?" Rose asked her husband.

"Imagine we had $100. Then if we gave away $10, we'd only have $90 to live on."

"Okay," said Rose. "That's what I mean – giving is losing."

"Okay. Got it."

"But," Rolly went on. "These days, Westerners want to give without losing."

"Okay," I said, "because they give away other people's money, money that they have raised so that they can give it!"

"Yes," said Rolly. "I can see a sense in which that can be immoral, as it is a way for an individual to utilize his connections in wealthy parts of the world to control people in the places he is reaching. As I see it ..."

"Okay," I added as Rolly paused.

"... the problem is trust. Donors trust their own people; hence they load fellow Westerners with money. They don't trust Africans. And this is sensitive because if you became known for not trusting African people, you could be considered a racist. However, it is not always racism, it can merely be a recognition of the difference in culture."

"In a way, it simply recognizes that other people can be different, but that doesn't mean that they are inferior," I said, "as we discussed before."

"Right," said Rolly. "It can be merely a matter of understanding being limited. Like, if you wanted to employ a German to work in England, you may well first want to insist that they know the English language. In addition to the language, we are saying that there is a logic and a culture that underlies a language. African people may not 'get' that logic and culture. Of course, the reverse will also apply, so that Africans might find that Westerners are not trustworthy."

"Plenty of food for thought there!" I said.

"Your turn, Dave," Rolly said.

"I was thinking of the so-called 'prosperity gospel,'" I went on. "We accuse Africans of following the prosperity gospel. We think that we don't need the gospel to prosper because we do our 'prosperity' in a secular realm. We think that the secular realm is not gospel. We also think Africans should be able to 'get it.' But they don't! It doesn't make sense in Africa. The only way that makes sense in Africa, it seems to me, for someone to be more prosperous than someone else, is through God's intervention or some kind of blessing. It is silly to condemn African Christians for adhering to the prosperity gospel when that is the only thing that can make sense to them."

"Another profound point to be expounded on another day," said Rolly.

Rolly prayed and we retired, each to their bed.

CHAPTER 33: ATTEMPTED MURDER?

The room in which we had breakfast was basic but satisfactory. We sat down for breakfast around 9 a.m. We were looking forward to a relaxed start, before embarking on our three-and-a-half-hour trip to Philo's next destination. Once there, we would, of course, be reunited with Mel.

"Mel tells me that she got to bed at two o'clock this morning," Rose announced.

"Two o'clock!" we started.

"I'm sure she will tell us more in due course," Rose added. "When she got to bed, she shared a bed with the two girls who we met yesterday, with two men sleeping on the floor beside their bed. The poor girl was desperate to relieve herself in the middle of the night but was too reluctant to leave the protection of having a woman on each side, in order to step over men in the dark, who she had only got to know the same day. The bathroom anyway was a communal one, ten yards outside the door of their house, so she wouldn't know who she might meet on the way there."

"That's the kind of story you might relish telling your grandchildren," Rolly reflected, "but not the kind of life you would want to live for very long."

Rolly thus summed things up pretty well! Queues of short-termers might line up to have that kind of experience, as long as it was only once, then they go home and save it for their grandkids!

We were getting used to having unexpected experiences crash into our planned programs. Unbeknown to us until a few moments later, this morning was to be no exception. There weren't many people in that small restaurant. We had tweaked our ears to tune-out conversations going on around us, even lively ones. That was relatively easy to do if those conversations were in a language that we did not know.

The first we realized of an argument going on a couple of tables away from us, therefore, was when we heard the sound of a crash, followed by a thump, followed by a male voice crying out in pain. Instantly, we all turned our heads in the direction of the noise and commotion. There was a man, seemingly a relatively short man with a beard, lying on his back on the floor. He was wearing a blue short-sleeved shirt and jeans. Between him on the floor and another man standing was an upturned chair. That was presumably what had crashed. The man standing, about six-foot tall, called Bill we discovered later, had a shocked look on his face. Meanwhile, the man on the floor, called Hamsi, was shouting profusely. What he was saying were presumably not nice things, making Bill who was standing there, look more and more worried. Funnily, the T-shirt Bill was wearing had a couple of words etched onto it in large letters in English. It said: 'No worries.'

In no time, we heard Hamsi shouting amongst other things "... *polisi.*" Actually – "*iteni polisi*" (call (plural) the police). At that point a man sitting at a table alongside where Hamsi was laying started contradicting him: "*Polisi la,*" repeated in English, "We don't want the police." Clearly, Hamsi wanted the police called to deal with Bill.

"He is accusing Bill of wanting to kill him," Rolly said. I was aware that if such an accusation of attempted murder went to the police, things could get very complicated very quickly. Although it appeared that Bill might have pushed Hamsi backward over that chair, it transpired later that actually, Hamsi was two yards away from Bill when he fell and tripped himself as he walked backward too quickly, unaware that there was a chair behind him. Which story the police might believe was another question.

The man refusing the involvement of police turned out to be the father in charge of that Catholic parish. His most outstanding feature was his flat nose – that looked as if someone hit his face with a spade when he was a baby. Actually, this feature was not so unusual amongst his home tribe, the Lile. Discussion between the father, Father Samuel, Hamsi, and Bill continued. We went on with our breakfast. Five minutes later, just as I was about to ask Rose if she would pour me another cup of tea, Father Samuel came and occupied the fourth seat on our table. The tea was good by the way. Water and milk had been pre-mixed then boiled with tea leaves added – that was true East African style.

"Good morning," Father Samuel said to us. We exchanged greetings and names. "I think you have seen and heard that we have a bit of a problem," he said. We wondered why he was telling us about the issue that didn't seem ought to involve us at all. "I think you are aware of what has just happened." We nodded. "I am trying to discourage Hamsi from taking this case to the police (very, very wise, I thought!). I am offering myself to arbitrate (very good of you, I thought), but Hamsi says that he will go to the police unless you come and sit in on the case."

In my mind was Paul's admonition that cases between believers should be judged within the church. I also had in mind that we wanted to get to Entio the same day. I looked at my colleagues. "Look, we only have a short time," I said to Father Samuel, who proceeded to breathe a sigh of relief. Why Hamsi thought we should be on the arbitration team, of course, I did not know. Perhaps he thought we might give him money should he agree not to go to the police?

Ten minutes later we were sat in a circle in, in fact, the same small hall which we had occupied the previous evening. The two men whose case we were considering obviously weren't at peace. Father Samuel stood up and announced, with a summary to us in English, why we were there. He agreed to translate everything that was said so that we could hear. That was a condition of Hamsi not calling the police!

"So, what is the nature of your dispute?" Father Samuel asked.

Little did he realize, I guess, how fast the question would reopen the floodgates! The two men went at each other verbally, hammer and tongs! I am glad I wasn't expected to follow all that in Swahili! Father Samuel did insist that the two men stay sat down and speak reasonably quietly – I guess he didn't want one of them to fall! Then he translated for us as fast as he could, staccato style:

"Hamsi's wife ... was teacher ... road accident ... with their three children ... all four were killed ... six months ago ... they remain unburied ... Hamsi had not paid bride wealth ... Hamsi says he has paid ... Bill is Hamsi's brother-in-law ... he says Hamsi has not paid ... Bill says Hamsi was a terrible uncaring husband ... Hamsi denies ... Bill insists that because bride wealth is not paid ... Hamsi's late wife and children ... should be buried at his wife's parents' home ... unless Hamsi pays full bride price ... Hamsi says ... why should he pay ... full bride price ... and all the people concerned ... are dead ... He agrees ... to pay two cows ... after all ... Hamsi's wife has no sisters ... and no sign of a replacement being made available."

"This matter has been in court for six months," Father Samuel went on. "Bill and Hamsi agreed to meet here to try to make progress out of court on this case. When they started arguing, tempers flared, and Hamsi found himself on the floor, as you know."

Now Hamsi began his appeal to us as authority. This was not over an accusation of attempted murder. That appeared to have become a non-issue. The issue now was – should he pay and how much, to have his wife and children buried at his home? He, after all, was the father of the children, and I guess we would say in English, the common-law husband. Father Samuel translated:

"Why on earth ... should I pay ... for a dead woman ... and dead children ... where in the Bible ... does it say that ... bride wealth should be paid ... for dead people?"

"Where in the Bible does it stipulate whether a woman should be buried at her father's or her husband's home?" I wondered. Philo had explained some of these issues to me in the past. This was a key concern to the Striden people. To have one's wife buried at her home-of-origin was an enormous embarrassment, and likely to result in various kinds of misfortune arising subsequently. Now though, what on earth was to be our legitimate role in this case? I realized that underlying the tradition concerned was an orientation to works as against grace.

"The foundation of marriage is love," I said. Father Samuel translated. "I believe you ought to take account of God's love, especially as expressed in his giving of his only begotten son on the cross for our sins." That was translated. Even as I was talking though, I hated myself. Imagine it had been America, and someone was having a case decided by someone from a foreign land, using a language they did not understand, in the light of a culture other than one's own! Also, this was a domestic dispute. No doubt there were numerous intricacies that I was not aware of.

I appealed to Father Samuel. Father Samuel adjourned the proceedings. The three of us sat with him.

"Look," Father Samuel said. "I very much appreciate you taking time out to help us to solve this case. You told me you need to get to Entio. You have listened to Hamsi, as he had requested. Dave – you have said some wise things. I suggest that unless you particularly want to be more involved, you quietly get on with your day's program. Leave this case to us, and we will handle it."

I looked at my colleagues. Those seemed like sage words from Father Samuel. We accepted his gracious suggestion. Father Samuel said, to make sure no issues arise, that he would wait till we were gone before continuing the case. In the meantime, Bill and Hamsi could stew.

"Good evasion?" asked Rolly.

"What do you mean?" I asked. We were in his and Rose's room. I was sitting in a chair, they on the bed.

"I mean you were expected to decide the case! Instead, you said some foundationally wise Christian things, and then you backed down from getting involved in a morass of issues that you did not understand. I just thought you handled that well."

"Well, thanks, Rolly," I responded. "I was struggling a lot, so said what seemed wise to say."

"If you had carried on," Rolly said, "I think everyone would have made out that they were listening very intently. They would have said you had wonderful wisdom, and then they would have done their own thing!"

"Interesting you say that," I commented. "That would have been my view. But I think not everyone would agree. Sometimes Westerners get very involved in complex African issues: marriages, disputes, arbitration, and so on."

"From an assumption which is that issues in Africa parallel those in America," Rolly said, confirming my own thoughts.

"That is what I thought as I spoke," I said. "Imagine an African coming to America and adjudicating a domestic issue for you, using an African language, as if we in America had the same culture as they," I added. "So he might advise you in a certain domestic dispute that you should take another wife, for example."

"Something that you know would land you in prison!"

"But," I added to Rolly's comment, "in such a situation you might say 'yes' to a foreigner, with your eyes rolling, thinking that to say 'yes' may be the best way to shut him up and leave you alone, with his crazy ideas!"

"You got it," Rolly said. "Generally, in my experience, African folks have more sense than to advise us on our domestic disputes. We are the ones who are not so guarded."

"Agree with you," I said.

At that point, we packed our bags. Before long we were on our way to Entio. We carried on talking as I was driving. The road was generally very good. Except, that is, for the big trucks one had to keep overtaking.

"Fancy fighting in the courts for six months over a dead body," I said as I drove.

"Yes, such an important issue for people here! You know, it reminded me of the genealogies in the Bible. The biblical authors were clearly very concerned to show that people's pedigree was known. That they could trace their ancestry back to known forefathers. To some of us now that seems a waste of time and space. But it did not to them," Rolly said.

"That's a good insight," I agreed. "But what about dead bodies?"

"Remember that the way some people think these days, that it is supposedly unimportant how one handles a dead body, is quite recent," Rose suggested. "Cremation has become common, certainly in the UK, thus ignoring any ongoing relationship between a corpse and a departed human spirit."

"I think it is a kind of self-deception – actually people are very fearful of dead bodies," Rolly suggested.

"Right," I said. "Having a corpse, no four corpses including the children, sit in a mortuary for six months as one argues over how many cows have been paid, is pretty extreme though!"

"It is," said Rolly. "It seems the dead are more important than the living."

"Why?" I asked. An answer was not immediately forthcoming. "Maybe a way of avoiding the more complex relationships of the living," I suggested to myself.

"Tell us what you think," Rolly said.

"Just by way of example, widows can be very complicated. The New Testament tells us as much. Sick people can be very demanding, and they can go on being sick for ages – especially if one treats them well. That's a lot of hassle for a long time, for no gain."

"What do you mean, 'no gain'?" Rolly asked again. Driving was proving conducive to conversation. The road was decent. None of us seemed to get tired at that point.

"They don't work, sick people like that, or have children, or even satisfy people sexually. They are just a drain on the community. I mean – I don't mean that is how I see it, but is it how others might see it?" I added.

"Okay," Rolly said. "So I see, once someone is dead, they can be handled much more easily. They just need to be put away, buried. That is an identifiable, manageable, predictable and accomplishable task. That brings a clear end, once the burial is done. Not only that – but a burial is also a major social event to which people can come to meet their friends, eat, sing, even dance, listen to interesting tear-jerking stories (of the last days of the late), and so on. But, why fight over a dead body?"

"Well, there is the shame to be avoided. There are cows to be gained. Then there is the likelihood that one might be haunted if one gets things wrong."

"Gets things wrong?" Rolly repeated my final phrase.

"Yes – I mean, if the body gets buried in the wrong place. If one gets things wrong, and the deceased haunts people, then one will incur other expenses, to rectify that."

"Like what?" Rose asked.

"Like having a ceremony involving the slaughtering of an animal so that its blood pacify the spirit of the deceased."

"How can one know that one has ..." Rolly started saying.

"Hey, look," Rose interrupted him. "Look where?" I asked.

"Ahead!" she said. "Look. It's a zebra crossing!"

Looking carefully indeed, ahead of us, a zebra was crossing the road. Then a second, then a third, then a fourth. I slowed down.

"Who has priority at a zebra crossing," quipped Rolly, "us or the zebra?"

"Ha, ha," said Rose. I was trying to think of how to make the joke, but Rolly got in before me! (For American readers, a zebra crossing is a name given in the UK to a crosswalk.)

"Impala," Rolly said.

Indeed, out of our left-hand window, there were impala scattered across the landscape. It was good to see some African wildlife.

"I do believe that is a warthog," Rose said. We looked. (By this time I had stopped the vehicle.) Only Rose saw that warthog. We opened the hatch. We had previously thought of it as our 'spying hatch.' Now we were able to use it for its intended purpose – observing African wildlife, on safari.

After that exciting interlude, we went back to our conversation as we drove on. (We left Rose as 'lookout' sitting in the back, but with the hatch closed.)

"How can you know if the deceased is upset?" Rolly asked.

"Good question," I said. "I guess you have to be an *ajuoga*, that is, a witch doctor as he is commonly known, to be able to do that."

"Hmm," said Rolly.

"Lion!" Rose exclaimed. We stopped again. Indeed, there was a pride of lions, although at a distance. Even further away, we spotted an elephant.

"It is also 'guesswork,'" I said. "You have to guess about the heart of the deceased. Was she unhappy at her husband's unwillingness to part with bride wealth? Would she rather be buried at her parents' home? What of other relatives – dead or alive? What is the consensus?"

"That is all rather mind-boggling," Rolly conceded.

Rose was, in the meantime, struggling with a related issue. "Look, gentlemen," she said. "In your many philosophical pontifications, you seem to have missed something."

"What exactly, dear," Rolly responded, tilting his head slightly to better carry his voice behind him.

"Here we are. We are exploring Africa. But – what we are doing is illegitimate."

"Illegitimate, how?" I asked.

"Well, these days African scholars are the ones who are supposed to be those who report on Africa. People want emic reports. That is – western people want to get their knowledge about Africa from Africans. Not from Europeans."

Rose was right. Indeed, in many scholarly circles. In the media, perhaps, even more so. People were a bit tired of getting white people's reports about Africa. Reputable news agencies and respectable scholarly interests wanted black people reporting on Africa.

"But we seem to be learning things about Africa that go unreported," Rose said. "The media rarely tells us that in Africa, a struggle over where to bury a dead woman can be in court for six months."

"When they do tell us, it is like it is something extraordinary, not something normal. You should hear Philo wax lyrical on that issue." I said. Of course, we couldn't hear Philo, as he refused to keep our company. But, we were also discovering that it was because he was avoiding our company that he was enabled to get deep insights into Africa! "Let us say, that African people do not know what Westerners do not know about

Africa. They tell a story as if the background to the story they are telling is normal and familiar. Whatever that story might be! Even if they tell the story 'accurately,' they might still be inaccurate because they are leaving their (implicit) western reader with the wrong assumptions about the background to the story."

"You're getting too complicated for my brain again," Rolly said.

"Related issues keep coming up," I said. "Last time it was about language. It is like the issue of race! But I am glad that Rose noticed it, and brought it up again. The problem with it is, or at least one of them, that one does not notice the issue if one is confined to the West! Many of the things we are learning about African culture are invisible to the West. They would be visible if European people were to be reporting about Africa. That is because Europeans would notice what is different between Europe and Africa – where Africa is different. But – the West and everyone else is in denial about those differences. They do not want to perceive them. The implications are just too great. One implication would be – that it would make young people in the West aware of the importance of carrying out Christian mission to Africa."

No one, neither Rolly nor Rose, raised a further question as a follow up to Rose's initial concern. I was happy that this matter was getting raised, again at least between the three of us. It is a theme that kept coming up in our trip. And rightly so.

CHAPTER 34: DECENT HOTEL

We were not far from Entio when something strange happened. We were singing in the car at the time it occurred. Rose was a contralto and was very good as a lead singer. We were still not in town, but the density of the houses was growing, when we came upon a roadblock. A pole had been extended across our half of the road. Two police officers were standing alongside it. Usually, roadblocks stop traffic in both directions. For some reason, this roadblock was only for traffic entering the town.

When the roadblock came into view, I announced "Roadblock. What to do?" It might have been bandits or highwaymen after all. But – in broad daylight and so near to town? We could easily have accelerated, moved into the other lane of traffic and passed the barrier. If in doubt – we could then drive to a police station to alert the authorities that we suspected the roadblock was illegitimate.

"Stop, I think," said Rolly.

I pulled our vehicle over to the side of the road. There were a few kiosks, small shops, just about forty yards from where we stopped, with people milling about them. It might have been difficult, much more sinister, had we been stopped in a bushy, wooded, or more isolated area. One of the two police officers was a woman. It was the man, however, who came to my window. I shut off the engine. I stepped out of the car, as did Rolly, leaving just Rose in the back seat. Somehow, it seemed that doing that indicated the most clearly that we were innocent of whatever we were suspected of.

"Driving License," said the officer, the male officer, in English. I stepped back into the driver's seat and sifted through my things. I found my international driving license. The strangest thing was the comment that both Rolly and I heard the male police officer, a man of average build, maybe forty years old, tell the female police officer. (She might have been forty-five, with closely-cropped hair.) *"Wanaume wawili na mwanamke mmoja,"* the male officer said to his companion. That is what both Rolly and I understood him as having said. The woman we also both understood as saying *"Sio hawa, wacha waende."* They gave me my license back. The wooden pole had already been withdrawn from the road and was not to be seen. They waved us on. I started the engine, put us in gear, and drove off slowly.

"What did you hear him say?" I asked Rolly.

"Two men and one woman," Rolly related.

"Well, that is what I heard," I said. "What did she say?"

"Not them, let them go."

"Absolutely," I responded. "That was strange. It seems to me that there is not normally a roadblock there."

"So what are you thinking?" Rolly said.

"Well," I said. "They'd been told to stop us. They would have seen our vehicle with white people in it. They deliberately stopped us. They had some agenda. Because we didn't fit the description they were given, they let us go again. Whoever gave them the description did not realize that Mel had gone ahead of us by herself!"

That was a strange incident. We, at the time, had little clue as to why it had occurred. Even later we could only guess – was this somehow Professor Nancy's doing?

* * *

Moments later, just a mile or so from the roadblock, we received a phone call from Mel. "Where are you?" she asked.

"Entering Entio."

"How far from the city?"

I had just seen a sign. "Eight kilometers," I said.

She paused. "Good!" she added. "Within the next two miles, you will come to a place where there are a lot of buses parked alongside the road. People are milling around on the roadside. That's where I am. Can you stop and pick me up?"

"Mel is getting around," I thought, "for a young woman." We were looking forward to hearing how she was getting on.

As we reached that spot we could see Mel was there and I pulled up alongside her. She jumped on board, and off we went! Mel gave us a report of her time. The gathering she was at was for a funeral.

"How was the funeral?" Rose asked Mel, who was sitting beside her.

"Speak up so that all of us can hear," I encouraged her.

Mel spoke loudly and clearly. "Good to be back with you all," she said. "I've had some adventure! I've been 'vulnerable,' as Philo generally is. It certainly helps one to learn things!"

"Well," I thought. "You have been more vulnerable probably than Philo ever is, you being a young woman!" I did not tell her that though, at that point. Neither did I remind her that Philo's style of vulnerability also required being able to understand and use the people's indigenous language.

"That was a big and well-attended funeral. African people certainly know how to organize events, and they do it all in the middle of nowhere. That is, I mean, at people's homes. We might arrange some big communal events in the UK, but not as frequently or as big as people here do. When we want to do that, we might rent a hotel that has all the facilities on tap, set up I mean: kitchen, hall, bathrooms, car park and all that. Here people arrange massive events, attended by hundreds of people, all of whom eat, many spend the night and need to wash and so on, and they build all the facilities almost from scratch, out of nowhere! If people in the USA have twenty visitors come to spend a night and day, that's probably the largest group they will ever host in their home. Here people have hundreds come, and manage to keep them all!" Mel paused. "There is one memory I won't be able to get rid of quickly though," she added.

"What on earth is that?" I thought.

Mel's voice changed as she spoke, and as she recalled something that she had just seen. She was choking a little on her words. "I just saw a skinny lady. When I saw her, I went up to her. I realized she was blind. Her daughter was leading her. The daughter was around nine years old. I greeted her. I asked someone to translate. I asked how she was. The translator knew her. She explained that, because she had been blind from childhood, this woman had had trouble getting a husband. There was a man in a neighboring village who, because he was addicted to alcohol, had trouble getting a wife. When her family heard about that man, they had found a way to solve their problem. They took their blind daughter to the man's home and left her there. That was about fifteen years previously. Now they have four children. But life is so difficult for them! Now their drunkard father is sick. He cannot even help his family. Instead, his blind wife has to keep him. But, she can't do much work. Even the older children cannot earn money. Discipline was never kept, so they never went to school properly. The children are wasters – used to idling and stealing.

What hurt me though, was to hear that the family, I mean like his brothers and other relatives, don't seem to do anything! They let this lady grow thin and ignore her pleas for help. She has no one to help her! While the funeral is going on around her – vast amounts of money are being used to celebrate the death of the deceased – the prospect for this woman was to go home to a sick husband and hungry children, and no food."

"Do you know this was really the circumstance?" I asked.

"I went to the home," Mel said.

Well, that doesn't mean that Mel knew everything. But I accepted, she had clearly found a lady who was in dire straits. Plus, the children.

"It was so sad," said Mel, her voice breaking up. "Why did the people who had been generous enough to help the funeral not give her something? Why did they not help her?"

"Why did you not help her?" Rose asked.

There was a pause. "I didn't help her because I want to help her," said Mel, her voice on the verge of tears. "I have understood enough from Philo, much of it through all of you, to know that coughing up a bit of money is not the solution. One must be able to do more than that. If I had given her something – I could not replace what to me the family should be doing unless ... (a pause), unless ... " she said, "I committed myself to stay in that village permanently ... (another pause) ... rather like Philo has done. But I was scared. I still am scared. I mean – could I just live there like that? I am beginning to follow you in realizing something else too," Mel added. "That is to say: it is true that people here don't think like we do! I mean, they do what they know to do, and do it well – like arranging the massive funeral event. But they cannot go further than that. Their language and understanding hits, from our point of view, a glass ceiling. They cannot discuss their issues in school, for example, because the curriculum dictates that they discuss western issues, from a western perspective in a western language. They cannot write about their issues, as writing must be in English, which makes no sense of who they are. Their issues are much to do with God. What does God want someone to do if their brother is so drunk that his family is suffering so much from hunger? I see people are scared to intervene. Their culture won't allow them to intervene. But neither can they make enough sense of the Bible to realize, together, what action they should be taking. They are not even allowed to study the Bible in their own language. I mean – anyone who does that is considered a fool."

We had explained this to Mel. Studying the Bible in English can give someone a career, a salary, maybe travel overseas, even a life abroad, prestige, et cetera. But then it cannot be addressing their own people's issues. Because of all the benefits of studying in English, few people study their Bible seriously in their own languages, hence their people's way of life can stagnate!

"The people are so stuck. Yet, we are not helping them. I was scared. I'm still scared. But will my fear of their poverty make it go away? Will my denial of their poverty, saying I do not want to think of them as different so don't want to accuse them of not being able to look after themselves, make their poverty go away? No!"

"Did we have to turn left here, or go straight on?" I asked Rolly, who looked at the scribbled directions in front of him on how to find the hotel. No satellite navigation map here!

"It's the next left," he said. The streets were congested. As well as hand carts, cyclists, motorcyclists, motorized rickshaws, pedestrians, children, beggars, roadside-traders converging into road space, and all shapes and sizes of vehicle, there were also goats wandering around. We took the next turning left. We came to a quieter piece of road and approached a large gate. A security guard came to check our credentials. The man opened the gate, and we entered into another very much more peaceful world.

* * *

We were met as soon as we parked. Very helpful men were quick to take our bags from us. They accompanied us to a spacious reception area, surrounded in its perimeter by comfortable seats, and gave us a wet towel with which to remove the dust from our faces as our booking was located and confirmed.

"Four people, two double rooms for three nights. Confirmed."

Rolly handed over his debit card. In total, not including food, that was to put us back $1,600. That was not even the top hotel in the city! We agreed that we would all freshen up, then meet again at 8 p.m. That had pretty much become our custom. Again, the two ladies shared a room, and we two men shared the other.

At eight o'clock we sat down at a quiet table (or so we thought) overlooking a grassy area, planted with intermittent flowers and ornamental plants. There was soft music playing in the background. A bit later, there was to be a soloist singing and playing on his guitar. Lights were strategically placed in the grounds to make everything look attractive. There was a regular swish of sprinklers making sure that the hotel grass kept a deep-green color. The waiter came and asked us for our drink orders.

Mel was getting the day's experiences off her chest. "Do you think I should have given that blind woman some money?" she asked us. None of us responded to her question. "I mean, it would have been straightforward for me," Mel said. "Possibly ten dollars would have gone a very long way. But, I thought, we white people already have a sufficiently bad reputation for thoughtless generosity without my adding to it. Maybe she was a con man (woman)? Had I given, after she had told her story, I would also have encouraged others to be con men, or for her to be a con man next time she faced the prospect of meeting white people. The point was, though, that her dilemma was caused by *abuses*, as we would see them, that she had received from her own people. It's like if one meets a battered wife, bandages are not the answer; there is a relationship that needs healing. There were so many needy people at the funeral. Maybe someone directed that blind woman to walk towards me? It somehow seems dishonest to provide help when one is there, when one is convicted by having to stare the poor in the face, but then not to be committed to staying, and not to do so when one happens to be far away from them? That is – it seems wrong to make a one-off donation without commitment."

Mel was getting things off her chest.

As Mel was talking, the area we were in began to fill with young people. These were not, however, African young people. Judging from their accents they were Australians. Our table had space for six which meant that we had two spare places where we were sitting. Two Australians sat down in those spaces. Although they probably intended only to keep each other company, we challenged that intention by asking them about themselves and their group.

"We're from Australia," they said. Well, so much had been pretty evident to us. "We are a group from a Presbyterian church in Sydney," they further explained.

"So, what is a group of young Presbyterians from Sydney doing in Holima, in Africa?" Rolly asked.

He pretty much knew of this kind of short-term trip by western churches, but he wanted to ask anyway.

"We've come to help the poor, you know, the needy and all that," said a young man with short blond hair.

"That's admirable," said Rolly, perhaps tongue in cheek.

"What do you do?" the young man wearing a sporty jacket asked Mel. His friend, a girl wearing a kind of tracksuit, was listening inattentively.

"I'm a journalist," she said. Mel thought she might be given an opportunity to talk about her intended feature article.

Instead, both the young people said in unison, "A journalist!"

"We need a journalist. Look, do you think you can help us out?" the blond-haired fellow, we were later to learn that he was called Ran, asked.

A little taken aback, "Well, I don't know. What do you want?" Mel replied in response.

"Look, I don't know so much, but my colleague does. Can I bring him to meet you?" Ran asked.

"Well, yes, if you want to." Mel could hardly see the harm in that. Ran left in the direction of the hotel accommodation with the young lady, to whom we had not been introduced.

Five minutes later Ran came with another man and a woman. The man pulled up a seventh seat to our table. He was called Euticus. There was some issue with the skin on his face, causing it to be mottled. He had a noticeable scar above his left eye. The girl, Beatrice, looked as if she was a little older than the rest of the group members – perhaps Mel's age.

"Good to see you folks," said Euticus.

We introduced ourselves.

"Look, let me be frank, my interest is in journalism. I was told one of you is a journalist? Perhaps all of you are?"

Rolly answered, "We are certainly not all journalists. The journalist is Mel here (pointing at her). Do you need her services?"

"You bet!" Euticus responded. "It's true is it Mel? Who do you work for?"

"SES, Scottish Evening Standard," Mel responded.

"Wow," said Euticus.

I noted that there was no interest in what Mel might be reporting. Euticus was interested in recruiting Mel. The pressure to that end became intense! "Look, Mel, would you mind reporting for us, I mean 'on us' I suppose?" Euticus asked. Beatrice's looks indicated that she was on board with Euticus's intentions and lively spirit!

"You've been reporting for long? You must be good. I hope they pay you well in Scotland? ..." Euticus had an endless stream of questions to throw at Mel. We were not sure he expected answers to all of his questions, he just kept on asking, not giving Mel any opportunity to respond. If Euticus was the tough cop, then Beatrice now played the role of 'gentle cop.'

"I'm sorry, dear," she said to Mel. "Euticus here comes across a bit strong. It is just," she said in a very alluring tone, "that we'd love to have someone with us who could do some good journalistic writing, and we would be prepared to pay."

That is how the conversation went on for about fifteen minutes. The rest of us and our interests were totally ignored. All the attention and efforts were on getting Mel to do some journalistic writing for them! We tried to put in an occasional comment, like "leave the poor girl alone," but to no avail. Eventually, the carnivores got their prey. Mel agreed to go with her new friends, seducers, or whoever they were, so that they could show her some things they desperately wanted her to see. They even said they would feed her! We were de-Melled.

Mel returned about ninety minutes later. "Wow, did they, and do they, want me!" she said. "Their church is involved in various projects around here. They want those projects written up. They want a third-party to do the writing. Preferably a professional – like me! What was, of course, made clear, is that they expected whatever comments I made to be positive about what they are doing."

"So, will you help them?" Rose asked.

"I accepted to accompany them tomorrow, but no commitment to writing up. I'll see if what you do is interesting, I told them flatly. I hope it's okay with you."

"Yes. That'll be fine if that's what you want to do," Rolly said when she asked.

We would learn more about the reasons they wanted Mel so desperately in due course! Mel did add that she wanted to go 'Philo hunting' at 4 p.m. the following day.

The next day, Mel's enthusiastic friends picked her up at 9 a.m. sharp. We saw her getting into a car with Euticus, Beatrice, and Ran. Mel was clutching her camera.

"Whatever happens, it should be an interesting experience for her," I thought. Mel came back at three o'clock.

"That was amazing," she said. "Now I know how one can buy a journalist! Since nine o'clock we have been to about seven different project sites within the town. At each place, I was encouraged to take photos, and ask all the questions I want – of the Australians and of local people we found on site. I recorded all the conversations. They tell me they'd like me to give them a 1000-word illustrated report on each project at each location. And I tell you what else – I will be paid $5,000. I realize that journalist-types are in demand! The Australians needed a 'neutral' journalist to report on their projects. That could aid their credibility to donors no end!" She laughed, and added: "And the more they pay me, the more they think I'll be *neutral!*"

Philo had not made it to Entio the previous day. That was apparently because the bishop he was to have visited canceled out. Instead, he was to arrive in town that very afternoon.

We had done some research on the location of the church he was to visit. It was on the side of a certain hill. Mel planned to locate herself on a facing hill, to be able to observe (or spy on) what Philo was up to! It seemed a crazy venture, but then crazy experiments seemed to be the order of the day. She was the journalist, so in that sense, she was in charge.

The children we met on the way were somewhat intrigued by what we were doing. Mel and I traveled by bus, and then we walked up that hill facing Philo's church. We found a big boulder that we could sit on that also offered us shade from a tree. "Perfect vantage point," I thought.

Mel had carried her binoculars. It took us a long time to pinpoint the location of the church where Philo was to be. Eventually, we found a building that we were sure was the church. People's living circumstances certainly were amazing! People were building houses on boulders, in front of or behind rocks, on incredibly steep slopes, wherever they could find space for a dwelling. The reason – space was short, but jobs were relatively plentiful. This was a city in which many people wanted to live. The only way for many to live there was to live like a mountain goat – always going up and down steep slopes, sometimes having to hop from one boulder to the next.

Mel and I were on that boulder observing the church for about half an hour when we were finally rewarded. "There he is!" said Mel. Philo was hardly visible at all to the naked eye, but when I put the binoculars to my eyes, there he was. Mel was suddenly excited.

"This is what love can do to you," I thought to myself, "getting excited about a white fleck on a distant hill!"

Conveniently for us, Philo moved in visible places. We saw him go to the building we had taken as being the church. Well – we must have been right on that one. Then he climbed up the hill a little behind the church. He looked in our direction. Funny if he'd had binoculars, he might have seen us! Philo was walking and talking with two or three colleagues. He went back into the church. Then a few hundred yards from the church, he leaped up some boulders, like a goat (as one had to in those parts) before disappearing into someone's house at the top of a slope. "Now," I asked myself, "how long is Mel going to keep us on sentry duty in the hope that Philo might re-emerge?" My body was not designed to sit for long periods of time on a boulder. I was getting sore. I had already put my hat under my buttocks. That didn't help much. "I'm just going to get some leaves," I said. I went and pulled some leaves off a tree. I sat on the leaves, and on my hat. Not sure that was enough help either.

* * *

About five minutes into our ongoing sentry-duty, Mel's phone rang. "It's a call from America," she told me, before answering.

"Hello, this is Mel," she said. She lifted the phone away to turn it onto 'loud volume' mode.

"Hello, my name is Gertrude," said the voice. "You don't know me," the voice added. "Look, Mel, are you alone? I need to talk to you alone. Tell me." Mel glanced at me, no doubt wondering who she should not be with.

"I am alone," she said. The voice speaking to her on the phone sounded to be that of an elderly American woman.

"Who is Gertrude though?" I wondered.

"Look, Mel, I've got to warn you," the old lady said. "You are about to be seduced. Perhaps you have been already. That is, by a group of young people on a mission trip. They will ask you to do some reporting for them. They want to take you away from Philo."

"How does this old lady know all this?" I asked myself. She wasn't any old cold-caller! I sensed Mel becoming tense, her body stiffened, especially when Gertrude mentioned Philo's name. "Does Gertrude know I'm interested in Philo?" I guess Mel was asking herself. That would have been a serious case of 'cat-out-of-the-bag' for Mel.

"Don't do what they say. They will offer you a lot of money to report on their projects. Look out – the money has been put up by people who don't like what you are doing. Even more – they don't like what Philo is doing."

"I hear you," said Mel, obviously stricken and shocked that someone else could know so much of what was going on around her.

"Look out. Professor Nancy is all fired up," Gertrude went on.

"Did Mel even know who Professor Nancy was?" I asked myself.

"They have had a meeting. They have decided that there is too much at stake. They want to use you to their own ends. Look, Mel, what I want you to do is to stand with Philo no matter what. I think Philo has something important to say. His audacity is unnerving people. They are kicking back at him. But – his love for the African people represents a truly godly orientation. Can you stand with Philo?"

"What a question to ask Mel!" I thought. "It seems that, after all, Gertrude did not know about Mel's romantic aspirations!"

"I will," said Mel. She asked carefully "But ... can I ask who you are?"

"I am Sam's mom," said the voice.

"Sam?" Mel asked.

"Yes, Sam, the close colleague to Professor Nancy," she explained.

"Oh, okay, don't worry!" said Mel, not knowing what else to say. At that point, Gertrude put her phone down.

Mel looked at me. There was puzzlement all over her face. She quickly remembered Philo. She raised the binoculars to her eyes and looked again across the valley. The roar of vehicles in the valley seemed to be getting louder. It was rush hour, and people were rushing home from work.

Eagles could be seen hovering over the hills. More distantly, some marabou storks. It seemed that Philo was still in that house. Then, at that very moment, Philo called through to me!

"Dave, how are you doing?"

"Fine."

"You wouldn't believe where I am now," Philo told me.

I looked at Mel with her binoculars! This was too funny to resist: "Haven't got a clue where you are," I said. I guess that wasn't exactly true. I was about to find out whether Philo was apt to tell lies over the phone!

"I am in a little house up a steep slope on a mountainside in Entio," he said.

"Wow," I responded.

"We are here watching a program on BBC," he added.

"Hmm. The world is a funny place these days," I thought. "BBC!" "What are you watching?" I asked.

"The Queen," said Philo. "How is Mel?" he asked, adding "Are you all well?"

"Yes indeed," I said, "we are all well."

"You know I've had a thought," Philo said. "In a few days, I'll be in Kosompa. I plan to stay with some Germans. Why don't you join us? I know it's a long way. But – if you could, that would be great. I should be there for three nights. Let me know if you can all make it, Monday to Thursday. It should be fun."

"Will let you know," I said.

"Greetings to the others," he added.

"There he is standing outside of that house," Mel said, at that point, in a hushed voice. We laughed.

Philo cut the phone.

"What's up with Gertrude?" Mel asked when we'd finished our conversation with Philo. "Who is she, and who is Sam?"

That was all a bit of a long story. In the hour we had left before we had to descend so as not to be caught out by darkness, I explained what I knew.

I told her about our prior meeting at Western University in Seattle, and all that. What I could not explain was how Sam's mom had got in on the act. Rolly would value hearing about these developments, I thought.

"Perhaps Rolly knows Gertrude?" I suggested to Mel.

"Let's ask him," she responded. In the meantime, we had got a few more sightings of Philo in and out of the little house, halfway up the hill. Then it was time to go back to our hotel.

We had not brought the vehicle with us. Had we, parking would have been difficult. We went back in a public minibus. While we were on that bus, Mel's phone rang again. I couldn't hear much that was said because of the ambient noise. It was evidently a man who had called her. She seemed to agree with whatever he was saying! (I don't suppose many people had her Holima number.) She called off. She did not explain that phone call to me. I could only guess that it was related to her making a mysterious disappearance the following day.

CHAPTER 35: OUT WITH THE GIRLS

That evening, Mel took the time to tell me of the adventures she had the night she preceded us on her trip to Entio. Here is her account:

"I went to the bus station and waited. I can't say I waited peacefully though," Mel confided in me. "Children were coming to me, pointing at me, shouting *Mzungu* – that means white-man – yes?" I told her that it does, although not exactly. We were sat in the reception area of the hotel. That means, that as we sat, various people walked past. It wasn't a planned location for our discussion. It is where we were, and conversation happened.

"Then some young men came along. They chased away the children. Then they sat with me, three of them. Let's say they were a bit intimidating. They each in turn offered to marry me. Not that they knew English. But they knew some keywords, like 'marry me' or 'me marry you' and 'give me money' and 'I go with you'! I couldn't get rid of those lads!" Mel used her eyes to communicate the agitation she had felt at the time. "Eventually, an hour later than anticipated, the two girls, Adhis and Adongo, came along. They weren't alone though. I thought we were going for a ladies' night out. They each came with a 'brother.' That's how they described their companions, a 'brother.' Was I glad to see them though! When they turned up, at least the three men who had been troubling me left me alone."

As Mel spoke, my attention was caught by some ants on the floor. Initially, there were just three of them, carrying what seemed to be a particularly fat fly, in one direction, towards the reception.

"I had been looking forward to chatting for the four hours we were to be sitting on the bus. Actually, it only took three and a half hours. They say it used to take four hours or more before the road was tarmacked. That did not happen. They each sat with their brother, with whom they talked, and amongst the four of them, but not in English, so how could I possibly join in the conversation? At least the ride was reasonably comfortable. I say 'reasonably' because we were a bit squeezed. The shocks though came when we arrived." Now Mel's eyes had a kind of 'penetrating' look.

"By the time we arrived, it was already latish – 9 or 10 p.m. Of course, it was dark. I was quite intimidated by all that was going on around us. But I didn't want anyone to know that I was frightened. So I acted all confident. I can't believe the places we walked through. Narrow paths, dirty, jumping over puddles (or was it sewers?), often in almost pitch black. Sometimes, we walked through wider spaces, like avenues between rows of houses. There were drunkards on the road. I can quite see why Adhis and Adongo would not have come by themselves. Of course, I was always the center of attention for people we passed who saw us – 'a white, and a woman at that.' When we stopped and chatted with people, I was the potential prize catch. If on other days people might have noticed how beautiful were Adhis and Adongo, they did not seem to that night. That night, my presence seemed to eclipse them completely!"

"Look, Mel. I hope you don't mind my watching these ants' antics as you talk. They started carrying this fly in that direction. Now they are moving in a different direction." Mel didn't seem to be over-impressed by my preoccupation but did not tell me not to follow the drama. Looking at the ants didn't stop me concentrating on what Mel was saying.

"We eventually reached our destination. It was a large hall, with a disco blaring away in it. As we approached the hall, we passed couples sat or laid in each other's arms. There was a stench of alcohol and urine everywhere. The hedges providing some shadows in which couples tried to conceal their activities were the same hedges, it seemed, where men urinated periodically when they emerged from the hall having had too much to drink. In the hall, when we got to glance in, there was, well, chaos. Writhing bodies jigging to the mega music, there was hardly a space to stand in."

"The conversation that I then had with Adongo made me think. Now Adhis and Adongo didn't become a part of that writhing mass of bodies. Whether that is because I was there I do not know, I cannot know. I asked Adongo 'Why have you brought me here?'

'This is where people gather,' she said.

'I thought you were Christians,' I said.

'We all are,' she said, 'unless there is a Muslim here.' She paused, then she said, 'Don't think that for us being Christian is being moral.'

I was very struck by that statement. But I am not sure that I understood it.

'What do you mean?' I asked.

'We become Christians because we need help and we need power,' she said.

'What do you mean?' I said.

We were pretty much shouting at each other to be heard above the crowd. A drunk man with a girl in tow crashed into me. 'Sorry, sorry,' he said in English. Other people were whispering noisily to each other.

'What is a white woman doing here?' I am sure they were saying. I was asking myself the same question. I could have been quietly going to sleep in the Catholic guest house, I thought to myself. Instead, here I was in this hell-house, with two girls who didn't seem to care, miles from anyone who knows me, the center of attention at something that, I thought, approached an orgy.

'Thieves will go to church and pray, and be prayed for, before they go and steal,' Adongo told me. I was surprised that Adhis could hear us given the din, but she added, 'An adulterer also.'

'Believing in Jesus is here about getting power to live by,' Adongo said, 'but it is only one means of power. There are others. It is hard for an African to be exclusively Christian. We also have other means of getting power,' Adongo emphasized.

'You mean sex,' I said. 'Can we go somewhere quieter?' I asked.

Adongo consulted with her companions. They seemed to agree. So we moved on. We walked back the way we had come. Then I don't know where we walked! Paths seemed endless. I guess we walked for about fifteen minutes. At least we got away from the din. We reached a bar and sat down."

As Mel recounted her story, I could see her becoming more relaxed at that point. As a storyteller, Mel told her stories with heaving breasts, eyes full of a quandary, and a shaking head, I noticed.

"We all ordered soft drinks. We were a group of five. The place all-told was pretty crowded. A conversation going on there helped me to understand what Adongo was trying to tell me." Mel moved her hand as if she was lifting a drink to her lips, as a means of helping me identify with the situation she had been in.

"'I drove one of those buses for twenty-four years,' said an older man, loudly enough for us to overhear him. He was talking with three women and a man sitting opposite him. The bus company, called *Verish*, apparently started with him as the driver and only one bus, so he explained. Then some years later there was a fleet of ten buses – carrying the public on a particular route. Then they expanded so that they were covering two routes. Before long the company had twenty-four buses. The question being discussed was the basis for their success in business. It was as if others in the discussion wanted to suggest this and that reason. The older man would not have it. He knew *Verish* better than anyone else, he insisted. He had, after all, been with them for twenty-four years. He would accept no other cause for their success. 'Only God,' he said. (Except he said, only *Mungu*.) Now he was mixing languages a great deal. I was asking Adongo to help me understand what he was saying. Fortunately, he could not see me as I was sitting behind him, or he might have stopped out of deference to a white person and ask me instead if I would agree to be his wife!"

"Now what I found is interesting," Mel told me, "was that no other explanation for the success of that business was permitted. It had to be God."

"Well, that is how it is," I said. "It is like if there is a road accident. No one will look at the blind corner, or even oil on the road that made a vehicle skid, et cetera. Instead, it always has to be 'god.' That is, a god of some sorts."

"A god?" Mel replied.

"Yes. I wish we didn't have the convention in English of having to write 'God' with a capital letter! I mean, bewitchment, a curse, an ancestor, a spirit, a wind, a presence, et cetera."

"Like fate?" she said.

"I guess so," I responded. "Look at those ants!" I had not been paying attention to them latterly as Mel talked. When she paused, I stole another look. A group of about six ants were carrying their carrion up a vertical slope! Who knows where they were going. I am not sure that they did. Mel came and had a look, perhaps through interest, perhaps just to please me.

"Well that does help to explain things," Mel said. "I see that, because of development that the white man brought, the white man's god is considered more powerful. But," Mel added, "that need not have anything to do with morality unless the morality itself is perceived to lead to prosperity."

"That's right," I said. "Hence a thief will go to church to pray before he goes to steal."

Mel went on with her account.

"We sat in that bar talking for a while. Then it was 2 a.m. Adhis suggested that we go home to sleep. I did not object. We set off again walking. We walked for about five minutes; then I heard a voice over a loudspeaker or megaphone or something. We got nearer and nearer. We could hear him more and more clearly.

'What is he saying?' I asked Adhis.

'Do you want to go in?' she asked me.

'Okay ...' I said, a little hesitantly, 'if that is okay, for five minutes.' When we went and sat, heads turned, wondering what a white woman was doing wandering around on their patch. Otherwise, people were too focused on the message being shared to pay much attention. The one speaking turned out to be a preacher. Adhis translated for me:

'The devil does not want us to be saved ... but Jesus died on the cross for us ... those who go to a witch doctor will not receive salvation ... people who follow our ancestors' traditions will not receive salvation ... if you want to be wealthy and successful you should be born again ... my uncle was born again, then his car-sales business boomed ... we've heard today from Clarice ... she was saved, then she found a husband ... my wife was barren, when I received Jesus, she started having children ... my cousin was injured in the army ... he left the army and was saved ... now he earns more money in business than he used to get in the army ... Jesus is the way to money.'

The crowd was not only attentive, but they were punctuating the preacher's words with a frequent and loudly declared 'Amen.' (Someone was translating, but not into English.) I was amazed at how awake the people were – and it was after 2 a.m. It was in town – I imagined they all had jobs. It was Monday night! Then, I also understood more of what Adhis was trying to explain to me. The West has all kinds of processes and mechanisms they use to produce and understand 'success.' African people here wanted none of that! That, to them, did not make sense. To them, it is God who brings success, in whatever you are doing! 'Morality,' then, was what brought money and success.

We did not hang out there for too long. Even my companions were tired. We walked for ten more minutes until we finally got to a house. The house only had one room.

265

'Where can I sleep?' I asked.

'Wait a moment,' I was told.

The ladies started cooking. Half an hour later, we had a meal. Only then did we think about going to bed. The bed was separated from the rest of the small room by a sheet.

'Where do you want to sleep – wall, middle or edge?' Adongo asked me.

'I don't mind,' I said. I didn't know what she was on about!

'Okay, I'll take the wall, you take the middle, Adhis on the edge. You'd better have your head that way. I hope our feet won't disturb you,' she added. As the three of us maneuvered to sleep on the bed, the two men slept on the floor beside the bed.

I had a strong urge to go to the bathroom later in the night. I resisted it! I did not want to have to step over the men – and the bathroom was communal, a pit toilet, about ten yards from our door."

"Well, it is little wonder people don't build capacity to make life more comfortable," I thought to myself on hearing Mel, "if they also calculate success as being from God! There's an irony for a western Christian to deal with – people sometimes seem to have too much faith!" I interrupted Mel at that point. "When people say God, they often mean white people. It is white men who provide the means that enable them to succeed in life, way beyond the capacity of their ancestors," I explained. "Carry on," I said then, encouraging Mel to continue.

"You know Adongo and Adhis made us breakfast in the very room," Mel said. "Then at eleven o'clock, they took me to the bus station. We boarded a bus and alighted at a funeral, and that is where they left me." Mel paused, then added "You know, I had a Philo-style experience. That is, somewhat inadvertently, I made myself vulnerable. As a white person, I was alone amongst Africans. I didn't buy myself any privileges that night. My problem remained, of course, that I couldn't understand what people were saying. But, I would never have had that experience if I had not been such a fool as just to set out with those two girls alone. I had that experience just once. It has taught me so much. Philo, I guess, has those kinds of experiences all the time, and because he knows the language, he understands what is going on. No wonder we have so much to learn from him!"

CHAPTER 36: DARK CLOUDS OVER JOURNALIST

That evening we were sat at the same table as we had twenty-four hours previously. Various members of the short-term mission group came to greet us politely. They expressed appreciation especially for the time that Mel had taken to be with them that day – something they thought could make a make-it-or-break-it difference to their projects. Yet, the tone of things was markedly different from what it had been the day before. The young people were not as lively and animated as they had been. We noticed some gatherings of young folks, speaking in hushed tones!

Mel and I had decided that it would be best to be entirely open to Rolly and to Rose about the day's developments. They already knew about Mel's ventures as a journalist. They did not yet know about our sightings of Philo, or the phone call out of the blue from Gertrude. Neither were as excited as had been Mel over our sightings of Philo. At that moment, though, it struck me in a new way. We, our small group, was really 'no different from anyone else.' Okay – Rolly and I (plus Rose) had long experience in Africa. That was helping us. But, here we were sitting in the same expensive hotel as the short-term team from Australia. We were also on a short-term mission trip. The only thing that set us apart was that we had this tentative link to someone who was doing things in the community. Philo had not 'succumbed' to the pressure to be with us, and the pressure often surely was intense, to be here in the hotel. He was, instead, staying in that little house on the hillside, one white man in a forest of black Holiman people. I realized, subtly in a new way, just how valuable was that link. Hence my appreciation for Mel, as someone who valued Philo and what he was doing, rose, even if her aspiration seemed to be somewhat personal!

Talking about the group of Australians, Mel had a concern: "There is something wrong. The way they tried to drag me into being a journalist for them wasn't right. I am not for sale."

When we mentioned Gertrude, Rolly and Rose came alive. Yes, they did indeed know Gertrude and had known her very well for many years. She was Sam's mom, they said. Of course, we already knew that. What we did not know that Rolly was able to fill us in on, was that Gertrude was also a very close friend, and in a sense confidante, to Professor Nancy.

"Gertrude was a close friend of Professor Nancy's mom," Rolly told us. "Since the death of her mom, Professor Nancy has been spending a lot of time with Gertrude. Gertrude does resemble Professor Nancy's mom a great deal. Some people used to think they were sisters. Even twin sisters."

That made it all the more amazing that Gertrude would break ranks and leak information to us. Her report was accurate; the things she told us would happen had already occurred earlier on the very same day. Gertrude had told Mel to stick with Philo no matter what! Well – those words were undoubtedly music in Mel's ears. Mel now had double justification to embrace, metaphorically speaking, Philo.

In due course, Beatrice came along to us. "Mind if I join you?" she asked.

"No problem. Welcome," I said, as did the rest of our group.

Beatrice began telling us more about the group she was with from Australia. She seemed to be heading for where she wanted some help from us.

"Things are usually more complicated than they first appear," I thought to myself as we were listening to Beatrice talk. After a while, I noticed Mel's eyes glaze over.

A little later, Mel said, "Hey folks."

Beatrice did talk a bit like a non-stop machine gun! Beatrice paused. We turned our eyes to Mel.

"Breakfast, normal time is it?"

Rose suggested 9 a.m.

"Okay," Mel said.

That seemed a good time for breakfast for people on holiday. One couldn't help but feel on holiday when one stayed at a hotel such as this.

"I have a meeting at 7 a.m. If I am late coming back, please don't wait for me," Mel said. "I'm tired and off to bed," she added.

"Good night," we told her.

Mel left, and Beatrice carried on. My mind, though, was troubled. There was something mysterious going on. Mel knew exactly where Philo was. She also knew which bus to catch to get there. Who on earth might she be meeting in that strange town of Entio at 7 a.m. if not Philo? The phone call she had received while we were in the bus came back to mind. "If Mel goes to Philo, she will blow it!" I thought to myself. We knew that as long as we weren't around, Philo did not have to justify his spending time with

African people. He wouldn't seem to be turning his back on his own people. Then African people will know clearly – that he is their responsibility. If they know that Philo's friends are in town, all that will change! I felt I had no choice but, in the morning, to follow Mel.

* * *

By 6.15 a.m. the next morning, I had placed myself strategically between some bushes, alongside the exit to the hotel. I had carried a jacket – early mornings could be a little cool. It was a beautiful spot! Although the roar of traffic was evident, it was background. I had determined to follow Mel to see where she went. I knew the bus to Philo's area. I did not want her to know I doubted her, but should I see her entering that bus, number 41, then I would call her and do my best to dissuade her from making such a rash move. Someone walking towards the gate could not see me in my location. Should she look behind, she'd see me. Well – I would say I was enjoying the cool of the early morning and watching the birds – as indeed I was.

At 6.30 a.m. I heard what sounded like female footsteps. Mel came into view. It was indeed her! So it wasn't just a story! She chatted with the gateman. He opened the gate. I stayed where I was for two minutes. That was excruciating, in case I lost sight of her, but I did not want to follow her too closely. Two minutes exactly after the gateman closed the door on her, I emerged from my bushes. The gateman suspected nothing. I reckoned Mel should have been about 200 meters ahead of me. A relief – there she was. I noticed again – she was smartly dressed. That was suspicious! I followed her, hoping, hoping that she would not turn around and see a white man on her tail! I was careful to avoid the potholes. The road was already busy with traders making their way to their stalls.

"Maybe it is a market day?" I thought. I kept following Mel. At least the bright colors she wore made her easier to see. *"Pole,"* I said, as I almost bumped into a woman carrying a container full of tomatoes on her head. Then Mel turned around! I took my eyes off her, and sauntered on, looking sideways. "So much better if she does not see me, or that would raise suspicions. The last thing I want is for Mel not to trust me." She walked on. I breathed a sigh of relief. Eventually, we got to the buses. I saw Mel talking to people. I stood behind a kiosk. Then I stood as if to buy a newspaper. I was watching out of the corner of my eye. I saw Mel board a bus. It was number 50! What a relief!

Now I felt a bit of a fool. "Let's actually buy a newspaper," I thought, so that if she saw me and asked what I was doing, well, it was clear that I was buying a newspaper, and didn't even know that she was ahead of me. Her number 50 bus pulled away with her in it.

Mel later filled me in. She took that bus as far as *The Grand*. That was a hotel in town that was favored by journalists. She made a beeline for the restaurant that was just opening at seven o'clock. Sat at a window was a smartly dressed white man.

"Good morning, Darren," Mel said to him.

CHAPTER 37: THE BOSS HAS COME

Darren turned. "Ah, Mel, good to see you," he said, standing up. Darren walked up to Mel and gave her a big hug.

Mel said later that she enjoyed that hug, but at the time wished that Philo had done the same thing to her when they first met in Holima.

"Well, good to see you too," Mel said, "and what a surprise."

"We like to keep an eye on our journalists," Darren said, "and give them a supporting hand."

They sat. Since Darren had told her that *The Grand* was the usual journalists' hotel, she was a little intrigued as to just what kind of people she'd find there. She looked around. It was still early. There were two white women at another table. Otherwise, the other people looked pretty much like normal Holiman fare. The tables seemed to Mel to make the place resemble a school dining hall. The restaurant space was round – not a perfect circle, but the walls of the restaurant were curved. Darren sat on the left, from Mel's vantage point walking, alongside the wall, alongside some narrow windows.

"I gather you are having an exciting time," Darren said.

Mel knew nothing of the purpose of his visit. Only that she was to meet him discreetly, so she had no answer to give him there really. She nodded. Darren was her boss from SES in Scotland. He was in a bubbly mood!

"I've been receiving a lot of communication from Professor Nancy," Darren said. "It was all kind of confidential, delicate stuff. It took me a while to realize what was happening."

"Well, what on earth was happening?" Mel thought, recognizing the name, and being increasingly aware of some intricate plotting going on.

"She mistook me for the previous incumbent. Professor Nancy had not realized or had forgotten that her friend, the one-time-director of SES, had moved on. She thought I was he!"

Mel was still very puzzled. Darren noticed that in her eyes.

"The things she was telling are not things you would say to someone you don't know," he said.

"Oh," said Mel.

"At least, I wouldn't. It was about maneuvering for donor funds."

"I see," said Mel.

"Also, about this fellow, Philo. You still on his case?"

"Yes," said Mel.

"Professor Nancy doesn't like him, one bit," Darren said. "The sums of money being bandied around, earmarked for support to Africa, are large," he added. "Let's finish a quick breakfast, then you and I go to meet Philo face-to-face. I am really looking forward to getting to know him." Darren was happy to cover Mel's bill. They ordered some breakfast. "What do you say?" Darren asked.

Mel was quiet for a while. "You want us to see Philo?" Mel asked.

"Yes," said Darren.

"You mean, like, from a distance, through binoculars?"

Now Darren looked puzzled. "Through binoculars?"

"Well, you said you want to see him?"

"You are shadowing him, I believe?" Darren asked.

"Yes," said Mel.

"He is in town?"

"Yes."

"Tell him to come."

"What, here?" Mel exclaimed.

"Hmm," said Darren affirmatively.

"But he doesn't know I'm here," said Mel.

"Well, tell him. I am sure he can find *The Grand* easily enough."

"No, you don't understand, Darren. He doesn't know that I am in town." Mel looked down after she had said that. She had got so used to the idea that they were secretly shadowing Philo, that to her it was no longer a big deal, but to Darren, of course, it was!

"But you said you were following him?" A few beads of sweat emerged on Darren's forehead. He was glaring intently at Mel.

"Yes, using binoculars."

"Look, Mel. What are you on about? If you are following and shadowing Philo, he must know about it?"

"No, he does not," Mel said.

Darren started laughing. "This is the most ridiculous thing I have ever heard. He's not a terrorist, is he? Look, let's go then to where he is. Then we can interview him, and the people he is working with. That way we can find out the truth. Then we can refute Professor Nancy. Then we have a big scoop."

"We can't visit him!" Mel emphasized.

Now Darren was getting angry. "You know where he is?" The few beads of sweat grew!

"Yes," said Mel. "Darren wasn't actually angry," Mel thought. Mel knew that Darren had a lot of time for her. She was also aware of his capabilities. He was exasperated, she thought, but it was the kind of exasperation that could become a smile within a fraction of a second. At least she hoped so.

"Take me there."

"No."

"Why not?" Darren shouted, his face becoming red while spitting saliva. Other folks were looking at them. (By this time, Mel was getting a little alarmed!) More quietly, Darren said, "What is going on?"

Mel took a breath. "Look, listen in Darren." Darren's eyes were incredulity-filled. He forced himself to listen. "You want to know what goes on in Africa? Well, I think Philo does know a lot. But he does so by being vulnerable."

"Vulnerable?" said Darren.

"He moves alone."

"Oh."

"And," Mel added, "he uses local languages and local resources."

"Aha!" Darren said. "That's what is grating with Professor Nancy!"

"Certainly. But now think for a minute. You are a white man, yes?"

"Yes," said Darren. He mopped his brow.

"White men in Africa are renowned for being rich and generous."

"Yes."

"Well, if we go to Philo, and people realize that we are his friends, then Philo's African friends will want to take advantage of the money that we have."

"Okay."

"But don't you see that if Philo introduces the African people he is working with to friends of his who are generous, then he will effectively be a donor to them."

"Oh, I see. We get to know people through Philo. Because our relationship with them has originated because Philo introduced us to them, then that might as well be Philo giving to them. That means that African people around will respond to Philo as a patron, i.e., as a donor – which is exactly what he doesn't want." Darren paused. "So, the only way for Philo to resolve that issue is not to bring other white people into relationship with the people he is ministering to."

Mel paused at that point to let Darren's own words sink into his head!

"That is crazy! That is masochism! That is barmy!" Darren added. At that point, he was tapping the top of his head with the palm of his hand.

"That is folly," said Mel. "Perhaps the kind of folly the Apostle Paul talks about in his first letter to the Corinthian church."

"So then," Darren was trying to get his head around this. "Philo is in town, but you don't go to him. I see."

"Except binoculars."

"Hmm?"

"We can see him through binoculars."

"You are also crazy, Mel," Darren said, "unless you are in love with Philo." (He seemed to say that, Mel thought, as if he was just joking.) "But," added Darren, "all the above doesn't mean that Philo shouldn't know that you are here. He just has to learn to avoid you!"

A picture came to Mel's mind, maybe it was in Darren's mind as well, of Mel and Philo meeting in town, but each was just putting their nose up and pretending that they don't know each other. As Mel contemplated this, she pursed her lips.

"Oh, come on, Darren," Mel said. "People aren't made that way. People relate! Imagine you are a missionary, then your friends come to visit you, but you ignore them!"

"People would think there was something wrong with you," Darren said.

"Yes!" Mel emphasized. "Having one's own people around puts one under a moral obligation to relate to them. To avoid that obligation, they must be not around. Or, they can be around, but Philo must not know!"

"So," Darren added, "you are stalking Philo?"

"Well, yes," said Mel.

"To what avail?"

Now Mel was thinking 'because I love him,' but that wouldn't do. "Because we want to report on what he is doing," said Mel. Then she realized how she could explain that. "So that people, i.e., western people, can know – that is really what he does and how he does it."

Darren was perhaps not so convinced this time around. But all in all, he was well and truly intrigued.

"The problem though, then," Darren said, leaning back in his chair like a business executive, "is us."

"Hmm?" Mel encouraged him to carry on.

"Our generosity, as we call it."

"Hmm!"

Darren was quiet.

"Which, of course, is not actually generosity at all," Mel said.

"How come?" Darren asked.

"Because the money many of us give away is not ours! We get given it by our fellow Westerners. They give to us, as they don't trust the African people. They don't trust them – but then African people don't understand our strange ways with money anyway. The outcome is a big *GAP*. White people wealthy, powerful, *generous*: African people begging, pleading, conniving to get money. A massive racial divide – caused by our so-called generosity!" Mel paused for emphasis, to make sure that Darren got this key point. "Whereas 'real' generosity means giving out of your lack, as Paul said, not giving out of someone else's surplus!"

Darren was starting to see that all this was great fun. "Does Philo know that you are here, but that he doesn't know?" Darren said. Both Darren and Mel laughed!

"Maybe," said Mel. "It doesn't really matter as long as he doesn't know, I mean, as long as it is not known that he knows!"

"So, if Philo's people were to know, and they know that he knows, that would be the problem."

"Look. We are laughing. And this is funny. But it is also terrible. The white man is like a walking curse of money," Mel added.

At that point, Darren said he was keen to join the sport of 'missionary watching.' "Can we go and see Philo, from a distance?" Darren asked.

"Yes, sounds good," said Mel.

"I'll get my keys," said Darren.

"Keys?" Mel answered.

"Car keys."

"No, no, we can't drive. Too conspicuous by far. More to the point though – nowhere safe to leave a vehicle. Leave your car here in *The Grand* car park. We'll take a bus. It's number 41. Before we go, let me tell a friend."

Darren went to pay the bill, as Mel phoned me.

"Dave," she said. "I've met a friend here. We are going to see Philo. I'll bring him to meet you later. He's my boss." Mel put the phone down and went her way.

Meanwhile, at the hotel, I panicked! I guess I shouldn't have. When she said, "we are going to see Philo," I didn't know she meant "see," as per through binoculars! I thought she meant "see," as per go to visit to talk to! I was panicking and panicking! Ten minutes later, I called back. "Mel, look. You are not going to see Philo, surely? You know that would mess up all the plans."

I could hear the noise of a bus, and people in it talking in the background as Mel spoke.

"Oh, poor you, Dave," Mel said. "We want to see if we can see him through the binoculars. That's all." I put the phone down, relieved.

276

Darren laughed all the time as Mel and he climbed the hill that I had climbed the previous day with her. Mel grinned as Darren laughed! Fancy spying on your friend like that. Darren was amazed by the hills around there. The way people squeezed their house onto the slopes was incredible to him; true feats of engineering. As he climbed with Mel, still shaking his head in disbelief, a question came to mind.

"Okay, I am getting this now, about money and resources. But what about language? What is wrong with using English?" Darren asked.

"Tell you in a while," said Mel. They had arrived at the rock, although in the morning, unfortunately, it was not in shade.

"Let's sit here," Mel suggested.

They did. A group of boys was eying them. One came to them. He asked them for some money. Mel declined to give him any. He went back to his friends. He told them, presumably, that the couple sitting on the rock didn't seem to be interested in making handouts.

"See that hill there …" Mel pointed.

Darren eventually located the church. He surveyed the scene with his binoculars.

"Language is money," Mel said at that point.

Darren glanced aside from his binoculars.

"Are you sure he's there?" he asked Mel.

"No," she said, "but we saw him there yesterday."

At that point, Rolly phoned Mel. "Look, Mel," he said. "You are wanted here at the hotel."

"Wanted by whom?" Mel asked.

"The Australians," said Rolly. "You don't have to come right now, but I wanted you to know – we do need you here as soon as possible."

"What do the…" Mel said before she had realized that Rolly had cut her off.

"That was strange," she thought. She went back to the issue with Darren.

"Language," Mel said, "that's a complicated point. Let me just say for now that – language is money. That is, English is an extremely valuable language to have the world over. Use English with people, thus enabling them to get more-like-native English, and you will make others jealous of them. That kind of education, being taught by native English speakers, costs a lot of money. If they don't want to be known for money, native-English speakers should not use English. There are many other reasons too. Perhaps my colleagues will be able to explain to you later."

Darren was listening intently enough as Mel spoke, while scanning the hillside with the binoculars. Then – before Mel had finished talking – he said, "Got them!".

"Where?" said Mel.

"To the right of that tree in front of the church. Under that next tree," Darren said. "There's a man there with white skin, sitting with, and I guess talking with, four African men."

Mel trained her binoculars until she also saw Philo there.

"If that is Philo teaching, then he only has four students," Darren said.

I guess, given his reputation, Darren had expected to find Philo teaching large crowds. Maybe of thousands!

"If you don't have so much money to give out, then you don't get so many students," Mel said honestly.

In due course, Darren and Mel started their way back down the hill. As they descended, the sun was already high in the sky.

"I sure could do with a drink," Darren said.

"We should have carried some water," Mel replied.

In due course, they found a small shop. Someone had established it as an informal business alongside their house. The shop was precariously propped up on top of a large boulder. Getting to it required climbing up some smaller boulders. Fortunately for the shop owners, the rocks were like a set of steps, but rather large steps, more suited to a tall man with long legs than they would be to a short woman.

"Tell you what I could drink," said Darren, "some milk."

"We'll ask," Mel said. She climbed up the boulder steps. "Do you have any milk?" Mel asked. The lad in the shop looked at her blankly. "M-i-l-k," Mel tried to pronounce clearly.

"*Maziwa?*" asked the lad. He was probably about fourteen.

278

"Yes … Eee," said Mel, presuming that was correct.

"*Freshi*?" asked the lad.

"Fresh?" said Mel to Darren.

Darren moved closer, his head cocked, listening. "Would that be safe? No, I'd prefer pasteurized or UHT."

"*Da*, not freshi," said Mel, trying to say *freshi* the way the lad had said it.

The lad gave her a 500ml container of milk. It said *lala* on it. Mel did not know what that meant. She paid and gave the packet to Darren. They carried on walking down. Darren found a pair of mini-scissors in his bag. He was well equipped! He cut the corner of the packet and raised it to his lips.

"Ugghh," he said moments later, as they had begun to walk away. "It's gone off." Indeed it had – it was all lumpy and coagulated.

"Let's go back," said Mel.

They walked back up, Darren with her to the mouth of the shop. Now, how to explain. "Milk gone off," said Mel pointing at the container. She dribbled some milk onto the floor to make her point. The boy went. Moments later his mother came.

"We wanted milk, it has gone off," Mel said.

Mom was a bit better at English. She took the packet and pointed to it. "It says *lala*," she said. "You want *freshi*."

"We don't want *freshi*," said Mel, "we want UHT." She thought she might as well spell it out! A light seemed to go on in the woman's head. "People around here don't seem to understand milk," Mel said to Darren.

The lady came with a packet. On it was written *freshi*. "So fresh milk is put in packets," Mel thought to herself. The lady pointed to where on the packet it was written 'UHT.' There it was! "*Freshi* means UHT," Mel said out loud.

Darren drew nearer and had a look. He saw the same combination of words! 'Freshi milk, UHT,' on the same packet! They bought a packet of *freshi* for Darren to drink. Then Mel laughed out loud. "You had asked 'what's wrong with using English,'" Mel said to Darren. "Well, you have another answer – English in Holima might not mean what English means in Scotland!"

CHAPTER 38: ACCUSE THE JOURNALIST

Approaching the hotel, Mel was a bit nervous.

"What on earth do they want to talk to me urgently about?" she asked herself. "Darren, you realize there is some issue brewing here?" Mel asked.

"No," he replied. He had not paid attention to that phone call of Mel's.

Mel braced herself as she entered the door of the hotel. They walked into the restaurant together. There seemed to be nothing untoward going on. In fact, Mel's colleagues, Rolly, Rose and myself, were sitting in the usual place! Mel carefully surveyed the scene, should there be any lurking Australians there who were after her. When she didn't see any, she walked to our table, followed by Darren.

"*Habari za asibuhi*," said Mel. She had picked up some Swahili. She caught us with our heads down! We were reading a document we had just been given.

"Hi, Mel, welcome back," I said, as my colleagues welcomed her with equal enthusiasm. We all stood to greet Darren.

"This is Darren," said Mel. "He is my boss in SES."

"Very glad to see you all," said Darren, shaking hands. We all sat down. "Sorry I did not come here straight away," said Darren. "I took a room at *The Grand*, where journalists generally stay. I wanted to talk to Mel. It was me who asked her to come incognito, early in the morning, to see me. We journalists like to check on the lay of the land before we put our foot in it."

"Very wise," said Rolly. Rolly had, however, a puzzled look on his face. We all introduced ourselves.

"I am the editor-in-chief of SES," Darren said. "I don't often make international trips, but especially wanted to come out to find out how Mel was getting on."

"She's doing very well," we all assured him.

I noticed Rolly still looked as if something was amiss. "What's up, Rolly?" I asked.

"Oh, nothing," he said. Then he said to Darren, "You are directing SES?"

"Yes," Darren responded.

"What about …?"

Darren knew what was coming. His predecessor had been in the job for years and years.

"Recently retired," Darren said.

Rolly looked embarrassed.

"Do you know someone called Professor Nancy?" Rolly asked sheepishly.

"Yes, I've been getting a lot of correspondence from her," said Darren, candidly.

"Spill the beans," I said to Rolly.

"Nothing," he responded.

"Mel has told me a little of what she is doing here. You are all helping her with her investigations, I gather?" Darren said.

"Yes," I replied.

Suddenly Darren looked a bit nervous. He looked at Mel. "Okay to discuss that?" he seemed to say with his eyes. She nodded and raised her eyebrows. "I know that the person you are shadowing doesn't know, or at least, if he does, doesn't make it known that he knows, that you are shadowing him." Darren seemed to have looked forward to saying that line. He laughed as he spoke. "Great, isn't it!" he added. "More seriously, Mel has filled me in on some things. We've just seen Philo this morning." Darren made a motion, like that of someone putting binoculars to his eyes, to illustrate what he meant. We nodded.

"Glad you are keeping an eye on him!" I said.

"It's probably good that you have come …" Rolly said, then, "… as we are also now facing another issue." Rolly told me later, he was processing the fact that it seemed that confidential correspondence from Professor Nancy that was intended for Darren's predecessor might all have gone to Darren. Darren might, therefore, be very well informed on much that was going on. It later became clear that Darren also assumed Rolly to be Professor Nancy's 'plant,' hence he did not trust him.

"What is it?" Darren asked Rolly.

"Mel is being accused of money laundering," Rolly said.

"Money laundering! Mel?" exclaimed Darren, and stroked his head with his hand.

"I am afraid so, and corruption," Rolly added. "Look, we'd promised some of the Australians that we would let them know when you came, Mel. Let me go and inform them. Don't be overly worried, though. They have nothing they can convict you on! It is entirely suspicion only on their part." While that may all have been true, Rolly's words made Darren yet more suspicious of his true colors! Why should he intentionally call people who have accusations to make against Mel?

Rolly walked off. While he had gone in one direction, moments later we heard sounds coming from the opposite direction. Sounds, that is, of people talking in Australian accents! The sounds got nearer and nearer. Then we saw the Australians entering from the front, the same entrance Mel and Darren had used to enter the reception area to the hotel. They came in in twos and threes. They were aggravated about something, so were debating animatedly amongst themselves. As they filtered in, one of them noticed Mel and pointed at her.

"There she is," he shouted to his colleagues.

They made a beeline for us. Others also spotted Mel and came in the same direction. All of us men instinctively stood up and moved between Mel and her accusers. They kept on coming, till there were about twenty of them, young men and women, standing in front of us, as we kept Mel behind us. Darren was perhaps the most alarmed, having little idea of what had led to this, but feeling duty-bound to protect his journalist.

"What's going on?" he said in a loud voice that made it utterly clear he was not joking.

"Calm down, folks," said a female voice. It was Beatrice. "Look, let's sit down and do this properly."

Fortunately, there were no other customers in the restaurant right then who we might have upset. The group of twenty or so sat in the various chairs.

"Mel," Beatrice said, "my colleagues have questions for you. But I am not sure that this is the right time or place."

It seemed to Darren they wanted a press conference. They certainly were intent on making a scandal. Mel was alarmed. Not enough to prevent her from speaking up, though.

"This seems a good time," she said. "But I'm not sure we ought to have a gathering like this in this restaurant that could put off other customers. I propose we sit under those trees."

"Good of Mel to be cooperative," I thought. The gathered throng followed her recommendation. Before long, we sat out on the grass in the shade of trees. Rolly, Rose, Mel, Darren, then myself, sat in a line. The Australian young people sat on the grass in front of us. We were looking over the hotel. Behind us were bushes and low trees. Behind those was the wall that surrounded the whole compound.

Beatrice stood. "I am going to chair this meeting," she declared. The Australians respected her, so had no objection to that. Some of them were fidgeting. "Ran," Beatrice said, "please fill us in regarding the problem you have."

I looked at Mel. She was pensive, wondering no doubt what on earth she had let herself in for. I guess, wondering whether she would have to defend Philo from something.

Ran stood up and began to speak. "We are sorry Mel if we have somehow frightened you. Allow me to tell you what has upset my colleagues. It was indeed on our request that you came yesterday, and we drove you to various locations here in the city of Entio. We encouraged you to take photographs and ask questions of people. We even offered you £5,000 for you to produce write-ups in the form of reports on the various projects you had seen. We had thought that would be a good idea, to help us to raise more money for the victims of poverty we were seeking to help." Ran paused, in case there should be a counter-narrative. But his Australian colleagues seemed happy enough with what he had said. "Following the service that you did for us," Ran said, "we went, that is about ten of us, to visit a certain church. We were there specifically to *listen* to Holiman people. You know, how short-termers are encouraged to be listeners." Mel nodded. "Well, this man was there. You might describe him as an agitator. I don't know. But he raised questions that none of us had thought about, and those questions indicted you." Mel said nothing. "He told us that endless projects that we foreigners were running on their behalf were not on their behalf at all. He said that they were meant for us, I mean like us Australians, to make money. He explained that if you tell African people, his fellow Africans, that there is money coming, then they will agree with whatever the white person proposes. Therefore, according to him, foreigners who come around on short visits evaluating projects by taking pictures and talking to people are con men. Of course, they will be told what they want to hear. The objective is to keep money flowing, but most of the money does not help the people at all. Instead, what happens is that it only helps the wealthy in Holima, and especially the people running the projects in the West. Therefore, to him, foreign-funded projects are a means to exploiting the people. Now I think you will understand why members of our group thought of you – because you agreed yesterday to receive a lot of money to do just the kind of deceptive evaluations that we were later warned about."

I think such accusations were the last thing Mel expected to happen to her on this trip! She was at this point white as a sheet.

Darren motioned to Beatrice. She nodded. "Thank you …" (Darren had forgotten Ran's name).

"Ran," Ran said.

"… Ran, for explaining what you have. You have presented a clear argument. You can also see that Mel is quite upset." (Although he said that, I guess for effect, the truth is that Mel was coping well with her position, and had regained her posture.) "I would like to ask Beatrice to allow a twenty-minute recess. Remember your accusations have come entirely out of the blue to Mel, and you have conceded that you were the ones who asked her to do what she did. If Beatrice agrees, we will break for twenty minutes. People can get a drink, then we will come back together and either Mel can speak, or we can speak on her behalf. Oh, apologies, I have not said who I am. I am Mel's boss, and it was me that asked that she take up this assignment. My name is Darren, I am the editor-in-chief of SES."

Beatrice agreed to Darren's proposal, giving us time to pause and gather our thoughts. We formed a huddle.

"Look, chaps," Darren said, "I think this is Professor Nancy's doing. What do you say, Rolly?" Darren was looking accusingly at Rolly. I could only guess that Darren considered us unaware of Rolly's 'double agent' status. It seemed right to let Rolly speak for himself.

"You are right," Rolly said. "I think this was Professor Nancy's doing. She knows the leader to this group, I mean the one in Australia, not here. She put up £5,000 in the hope that such a financial incentive would draw Mel away from her interest in Philo into conventional project evaluation. I do not think that Professor Nancy had any idea that this outcome would arise from the group's engagement with a Holiman 'agitator.'"

Darren was satisfied with that response, at least for now. "Did you approve that contract?" Darren asked Mel.

Now, I think Mel had seen things quite differently. She had just wanted to be helpful! "I agreed, I took photos, I talked to people, I was planning to write-up. I was not doing it for the money, but the money, £5,000, was mentioned. I thought that if they were to pay me, that would be useful, but I did not do it for the money."

"Did you sign a contract?" Darren asked.

"Of course not," said Mel. "I would have consulted you first."

"I think it is fortuitous that I am here," said Darren. "I propose that I speak on behalf of Mel. If she did not sign, it is unlikely that anyone can make a case against her hold water. Our newspaper does have insurance for this kind of eventuality. I do agree with Ran and his colleagues, and even with the Holiman 'agitator' who spoke to them, that journalists and others should be careful before taking on evaluative projects in international contexts that they do not understand, to which they have not been officially assigned, especially when there is money involved." Then he added, "I suggest that Rolly have a word with Professor Nancy."

"I've been fired," said Rolly, but I am not sure if Darren heard him.

In due course, the Australians were gathered again in front of us. Beatrice opened by saying that only ten minutes were available because a bus was waiting to take the group on a visit. Darren stood. He apologized on behalf of Mel. He thanked the group for their astuteness. He said Mel had agreed to destroy the photos she had taken. She would not write-up, and she would not accept any payment. He explained Mel's attitude and reminded them that she had not signed or accepted money at any time.

Mel stood. "That is so," she said. Mel was battling back tears.

Ran stood and asked his group if there was anyone dissatisfied with Darren's response on behalf of Mel. No one spoke. Ran sat down. Beatrice prayed, then dismissed the meeting. There was a buzz of conversation amongst the Australians as they stood up, brushing grass from their clothes. The tone of the discussion indicated, it seemed to me, that they were content with the proceedings they had just been a part of and witnessed. They were just beginning to realize that they had been forced into a dirty game.

CHAPTER 39: THE GRAND

"I agree with you, Rolly. We ought to take advantage of Darren's presence. We also need to explain your status to him. At the moment, he thinks that you are still with Professor Nancy," I said to Rolly moments later. We were still standing out in the grass.

"I know," said Rolly, grimacing.

"We should also invite him to join us in Kosompa, at which point he will be able to meet Philo face-to-face."

Rolly and I walked straight up to Darren and addressed him. "Darren, you came at the right moment. And I think you handled that issue wonderfully. We don't know what we would have done without you."

"No, indeed," Darren responded dryly, eying Rolly!

"You know Rolly was fired?" I asked Darren.

"No! Tell me," he said.

"A few days ago," Rolly said.

"Why?" Darren asked.

"Intransigence," Rolly said.

"After all those years!" Darren exclaimed.

Darren seemed to have done his homework. I thought that he probably knew much more about Rolly than we did.

"Well, I guess I can say that is good to hear," said Darren, "at least in terms of the current company."

"Look, Darren. We are glad that you are here. We are wondering now – whether you can help us?"

"What do you have in mind?" Darren replied.

"Can we sit down and discuss. I don't know your plans for this afternoon? I think we are all pretty worn out right now, probably you more than we. I propose that we convene a meeting for three o'clock."

"Mel!" Darren called. Mel came over. "I am really here to engage with you. I do have some time free today. Would you want us to meet together – with Rolly, Dave, and Rose? They propose three o'clock. Let you and I sit for thirty minutes now. Then I will go back to *The Grand*. But by 3 p.m. I hope to be back here."

"Also," I said, "in a few days, we may be able to meet Philo face-to-face."

"Oh!" Darren interjected.

"Yes, in Kosompa."

"Well now, I should be in South Africa for three days. After that, will it work?"

"Should do," I thought.

"Let's talk some more this afternoon," Darren said.

Rolly and I withdrew. I put my thumb up! Rolly was smiling. I needed to check my email account. Rose had told us she had a headache, so had gone to bed. Rolly wanted to attend to her.

"Look. We've talked a lot. See you at three o'clock." I said.

"Where?"

"Here, I guess."

"Will do! Bye for now."

* * *

At 3 p.m. there was no sign of either Darren or Mel. Five minutes later, Mel showed up, puffing a little.

"Sorry, chaps," she said. "Darren can't make it. But he can talk to us."

"How come …?" I said.

I was obviously too old! Mel propped her phone onto the table. There was Darren!

"Sorry I can't make it. Don't really have long enough. I can give you up to half an hour now, though," he said.

"Can you see us?" I asked.

Mel put another device into the middle of the table.

"I can now," he said.

"I'm not sure we have an agenda as such," I said, "but we thought your head together with ours might help us to crack a nut."

"What's the nut?" Darren asked.

"Well, here's the nut for you. Here we are, bouncing around with our own people, even though in the heart of Africa. I'm not sure that we are really *meeting Africa*. Then, we have our friend Philo, who *is* engaging closely with African people, even knowing their language and so on. But, *ne'er the twain shall meet!* We look at Philo through binoculars! He acts as if we are in Imbigen. There is a massive rift there. Can you journalists help us to bridge that gap?"

"That is what I am here to do," said Darren, through Mel's phone. "I am tired of relating to African people only through money. It's a good topic for our newspaper. I am also shocked that you end up relating to Philo using binoculars! That all presents us with a big challenge. You're the ones, though, who know Africa better. Give me a clue. What do you suggest?"

Rolly and I looked at each other.

Rose said, "You have got to connect with the heart."

"How?" Mel asked her. No answer.

"There is something I can do for you," Darren said. "Here I am in *The Grand*. This is the journalism mecca of the city. I have time, till tomorrow morning, when I leave early. Are you free this evening?"

We looked at each other. "Yes, of course," I said.

"I have lots of contacts in the media business. Time is short, but journalists are used to jumping at unexpected opportunities. I can also get my office in Scotland to help out. I want to get the word out to all the foreign journalists in town that we are calling a special meeting. It will be in *The Grand* at 7.30 p.m. I will tell them I have some 'experts' coming. That is you guys. As many journalists as possible should be there. We will have till, say, nine o'clock. That is, providing something more exciting doesn't happen in Entio, because then, journalists will run to report on that. If we do this, then I will introduce you. Once I have introduced you, then it is over to you. I will be relying on you to say more than you have just now – when you met my questions with silence. You will need to give those who show up something original. Something that will stimulate them! Something they have never heard of. You might tell them about Philo. You might not. If you do, remember – you cannot tell what a journalist might choose to report on, or what his media outlet might choose to broadcast or publish. If there's not much other news, then Philo might become a front-page item. Use wisdom. Keep your interventions short and to the point. What do you say?"

"Yes," Rolly said.

"Agreed," I added.

"Good," said Mel.

"Heartfelt," said Rose.

"See you here ahead of 7.30 tonight," Darren said. "I hope that is it?" he added.

Silence.

"See you later."

"Bye for now."

He was gone.

* * *

Six journalists had introduced themselves. Two were from the USA – one man and one woman. The others were from Germany, Australia, the UK, and Romania. There was just one woman in the group of six. We were in a meeting room provided by the hotel that was regularly used for press conferences, gatherings between journalists and celebrities, and so forth. We were sat in a row at the front, facing Mel's six fellow journalists. Darren was to our right, and to the left of the journalists. We were on a slightly-raised platform. There was a table in front of us. I had been designated to present what we had to the journalists, after consultation with the others. I will give here only an abbreviated version of what I said on the day. I perhaps ought to add that, unlike at a press conference, these journalists had no evident cameras or microphones. They had little else to do that night, so they decided to respond to Darren's invitation.

I began by talking about God. I am not sure in hindsight that to have done so was necessarily the best approach. I wanted to pin my colors squarely on the mast. As I talked, the man from America walked off. He came back two minutes later, so perhaps his urge had been for a visit to the bathroom! Second, I talked about truth. I think I was there in mainstream-journalism-talk mode. They were used to discussing issues of truth, *ad nauseam* probably. I then went on to issues of culture. How can we report things that pertain to a culture that is foreign to us? At that point, the Romanian, in a thick Romanian accent but comprehensible, said, "No point in reporting what our readers cannot understand." Fourthly, I talked about language and complex issues of translation, and problems associated with the dominance of English. At that point, they all seemed to listen intently. Fifthly, I talked of money, and people's proclivity to pleasing the person who has money, resulting in their being quite disinterested in truth. In other words, that what brings power is what is true.

In the above, I seemed to be in familiar territory for the journalists. I then took a different tack. I explained that we had a friend who had set out to take the indigenous language and culture very seriously. As a result of doing so over many years, he had achieved a singular level of identity with the African people of Holima. "How long?" the American woman asked.

"Over thirty years in all," I said. "My point, or my difficulty, now, however, is how we can helpfully communicate insights that someone like that can get to a western or to a global audience. His insights won't translate into English. Local people are not keen for his insights to be known, whenever they might seem to contradict short-term means of making money. Even associating with him, as foreigners, changes the dynamics he works under. That's in at least two ways. Firstly, it turns people to speaking English, thus resulting in immediate loss of local cultural contextual peculiarities. Second, it turns all relationships back into being paying homage to a patron, i.e., bending whatever other notions of truth they otherwise work from into a presentation of that truth that will bring them the greatest evident short-term reward."

"This is not a press conference," Darren said when I was done. "I would like our six journalists to put their heads together for fifteen minutes first. Then to give us a response to the challenging insights that Dave has given us. I think I can add – please do carefully consider the gravity of these issues."

The six journalists did exactly that. We moved a little out of earshot so that they could prepare the way they wanted to respond in a unified way. After fifteen minutes, Darren even went so far as to reverse our seating positions. The journalists sat on the platform facing us, we sat where they had sat. The group of six had appointed their spokesperson, the Australian. Here is a summary of what he said.

"Thank you very much … and all that. I feel, and my colleagues agree, that we have today been presented with an extremely succinct and penetrating challenge to the art of journalist's reporting, and especially journalistic neutrality. While these issues are not unfamiliar to us as professional journalists, they are rarely presented as succinctly and pointedly. We ask that what we say, i.e., what I am about to say on our behalf, not be cited in relation to our names or our employers. We would prefer to say these things anonymously."

"Amazing!" Rolly whispered to me.

Darren spoke up at that point. "Are we in agreement on that?" he asked.

We, on our side, all nodded. That was as far as the formalities went.

"What you mention is a set of issues that very much trouble us," said the spokesperson of the journalists. "Except, that is, that making certain assumptions has become so much the norm, not just here in Holima, or just in Africa, but everywhere, that it is easy to continue on auto-pilot. In that sense, one can forget and no longer be troubled by the immorality involved in always using the same paradigm to present everything that goes on. We are anesthetized to the pain of it all. *That is grossly immoral.*"

I elbowed Rolly and shook my head when the Australian said that!

"We are required, by journalistic convention if you like, to Europeanize everyone around the world. We are also required to assume that whatever translation into English is chosen, is the legitimate one. We are required, that is, for pragmatic purposes, in all but the rarest of cases, to ignore intricacies of translation. We are also required to ignore any differences between people that might seem could be of racial origin. It is the most ridiculous thing, but we are required to expect, say, African people to behave like Americans, whether they do so or not, and that continues to be a requirement no matter for how long or how consistently they differ from that norm. You will imagine that such reporting, in turn, makes an absolute mockery of efforts by scholars and others to build on what we report to try to make sense of life in Africa. Speaking personally – I have lost all real faith in secularism. It is secularism that we have come to worship. Secularism is a de-divinized interpretation of Christianity. But, we as journalists are required to assume secularism to be God-ordained and set in stone, for eternity, forever and ever. Amen!"

After our time was over, we dispersed, and I thought of asking the Australian, who agreed to identify himself as Les, a question. I asked him why all the journalists who came along to our gathering were whites, why not Africans? He explained that African journalists tended not to stay in

The Grand. Les showed us a picture of his family. He had just one week left, and he'd be going back to them, he told me. His wife was blonde. He had a girl and a boy, aged around six and eight. He must have been missing his family. Then Les suggested, "Well, why don't you come with me?" The way he presented us with that invitation was strange. He didn't tell us where he was inviting us. He just said, "come with me." He obviously didn't mean for two minutes.

Rolly looked at me, then at his watch. "I'm ready for bed," he said. He and Rose set off for bed, leaving Mel and me to go with Les, or otherwise. There didn't seem to be an 'otherwise.'

Moments later we were outside and walking down the street, not knowing where we were going, but following him anyway. The streets around *The Grand* were well lit. By that time, after 9 p.m., there was little traffic. There were groups of men sitting around and walking around. I was struck – that some beggars were still plying their craft. We walked alongside Les. We had to be careful – walking the streets of Entio, or any African town it seemed, pedestrians were required to be vigilant. At any time, one might meet an open drain, a sudden step, a missing pavestone. Should an unsuspecting pedestrian stumble and twist their ankle, there'd be no compensation and no suing of anybody, just the pedestrian lying in the hospital looking for money to pay their bill. Walking three-abreast at night, therefore, was hazardous. We did it.

I did say to Mel, "Look out where you put your feet." She nodded.

"Great message you brought for us tonight," Les said. He didn't elaborate. We'd been walking for about five minutes. "I don't usually take other people to this place," Les added. "Somehow, I figured you would cope, and appreciate it."

We kept on walking. Not for long. Then we went through a doorway on our left. Above the door, in faint letters, was written 'Cinema.'

"Was Les taking us to see a movie?" I asked myself, although I had guessed that it wasn't that. We had come to what was once a cinema. It was crowded. The people crowding it, though, weren't watching a movie. They were singing! Loudly, noisily, heartily. Les was evidently no stranger there. He was welcomed, and then we were shown some seats. Les started singing along enthusiastically, even though I could tell he really did not know the words. He put his soul into it. This was one of Entio's Pentecostal churches, having rented the cinema, or maybe bought it, for use as a church. They had regular all-night gatherings there (sometimes that meant till about midnight). I couldn't see another white face in the whole place.

"I've never believed in God," Les told me, "but, I sure do like to come and join these folks in praising him." We sat for a few minutes as someone on the platform spoke. We stood and sang again.

"There is hope for people stuck in the secularist deception," I thought to myself.

After we had stood for a while, singing, I heard a beeping sound. Someone had not turned their phone off. Les reached into his pocket. It was his phone! He read the screen. "I've been called," he said, then added between lines of the song; "an incident. Journalists to go. We leave?"

I didn't intend to stay there without Les. We followed him out. "We need to be quick," he said. "Why don't you come with me?"

We fairly ran back to *The Grand*.

"Shall we go with him?" I asked Mel.

"Yes," she said. "Where?"

Les overheard and explained, "Report of a collapsed building, fifteen-minutes' drive from here. Journalists to go. Scores trapped."

Back at *The Grand*, the minibus was already half full. We dived in with Les.

"That's it?" asked the driver, in English for the benefit of the journalists.

No response, so we sped off. Ten minutes later, we arrived at the edge of a growing crowd. Now we had to find out what was going on and what had happened.

"You know some Swahili?" Les asked me.

"Yes, some," I said.

"Mill in the crowd, learn what's going on," he said.

Les was searching for the ideal location for a good picture. He gave me ten minutes to meet back there again. Mel went with Les. Trying to press through the crowd to get a good vantage point for a picture was no mean task. I was surprised Mel chased Les like that. Then I thought, "She had little choice unless she wanted to be left alone." I was surprised once again, at my brief moment of jealousy. Something was wrong with me! I mixed in the crowd. I tried to overhear what people were saying.

"Fifty dead," someone said. "The building belonged to the governor," someone else said, from what I could understand with my limited Swahili. "Thirty dead," said someone else.

"Ilianguka saa ngapi?" (when did it fall?) I asked a woman wearing glasses and a red dress. "9.10 p.m." I was told. Eventually, I got back to Les.

"What have you got?" he asked.

"Suspected between thirty and fifty people dead. The building that collapsed belonged to the governor, and it collapsed at 9.10 p.m." I said.

We got back to *The Grand*. Les had despatched the account that included a short clip of him standing by the crowd verbalizing a report. In his statement, he had repeated exactly what I had told him!

"Was I your only source of information?" I asked Les, amazed.

"We don't know Swahili or Striden at all, you do," he said.

"Surely people there could tell you in English?" I asked.

"You save a lot of money by getting your own information," Les responded.

"But … how do you know my information was correct?"

"Here, you can pay a lot of money for the wrong information. You noticed that I used words like 'preliminary' and then I said the police had no precise details at this time." Les explained.

I had nothing more to add.

CHAPTER 40: PREACHING ON THE BUS

The following morning it was time for another trip. This time, we anticipated being on the road for eight hours. We left after breakfast, around 8 a.m. We soon hit an unexpected snag. Nearly all the fuel stations were closed, but we had hardly any fuel in the tank. The reason they were closed – presidential decree! The president had given an order. Many fuel-station owners were not paying their tax-dues to the government. The solution – stop people selling fuel until they had paid up. Some businessmen owed the government vast amounts of money. From what we could gather, for miles around, in the whole city, only one or two stations were open. We drove to one – we got to the queue a mile, or at least it seemed so, before the actual station. A quick discussion and we said 'no way!' It could have taken hours of creeping forward in that line to get fuel. That would likely mean we would have to postpone our trip anyway. We parked to consider our dilemma.

As we parked, a man came to our window. Alongside this piece of road was not pavement or even a sidewalk, but sandy dirt. The man was wearing the uniform of a private security company. That seemed to give him credibility – so we thought. We explained our dilemma, which I guess did not surprise him overmuch.

"Look," he said after some thought. "I can get you some fuel, but the price will be higher."

"So why don't other people take advantage of your bargain?" we asked.

"They are Holimans. The government has an alternative scheme for foreigners like yourselves."

"We don't pay till we get the fuel," I said.

The man stood aside and talked on his phone. At that moment another man was walking by, clutching a Bible. "*Bwana asifiwe,*" Mel said to him through her window as he passed.

That was a standard greeting between Christians, literally "the Lord be praised." The man stopped to see who had so greeted him out of the window of the vehicle. He found it was a white woman. Mel was encouraged by seeing someone walk by unashamedly carrying a big Bible. Now, his English was a bit limited, but he was trying out what he knew on Mel. As that conversation was going on, the security man came back. He said he had found a garage that would sell us fuel.

"Let's give it a try," I think we all thought.

I looked around in the vehicle. The others shrugged their shoulders. It seemed to make sense that the government would not want their issue of taxes to interfere with tourism interests. We told the security man to jump in. Before we set out, though, Mel had a suggestion. "I've just been talking to this man," she told us. "He tells me that he preaches in buses. I couldn't believe it. If you preached in a bus in the UK, chances are you'd get things thrown at you, then get kicked off, then prosecuted! He has told me that people in Holima like it if someone preaches to them on a bus. Then I asked him if I can join him. I want to see this happen! He agreed."

"Will you be okay?" Rolly asked.

"He's heading on the route we are to be heading out on to Kiridos," Mel said.

"Be careful," I said.

"I will," said Mel. "All we need to do, though, is communicate by phone. When you've got your fuel, you pick me up wherever I have reached." Mel was very keen, so we agreed.

"You are going with him from here?" I asked.

"Yes," she said.

Mel ran off with this stranger preacher-man! A few minutes later we turned up at a fuel station. There was no one there.

"He is coming," said the security man.

Sure enough, a man appeared at the otherwise deserted station, wearing the kind of clothes you might expect a fuel attendant to be wearing. He waved, and we pulled over to a fuel pump. Well, he had a key and unlocked it. We counted as the dial moved. He gave us sixty liters.

"No receipt, cash only," said the attendant.

He named his price. It was twice the regular price.

"Just pay," said Rolly. I gave him the money.

"Well, that was good," I said as we drove off.

"Let's have a cup of tea first, to give Mel the chance to hear her preacher," Rose suggested.

That seemed a good idea. We stopped at a small restaurant on the edge of town. Just as I was about to turn off the ignition, I thought of something. We had not thought to check that the fuel gauge had shifted. When I looked at the fuel gauge, it had not moved – it still read close to zero! I turned the ignition off and on again. Rose and Rolly were waiting for me.

"Come and take a look at this," I said to Rolly. He leaned forward through the open door of the vehicle. "See the fuel gauge. Still only just above zero," I said. Rolly looked carefully. So it was! "So, how do we know that we received any fuel into our tank when we were at the fuel-station?" I asked. Rose was also peering in. "I am not aware that the fuel gauge doesn't work," I said. "I think we've been conned." Our joy turned to mourning! Rose looked somber.

"No point in going back there now, even if we could find that garage again," Rolly added. "The culprits will have scarpered. The only thing to do … look, let's drive back to the garage that does have fuel. Let's not join the queue. Let's drive up and ask them if there is an alternative to joining the queue. If not, then we book ourselves back in the hotel, then we put our vehicle into the queue and reckon on traveling to Kiridos tomorrow."

That seemed the only reasonable course of action.

"Someone will have to go and fetch Mel back," I said.

"Yes, at least we are in phone contact," said Rolly.

"Providing, that is, that she doesn't get to an obscure location with no network." None of us had thought of that! "Rose, why don't you call her?" I suggested.

She did. "I am told the phone is out of network," said Rose.

"We shouldn't have let her just go like that," Rolly said. Now, with Mel having run off with a strange man, and no fuel despite having paid for it twice over, things were looking difficult!

We approached the fuel-station from the direction in which there was no queue. I parked, and Rolly went up to one of the fuel attendants. He explained our dilemma.

Rolly came back, jumped in and closed the door. Then he said, "Options look bleak. This seems to be the only place in town at which fuel is available. The queue is indeed incredibly long." He said that and paused. Then he added, "And the petrol attendant told me that he'll let us in front of the queue." One of the advantages of being white, I thought with a smirk.

It was one of those situations, in which one feels very torn! Someone had offered to help us – to give us privileged access to a resource that was scarce – because we were Whites. Should we refuse, and insist on queueing like everyone else? That would mean Mel wandering around by herself miles away from us ... Holima was a very donor-dependent country. They were constantly getting resources from the West. This was a small way in which they saw themselves as able to repay, by giving us Westerners fuel without our having joined the queue! I was not about to play the hero, and I was at the wheel. I started the engine and pulled across the road into the petrol station, effectively pulling alongside the queue. The station-attendants indicated that others should make way. We were put in line with just two vehicles in front of us. Moments later, we were at the pump, and our tank was filled.

Some people probably think that 'white privilege' is only what Whites take for themselves. Here, though, it was something that we were handed on a platter by black Africans! Maybe we should have refused it?

This time I checked carefully, and as the tank filled, the fuel gauge responded. This time we were given *real* fuel, and not air for sale by a con man!

* * *

"Mel, how are you doing?" said Rose on the phone.

"I'm fine," we heard a response, though with a lot of noise in the background. There was the unmistakable roar of a bus engine. We could even hear the preacher preaching. Mel was obviously near him. Also, there was the sound of one or two children crying.

"Where are you?" Rose asked.

"Hang on," Mel responded. She was asking some people on the bus. She then told Rose the name.

"They are at Edomi," Rose told us.

"Tell her to alight at the next opportunity. Then she should call us, and tell us the scene where she is at, and of course, she should wait, stood on the side of the road looking out for our vehicle."

Rose relayed that information to Mel. Ten minutes later, Rose tried calling Mel again. No network.

"We're in trouble," said Rolly.

Rose kept trying to call Mel, but consistently to no avail.

"Look, Edomi!" I said. There was a road sign indicating that we had just entered Edomi. "Keep your eyes skinned," I added.

Eventually, there in front of us stood under a tree next to an African man, was a white woman. We pulled up. The preacher-friend seemed happy to have found a colleague for a few hours. He smiled and explained some things, most of which we did not understand. He asked for some money, which we refused. Mel climbed in the back, and we left the preacher smiling at the side of the road as we waved our goodbye to him.

Stopping and starting on the road reminded me of what had happened a few days previously. "You remember when we were stopped on our way into Entio?" I asked my colleagues.

"Oh yes," said Rose.

"What was that?" Mel asked. Rose explained to her.

"What was all that about then?" I asked.

For a while, no one answered.

"I guess it was about Professor Nancy," Rolly said. We couldn't be sure about that. We left the matter.

"A real shame I couldn't comprehend what the preacher was saying," Mel said. "It would have been much more interesting had I been able to understand! But he was certainly right; people do appreciate being preached to on the bus. Very much so! I mean, I don't know if everyone does. One can't necessarily tell what people are thinking or otherwise from their faces. But most of the people on the bus were attentive. When he said we should pray ('*tuombe*, let's pray, yes Dave?' I nodded), I closed my eyes and bowed my head. Most of the people on the bus did the same."

"Then there was a collection," guessed Rolly. He sounded a bit cynical.

"Yes, there was, and people gave generously," Mel said, lifting her head as she spoke.

"So was it all genuine?" Rolly asked.

"I believe so," Mel responded.

"So why is it," I asked, "that in the UK people would be horrified that someone might preach in a bus or train, but in Holima people love it?" We were all silent for a while.

"I noticed, rightly or wrongly, that our preacher connected with people," Mel said.

"Well, here is my theory," Rolly said. He spoke slowly, apparently thinking through what he was saying as he went. "British people have a concern for truth. They do not like to accept deception."

"You mean Holiman people don't mind being deceived?" Mel asked.

"Not exactly," Rolly said.

"Hear him out," I suggested.

"People in Holima have been very concerned to know about God for many years. Maybe even forever," Rolly went on. "But they have not been able to discern what he is like. If someone tells them what he is like, they are amazed, impressed, and love to listen. British people were also so, but they have been deceived."

"Deceived?" said Mel.

"Yes, deceived."

"By whom?"

"Listen in," I interjected. I was interested in what Rolly was saying.

"British people used to know God overtly. That is to say, British people were very Christian. Now they know God covertly!" Rolly was laughing to himself as he spoke.

"I don't understand," said Mel.

"When, especially in the nineteenth century, British people went exploring the world, they brought back many reports of strange things that they observed. Things about temples, elaborate rituals, beliefs in what appeared to be the supernatural. All that kind of thing."

"And ..." Mel said, encouraging Rolly to carry on, nodding as she spoke.

"The British lost their nerve," Rolly added. Rolly was never one to be sensitive to other's feelings, except when Rose put her foot down.

We had a long drive that day and a delayed beginning to it. I had my foot down. Every so many miles, we would come to a settlement. There'd be a few houses and shops alongside the road. Then for miles, basically, bush – grass, trees, bushes, interspersed cultivated land. Occasionally, there'd be a herdsman with a large herd consisting of a mix of cattle, sheep, and goats. When we approached the settlements, there'd be bumps on the road to slow the traffic down. Sometimes we could go for a mile without meeting ongoing traffic. On other occasions, there was a vehicle coming the other way every few hundred yards. While there were occasional spots with potholes, the road was mostly good – enabling me to maintain a decent average cruising speed for the region, perhaps forty-five miles an hour.

"When I say the British lost their nerve, this is what I mean," Rolly went on to explain. "For a while, the British saw one of their roles as being to spread the good news of Christ to the various people they'd discover around the world. Then, however, some who came across the various strange customs of various strange people doubted! They began to doubt – is there really only one God? Are these people all misguided?"

"Had they read the book of Kings or the book of Chronicles, they would have realized that they were!" I quipped.

Rolly carried on. "Ironically, two things happened in parallel. One, people doubted. Two, people re-interpreted what other people were doing as if they were Christian."

"What do you mean by that?" Mel asked.

"British people were steeped in Christianity," Rolly went on. "They ate, breathed and lived the teachings of the Bible. When they came across other people in other parts of the world doing things differently, they could not help but interpret what they did in Christian ways. They, therefore, as if by default, automatically categorized and classified what everyone else was doing as if it was all Christian. That is, often regardless of the reality on the ground."

"Regardless of reality on the ground?" Mel repeated.

"Yes, that's right," Rolly went on. "A classic instance of that is Buddhism. Western scholars interpreted ancient Buddhist texts as if they were Christian texts. Then they invented the religion of Buddhism as if Buddhists were Christians doing Bible study, but on those Sanskrit documents instead of on the Bible. Hence, they invented, in their mind's eye, what Buddhism ought to be, even though such Buddhism was not actually happening anywhere. That is the Buddhism that, when some Christians heard about it, caused them to doubt. It was not 'Buddhism-as-was,' let's say, but 'Buddhism as invented.'"

I suddenly got where Rolly was going with this. "It led people to believe that all religions are equivalent, as they were interpreted in terms of similarities with Christianisms," I said, and Rolly confirmed that it was what he meant.

"Why was that a 'loss of nerve' on the part of the British?" Mel asked.

"Well, in another way, you could say it was a 'loss of faith': people ceased to believe, at least officially, in the uniqueness of the message of Christ. It was a loss of nerve insofar as it was also a failure to believe in oneself. A Christian who no longer believes in Christ will begin to lose faith in himself, lose confidence, lose nerve – can that on which he has been relying really be as good as he had hoped? Well, yes, but the official answer became 'no.'"

"Okay," said Mel.

"Well, that brought the question – is something else, or someone else, as legitimate as is Christ? While the answer was 'no,' then everyone was happy to have preachers on a bus, let us say. When the answer became 'yes,' however, that raised the question as to whether that preacher-on-the-bus, metaphorically speaking, was trying to mislead people with a pack of lies (i.e., is faith in Christ just one of many equally valuable and true options?). So, if someone stands up in a bus in the UK and preaches, people immediately doubt."

"Well, yes, especially though if that were to happen in a place like, say, Bradford, that has a strong Muslim community," Mel said.

"So, you mean Muslims do not need to know God?" Rolly replied. "Well, yes, but ... Fewer buts here in Holima than in the UK," Rolly emphasized. "I don't suppose we'll be able to conclude this whole debate in one go. There is much that I have not mentioned. For example, some British people have been convinced that causation is entirely physical. It is not. That belief should have died with the discrediting of positivism. But – many people still believe it. If, they reason, causation is material, then how will believing in God help anyone? In Holima, people believe that God can bless people. Thus, God can make a difference. Thus being preached at in a bus, being reminded of God's grace and law, can be a very real encouragement to people, bringing them blessing and prosperity."

"Well, you seem to be right, Rolly," Mel said, "because people here sure seemed to value what the preacher had to say."

"So tell me," Rose asked, "did you stay just in the one bus the whole time?"

"No," Mel replied. "We would board one, at a point at which it was anyway traveling slowly. Then after the preaching was done, the preacher and I would alight at some place at which the bus was traveling slowly or stopped. Then we'd board another bus. So, I was on a total of three buses."

"Did the preacher always give the same message?" Rose asked.

"How was I to know? I didn't know what he was saying." Mel replied.

"Oh yes! I'd forgotten that," Rose responded.

"When we are in Kosompa, you will have to ask Philo about that," Mel said.

"A question from me for you, Mel," I said. Mel leaned forward. "Were there any Muslims on the three buses you boarded?"

"I don't know," Mel answered. Then she added: "Oh yes, there must have been. In fact, I saw some people dressed like Muslims."

"What do you think they thought?"

"I don't know," Mel said. "What do you think?"

"I can tell you," I said. "I am convinced that most Muslims who understand Christianity would rather be Christians, but they are afraid to change."

"Really?"

"Yes. Not all. Especially not men who prefer to have four wives. But most, especially women."

"So, they only stay as Muslims," Mel asked again, "because they fear to change?"

"Yes – and they fear for it to be known that they want to change. It is a very serious crime in so-called Islam for someone to make it known that they want to be a Christian. But it is not a crime to desire something as long as it doesn't show on the outside."

"Wow," Mel said. "That's another reason why it's good to preach on a bus. That gives Muslim people on the bus a chance to hear the gospel without risk of persecution – because they have not gone to church. If one asked them, 'Are you in favor of preaching on a bus?' on the other hand, of course, they would have to say 'no!'"

CHAPTER 41: TWO GREAT MEN

Driving was getting monotonous. Eight hours was a long time for a non-stop drive. "Do you mind driving?" I asked Rolly. He agreed. "According to that sign, there is a place up ahead that has refreshments. Why don't we stop there, and have a bite to eat? Then you can drive from thereon. What do you say in the back?" I asked.

"Good idea," was the response from the back.

We pulled in. This was a place for buses to offload their passengers for them to do all that is necessary. A bus would arrive. Everyone would disembark. Bathroom, food, back on the bus twenty minutes later, and it was off again. We did not have the same rush. We sat around a table with the food we had acquired and started eating.

As we were eating, a group of five men came. They also had their own private vehicle. They sat at a table once-removed from ours. There were four African men and one white man. They were having great fun it seemed – laughing, discussing, joking, generally living it up, I mean – not drunk. They just seemed to be enjoying each other's company.

At that point, Rolly made an extraordinary remark that would lead to much discussion. "See the white man over there," he said, "with those four African men, laughing and all. He is paying them." The remark startled me. I think I also saw my companions eyebrows shift up a notch or two.

"How do you know who might be paying who?" I asked.

"Yes – how on earth do you know that?" Mel asked.

Rose did not ask him that question.

"That was a suspect statement," I said to Rolly.

"I am sorry," said Rolly, "seeing them reminds me of the position I have been in repeatedly. It saddens me."

"Why, Rolly?" Mel asked compassionately. (This time Mel added some honey to her words, and she wasn't even talking to Philo!)

"The cultural and economic gap between Westerners and Africans is not overcome easily," said Rolly. "Now, you may condemn me for saying that. I feel like condemning myself in fact. But – it struck me with such a force that such is happening that I thought I just had to make that comment."

The white man in the group had a large beard and a full crop of black hair on his head. He was of medium height. One wondered whether his wife ever paid any attention to what he had on. That day he wore a thin and worn cardigan. It seems he had a wardrobe full of thin worn-out cardigans, as the color of the ones he wore changed from day to day but they were all threadbare, we discovered over the following days. We were to discover later that his name was Dennis. The names of the black men were Omboko, Siske, Madimbo, and Alphonse. As we talked, they kept on laughing together. I would guess that all of the men were either in their late forties or their fifties.

I thought about that statement of Rolly's. It was indeed a hard one! If one saw black African and white men enjoying each other's company and laughing together, did one have to conclude that the African men had been bought? I had never quite thought about it that way. I also saw some truth in Rolly's words, however. It was very common for white men to relate primarily or even almost exclusively at depth to African people who they had bought. They rarely saw it that way. They were, however, looking for collegiality. They would forget that they were footing the bills, and that the fact that they were doing so could lead to some contrived relationships! Later things might fall apart, but in the meantime, an optimism is produced, that might be false optimism. At a time like that, one wanted to go to the white man and talk to him. To explain to him – that there is a place for relating to people that one has not 'bought'! That is, that there ought to be a place for Whites to relate to African people 'on the level.' Whites don't always have to be the boss, superior, providers of wisdom, and solvers of other people's problems. When such is not on the agenda, white folks tend to lose interest in the relationship – which means that all their relationships come to be of domination! We were still finishing off our tea when the group of five went back to their vehicle and drove off.

"You are suggesting that black people's relating to Whites is usually an outcome of African people's desire for prosperity," I said to Rolly. "But then what about us here?" I went on. "Aren't we also all in it for profit? I mean – a profit of some sort or another. Mel needs us to keep her company and guide her in her journalistic quest. I am a single man – I like to come on a trip to get some company. You ..." I said looking at Rolly, "you are here to kill time before you have to face the music in the USA. (I said that tongue-in-cheek, but I felt there was truth to it.) Businessmen meet because they think they can make more profit by working together. So then – are African people who might be only interested in us in this way different from what we do all the time – using other people for personal gain?"

"Yes, they are different, and yes, there is a difference," said Rolly. "It is a difference that, admittedly, is hard for the secular world to perceive. That is because its content is not secular. Yes, we are all here with our own personal interests at heart. We are also all here because Christ died for us."

"What do you mean by *that*?" Mel said, with the emphasis on *that*, that is, 'what are you on about?'

"The understanding that Christ died for us is very deeply ingrained in us and is very foundational to how we as Westerners relate. That fact has attenuated the sharpness of interpersonal selfishness. That attenuation has not happened everywhere. Notably not in the history of sub-Saharan Africa, that until recently was basically unfamiliar with the gospel. That means that African people are especially inclined to relationship for personal gain."

"Oh, I see," said Mel.

"You could add there," Rose said, "that Westerners have an orientation to the common good that many Africans do not have. They have a kind of universalist ethic, arising from the universality of the gospel that African people do not share."

"Of course," Rolly added, "many western people these days do not openly concede the origins of their peculiar values, or even that they have peculiar values."

"The latter is so hypocritical," I said.

"Why hypocritical?" Mel asked.

"Put a group of, say, a hundred black people together in a forest to live, and you will find them living in strife and poverty. Put a group of a hundred Brits or Americans together in such circumstance, and the chances are much higher that they will soon be prospering. Just look at how America prospers more than Africa, but Africa has many 'natural resources.' These kinds of differences totally fox secularists: their origins tend to remain invisible to them!"

"Even though their outcome is so grossly visible?" Mel asked.

"Yes," I replied. "While secularists are desperately looking for solutions to many issues today, the solutions are there under their noses in the gospel they are rejecting."

Arrival in Kiridos found us all somewhat worn out! We went to a hotel we had found registered on the internet. It was expensive but otherwise seemed satisfactory. We understood that Philo was to be fairly central to the town, hence Mel was satisfied that our location couldn't be too bad. We washed and rested, then at about half-past seven, I took our group (Rose didn't want to come) on a 'drive-past' of Philo's location. There was a small church on the side of the road, and he was staying in a house alongside it. We didn't make a 'sighting,' so, for the time being, just had to accept that he was probably there.

We sat in the dining room for supper at eight o'clock. Hardly had we sat when a very chatty talkative white man made a beeline for us. "Good evening, and welcome to Kiridos," he said.

We told him we had just arrived, to which he responded that he had already been in Kiridos for three days. He was from Ohio, and was called Potrix, but preferred to be called Potter. I am not sure whether there was even one hair left on his head. The other noticeable thing about him, from my point of view, was that his trousers were held up with braces. Potter was a man full of the gospel, we soon discovered. Every other word he said seemed to be 'Jesus.' A close second to 'Jesus' in his vocabulary was 'Holy Spirit,' beside 'saved,' 'healed,' 'born again,' and 'power of God.' Potter was excited. He was making breakthroughs. He had acquired a faithful following, he told us, during his three days in Kiridos. He and 'the brothers' were meeting every morning for breakfast and then engaging in an evangelism program for the rest of the day. When we told him we were in town to look at how missions should be happening, he told us to spend time with him as he had it cracked.

"God is good!"

It was a little ironic how repeatedly during our stay in Kiridos, Potter would disappear, then moments later, Dennis would appear. We are not sure that they even actually met each other! Every time, however, that we saw one or other of them, we got an update. Moments after Potter had left, Dennis came in. He sat at a table alongside us.

"Aren't you the man we saw at the restaurant on the road from Entio?" Rolly asked.

"Is that right?" he said. Dennis was engrossed in reading something.

"Ah, yes," he said. "I recall. Good to see you again. I am Professor Dennis." Dennis introduced himself. So did we in turn. (While Dennis would never normally have introduced himself in informal circles like that as a 'professor,' his Holiman colleagues had advised him to do so in Holima, as it would make his work easier. He was thus practicing overcoming the American tendency not to mention one's title, so as not to appear to be proud.)

"Good to meet again. We saw at the restaurant that you are part of a team," said Rolly. Rolly seemed to be leading Dennis a little by the nose. I guess it worked.

"We are an African team of five," Dennis said. "I am the only non-African." At that moment, his colleagues came in. "This is Professor Omboko, this is Dr. Siske, he is an anthropologist, this is Dr. Madimba, University of Cape Town, and Dr. Alphonse, chair of theology, Africa University in Imbigen," Dennis told us some of the cutting-edge research they were doing on the nature of the Trinity, while his colleagues nodded profusely. "You will appreciate that despite being from vastly different parts of the world, and I being the only Westerner, we relate on the basis of our educational status, which has rendered us as equals."

We nodded.

"I wonder what form your research takes," I asked Dennis.

"We follow the latest findings regarding research methodologies in the West," Dennis explained. "All of my colleagues here are experts on research methods at their respective universities. Look, you said you are who?" I told him. "Dave, if you are interested, why don't you join us for a discussion we are to have tomorrow morning at nine o'clock? I think you could learn a lot."

When Dennis had said that, I thought of a problem. "Won't that spoil things, Dennis?" I asked. "Because then there will be two white men. I mean, didn't you want to make sure that white men were not too many, or it might seem like we are engaging in neo-colonial imposition?" I did say that a little tongue-in-cheek. I knew that it could be stimulating for white people to find themselves alone in a crowd of Africans. Especially when the African people concerned are very compliant with what the white man wants to do. They usually are willing to be compliant because of the enormous prestige of white skin in Africa. Even if a white man himself doesn't have money, they will almost invariably have contacts that lead to money.

"I don't mean that you should join our team," Dennis said. He was hesitating a little. "Only that you are welcome to the session tomorrow at 9 a.m."

"Even though I do not have a PhD, as do your colleagues, and I am not a professor?"

At that point, Professor Omboko spoke up. "You are welcome, Dave," he said.

"I feel very honored to be invited to join such a select group, given my lack of academic credentials," I replied.

It would not be easy from that point for Dennis to deter me from joining him, because he had already opened the door, and his African colleagues may well have been hoping that I would add finance or at least prestige to the group. I don't know if Dennis had realized that his theory was scuppered. He had told me that they were equals because they had comparable-sounding academic credentials. By inviting me to join them, as an equal, however, he was implying that a white man without academic credentials was comparable to an African man *with* academic credentials.

I was aware that, should we meet, there was little risk that Dennis' African colleagues would disagree with him or oppose him. They were people who held the white man's knowledge in awe, and were hoping to use their relationship with Dennis to advantage themselves. What now though of me – as I had little reason not to disagree with Dennis if I wanted to disagree? Not that I intended to disagree. Africans know, however, in my experience, that for something to be truly African, didn't need 'only one white man,' it needed 'zero white man'! Or, just possibly, someone like Philo, who had spent his life consistently proving to people that he was sincere and did not have any spare money. Even for Philo, though, unlikely really!

That made me think – it was probably a good thing that Philo was not with us in that hotel. Had he been, and had he entered into conversation with Dennis. Well! Philo's whole life was designed to overcome the difficulties and traps that Professor Dennis was falling into (or was about to fall into), but Dennis did not even yet know that those traps existed. Had we told him about them, he would most likely have become angry.

As I was still contemplating, Rolly walked into the room, closely followed by Potter. By this time, Dennis and his colleagues had left. (As I said before, this seemed to keep happening – after one of Dennis or Potter had left, then the other came!)

Potter was waxing lyrical: "There must have been 300 people in that building, Rolly. They had me preach. I felt fuller of the Spirit of God than I think I had ever been before. The building seemed to vibrate by His exuberant power! By the time I stood up, the Spirit of Jesus had already moved people's hearts. I don't take all the credit! All I was able to provide was that final anointing. I stood and clutched my Bible as I had never done before. My translator did an excellent job."

At that point, I thought, I don't know if Rolly was thinking the same – how could Potter have known that his translator did an excellent job if he hardly understood a word of either Swahili or Striden?

"People were transfixed," Potter went on, "as if they had never heard the gospel before. I imagined them, all their lives, shaking in fear before a witch doctor trying to kill them, and now here was an offer of life. People were so attentive that I went on and on. Then people started crying! Would you believe it! *My* preaching, and people started crying! First, there was just one man, yes, a man, not a woman!" Potter emphasized. "Then two or three people. Then, not only did they cry, people started shouting. Then a man ran forward and knelt in front of me, begging out loud to be forgiven. At that point, I said, 'Hallelujah.' Then he cried, 'Hallelujah!'"

"Take a seat," I said to Rolly and Potter.

"Thanks," Potter said. He sat down. Oh no! I had noticed that chair didn't seem to be very robust. Potter sat on it so suddenly that the legs of the chair splayed outwards as if they were made of rubber. "Youch!" Potter cried. Momentarily, there on the floor, he was silent. I looked at Rolly. Had he hurt himself badly? Then Potter started laughing. We were relieved.

"Satan!" Potter shouted, lifting himself up. Then he remained standing. He decided not to sit down again. There was a rather sad-looking, collapsed chair there on the floor. Rolly picked it up and propped it against the wall.

"Then ... Look, I'll be alright ... then, more and more people came forward. They poured forwards. While they did that, I was shouting 'thank you, God, thank you, God' over and over again. More people kept coming!" Potter paused. "What I am saying is – that God worked powerfully!" he added.

"That is fantastic," I commented.

"Unbelievable," said Rolly. (I was not sure Rolly said the right thing there. – I don't think what happened was 'unbelievable' at all, because it happens a lot in Africa anyway.)

"Coke?" I asked Potter.

"Orange, fizzy if possible," he responded.

"So how many do you reckon were saved or healed?" Rolly asked.

"Nearly everyone," answered Potter proudly. "My Holiman colleagues were also amazed by the movement of the Spirit. Wait till I tell people back home! The next revival meeting will be at 1 p.m. tomorrow," Potter added. "You really ought to come."

"We should try, Rolly," I said. "Where is it to be?" Potter gave us directions.

"So, should we tell Potter that the way he described the service he preached at is the way it happens every week around here?" I asked Rolly after Potter had gone.

"I don't know," he said.

"Probably not. Probably there is no point. Visitors usually don't want to hear things from other white men. We need to look out for that if we go with Dennis tomorrow," I suggested.

"You're right," Rolly said, "but it is sad. Why do white men become big egoists when they come to Africa? Well, there you are – I am not sure everyone will appreciate what I have just said! I mean – they don't. But they do. The amount of respect our African brothers and sisters give them can be more than they can cope with."

"Us included," I added. That comment gave me pause for thought. I was sure I was as guilty as the next man. Africa easily gives us white men an ego trip. "We are here like kings of the castle, driving our big vehicles. It is as if Africa is a show put on for us. Saying that, where is Rose?"

"She's in her room reading," said Rolly.

"What about Mel?" Rolly didn't respond.

"Don't know," he said in due course.

Neither of us seemed to have seen her for a while. "Where was she?" we asked ourselves. "We'd better look ..."

We walked around. "Mel! Mel!"

Then Mel appeared from a corner of the courtyard, phone to her ear. "Yes?" she said. It seems she was spending a very long time talking to someone on the phone.

"Who might that be?" I asked myself.

Mel herself didn't tell.

* * *

The next morning at 9 a.m., Rolly and I did indeed join Dennis for his meeting. It was in one of the rooms of the hotel. Obviously a conference room, with chairs and desks. Dr. Omboko was to give us an exposition of the nature of the Trinity in an African context. He told us ways in which the doctrine of the Trinity had been differently interpreted, starting in the second century. He went into even more detail for the Reformation. Then he outlined some of the discussion that went on in the post-war years. Finally, he explained how the Methodist church had successfully communicated the Trinity to his tribe.

"Any discussion?" asked Dennis, when Dr. Omboko was done. I wondered – had Dennis hoped to have more people in the room? Twenty people could easily have fitted into the place. There were additional chairs up against one wall. Outside, we could see the car park, with various hotel visitors' 4x4s parked in rows.

I wrote a note on a piece of paper. "It seems all that came from Lewis," I wrote. I passed the note to Rolly. Lewis is an American author of a book on the Holy Spirit. "Yes," he wrote under my note. "Will you say anything?" Rolly glanced in my direction. He passed the note back to me. I read it. Then I wrote "No," adding "Did he talk about the Trinity in his tribe?" "No," was the response from Rolly.

After discussion and a short break, it was Dr. Siske's turn. He was from South Africa. Rolly and I were skeptical as he, without giving any credit to the author at all, recalled chunks of the chapter of a book on Christian theology, known to both myself and Rolly, that was on the Trinity. All he really said about the context of the Trinity in his own tribe is that they did not have a term for Trinity, so instead, they used the English term. (Unfortunately, the word they have that could be used for Trinity in their language sounds like their word for fire. Hence Siske's people were often confused between the Godhead and fire for cooking.)

After those technical discussions, for which Dennis took copious notes, the discussion moved on. I can only imagine, surely Dennis realized that his colleagues were merely re-telling things written by white scholars? This was not African scholars contextualizing the gospel into their own communities as Dennis had told us would be happening. It was more like plagiarism. I do not to this day know the answer to that question, though did Dennis know? I did not dare to confront Dennis about it. The rest of the discussion centered on the mutual responsibility of Dennis as against the African professors. I must add that Rolly and I said very little throughout, and certainly were careful not in any way to undermine Dennis' authority.

The time came for Rolly and myself to analyze proceedings, in Dennis' absence, over a cup of tea.

"Did Dennis know they were borrowing things from white scholars? Surely he did?" I said.

"He must have!"

"So why say nothing?" I asked.

"Non-question," said Rolly. Rolly crossed his legs. That was usually a bit of a feat for Rolly, given his 'shape.'

I nodded. In short: Dennis did not have the guts, or whatever it was it might have taken, to shame the African scholars.

"Why do Westerners always seem to expect African people to do what is impossible?" I asked. "The measure is always us Westerners! If ever they fall 'below' our standard, we are too scared to tell them, never mind too afraid to ask ourselves why."

"Why?" Rolly asked, although he knew the answer.

"Because someone who does can wrongly be accused of being racist."

I knew he also knew that answer. Racism is clearly a very sensitive issue. Both of us were aware that it is very bad to be racist in the West, treating people differently according to their color. I think Rolly also understood that was on the basis that Whites are the norm. Within the West, that works. But now, what to do in Africa? Does one have to treat Africans as if they are Westerners? That seemed to be a strategy, or if not a 'strategy,' then nevertheless a process, that would guarantee western domination over the whole continent of Africa!

"We Whites are always the standard. If Africans fall short, we are afraid to tell them. We think they should imbibe our particular history through osmosis, through the air or something! We not only expect them to be transformed into us as a result of a few years in school. We demand it! This is so crazy because it ignores the long, complex, historical process that brought us to where we are."

"And the impact of the gospel on that history!" Rolly added.

"So," I added, "Dennis is forced to tell lies to conceal the weaknesses of his African colleagues, while what he expects of them would require superhuman, i.e., supernatural, feats of intelligence. Why is no one prepared to accept that maybe African people really are different from us, and that is okay?"

We left my question hanging for a moment. Both of us knew that for many African people, it did not make sense to condemn plagiarism, which they understood as 'helping each other.'

"So what do you reckon of the way they have divided up responsibilities?" Rolly asked me.

"Why ask me rhetorical questions for which you know the answer?" I responded.

Rolly laughed. We both knew that typically in such situations, what the white man says he will do, he does. What the African says he will do he doesn't. But – that's okay – because even if a car works on one cylinder and not on two, it can still shift. Plus – there seems to be plenty of spare capacity in western capitalism to compensate. The thing we need to remember is that the African has responsibilities that the Westerner does not have – like the mandated requirement to attend a lot of funerals. The agenda always seems to come from the white man anyway. If the African doesn't do what he said he'd do, you're not going to label him *lazy*. Such accusations, given the way that the western standard is held high as the global norm, could be considered to be racist. Not that he should be called lazy. That English term doesn't necessarily fit *at all*. Lazy might be a component of the western worldview. But does the implication of that term, whatever it is, necessarily fit Africa? Why should it?

* * *

It was not long till 1 p.m. Rolly and I had a quick lunch in the hotel restaurant. We munched; hardly time to talk. Then, as we set off for the meeting that Potter was holding, Mel also joined us. We decided to try to walk. As we walked, we were impressed by the road system that was being built. What had been just dusty dirt tracks, were in town being transformed into nice tarmac roads. The roads seemed more beautiful than the houses.

"Why do people leave their house so decrepit," Mel asked.

I could see why she asked that question. Not all of them – but a good number of houses – seemed to be in pretty poor condition.

"The less impressive one's house appears, the less the likelihood that one will be bewitched," I said.

"Really?" Mel asked. "You mean people will allow themselves to appear to be poorer than they are to avoid others' jealousy?"

"That's it," I said.

"Does that only apply to their houses?" Mel asked.

"No," Rolly came in. "It can apply to almost anything."

"You mean," said Mel (at that point I wondered how she was going to include this in her feature article), "that when we Westerners respond to people's poverty, like try to lift them out of their poverty, we may be trying to counter an appearance that they have intentionally?"

None of us responded to that comment. How should one have responded after all? We followed the directions that Potter had given us, until we came to a large structure, covered by iron sheets, with metal struts but no walls. There was Potter!

"How-do Potter," Rolly greeted him. Potter was happy to see us, but also a little stressed. It was five minutes short of 1 p.m. The seats were many, the hall was expansive, but, including the three of us, there were only ten people there. We tried to help to calm Potter. Indeed, in some parts of the world, 'meeting at one' might mean that 99% of your congregation are sat by one minute to. In other parts of the world, however, here being a case in point, 1 p.m. might mean 2, 3 or even 4 p.m.

While before then Potter had relied on whatever translation the people could provide, this time he made a special effort, and had put up some money to get a good translator. I guess that was in part because he knew that we were coming. Perhaps he'd have been better off not to do so – as ignorance can be bliss. By 2 p.m., we were about fifty people. By 2.30 p.m., there were about 150, so the meeting began.

"God will bless us," said the translator. "Look at this. Isn't it amazing? Yesterday we had just one white person. Today we have four. That is how God multiplies his blessings. Today we need to trust with great faith, and showers of money will fall on every person here. Let us all pray that today money will fill our bank accounts, our purses, our bags, our pockets. Pray that our children will be wealthy. Give thanks that the white people have come to bless us!"

By that point I think Potter wished that either he had not invited us, or at least that he had not invited that good translator; did he want us to hear that translation? The four of us were sat on the platform in front of the crowd, that I estimate at that point might have been of 300 people (i.e., adults). In front of us, with the two microphones, was the person leading the service and the translator. Although there were perhaps just 300 people within our building (that is, under our roof), loudspeakers were broadcasting the message far and wide.

"If we do what God tells us, we will prosper majorly, not so?" said the translator. As he said that, the speaker looked behind at us. What to do? I wasn't a great proponent of the prosperity gospel. But the speaker was looking for affirmation from us. I nodded, smiling. I think Rolly and Mel did the same. Mel seemed to be looking at me to know what to do.

At that moment, Potter stood up and walked forward. He took the microphone from the leader of the meeting. "Look," he said, "we all need food and shelter, and I don't mind helping out some people who are struggling. But I want to emphasize that the gospel is about suffering. We should be ready to suffer with our Lord."

The congregation started murmuring. They did not know what was going on. There was Potter's hire car – a Land Cruiser, and his driver. They knew that Potter was staying in the most expensive hotel in town. What did all that have to do with suffering? Potter didn't know how to go on. He had said what he felt he had to say. He sat down again.

He turned to us and apologized. He was embarrassed. "It has not been like this before," he said to us in a low voice.

"Well," I thought, "'before,' you didn't bring in a professional translator."

The meeting went on until about 6 p.m. It was, as Potter had told us before, impressive to see so many people respond so enthusiastically to the gospel. Indeed, they came forward in their droves, before any altar-calls were even made. Many cried loudly, and many evil spirits were removed. The tone of the whole event was just marred a little by the revelation we had received, that people were there for the money. And, that we white people sat prominently at the front were expected to provide it.

* * *

We had every intention of walking back to the hotel after the meeting.

"No, you mustn't," Potter insisted. He told his driver to take us back. It seems we could not refuse. We were soon back.

I was looking forward to discussing what had happened that afternoon, so we sat in the lobby of the hotel. No sooner had we sat down, however, when Dennis came in with two of his African professors. I did not know that professors were necessarily noisy people. That day, though, it seems they were!

Dr. Siske was the first to walk into the room, followed by Dennis (Professor Dennis), followed by Dr. (Professor) Omboko. Neither of them noticed our presence. They sat alongside a window, all three facing outside.

"An academic program in Africa needs to be headed up by an African," Dennis was saying, as the three of them walked into the room. They were so noisy that they startled our little discussion into silence.

"We do not want to be an African program, we want to be an American program," said Omboko.

"No way will I get funding for yet another American program in Africa," said Dennis. "Okay. It's not 'no way,' but it could prove much more difficult. Donors want to see Africans taking the initiative."

"You be the boss, you give us the credit for initiatives," said Omboko.

"You must realize, Dr. Dennis, that is how things work around here. You use our pictures, but you be the boss."

"Why must I stay as a boss?" Dennis asked again.

"If you are not the boss, it might get hard to get donors, Dr. Dennis. Remember that donors are white people, and they don't trust us."

"Well then, you should learn to be trusted," said Dennis.

"What, with your way of life?" said Omboko. "Don't you see, we have obligations. Especially to our families. Those obligations must come first."

"What do you say, Siske?" Dennis asked the other African.

Siske had a bigger build and seemed older than his two colleagues. Omboko was not slim. One got the impression, though, that Omboko might have been slim had he not been a professor. Siske was built more like a sportsman, so would have been that way, professor or not professor. Both were very focused on the conversation.

"Siske and Omboko had worked this out in advance," I thought.

"You are telling us, Dr. Dennis," said Siske, "that you will continue searching for funds for us. But – how do we know that you will continue searching for funds, and give them to us?"

"You have my word," said Dennis.

"So, will you continue sending funds even if we do not do everything the way you want us to?" was Siske's next question.

"Now, that was a good question," I thought.

By this time, it was dark outside. After Siske had asked his question, suddenly the power went out. That was not such an unusual event in those parts. We all sat in darkness. Ten seconds later we heard the roar of a diesel engine. The lights came back on. I was aware that people in less expensive hotels, that did not have backup generators, and those in their homes, remained in darkness. I was looking forward to hearing Dennis' answer to that question.

"What was your question again?" Dennis asked. Siske repeated it. I had the impression that Dennis was playing for time!

"You mean you want me to write you a blank cheque," said Dennis. Omboko and Siske were quiet. "Of course, I cannot just keep giving you money if you don't do what I want," Dennis answered.

"At least he is being honest," I thought.

"Don't you see then," Omboko said, "you will want to control us using the purse strings. Well, then you might as well be the boss in the first place. In fact, to make out that you are not the boss would be deceptive."

"Most people don't seem to care two hoots about that kind of deception," I thought to myself. "Good for Omboko for being honest!"

"I will not control using money," said Dennis.

"Then you will drop us when you no longer like us," Siske came back.

"No I won't," said Dennis.

"How do we know that?" Siske said. "You could drop us and blame corruption in Africa. That won't do too much damage to your credibility."

"Once you are no longer the boss, we can't trust you," said Omboko. "If this is going to fail, then we want you to take the blame, not to blame it on corrupt Africans."

I heard Rolly take a deep breath at that point! This was hot stuff!

"But donors want to see African leaders," Dennis said.

"Donors want to see African puppets," Omboko corrected him. "Just look at the education systems in so much of Africa. In English. Why?"

Silence.

"So that donors can control," Omboko answered his own question. "Do you think we use English out of choice?" he added. "Of course, we do now, but we were never really extended a choice in the first place."

At that point, the discussion of the three professors came to a temporary end. Rolly took advantage of that opportunity to cough. Dennis looked at us at that point, then looked rather sheepish and embarrassed!

"Good evening," he said. "I guess you heard our conversation," he added.

"So did Mel, our journalist here," I responded.

"You've been listening?"

"You didn't give us much choice," Rolly responded.

"Ever since we walked in?" Dennis added.

"Yes," said Mel this time.

"Well, what do you think?" Dennis added.

This may have been his way of saving face! I'm not sure he really wanted our opinion.

"You started it, Dennis, you finish it," said Rolly, who had no doubt been in endless such discussions. "In other words, you need to be the boss, Dennis, and not try to get out of the hole by pretending that you are handing over."

"But don't you see," Dennis said to Rolly, "that if everyone followed that advice of yours, then Africa would still be being run by us?"

"If everyone had followed my advice, then Africa would still be run by the white man one can see, instead of the white man one cannot see," Rolly replied.

At that moment Rolly's phone rang. It was a female voice.

"Rolly? This is Professor Nancy," she said.

"Hello, Professor Nancy," Rolly responded.

"Are you free for me to chat with you?"

"Go ahead, Professor Nancy," Rolly responded.

"I understand you will be in Kosompa in a couple of days?"

"Yes," said Rolly. He looked at us. – "Where on earth did Professor Nancy get that information?" his eyes asked us.

"Sam would like to come," said Professor Nancy.

Rolly flinched. "He's welcome," he said.

"We want to talk with Philo, and about Philo …" When Professor Nancy mentioned Philo, it was like a cat sprang up! Without apparently even thinking about what she was doing, Mel grabbed the phone from Rolly.

"Hello, Professor Nancy," she said. "This is Melanie, a journalist with SES." (I had never before heard her refer to herself as Melanie.) "What are Sam's plans concerning Philo in Kosompa? I can tell you that Philo is a wonderful worker for Christ. He knows what he is doing. He is serving God. And he does it according to Solomon's way of wisdom and not your way of serving mammon. You had better not be sending that Sam to do any harm …" She stopped. Professor Nancy had put the phone down.

I think Rolly and I were goggle-eyed at that point. "Who was this, and what was going on?"

"I'm going to bed," said Melanie.

Off she went. Perhaps to make a phone call.

* * *

Rolly and I at that point also left the lobby. We didn't need to overhear any more of Dennis' conversations. We walked outside into the car park, wanting to enjoy something of the cool of the evening. As we did so, or it may have been a minute later, Potter emerged from the hotel.

"Dave, Rolly," he said. "Perfect timing."

We looked at each other. "Perfect timing for what?" we thought.

"You must come. My translator is busy. He won't come. I am going right now to attend to the case of a sick woman. They tell me she is dying. This is very urgent. They want me to pray for her. They tell me that my prayer will make a difference."

"What, now?" I said.

"Yes – if you are willing?"

"Well, we have just ..." I started saying.

"Yes, we'll come," said Rolly. "Sounds interesting," Rolly said to me, as we climbed into the back of Potter's Land Cruiser.

Fortunately, the driver knew where he was going. We had not yet visited what it seems one could aptly call the 'slums' of Kiridos.

"Slums have many corners," I thought to myself.

"Why does Sam want to come to Kosompa?" Rolly asked me.

"Better ask Gertrude," I said.

"Whatever he wants to come to say or do, does he know that Darren from SES will also be there?" Rolly asked.

"Hmm!" I said. "Maybe not."

"That could be interesting, then," Rolly replied.

At that point, the Land Cruiser was ascending what seemed to be a thirty-degree angle. These slums were rough places. The Land Cruiser was larger than most of the houses, or at least so it seemed.

Residents did not seem worried by this monster that was invading their space. The headlights of the cruiser were lighting up otherwise dimly-lit impromptu stalls selling kale, tomatoes, and, in some cases, bananas and oranges. Children were moving around, often chasing the vehicle, presumably shouting, although we could barely hear them over the roar of the air-conditioning.

Suddenly Rolly elbowed me. "Look!" he said. I looked at Rolly's eyes, and then the direction in which he was staring. There was a white man up ahead, walking with two African men. It was Philo!

"Goodness, a white man!" Potter exclaimed at that point. "Don't stop!" he added to the driver. "If a white man is walking around a place like this at night, I am not sure that he can be trusted."

Philo, clutching his Bible, and his companions stood with their backs to a wall to let us pass. Then they ate our dust. It was dark in our cruiser, so we assumed Philo didn't spot us. Even if he had, it would not have made any difference. Potter wasn't in a hurry to stop to greet him. Five minutes or so later, the Land Cruiser ground to a halt. The driver stopped the engine. The lights went out. We were in a residential area in town, but apart from a few smoky flickering lights, it was pitch black. That was eerie.

We left the driver. Potter, his pastor colleague, Rolly and I stepped into a small house. Inside was one flickering smoky light. We sat on a bench against one wall. In front of us was a low table. The other side of the table were plastic chairs, three of them, lined up in a row. A young girl was sitting there. When she'd spoken to the pastor, she disappeared into the back of the house, presumably to get the sick lady, who was presumably her mother.

"Let's be in prayer as we wait," Potter said.

In fact, the pastor started singing some Striden and Swahili songs. We joined in as best we could. A few minutes later the girl came back, supporting a disheveled emaciated figure. She sat her mother on the middle chair, as she sat on her mother's right.

"How anyone can live in a place like this?" Potter whispered to Rolly, with me overhearing.

At a moment like that, one was reminded of one's mortality, and just how transient and decrepit can be human life!

This is where the dilemma kicked in. There was little doubt in my mind what Potter was thinking – "she needs to see a doctor!"

Indeed, Potter asked the pastor, "Has she seen a doctor?"

Potter was unaware, however, of the marshy territory that question immediately flung him into. In some parts of Holima, the English term *doctor* was translated into Striden or Swahili as *daktari*. In other parts, though, it was *Mganga* or *ajuoga*. The pastor heard doctor and chose to translate as *ajuoga*. That is, so to say, "has she seen a traditional healer/witch doctor?"

"Ee," said the daughter. Potter was told, "yes," with which I guess he had to be satisfied, not knowing that the lady had seen a witch doctor, not a biomedical doctor.

Quite likely, I postulated, to see a biomedical doctor could have demonstrated a lack of faith in God – not a road the sick lady most likely would want to follow. Hospitals could also be costly, which raised the question of who was standing with this sick lady in her distress to pay bills? Anyway, as a result of what he heard, Potter was satisfied. If she'd been seen by medical doctors, then he could enter prayer ministry.

"What is the sickness?" Potter asked next. The pastor looked at me. He was having trouble with Potter's accent.

"Vipi ugonjwa?" (which sickness) I asked the girl.

The girl was probably a bit too young to know that you shouldn't mention witchcraft when you are with white people. *"Oire gi nyieke,"* she said.

"A co-wife cast a spell on her," I said to Potter.

"Nonsense," said Potter.

"Should I translate?" I asked.

"Yes, of course!"

"Are you sure?"

"Why shouldn't I be? You don't believe in witchcraft, do you?" That was said somewhat disparagingly.

"Juok," I said.

"What is *juok*?" he asked.

"A Striden thing," I said, "whereas witchcraft is an English thing."

"Look, I only know English," said Potter.

"Then you don't know what *juok* is," I said, "so why call it witchcraft?"

"Well, is it?" he asked.

"You are out of your depth," I whispered under my breath.

"Tell me!" Potter reiterated.

"So if it is?"

"Then it's a figment of the imagination. There's no such thing as witchcraft!"

"So shall I tell her – a figment of imagination has made you sick?" (I wasn't sure I knew how to translate 'a figment of imagination' anyway, to be honest.)

"Ask if she believes in witchcraft," Potter ordered.

"I can't," I said.

"Why?" he turned to me.

"No word for 'believe in' in the Striden language," I answered.

"Look, I don't know what you are playing at, Dave. If this woman believes in witchcraft, we need to correct her before we pray for her."

"If she didn't believe in witchcraft, she wouldn't want you to pray for her in the first place!" I said.

"What are you on about?" questioned Potter.

I looked at Rolly. "The whole point of what you call prayer here, which we call *maombi*, in local people's eyes, is that it counters witchcraft," Rolly said.

"So you believe all that stuff too, do you?" said Potter.

Potter didn't seem to get it at all. It is like the gospel in Africa builds on the back of witchcraft fears. Sometimes it seems – if people didn't fear the impact of witchcraft, they might not see the point in going to church. Anyway, Potter did what he could. He explained what he was going to do, then he told the woman to put her hands together. He prayed quietly for her, culminating in saying 'in the name of Jesus.'

"If there was a devil there, he has gone," said Potter.

He stood, shook the hands of the woman and the girl, then walked out, motioning for us to follow him.

"Isn't he going to pray for us?" (that is, *ok obi lamonwa?*) asked the girl. What Potter had done did not count as 'prayer' in those parts. Prayer had to be at least a bit long and noisy. I shrugged my shoulders, we followed Potter out, boarded the vehicle, and went back to the hotel in silence.

Potter invited us to join him for a fizzy drink. "Thanks for coming along, gentlemen," he said. "The woman is so poor! I am glad we were able to pray for her."

"I guess you didn't know you were a witch doctor," I said provocatively.

"Now what is this about?" Potter replied. "Let me make it clear that I do not believe in witchcraft one little bit!"

"So then," I added, "you responded to something that you do not believe in."

"Oh, come on, the woman was sick!" Potter said.

"So, when you say 'sick,' what do you mean?"

"Sick!"

"You mean, like viruses, bodily misfunction, infection, inherited something, lowered immunity?"

"Yes! Glad you've got it. Not that anyone has been bewitched." Potter was glad that his point was going home, finally.

"I thought," I added, "that like deals with like. That is to say, biomedical aberrations have biomedical resolutions."

"Yes," said Potter, "but there is also the spiritual. That is why Jesus prayed for demons to leave them."

"As you did earlier this evening?"

"Yes!"

"So what exactly are demons?"

"You tell me, Dave," Potter responded.

"I have told you. They are *witchcrafts*…" (I realized that at this point I was decimating English, but I was trying to make a point.)

"You mean – witchcraft, as in Africa, works through demons, as in the Bible?" Potter asked.

"Yes!"

"So then, you are saying that Jesus believed in witchcraft?"

I didn't answer that question.

"Help me out, Rolly," I said.

"If Jesus hadn't believed in 'demons,' why would he have cast them out?" Rolly responded. "Bear in mind – that it is ancestors who stand behind witchcraft beliefs."

"What you folks are saying, is that it is the prominence of the spiritual realm of evil in Africa, that is in African people's minds, causing the powerful need for the gospel?" Potter said.

"Well put," I responded.

After a while, Potter added a question. "So, tell me, in my prayer, did I do well?"

"That's up to God, isn't it?" Rolly said.

"Well, yes, but all the same…"

"You mean, was she healed?"

"Yes," said Potter, "do you think?"

"Do you mean, 'will she say she was healed,' or do you mean, 'was she healed'?" I asked. Before Potter could respond, I added: "Do you mean biologically 'was she healed,' or *spiritually* 'was she healed,' or Africanly 'was she healed'?"

"What do you mean, 'Africanly'?"

"African people, foundationally, do not distinguish material and spiritual."

"What!" exclaimed Potter.

"Okay, here's my answer," I said. "'Biologically was she healed?' We cannot say as Christians, because biology as a discipline or understanding wasn't around in Christ's day. 'Will she say that she has been healed?' – yes, at least to you, because you are a big wealthy powerful person. 'Spiritually was she healed?' Hard to say, because in Africa the spiritual is hard to distinguish from the physical. 'Africanly was she healed?' Yes."

"Whatever it is you…" Potter said, when Mel burst in on our conversation.

"Philo is not answering his phone!" said Mel. "I've been trying for two hours! It just keeps ringing. Do you think he is okay?"

There was a lot more between Mel's words than in her words! She needed some reassurance. "Philo is fine. In fact, we saw him," Rolly said.

("Did Rolly know what was going on?" I asked myself.)

"You saw him!" Mel said. "Where?"

"Walking along the road, looking great."

"You know that white man?" Potter exclaimed. "Why didn't you say?"

The three of us looked at each other.

"Rose said to tell you to go to see her if possible when you get back," Mel said to Rolly.

"Time for me to go to bed," I said.

"Good night all," we said to Potter.

Potter nodded and waved. We left him there sitting alone.

* * *

The same small group of academics had gathered the following morning. We were in the same hotel room as the previous day. Dr. Dennis (or Professor Dennis) seemed to be very glad to have us with him.

"Welcome Dave, and Rolly, and Mel," he said. Mel had decided to join us that day.

"We have a professor from the local university coming to present a paper today," Dennis said, "which I am sure you will value."

Professor Memphis stood in front of our small gathered crowd. He was slim. He had a sharp pose and almost yellow eyes! The way he stood made you think he was about to walk forwards. His face was shaped like an arrow, I thought! Forward-looking! He had a big beard and a receding hairline. Professor Dennis introduced him, then handed over the podium to him.

(As previously, I will below give only a summary of what Professor Memphis told us that day.)

"My talk is entitled 'God made Invisible,'" Dr. Memphis started out. "I once split a group of students into two. Neither could see what the other group was doing. To one group, A, I gave three sticks, three inches, five inches and seven inches long. To the other group, B, I gave three sticks of the same circumference, but twelve inches, fifteen inches and seventeen inches long. I asked the groups to discuss their sticks for a few minutes. I then asked a member of group A to bring me a long stick. I asked a member of group B to bring me a short stick. When the person of group A held up his stick and said it was long, the person of group B did not agree. He said, 'no, your stick is short.' When the person from group B held up his stick and said it was short, the person from group A said, 'no, it is long.' The members of those groups could not even agree on the length of sticks! Two groups of people can look at the very same stick, and yet draw opposite conclusions," Memphis said. At that point, he paused and looked at us.

"I once went to a village," Memphis went on. "As I talked with people there, I was told that 'that man is so old, he has seen his own grandson being born.' Fellow villagers were amazed that he could be so old. I went to another community that did not consider someone to be 'old' unless he had great-grandchildren."

"I recently considered the English term 'honor,'" said Memphis, "from which presumably we get the term honesty. Honesty, it would seem, is that which preserves honor."

At that point I nudged Rolly. "Not sure where he's heading with all this," I said, "but I am enjoying it!"

"A boy observed his own father stealing eggs from his neighbor's chicken coop early one morning. When asked the following day whether his father had stolen, the boy said, 'to be honest, yes, to be honest, no.' There was a community in which much property was held in common. If a man had a bicycle, he would not (in fact, he could not) prevent anyone else in the village from riding it, as long as he was not using the bicycle at the time. This was an African village. One day a white man came. The white man said 'I saw a thief stealing your bicycle!' 'That was no thief,' was the local person's response."

"Two African tribes had had different missionary mentors. One taught his people that spirit (coming of course from the Greek term *pneuma*) was like a breath or a breeze; it resulted in an impact, the cause of which was not evidently visible. The missionary instructing the other tribe told them that there was something called a soul. When the soul became disconnected from a body, then its essence was spirit, or spiritual. Hence a spirit was a disembodied being. When a scholar from the West came, he asked a member of one tribe 'do you see spirits at work in your tribe?' He was told yes. When he asked a man from the other tribe he was told no. The foreigner concluded that the two tribes' traditions and cultures must be very different."

"One man, A, had just become a Christian," Memphis went on. "In the course of his discipleship, he had heard how Jesus had willingly gone to a cruel death on the cross to die for undeserving sinners. 'That is love,' he was told. Man B of another tribe was told about love, but no one told him what Christ had done. Both men had children. When asked whether he loves his children, the Christian man, A, with tears in his eyes, confessed that he did not. Man B stated simply 'I love my children.' This, of course, proves that non-Christians are more loving than are believers."

"I don't fear curses." Memphis went on. "A white woman said: 'I heard your husband say that he thinks you are a poor cook and lousy in bed, but he puts up with you because he couldn't face what his mother-in-law would say if he didn't.' The lady freaked out, packed her bags, and walked out on her husband. Another lady was told the same about her husband. 'That is a curse,' she said."

As Professor Memphis continued, I was watching Dennis's face. I hope Memphis wasn't watching it, because if he had been, I doubt he would have carried on talking as he was. Memphis was driving Dennis crazy! At the end of the curse example, Dennis could take no more. He stood up. "Round of applause for our visiting speaker," he said.

Memphis stopped in his tracks as we clapped.

Dennis went up to Memphis. "Marvellous presentation," he said. "Thank you very much." Then he turned around to the group. "Time is up, I'm afraid. We'll take a break." Dennis proceeded to encourage Memphis to pack his bag. Praising him all the while, he accompanied him, maybe half 'forcing him' to the exit. Outside on the street, so I was told later, he shook his hand, said goodbye and left Memphis there dumbfoundedly asking himself: "The session was to have been for one and a half hours – why had it been cut short to twenty minutes?"

The three of us had left the meeting room. Dennis went back into the meeting room. "Take a break. Next session in two hours," he said. Then he came back to us. "Sorry chaps. We get some liberals come along and try to undermine the faith of weak believers. I will have none of it. I appreciate you said you have another appointment with, who was it, Potter? You are free to join us for our next session in two hours, but if you are busy with Potter as you said you would be, I will of course quite understand." Dennis walked off!

The three of us sat dumbfounded. Eventually, I asked Mel: "What does the journalist say?"

"Memphis, I mean, he was a theologian, yes? He had come to tell us about how to disciple believers?"

"Yes," Rolly said.

"I wish we could have heard him out," Mel said. "The man had a sense of imagination that made you think."

"What was he going to say?" I asked. My question wasn't to anyone in particular.

"What he was going to say was quite devastating, I should say," Rolly came in. "He was pointing to ways in which communication has to adapt to context. He was saying that it is inadequate to bring theological teaching in one language and expect everyone to understand. He was saying that God's word, to make sense, had to be culturally grounded."

"If that is what he was saying, and I think you are right, Rolly, then what is the role of globe-trotting monolingual theologians?"

"I think Dennis realized that question," I added after a pause.

"Acts 14:8–20," Rolly piped up. "Paul and Silas went to preach the gospel to a people whose language they did not understand. The upshot was – that the evangelists were mistaken for gods."

"And that didn't end well!" I said.

"How did it end?" Mel asked.

"You know Mel, that Paul was stoned, and left for dead," I said.

"So why don't missionaries get stoned and left for dead today?" asked Mel.

"I think the answer to that question is easy, isn't it Rolly?" I asked.

"Yes," he said.

"Okay, let's count to three and say it together. One, two," Rolly and I counted in unison. Then still in unison exactly, we said "Three, money." At that point, we exchanged high fives.

"So then, contemporary missionaries buy themselves out of being stoned to death, but what they leave behind is confusion," said Mel. "I don't know about you," she added, "but I can more and more clearly understand why Philo doesn't want to work with short-term missionaries."

Mel seemed to gloat, as if Philo was already hers!

* * *

"The lady I prayed for last night. She is healed!" said Potter enthusiastically when we met him again. It was about noon. And was he excited! "You were wrong, you lads," he said. "You see, prayer does bring healing! Even my kind of prayer!"

I was verging on anger on hearing him. "Why do we always have to be superheroes?" I know, of course, that African people would make the same claim. But they knew what was going on. They weren't scientists, or pseudo-scientists. They knew that the next announcement may well be that the patient is dead.

As we stood wondering whether to try to explain things to Potter further, his phone rang. "Good job." I thought. "Trying to explain things to bundles of white enthusiasm like Potter is a sure way of becoming unpopular. I'm sure he'd like to own his miracles, for display value at home," I realized.

As Potter spoke on the phone, his face changed. He began to look worried. "Yes, we'll come straight away. You say at the junction of … Okay. Five minutes."

He cut the phone. "Pastor Seme has been hit by a motorbike. You are welcome to join me," Potter said.

"You go, I'll stay," said Rolly to Mel. She agreed.

"You drive," Potter said to me, "so that I can utter words of prayer."

I jumped in the driver's seat, and we set off, when Potter's phone rang again.

"Don't spread the word. Only the pastor's wife is to know," a voice said in stumbling English.

"A strange request," I thought.

I liked the feeling of being an ambulance driver. I wished I'd had a siren and a blue flashing light!

We found Pastor Seme, squirming. He was clearly in much pain, possibly in his thigh or hip. Fortunately, we had a board in the back we could lay him on. Then we placed him into the back of the cruiser. Mel crouched with the patient.

"Nilikuwa tu nakata barabara na piki ikatokea ghafla na kunigonga," said Pastor Seme. He was hit while crossing the road.

We rushed him to the hospital. By the time we got there, Seme was unconscious. We took him to emergency.

His wife was waiting for us. "Thank you very much," she said. "Please don't tell anyone."

"Are you ready to come to our meeting?" Potter asked once we'd left the scene. He was now driving. "Or would you rather I dropped you off at the hotel?"

"We might as well go to the meeting," Rolly suggested to me, once we had found him there at the hotel.

I lifted a bag with Rolly's and my Bible in it. "We're ready to go," I said.

"Strange, the secrecy," said Potter as we drove, thinking back to the incident with Pastor Seme.

"Not strange," I thought, but did not say anything.

"You know why?" Potter asked. Neither Rolly nor I were wanting to answer. We were tired! "Tell me," Potter repeated.

"Okay," I said to myself. "Ever seen a picture of emaciated African babies in the news media?" I asked Potter.

"Yes," he said. "What's that got to do with it?"

"Listen in!" I said. "Do you see similar pictures of dying babies in British hospitals?"

"No," he said.

"Do babies die in British hospitals?"

"Well, yes, they must."

"Even many, if you add them all up."

"But what's that got to do with…"

"Why doesn't the British media broadcast images of emaciated babies dying in British hospitals?"

"Don't know. Guess they don't want hospitals to be known as places of death and dying."

"Right. In the West, Africa is the place of 'death and dying.' That distracts us from our own human predicament as if we were living forever, whereas African people die. Europeans are afraid to die and afraid of the idea of dying."

"Yes, I see."

"The point is, pastors here also need to have that identity of success. They must have a reputation for being strong and victorious, or they may lose their congregations. The chances are that Pastor Seme will be 'found out.' That is, people will discover that he is in hospital. But at least, it is hoped, that by the time they see him, he will be smiling, and in a nice clean context, not tossed onto the roadside, dirty, confused, broken. Even then, some will see him as having become a victim of witchcraft. Remember witchcraft?" I emphasized.

"Yes," said Potter.

"If the witches can get him, then how can his congregation be sure that he can adequately protect them from the same? Perhaps his prayer life has become weak. Perhaps he has sinned, for example, committed adultery, giving the devil a foothold. He has a battle before him, reviving his reputation."

"That's sad!" said Potter.

We arrived late at Potter's gathering. The news of Pastor Seme's accident had spread like wildfire. Secret or no secret. What people were saying was, however, hard to ascertain. My and Rolly's ears were not sufficiently in tune with the African languages. While we could understand more when people addressed us, it was especially hard to catch what people said amongst themselves. Philo could have done a better job!

The fact that one of their pastors had just had an accident and was in the hospital, did not deter one lady testifying to what in the West might be considered a 'health-and-wealth gospel': "There are three levels of faith in

Christ," she said. Level one (which was her!) was no Panadol in the house. Level two, you might get an occasional headache, so Panadol is available, but you don't get malaria. Level three, you need to keep malaria medicine at home, because full-blown malaria is a common problem. That was low faith!"

"Is being admitted to hospital having been hit by a motorbike level four or level five?" I wondered.

As the service progressed, I realized that it constituted full (or whole) entertainment. That is, unlike some British Christians, African Christians didn't reserve extreme emotions for the football stadium. A church service was a full-emotional-release-experience.

At the end of the very lively service, Potter had some bad news for us. "The woman we prayed for last night. I have received word that she is dead," he said.

That was a lot of hope dashed, again. I did try to explain to Potter: "There was more going on than you might have realized, Potter. The report you received this morning that she was getting better, or was healed, was not a biological report. It was a faith report. Everyone agreed that our going to visit the woman, white foreigners, and with a big vehicle, was such a major investment into the woman's healing, that recovery to full health *had* to happen. It was not to be spoken against. That was a way of thanking you (and us) for what we did. A way of saying 'we really appreciate the trouble you took.'"

Tears were coming to my own eyes at the same time as I talked. I asked God, "Why, why, why?" Now there are more orphan children. I only hoped that the family would do as did Job in the Bible, and keep their eyes on God, and not on those of their friends who might advise them to take revenge on a witch.

* * *

After the end of Potter's session, the four of us decided to have something to eat in town, instead of making our way back to the hotel. We hired a motorized rickshaw that were very plentiful in this town. This part of Holima had a relatively high population of Muslim people.

"What did Muslim people do to win so many converts?" Mel asked, as we bounced along in the rickshaw.

"They took slaves," I said, holding on to the bar above my head.

"That's a strange way of convincing people to believe in what you do!" Mel said. "What do you say, Rolly?"

"It is interesting indeed," said Rolly, "especially concerning what Christians endeavor to do in mission. It is about you, dear," he continued, looking at Rose. She blinked.

"How is it about me, dear?" Rose asked. The four of us were squeezed somewhat. Rose was sitting to our left.

"If I was a Muslim man, chances are I would have four of you."

"That sounds frightening," Rose said.

We laughed. I tried to picture four Roses sitting with us in a row that day.

"More seriously, Mel" Rolly went on. "I think that is a very important question. Quite frankly, I think that African men got to admire the power, especially the power over women and the power over slaves, that Muslim men had. They also desired to have more wives. They also desired a system of power that was exclusive of their women, if you like. Islam also inherited a great deal from Christianity and from Judaism. Thus it was based on rules that, while up to discussion, were written. This gave Islam a solidity that people's own ways of life did not have. Add all of that to the scorning by the powerful Arab traders (yes, many of them slave traders) of men who had not become Muslims, and you had little reason for a man not to become Muslim. Once a man made a decision like that, then the women were simply included by default."

"Now we tend to think," Mel said, "that to bring people to faith in Christ, you have to be terribly nice to them. But you are saying that Arabs brought people to follow Muhammed in very different ways."

"Yes, indeed," said Rolly.

We reached our destination. Bending low to squeeze out of the motorized rickshaw needed a bit of effort. We were now in the center of town. We walked to and sat in the restaurant. Alongside was a cyber-café. There was a roof above our heads to provide shade, but no walls, so air moved freely around where we were sitting.

"So, what should we learn from the way that people have been convinced to follow Muhammed?" Mel asked once we'd sat down.

"Let's put it this way," I suggested. "We in the West are accustomed to leading orderly lives. Much of what brings that order is our governments, especially in Europe. We take that for granted. Hence missionaries, like to Africa, tend to concentrate on Christianity as a 'spiritual system' if you like. They forget that it was the same faith in Christ that brought order to our countries and governments. Partly they forget this because these days European governments ..."

A lad of about eighteen came to hand us menus. He was smartly dressed, I thought, and looked sharp. Then I carried on:

"European governments try to conceal it. They do not want their Christian history to be known. They prefer to be known as 'secular.' But actually – what African people appreciate about the message of the gospel is the order, and purpose, and peace that Christ brings into people's lives. That says a lot of what was there before, in Africa that is. Coming to Christ has brought people great improvement over 'what was before.'"

"So, what is the difference between becoming Islamic and becoming Christian?" Mel asked, "if both bring order?"

"Come on, let's look at the food options," I interrupted. We all buried our noses into menus. Meanwhile, Rolly went on with the discussion. He kept his finger on the item he wanted as he spoke.

"Many things of course," said Rolly. "Islam works by endeavoring to satisfy men's desire for sex and power over women. It also justifies taking of revenge. Islam teaches that if someone does something bad to you, then you should pay them back. Faith in Christ is a very different thing. You notice that churches often have more women than men?"

"Yes," Rose said. "Do they have pizza here?" We all looked again at our menus.

"They don't seem to," Mel responded.

Rose went on: "Men, especially, find it harder to become Christian. For them, it requires a kind of self-denial. That is – a denial of their aggressive, dominating side. Including, of course, their desire to have a harem – more women, as Christ taught clearly that an exemplary man should have just one wife."

"I think you've got something important there Rolly," I added. "For a man to become a Christian is hard for that reason. It requires an admission of a kind of weakness. Once conceded, however, especially once a man agrees not to take revenge on his enemies, becoming a Christian is an enormous harbinger of peace."

"African people seem to think that Christianity is all about healing though," Mel said, "and driving away demons and all."

"So it is!" I responded. "'Healing,' or 'salvation' (in the Bible these are overlapping concepts) are means to peace. African people are not wrong, but it is hard for the West to understand them. Remember that the West is on a big project to *deny* its history. This can result in western people being very blinkered."

"That is a problem," Rolly said, "because when they come to Africa, Westerners don't understand. They think they have to give people sweeteners for them to accept Christ, when, once people understand, and once men accept to drop a few pegs, then they want to be Christ-followers, even without gifts from far away. Of course, it is that ignorance of Europeans that forces Philo, to do ministry with African people without constant upset if you like, to have to tell the likes of us that we cannot just 'shadow' him, unless as now, we do so secretly, and at a distance. I tell you what as well – as we have followed Philo 'at a distance' and met up with fellow Europeans, we have seen much justification for Philo's stand. Frankly – mission should be done using people's languages and their resources."

"Sad about that woman dying," said Rose at that point. "Shouldn't we order now though?" She waved, and the same eighteen-year-old lad came back for us to tell him what we wanted, in English. Once he had taken our orders, carefully scribbling them onto a small pad, Rolly continued our prior conversation.

"Yes," Rolly said. "Potter did what he could."

"He could have taken her to the hospital," Mel interrupted.

"Yes, but…" I said. I did not complete my sentence.

"Okay. Got it," Mel said. "That would be like the powerful white man dominating everything again."

"Right!" Rolly agreed.

"So you can't drive a wounded person to the hospital for fear of dominating? Better let her die?" Mel added.

I looked at Rolly. He was glancing at me. Rose looked Mel in the eye. "You'd better tell us the answer to that one in the article you are writing," she told her. I felt sheepish. Mel had dug down to some hard realities. It felt that we now needed to order a debate on this issue by something as eminent as British parliament!

"So, Philo doesn't have a car ..." I stated. Mel was looking at me nodding. Her right hand was over her mouth in an expression of shock. "... out of choice. He could afford it if he wanted to. I mean, if he told his supporters he must have a car, many might well agree and buy one for him. Does Philo not having a car at hand whenever he prays for a sick person, make him guilty for not driving someone to a hospital?" I looked around at Mel and the others. No one said anything. All were attentive. "If refusing to access resources that one could access makes one guilty, then hey-ho, capitalism is the only way, and all us arty-farty missionary types should go into business. Mandatory."

As we were talking, a good-looking African girl had come to deliver our food. Food was indeed a lot cheaper here in town, at African restaurants, than it was at our hotel. Sometimes, as a single man, I wondered if married Westerners didn't think their wives were all spoilt, always insisting that they go to the most expensive places! We ate our fill. Walking back to the hotel, we elicited no end of comments like *"kwani Wazungu wanao miguu"* – so white people have legs. Many African people think Whites never walk anywhere. The example we set for African people to aspire to is often horrific, I thought.

* * *

When we got back to the hotel, there was Dennis with his four African professors in the foyer. "Dave, Rolly, please come and join us," he beckoned. "Mel and Rose, welcome," he added.

The ladies chose to leave, still debating the issue of just when a missionary might be guilty of *not* doing something, as our ways parted.

Rolly and I sat down. We were in the circle with the professors. For some reason, the Africans especially looked tense.

"Look, Dave, Rolly," Dennis said. "You might have come at just the right moment. We are discussing where to have our next seminar on contextualized African Christianity. I am suggesting Imbigen, or maybe Deja, or Kosompa. They are saying that it must be in London, or in a US city like Chicago."

We had arrived in the middle of a boiling cauldron, I discovered! Seconds after Dennis completed his sentence, one of the professors, Alphonse, who seemed to wear over-sized clothes, stood up. "We're tired of your seminars," he said. He beckoned to the other professor, Madimba, who in my head I called bean-pole, as he was tall and slim. Both got up and left. We were stunned. Moments later they came back. "We believe you owe us arrears," said Madimba. He wrote on a piece of paper. "Here's my bank details. Please pay." "Here are mine," said Dr. Alphonse, handing him another sheet of paper. They marched off again.

"If you live by the sword, you will die by the sword," I thought to myself. Words of Jesus. I wondered if an extension of that would also work, "if you live by money, you will die by money."

I could quite see why Dr. Omboko and Dr. Siske would want to travel to London, or Washington, or somewhere else, for the next seminar. Those were to them, and I do not deny, the real centers of power. People who came from those places, including Africans who had spent time there, were given enormous respect in Africa. Africans who went to those places, and especially if they *stayed* there for a few years, became world-renowned. Africans who stayed in their home countries were like 'the field,' whereas those who went and lived in those places became much more 'one of us' with western professors. I understood their point of view. But now – how to help Dennis, before his remaining two professors walked off? Dennis was in a dilemma. For him to make a trip to Africa alone, and pay some relatively cheap costs, was one thing. Donors were ready to cover such costs in Africa. It would be more difficult to get donors to pay for his colleagues to come to America. He obviously saw himself as 'reaching out to Africa,' not as just another professor arranging a seminar back on State-side.

Dennis no doubt expected Rolly and I to address his Holiman colleagues, to 'knock sense' into them. I had to take an alternative track. Of course, I was actually addressing them, but via an apparent attack on Dennis.

"What you have very effectively done," I said looking at Dennis, "is demonstrated the enormous power of the West over Africa. You are an outsider to Holima. Perhaps this is your first visit?" Dennis nodded! "Yet in the visit you have attracted some of Africa's top academics and made an instant stir in this majority-world town. You have amply demonstrated the power of the West, what the West can do. I think it is only natural now that your African colleagues will want to 'do what you do and not just do what you say.'" That exhausted me for a while. Thankfully Rolly could jump in.

Rolly told me later that he had major *déjà vu*! How many times had he been in these kinds of discussions, sitting in Dennis' shoes? Recent events, plus those opening words of mine, opened up avenues of thinking that had not previously (in previous such encounters in Africa) come to him. When he saw me exhausted, he knew he had to speak up.

"I confess, Dennis," Rolly said, "that I used to be somewhat like you. I thought God had blessed us in America so that we could arrange seminars like this in Africa. Then I realized, however, that this model has a problem. It is like buying people, and effectively (economically) forcing them to do things in our way, on our agenda, in our language, at our pace, and so on."

"Was Dennis squirming?" I asked myself.

"If we think that is 'charity,' we have deceived ourselves, because charity, true charity, leaves people free. The apostle Paul said, 'love does not insist on its own way.' I know you don't think you are forcing anyone, or insisting on your own way in anything, but because of the money that you offer on your terms, you are."

At that point, I thought, Rolly might have needed to explain that western donor money is always of this ilk. Accountability structures in the West mean that western money always follows and undergirds western agendas. Rolly did not mention that. I hope it was implicitly understood. As Rolly spoke, you could have heard a pin drop. Well, no pin dropped, but Mel did come back.

"Can I join you?" she whispered to no one in particular. She didn't want to disturb things by gate-crashing if she wasn't wanted.

"Sit down," said Professor Omboko. I hope my look communicated that she was very welcome. She took Madimba's chair.

"So what should we do?" Dennis asked.

"He is good at heart," I thought to myself, "but he has been guided by a system that does not understand itself."

Rolly glanced at the two remaining professors. They were tracking with him. I should say, looking at their eyes, that they agreed with him. They knew the system. But this is where they were now stuck. Of course, when a visiting scholar came, they played the game. There was money, never mind prestige, to be won. "Now what was Rolly going to suggest as an alternative?"

"The way forward," Rolly spoke audibly and clearly, his left pointer finger laid alongside his mouth as if to add force to his words, "has to be for western scholars to take a bold step. That is – they need to learn to travel, using funds to get to places. But, when they get there, they should not have privileged funds with which to pay indigenous scholars to work with them. They should instead rely on volunteers, or indigenous scholars raising their own funds, then to join them."

Once he had said that, I am not very sure how ready Rolly was for what happened next. Maybe he anticipated it? Maybe he did not? I never did get to ask him.

Both Dr. Omboko and Dr. Alphonse started laughing. "You think we'll want to cooperate with you if we don't get paid?" they both said. I looked at Dennis. He was reeling as a result of that revelation. We sat in silence as both of them wrote. "Here is our bank information," they said, each handing a piece of paper to Dennis. "Be sure you pay us what we are due. As to these friends of yours, Dennis, we are not impressed." Both professors walked out.

* * *

Poor old Dennis! Maybe our help hadn't been helpful. I dread to think what he thought of us at that stage. "What to do next?" was surely the question that troubled Dennis there and then. What to do?

We told Dennis about Philo. Perhaps Dennis was impressed because Philo had a PhD? Perhaps he was impressed because he had been through some rough times! Maybe he wasn't impressed at all? Hard to know.

Dennis did ask, "So, Philo tells what one should *not* do, and you are on board with him on that, it seems. So then – what about what one *should* do?"

Rolly gave him an immediate response there. "That's what the Bible is there for," said Rolly, "to tell us what to do."

"Okay," said Dennis. He could see some sense in that! "But it still seems as if Philo, and you lot, are saying, primarily, 'don't, don't, don't...!'"

"You may be right," I said. "There could be a few reasons for that, one of those being that certain contemporary practices by western missionaries are pretty plainly 'wrong.' Those practices include engaging people in the language of the missionary instead of using the people's own language. I suggest that for intercultural missionaries that is just wrong, wrong,

wrong! If it is just wrong, then as long as people keep doing it, one's message remains a negative one. It is like if a man is strangling his wife. As long as he still has his fingers gripped on her throat, you won't tell him to do anything else, like give her flowers. He has to correct that behavior first!"

"So, for you, that rule applies to two things: use of outside languages, as you say, and use of outside resources?" Dennis said.

"Yes. Use of outside resources to control people," I added.

"Often," Rolly came in, "foreigners do not realize that they are controlling local people. For example, a professor is used to having staff work under him in a university in America. He goes to Africa. He finds people with similar titles as were there in America, just of a different color (although, of course, there are also Blacks in America). They dress much the same and talk the same language. The professor treats them the same as he would academics in the West. There in the West, that treatment may be fine, but in Africa, he may be exploiting them."

That was probably a bit close to the bone for Dennis! "Why exploiting them?" Dennis asked, rocking back somewhat in his chair.

"I thought you'd just learned that," I said. "If they are not citizens in the West, then they have none of the guarantees, choices, pension options, privileges, alternative employment outlets, securities, and career ladders that Westerners enjoy. The dynamics they work under may be very different from those of academics in the West. Perhaps they aren't even getting paid. To assume that they will just produce academic work, as you would of a western colleague, could be a very misguided assumption."

"But they agreed!" Dennis said.

"In whose language? Under whose cultural presuppositions?" Rolly asked.

For a few seconds, Dennis didn't respond.

"So, first thing is that what outsiders are doing is plain wrong," Dennis said, "so you just have to tell them not to do it. Second thing?" Dennis wasn't entirely impressed.

"Second thing," I said, "what you learn you have to learn from the context. No university course in the West can tell you *what to do* because you must do what you do in response to what you find. The context, the local people, the environment, the peculiarities of the language you are dealing with – those, with God, and his Word, and his Spirit, are the teachers. One could even say that – what you should *not* do is everything. You have to start again. Question everything that you thought was simply obvious. Don't do anything … Now, in reality, you have to do certain things, like eat, but then you need to realize that you are probably doing it wrong!"

"How can you eat wrong?" Dennis asked.

"You slurp when you shouldn't, not slurp when you should, use the wrong hand, hold the fork the wrong way up, sit with the wrong pose, talk while you are eating when you shouldn't, or be silent when eating when you should be talking, sit at the wrong place, at the wrong time, fail to wash first, or wash first when you shouldn't have … come on. Lots of things," I said.

"But, come on, Dave, I was dealing with fellow academics!"

"Yes," Rolly said. "Academia is one of the landing strips in the majority world designed to entice western money-planes to land."

"You know what anthropologists call that?" I asked.

"No," said Dennis.

"A cargo cult," I responded.

"You mean, it isn't serious academics in relation to its own context, but it is a means of attracting foreign money?"

"You've got it," I said. We got the impression that Dennis was distraught. Maybe, he won't make the same mistake again? But, quite likely even if he doesn't, many others will.

* * *

"Oh no!" said Rolly at that moment, looking at his watch and appearing agitated. "I agreed to accompany Potter to a gathering. I'm late! Excuse me. Dave – I haven't even told Rose where I'm going. Could you please tell her? I'll be back when I'm done with Potter." Rolly was rising out of his chair as he spoke.

"Sure thing," I said, asking myself why he doesn't call her. "People of his generation don't always remember that they have phones in their pockets," I said to myself. I went and stood outside Rose's door. "Rose, Rolly says to tell you he's gone with Potter," I said.

"Fine," she responded.

I relay Rolly's subsequent report following his visit with Potter here:

"Noise, noise, noise, why always so much noise?" Potter asked me as we walked to the meeting. We had told Potter that the early evening was a wonderful time for walking. He decided to give it a go. He was even courageous enough to accept that on the way back, in the dark, we'd come back by motorized rickshaw instead of the Land Cruiser. Rolly wasn't quite such a *great* walker himself, but he did okay.

There was one thing that happened that evening that further convinced Rolly that Philo was right. That is to say – short-term missionaries should not reckon to accompany a long-termer *unless* they are totally committed to using the indigenous language, and don't use their access to resources as a lever to power.

Potter was frustrated. Rolly also said – he could not blame him for being so. That is anyone in Potter's position would have been frustrated. So, it was not the frustration that was problematic. What became problematic was that he, the frustrated one, was also in charge, the initiator of what was happening, almost the sole donor (nationals did contribute a little), and the only one who could not understand what everyone else was saying! This meant that Potter's frustrations were soon apparent to everyone at the first sign of a frown on his face, instantly affecting the whole group, but his mood was incomprehensible to everyone, as no one could grasp just what his issue was. Rolly felt he could, to some extent, more than others. He made some efforts at communicating what was grating with Potter, the fact that people in the church made too much noise, but he soon gave up. What resulted was something of a farce, he told me! As soon as someone walked into the hall, and there were more than 300 people, they knew that something was up. They did not know what. They soon understood, however, that it was an issue being brought by the white man, and it was very important because the white man had a lot of money. Everyone had to be on tenterhooks, that is, on eggshells. They did their utmost to please the white man. They knew if they didn't that their leaders wouldn't be happy. But they did not know the problem the white man had, or why he was unhappy!

Potter did open up to Rolly later. "I'm sorry, Rolly," he said, glad that at least he felt Rolly could understand him. "I guess I messed up," he added. "I was troubled. I guess I was homesick. I am tired. Yet the people kept on getting it wrong. I just didn't feel that what was happening could be of the

Spirit of God. It was too, what, coarse. Even demonic! Why couldn't they sing gentle songs? Why always all the noise? I wanted to correct them. But they did not understand me. I suppose I didn't realize how central I was to everything. How when I spoke, yet couldn't make myself understood, they were stuck. I suppose they were trying to please me. But they didn't know how to, because they didn't know what I wanted. Rolly – missionary work is tough! I did not realize it was so difficult. I thought it was just a matter of preaching. People tell me I am a good preacher. You have someone translate for you. People accept the gospel, then you disciple them. I mean – all those things happen; but how to disciple people who are living in a different world?"

"How long do you have left here?" Rolly asked Potter.

"Three more full days," he said, wavering. I think that meant, he was trying to work out in his mind how in three days he could turn the situation around.

"Do you realize we leave tomorrow?" Rolly asked Potter.

"No, I didn't know," he said.

"Well, now you know!"

"What am I going to do? At least Dave and yourself seem to know what you are doing," he said.

"You know, I think, Dave," Rolly said to me later, "that it can be hard to tell a missionary how to disciple. I tried. In the end, we looked at Luke 10. I tried to explain that Jesus said, 'don't carry anything.' I don't think he got it. He couldn't get it! Back in the USA, he's probably THE expert on evangelism in his college. How could he know that most of that will not help him in Africa? It's like he needs to start again. Almost – be born again into Africa!"

Unfortunately, we have no more updates on Potter, as we moved on and lost contact. Perhaps what remains is to comment on the issue that Potter focused on. Was he right to try to encourage people to be less noisy in church? He might have been. I could not say he was necessarily *wrong*. Unfortunately, though, the way he went about tackling the issue, without a cultural/contextual background, made it almost impossible for him to succeed. That is how a poor approach can pre-empt good action.

CHAPTER 42: RAINSTORM

"Ya. Vilcome," said the voice on the phone the following morning. Mel's raised level of excitement was presumably because on the same evening, we should finally be together with Philo. The reason Philo had suggested that we be together is that he was anyway planning to spend a few days with western people, in a western context. Philo, presumably, did not know that we were shadowing him, so was anticipating that we were driving to meet him in Kosompa from Imbigen. Hence, when the German lady on the phone asked us *"vere* are you?" we responded, "already on our way!"

"Hope you have been *vatching de veva* forecast?" the voice said.

The voice belonged to Iris. She had lived and ministered there in Kosompa for many years. She was a very accomplished Swahili speaker. She was also an excellent hostess. At least, so we were hoping then, and so we were to discover in due course. Judging by her voice on the phone, Iris was about forty. This was later proven accurate. She was slim, with greying shoulder-length hair.

"De *veva* forecast is *sery* grim," she said, "*sery, sery* grim."

"What is anticipated?" asked Rolly in response to that warning.

"Heavy rain," she said.

"It never rains very heavily around Kosompa," Rolly said later, "and even if it does, a bit of water won't hurt anything, will it?"

That response by Rolly was such that it closed any discussion that there might have been about whether to go ahead with our trip. Rolly had decided for us – who cares about weather forecasts? We might subsequently come to regret such a quick and poorly thought-through position!

As often happens when one is heading for a storm – there was no sign of anything inclement as we set off. Skies were blue, and we were happy campers. Mel, especially, was looking forward to spending more time with Philo – seeing him, and not through binoculars! As we traveled, the trip taking about three hours, clouds gradually accumulated. Rolly was the first to comment. He had obviously not been able to totally ignore the warnings of the Germans! Perhaps he was worried that he might have taken their warnings far too lightly. A few miles later he turned on the windscreen wipers. That, he told us, and I believed him, was already amazing – to have any significant rain at that time of year. A bit later Rolly turned on the lights, and it was only nearing midday in Holima. Then the windscreen wipers went to normal speed, then to fast speed! Now it was bucketing down.

For any drainage system to withstand that much rain would have been a challenge. The Kosompa drains, if there were any, did not stand a chance. Roads soon became rivers. Rolly determined to keep right on. He had been told that the mission at which we were to stay was on a raised piece of land. "Once we get there, all should be well." The getting there remained our major problem! There were signs of devastation around us; a kiosk (small shop) demolished, a motorized rickshaw lying in the mud, a dead animal, probably a small sheep, floating by. We saw a group of people escaping the floodwaters by standing on an upturned lorry.

It was when we passed by a hospital that I came to be amazed at Mel. The hospital seemed to be in devastation. At that point, Mel could bear it no more.

"I can't just go to take shelter in a mission house with this chaos all around me," Mel told us. "Look. Drop me off at the hospital. I want to help out."

"Are you sure, Mel?"

"Yes. I'll find you later," Mel said.

We tried to discourage her. Then, at a junction near the hospital, Rolly stopped to check traffic. Mel opened her door and leaped out!

"What shall I do?" I asked.

"Leave her," Rolly said, "if that's what she wants to do. She has her phone. She can find her way later, if necessary, using a rickshaw."

We saw Mel splashing her way to the hospital, clutching a small travel bag. We drove on. I wasn't sure just how she could help, but at least she was able-bodied, I thought. I could also understand her reaction – in the middle of a catastrophe – one wants to *do something*!

By the time we arrived at the mission, the rain had gone from very, very heavy, to just very heavy. It was a relieving and comforting experience to be able to sit down in a calm dry place, and while we could still hear the rain pounding on the roof, we were one further step removed from it than we had been.

"I gather Darren is on his way here. You have news?" Rose asked Iris. Iris turned out to be much as we had, or at least as I had, imagined her on the phone. She came across as a very capable lady. We would meet her husband later.

"He's taking a taxi. I gather he has succeeded in getting a 4x4 taxi," Iris said. "My husband has gone to fetch Sam. His taxi ended up in a ditch," she added.

"Wow. Things were rough! We were going to have a diverse well-populated gathering," I also thought. Before long Darren showed up. We saw him pay his driver, then dash in to avoid the rain – although the latter was merely 'heavy.'

Before telling more from Darren, let me tell you that at that time Mel was having an interesting time at the hospital. Mostly, though, a shocking time. If she had expected coordinated heroic efforts being made by hospital staff, frankly, she was disappointed. The hospital was overwhelmed, and that was that. Patients 'to be seen' remained just that – to be seen. Some staff had left to attend to emergencies, or anticipated or assumed emergencies, at their homes. Things were a mess, but instead of finding people pulling out all stops to bring the crisis under control, she found them resigned to what she guessed they saw to be a God-given fate for those of the sick who were struggling. One particular incident stuck in her mind. A nurse walked out of the outpatients' room shouting at a patient. The patient was walking away briskly. Well, as briskly as one might expect of someone who is sick, but had a reason to be in a hurry.

"What is she saying?" Mel asked a bystander. The bystander, who knew some English explained: "Come back. Your diagnosis was wrong," the nurse shouted. "You do not have terminal cancer, you only have malaria!"

The bystander explained that the man had walked through the gate saying he is going to hang himself. Hence the nurse's concern. Given the state of the floodwater, though, no one was going to follow him any further to tell him he had been misdiagnosed.

Mel did what she could at the hospital, which she conceded was not very much. "Why do they not care more for the sick and dying, though?" she was asking herself.

Darren came and sat down to join us. He had news for us. Although his coming to Kosompa was in response to our request, he discovered subsequently that there was a major conference going on in the city.

Sponsored by the World Bank, and bringing delegates from many corners of the globe, this conference was to do with development. In other words – how to do development right. While he intended to spend time with us, he would also be dividing his time. He planned to report on some of the discussions and outcomes of the conference. One immediate question was, of course – was the conference going ahead in the first place, and if so, how, given the general chaos in the city?

Moments later, Noel, Iris's husband, came in carrying some suitcases. Those were Sam's. Sam walked in behind Noel who was a big man, and very much a hands-on type. I thought at the time that the brains in their family must be Iris. Later, Noel was to prove that he didn't do too badly himself. (They had two children, but the children were not with them.) Noel liked to do building, repairs, and renovation of mission facilities. The kind of man it was good to have around.

Sam immediately started telling us his story. He had traveled into town by bus, due to a prior appointment in a nearby town. He had anticipated using a rickshaw to get to the mission compound. Because of the rain, he opted instead for a saloon car. Then he described how the saloon car had calmly slid sideways off the road into a ditch! That is where it lay, and no amount of revving the engine while spinning the wheels would shift it. (It seemed his driver thought that the faster the wheels spun, the more likely they just might have got some traction!) Sam was plastered with mud. He had stayed in the taxi and called Iris. Noel went to pick him up. He got covered in mud once Noel had arrived, slipping and sliding and falling back a few times, as he tried to make it out of the ditch and back to the road! Once he'd explained all that, Sam was sent into the decompression chamber, otherwise known as the bathroom, to change all his clothes and have a wash.

There was, though, no sign of Philo. Not even a phone call. We had expected for no good reason that Philo would be the first to arrive. It turns out there was at least one positive thing, if one considers such things to be positive; fortuitously, Philo's means of travel to Kosompa city involved his being rescued by Mel!

Philo explained later. His crowded bus, of course, hit the same heavy downpour as had troubled the rest of us. "Look. Accident," one of the passengers had said. Another small bus had tipped over as a result of the floodwater. The driver wasn't going to stop. He just wanted to slow down for people to take a look.

A woman rushed up to the bus Philo was in. "*Chung'*!" she shouted. "She forced our driver to stop by standing in front of the bus," Philo told me. "There were two badly injured people. We don't know *how* badly, but they could not stand. All the seats on the bus were occupied. But – those people weren't up to sitting anyway. They laid them onto the footway, between the seats. I felt, surely we should be applying some first aid," Philo said. "But how? One of the injured was a man, the other a woman. The man, maybe in his fifties, was groaning where he lay. All I could do for him was pray for him," Philo said. "Soon others on the bus, now going faster than ever, presumably in the interests of getting the injured to the hospital as quickly as possible, were also praying. In all that, of course, it was raining heavily."

"I didn't know where the German mission was, or how to get there," Philo said. "I had expected just to call through. Then I checked my pockets. No phone! I checked my bag. No phone! I checked everywhere. No phone! Now I was stuck," Philo added. "I was aware that the hospital was nearer to the German mission than was the bus station. It made sense to alight there. I ended up helping to carry one of the sick from the bus. The scene there was not a pleasant one. We carefully laid the injured we had brought, alongside others, on the ground. The hospital was overwhelmed, completely. I could only guess that rain and flooding had caused all kinds of accidents. Bodies, some maybe already dead, were laid in rows. No one was paying any attention to them. My bus left, and there I was standing amongst all those injured people! The sick and injured outnumbered the healthy a hundred to one! Do you know what I did? I started singing. I mean – I started singing a local worship song, in Swahili. Then I prayed, then I went into another song, and so on."

"You mean you didn't help them?" I exclaimed.

"Help who? There were so many. Help how? I'm not a medic. I did what I could while singing to encourage them," was Philo's response. "As I was singing, suddenly I found myself embraced," Philo added. "It was Mel. 'You are here love,' I thought she said. 'What did you say?' I asked her.

'You are here, bruv,' Mel responded.

Anyway, I didn't expect to find Mel at the hospital. 'Are you injured?' I asked.

'No,' she said. 'I've come to help.'

She'd been there, it transpired, for two or three hours. She looked more-than-worn-out. I don't know what she had been doing. She kept a hold of me and wouldn't let go.

'Time to go before we become patients!' I thought. 'Look Mel. We need to get to the German mission. I don't know where it is, do you?'

'Yes,' she said.

'Let's go,' I said. With her holding on to me, we kind of stumbled on. The rain had eased a lot. We found a vehicle. It looked a bit rough. 'Are you for hire?' I asked the driver. He was. 'Please take us to the German mission, at …' – the name Mel had given me – that I can't now remember."

"It was like a ride in a chitty chitty bang bang! We found our way to the mission. That's how you found us. That's why, as you know, Mel was a physical and emotional wreck! You know, when I rechecked for my phone, it was in one of the pockets of my bag. Yet – the phone appears to have been lost enabled me to rescue Mel, and Mel to rescue me."

* * *

Fortunately for all of us, Mel recovered rapidly from her ordeal. She spent an hour or so in bed, after having cleaned up. While she did so, Philo also took time to disinfect himself. Where he'd been sleeping, he said, there were a lot of bed bugs. He didn't want to be carrying them to and depositing them at the German mission station. I watched him as he piled up all his clothes, beddings and sundries, into a pile in the bathtub. Every layer he added, he sprayed with a new coating of insecticide. I don't know if all that helped or not. Philo felt it was important to do it.

The next morning Mel had one thing in mind. She was determined to go back to that hospital! She had had a taster. She wanted to invest herself more into the lives of local people.

"Look. The work you want to do, washing and cleaning people, you could much more easily pay someone to do," Sam said to Mel.

"No. I am not here to use foreign money to help people," Mel replied. (Mel had learned something!) "Either I do it myself and get my hands dirty, or nothing!"

I guess that was Sam also learning, not from Philo, or even myself, but from our journalist friend Mel, who had started all this and seemed to be the main center of attention at the time. The value of service, before God, may not be in what is or is not achieved, but in what someone has sacrificed! Mel was wanting to give sacrificially, not as a wealthy distant benefactor. I am not sure how much of an impact that had on Sam, but surely some on me!

We had to put our heads together. It certainly did not seem right just to expect Mel to go to the hospital by herself. The question was: who should accompany her? The answer to the problem was not so hard to find. Now some of us were biased, wanting to give the new anticipated 'couple' time together. Who better to accompany her though, anyway, than the person who culturally and linguistically was most in tune with goings on? The vote came that Philo should accompany her. Whether that for him was a negative, neutral, or positive decision, time would tell.

On the morning of the following day, Philo and Mel set off together by rickshaw to the hospital. Mel was going to find out what service she could offer. Philo went along as her cultural guide and translator.

"I have a difficult question to ask you," Mel said as they rode in the rickshaw. The diesel engine of the rickshaw was not the quietest. The lack of suspension in the rear wheels did not help either, as even in this city there were a lot of rough roads. That was especially the case after the destructive storm of the previous day.

"We hung on as the rickshaw rattled along. It seems this question was eating Mel." Philo shared.

The great thing about a rickshaw was that it could turn on a sixpence! So also it did, it seems repeatedly, maneuvering obstacles, many of which had been left by the floodwater.

"Go ahead," was Philo's response.

"But this is a very delicate and sensitive question," Mel emphasized.

"I'm bracing myself," Philo responded. At that point, they hit a part of the road covered by gravel. From then on, no one could hear anyone else. Thereafter, however, there was some smooth tarmac.

"Why do medical people not seem to care about the suffering people brought to them?" Mel asked.

Given Mel's courageous experience the previous day, that question might not have been so surprising to Philo. Participating in something can be an *excellent* way to learn about it. Much better than just observing from a distance. Certainly, much better than just reading about it. Issues related to language and culture must have been high in Philo's mind. Language – because African hospitals were modeled on western ones, when described in English, they could sound just like western ones. Sometimes just like slightly (or very) impoverished versions of western hospitals. That is – the impact of African culture on the running of the hospital could come across as the impoverishment of a western model. A bit like a tennis player may seem to be a hopeless football player! African people were inclined to believe in 'fate' (nothing one can do against fate!) or that somebody has cast a spell on the sick. The solution to the latter is prayer or sacrifice of some sort.

"To answer that kind of question requires a lot of wisdom," Philo once told me. "If you answer according to the way the question is asked, you can appear to be writing off a people." In this case, it would be writing them off as uncaring! Here was Philo's response, as I received it from him.

"Don't expect African people to be caring in the way that western people understand to be caring. Westerners have been trained to be so by generations and generations of Christian teaching and devotion. Don't expect African people to be able just to lay aside generations of their wisdom just because they are told, in English, to do so, then when asked whether they have laid aside that old wisdom, they simply respond 'yes!' Certainly, there are weaknesses in African systems of caring. So are there also in western ones. We play down the weaknesses in our systems and emphasize the strengths of our systems. In doing so, our (western) way of thinking accentuates, magnifies, and puts a spotlight on the problems inherent in African means of caring. It is naive to think that Holima's citizen should be able to run western medical services in a western way."

"Like what?" Mel responded. "Give me an example of a weakness in western medical care."

"Just an example," said Philo, "denying people hope by stamping on the truth claims of the gospel. When you discourage faith ..."

At that point, the rickshaw tilted to the left. Mel almost fell onto Philo. The driver had left the main road to take a short-cut. It was impossible again for Mel and Philo to hear each other.

Reaching the hospital, things were much more orderly than they had been on the previous day. There weren't wounded people lying everywhere.

"We did wonder how many of the living people we saw the previous day were now in the mortuary," Philo said to me.

The previous day, Mel's efforts at communicating had been almost entirely useless. So she just had to do what seemed right and sensible. Now things were less chaotic, and she had Philo with her to help her to make herself understood. The two of them approached the hospital administrator.

"I was here yesterday and tried to help out because of the emergency. I've come again today to offer my voluntary services," Mel said, with Philo translating.

It took the administrator a while to work out just what Mel was proposing. "No, we do not need your services," the administrator explained. "But," she added, "we are very much in need for finances for X, Y, Z...!"

"Sorry, we don't have finances," Philo said on Mel's behalf. Sometimes Philo was translating, sometimes explaining things to the administrator, and sometimes explaining things to Mel. It was hard to keep those three things apart.

"Can't I do something, even washing sheets, or cleaning patients?" said Mel.

"No!" said the administrator.

That reaction helped Philo to understand another reason why people who want to help the situation in Africa tend to end up as donors. Other services they offer may well be refused, yet they want to help! Ironically, the reason their services are rejected is related to the fact that they are donors. If, for example, Mel had been given opportunity, say, to clean the hospital. What then if she turned out to be unhappy with what was happening that she saw around her as she cleaned, perhaps it was not up to standard. Then she communicated with donors. Then she could tell donors; 'as an insider ...' Then she could interfere with incoming funds or create headaches for hospital administrators. On that score – once a Westerner begins to understand what is happening in Africa, if they want to continue to live and work there, then they should not tell anyone about it! Like, if things were happening wrongly at the hospital, perhaps even things that cause the patients to die. If a Westerner blew the whistle, funding could be at risk, or people might have to be fired. Consequently, African leaders in Africa love having Westerners around as donors, but they do not want them to stay too long to find out how things work, or to get to be in other ways intimately aware of the functioning of African-run institutions.

It was clear that neither Philo's nor Mel's services were wanted at the hospital if they did not have money to give. They began sauntering away. 'Sauntering' that is, because they did not really have anywhere to go, except back to the German mission. Plus, whatever else one can say about Philo, he was enjoying the rare company of a white lady, a lady – he must have realized – who enjoyed and coveted his company! Hence they sauntered out, both trying to think "what legitimate alternative way can we find to spend more time together?"

They walked past two nurses, talking in rather loud voices. One said to her friend *"nonyise en gi cancer, to ne ok en cancer, ne en aena malaria."*

Her friend was amazed by that report.

"Nodhi ka nowacho obiro dere. To ne wadich ok ne wanyalo konye," the nurse added to her friend, who continued to express amazement.

"Some poor fellow was told yesterday that he had cancer," Philo told Mel just as a means of chatting to her, "but he only had malaria. Having been given the cancer diagnosis, he said he was going to commit suicide. Yesterday, everyone was too busy to do follow up on that case, so the fellow ..."

"Really!" Mel interrupted. "I saw the man yesterday as he left! That is terrible" she added. "Has he been found?" she asked.

"Don't think so. Wait, I'll ask," Philo responded. He asked the nurses. They did not know.

"What was the man's name?"

"Mlula."

"Where does he live?"

"Msufa estate," and that is all they knew.

"Not found. What do you say, Mel? Let's try, eh?"

"Yes," said Mel.

Once out of the hospital, they came to an area of small shops. Philo asked a shopkeeper; "Would you know Msufa estate?" The shopkeeper was peering out from a crowded front to his little shop. Hanging on the wire mesh that served to prevent anyone from grabbing items should the shopkeeper turn his back were endless 'trinkets' on display.

"Yes," he said. He gave Philo and Mel directions. It was twenty minutes' walk to the edge of the estate.

They set off marching. Mel told me later, she was thinking 'finally.' She had longed to spend time alone with Philo. Now they were hardly 'alone' in one respect – they were walking around slum areas in this African city. The slums were densely populated. Children were everywhere. Little shops, women selling things sat on the roadside, men sitting and talking, bicycles, goats, dogs – much company and much paraphernalia! They were 'alone' insofar as they had no other white people with them. Part of Mel would much rather have been alone with Philo shopping in Harrods in London, perhaps walking in Scotland, or somewhere romantic like Paris.

On the other hand, if she was seriously contemplating offering life-long companionship to Philo, she needed to better understand him in context. Walking around an African slum seemed to offer the best prospects for doing that! It was the kind of place one might imagine Whites would be warned not to go to. That didn't seem to be Philo's concern. His concern perhaps was – the constantly repeated amazement expressed to him regarding his fluency in the Swahili and Striden languages. This was undoubtedly tiresome for him, and would become so for Mel. That amazement did illustrate just how rare it is to have a white man take African ways and languages seriously.

As they walked towards the slum, Mel asked Philo: "How has your trip gone so far?"

"Very slow!" Philo responded.

"Slow?" Mel asked.

"Yes, I mean, not much happens. Things happen slowly. As a Westerner one wants appointments and activities to be in quick succession; bang, bang, bang. Here it seems one should not anticipate getting more than one thing done in a day. The rest of the day one is likely to be sitting around."

Mel reflected on that. It's not what one wanted to hear from a missionary! One wants to hear of his great accomplishments! How busy he is! How much he is the center of attention! How, as soon as he arrives, lives are transformed around him. That's not what Philo talked about. Well, though

– Mel had seen another side of the coin of 'busy' missionary life at each of the stops so far. "Perhaps slow but steady wins the race," she thought.

"As soon as you start running ahead of people, then if you don't have money, well, they stop following you," Philo said.

It was time for Philo to complain. That's one effect that Mel had on him. Now he was relaxed with her. More relaxed, perhaps, than he had been with many people for a long time. (And there they were, walking to a slum. Maybe that also made Philo relaxed, Mel thought.)

"Things never seem to work," said Philo. "Things never go to plan. Unless, that is, you don't have a plan!"

Philo was quiet for a while. Mel let him think.

"You know one of the most depressing sides of ministry in Africa?" Philo asked.

"No," said Mel. Their feet were stepping in tandem as she said that, even though Mel was considerably shorter than Philo.

"It's that it doesn't happen the way it says in the glossy magazines, or the 'development' books, or the missionary manuals!"

Mel almost laughed out loud at that point. She had in recent days had some insights into what one might call 'missionary deception'! She'd seen the struggles that a few missionaries are going through. She'd seen how they are self-inflicted. That is – Westerners set themselves targets as to what they will do in Africa that are impractical. Then they are required to report as if they are doing what they said they'd be doing. They report castles in the sky while getting depressed about realities on the ground. "Perhaps Philo is intentionally painting me a negative picture," Mel thought, "to make sure that I don't get an over-inflated impression of what he achieves here."

By that time it felt as if they had reached the boundary to where Mlula might be living. Hence Philo began asking people, "Do you know someone called Mlula, who has recently been sick and diagnosed with cancer?"

"Yes," someone said eventually. Well, that was encouraging.

"Can we see them? Are they around?" we asked.

"Yes, yes."

There began an incredible trek! What made it incredible was not the distance covered or even the pace at which we were led. It was that our guide seemed familiar with every nook and cranny in the entire place! We cut every corner. This took us under everyone's washing line. Right through everyone's back yard. Everywhere were people sitting and talking.

"No wonder slums are places of poverty if people spend all their time talking," Mel thought, she told me later.

There were chickens everywhere. Suddenly, in the middle of washing lines and children playing and wearing rags, there was an enormous sow! Agriculture wasn't left out in the village. Neither was it separate from the people. People lived with their animals in the middle of residential slums.

"You know, Mel," Philo said, "if you are a foreigner, local people always know better than you do."

As Philo said that, yet another group of children shouted at us, *'wazungu'* (white people), and started running after us, laughing. (Either laughing at us blundering fools stumbling through their homes, or just generally laughing about us!)

"We are always behind. It is like being a child. Now, you may think I know a lot about Africa. For a white person, possibly I do, but compared to local people I am so ignorant! Like, you see all the children laughing at us? They know that!"

Walking through people's yards didn't seem to trouble our guide.

"Sometimes barely-dressed women were rather shocked to emerge from their door and meet strange people like us face-to-face," said Mel later.

Eventually our guide, a lad maybe of twenty-one, tall and smart looking, said, "Come in." (Well, he said "*donji!*")

We stooped through the door. Inside the house made of mud covered by cracking cement, we found a few chairs around a low table. Our guide, who the people in the house called 'Ayub,' indicated that we could sit, which we did, once we'd prayed. Ayub talked to someone behind a sheet that was hung from the ceiling, that divided the small one-room house into two. We heard some muffled groans. The creaking of a bed. The sheet moved. This was presumably as the man on the bed swung his legs down alongside the bed. He was not moving quickly. Eventually he emerged, bent double, evidently in some pain. He sat in one of the seats. Mel estimated that he might have been sixty years old.

Mel told me that Philo talked with him. He gave her occasional summaries of what they said. The old man, called Mlula, was staying here in the home of his grandson Ayub in Msufa estate. He was a farmer. He had started getting sick about a year before. He had been diagnosed with cancer. The hospital told him there was no treatment. He was going to a herbalist for medication. In a couple of days, he was to go back to his farm. It seemed evident that would be the last journey of his life. When Philo asked him if he had been at the hospital the day before, the old man did not seem to know what he was talking about. Philo looked at Ayub.

"He was at the hospital two weeks ago," said Ayub.

"But I told you we were looking for someone who might have been misdiagnosed as having cancer yesterday." Philo presumably said.

"I thought you might be able to help my grandad," said Ayub!

Two white people wandering around was too big a temptation, it seemed. Ayub probably impressed his grandad that he has wealthy friends. The fact that he was not helping us to find the person we were looking for was no issue to Ayub.

"I am glad that Philo was able to encourage Mlula," Mel told me. "Then we were on our way again!"

Mel had not known that she could feel so good in a slum, she told me later! To be in a slum with Philo was better than in the Ritz with anyone else, she thought. Maybe Philo's presence was like an immunization. It stopped her fathoming all that was going on around her. Mel went on: "Just then, another man came to us as we walked. Somehow, he perceived that Philo worked as a pastor."

"He asked me to come with him and pray for his wife" Philo explained.

The house was nearby. There we found a woman, heavily pregnant, in the early stages of labor. Philo led us in a song, either in Swahili or Striden, then prayed for the woman. At that point, the man seemed happy for us to go on again. Prayer is what he was looking for.

"I was really proud of Philo just then," Mel told me later.

"You were proud of Philo?" I asked her. "But he never left any help for the people you had visited?" I added.

"No," she said.

"How do you keep a list of appropriate encouraging messages?" Philo asked Mel. It was a rhetorical question. "Suddenly you are there in a situation of calamity. People look to you to encourage them. In my mind at times like that, I can draw a blank," Philo said. "Other people seem to know all the Psalms off by heart. They know just what to say and when. Thankfully, God always seems to give me a word, but it's not easy!"

Mel went on "We asked, or rather Philo asked, a lady washing clothes, if she knew a Mlula who had been to hospital the previous day and had been diagnosed with cancer?"

She had what seemed to Mel an enormous pile of dirty clothes in front of her. She was bent double while washing, with a baby attached to her back. Behind her, a TV was blaring out through the door of her small house. Philo and Mel could hear men in the house, talking with raised voices, apparently drunk.

"Pay me and I will tell you," she said, Mel explained to me.

"You know?" Philo said (presumably). "No money," Philo added.

"Can't help you then," must have been her response.

We went on.

"Needle in a haystack," thought Mel at that point!

"Have you ever slept with bed bugs?" Philo then asked Mel.

"I first thought he was asking me if I'd ever slept with a man. I had an answer ready on my lips: no. Instead, he talked of bed bugs!" Mel told me later. "No, I haven't, and don't desire to either," Mel responded. "Then I realized that might not have been the right answer," Mel went on to say.

"That's my battle," said Philo. "The idea of having the little critters just come and take a feed when they feel like it as one lies in bed is not an attractive one, but it is the reality. It seems here that all the beds have bed bugs."

"I'm disqualified!" Mel said she had thought!

"Get a man, enjoy his bed bugs," I mused. Poor Mel! I had thought Philo might just sleep with bed bugs and not care. Now I realized he was not quite such a toughie after all!

"Do you know a man …," Philo asked another woman if she knew Mlula. Instead of responding to his question, this woman reacted in amazement, how a white man like Philo could know such good Swahili.

"That was another much-repeated experience," Mel told me. "Instead of having conversations on matters in hand, people wanted to talk about how he, a white man, could know such good Swahili. I think Philo gets tired of those conversations," Mel added.

Mel realized that whereas English was like a language for everyone, languages like Swahili and Striden were considered to be exclusive to Africans. Whatever secrets those languages held were for Africans only! Philo was breaking the mold. Whether people understood 'why' was another matter. It had also cost him. Few of the Africans there in Kosompa could imagine how he lived, I thought.

The prominence of discarded packets of alcohol was a discouraging feature of slum life, Mel found. Wherever they walked, the little empty packets seem to be scattered about. Also scattered hither and thither were used condoms. Some children would pick up and play with them, not knowing what they were. Open sewers were another standard feature of life. Philo and Mel were constantly jumping over smelly stagnant water that contained goodness-knows-what.

"If you want a man to reveal his heart, put him with a woman who likes him," I thought. Mel gave me some insights into Philo's life that I might not have got any other way. While we were much amazed by his exploits, the pace of life could be excruciatingly slow for Philo. Often he seemed to do nothing! There was also a prescription there for Westerners: expect to be frustrated by things not happening! In the West, it is all about achieving and getting things moving. In Africa, in Philo's experience, it is not.

"Sometimes people say to someone on the phone that they are busy," Philo told Mel, "when they're sitting waiting for two hours doing nothing, expecting a meal to be cooked. That is 'busy'!" So, Philo's advice was to carry with you something to do or you might go crazy! For Philo, that is a book to read or a letter to write. Whether that means that Westerners should spend their time in Africa playing on their smart-phones – I never got a straight answer from Philo on that one. Philo probably thought reading and writing were more constructive pursuits than are computer games.

A young man approached Philo and Mel. He was wearing a tracksuit, Mel told me. English flowed smoothly off the man's tongue. Mel felt good. Then she felt guilty about feeling good! The impact of having an African speak clear English, and be able to laugh with the white man, was almost hypnotic to her.

"Aren't you afraid?" he asked.

"Of what?" Mel responded.

"There's a lot of desperate people here," he said. "Many white people fear walking around slums like these."

Mel wanted to say that she didn't fear while Philo was with her. She resisted.

The young man explained that he had lived the last ten years in New Zealand. His father was there with the Holima government.

"That explains his English," Mel thought.

The man in the tracksuit, which had *Nike* written on the front and back in big letters, invited Philo and Mel to his home. Mel was about to give a default 'yes!' She'd finally found a Holiman she felt relaxed with.

"Feel free if you want to," said Philo.

"Aha," thought Mel. "Philo isn't interested in following people who happen to know good English."

Mel politely declined. It made a nice change for Mel, though, to be the one talking instead of having to glean all her insights from Philo. She realized, though, that for Philo, he might have been a con man. From Philo's point of view – why go with someone just because he knows English?

Mel later told me another thing that she learned on walking through that slum with Philo. She had always thought that slums must be shocking places. Indeed, it was shocking for her to walk around there in Kosompa. People living in that slum did not keep to many western norms of behavior. They compromised on things that to Westerners are basic. For example, instead of finding people, as she had somehow anticipated, struggling and desperate to get running water to their homes, she found those whose whole way of life was simply oriented to the assumption that water was something you carried to your house on your head.

"Something has died," said Mel. Moments later Philo noticed it. A dog had died. It still lay on the side of the road, as it rotted in the hot sun. No one seemed to bother with it. Not many yards away were two or three women sat on the roadside selling tomatoes and kale. A bit further on, another was frying fish in oil. That's how many of the roadsides were! Next to the lady frying fish was another roasting maize cobs. Then there was a group of men repairing motorbikes – just out under the sun. After that, a place where you could sit under a tin roof to eat a *chapati*, or something similar. Then another hut, a woman would enter to have her hair braided. Then a shop selling home provisions – soaps, matches, margarine, school exercise books, pens, mosquito coils, cooking oil, phone credit, and you-name-it.

The last person Philo asked for information on the person with cancer was the lady in that final small shop.

"Don't know," she said.

Mel and Philo had drawn a blank. Mel was still about the happiest lady in town, however, for reasons my reader can probably guess. As they drew their search to a close and were headed back to the German mission, Philo commented. "I really like you, Mel," he said, and he smiled to her. Thus he made Mel's day.

CHAPTER 43: AID CHAOS

Unbeknown to us at the time, as we were driving through the rain to the German mission in Kosompa, Wycliffe, a Norwegian working with NORAID (Norwegian Aid) was on the phone to Oslo. Wycliffe was attending the conference in Kosompa when the rain came. He was tall and skinny and typical Norwegian in appearance (at least I thought so), who in his life sought for fame, but fame had always seemed to evade him. His hair was butterscotch, somewhere between blond and brown.

"This is an emergency. I am on the ground," he had said at the time to Adhula, who was in Oslo.

"How many trucks?" Adhula asked.

"Send three," he said, "to arrive here tomorrow."

"Yes, tomorrow morning and afternoon," was Adhula's confident response.

"Let them call me when they are an hour away," Wycliffe told Adhula.

After his phone-call, and doing other town business, Wycliffe went back to his conference accommodation. He was not prepared for what he saw. His room, and the rooms of many of his colleagues, were in up to a foot of water! He ran to grab his laptop bag. He had left it leaning on a table leg. There was no point. Absolutely sodden! There were four of them staying in that room. His three colleagues must still have been at the conference. They were probably advised, rightly so too, to stay put while the heavens opened. They would still be naively ignorant of the devastation caused in their house. Wycliffe realized why their home was in a worse state than that of others. Ironically, a gutter had dislocated in such a way that it had poured water into their dining room through an open window! Wycliffe stashed his belongings and those of his colleagues onto the kitchen table.

"They had not been so stupid as to leave their computers on the floor," he thought to himself. Although – earlier that day, no one would have considered that the floor wasn't a wise place to leave a computer!

Fortunately, Wycliffe knew his wife had a friend staying there in Kosompa. Moments later he was on the phone to his wife. "My computer is lost, but I'm okay," he told her. "Look. Please give me contact with Iris. I am hoping she will be able to accommodate us. I know accommodation in town is chockablock."

His wife did so, and Iris called him back. "Come," she said. "We have a spare house." That is how Wycliffe and his three friends came to stay at the German mission that evening.

Wycliffe was quite chuffed at his organizational ability. He had been mostly office-bound in Norway, but now he had the opportunity to be on the front line of aid distribution. Shortly after Mel and Philo had set off to see the hospital, Wycliffe arrived, and Iris introduced him to us. The most noticeable thing about Wycliffe was, without doubt, his prolific mop of butterscotch hair. I couldn't help but think that surely amongst his forefathers were the Vikings, who invaded England in who knows when. Wycliffe's colleagues had gone back to the conference. So, he was alone – waiting for his trucks to arrive. When he found us there, also at a bit of a loose end, he was overjoyed. "Why don't you come and help me hand out the aid?" Wycliffe said to us over a cup of coffee.

"Handing out aid? No way!" was my reaction.

Not so my colleagues, however. "Sounds like a splendid idea," said Darren loudly, and I think he meant 'splendid' by way of putting on a show.

"I'll join you too," said Sam.

Wycliffe was helping Iris wash the dishes when his phone rang. He quickly dried his hands and picked up his phone. "One hour and the first truck will arrive. You'll meet it?" asked the voice.

"Sure thing. At the junction," Wycliffe responded.

The three musketeers set off on their adventure. Now I don't know if they, especially Sam, might have been thinking, "Let's embarrass Philo by showing how we can bring in *real help*." It was in my mind though. This ought to be Sam in his element, implementing wealth distribution from the West! Then Wycliffe, equally excited, plus a media mogul to make up their number. In no time they were in their taxi and on their way. Wycliffe was sure, he told me later, that his truck would be one of the first to arrive at this site, the city that had been hit by a flooding disaster.

"I hope you are going to take notes and will give us a good write up," Wycliffe said to Darren, as he buckled his seatbelt.

"I'm ready," he responded.

"How on earth are we going to do this, the distribution I mean?" asked Sam in due course.

"We have police officers coming. All we need to do is to locate ourselves near the worst hit areas, then we set up a stall and begin handing out."

"Okay," said Sam.

Wycliffe seemed to know what he was doing. They had the driver park the truck.

"Where are the police?" asked Sam. No one in sight!

"Hmm," said Wycliffe.

Wycliffe was on the phone again. There were signs of flood devastation all around them, and not a few curious people eyeing up the truck. "One item per person. You," Wycliffe said to Darren, "record names and pictures. Sam – you're in the truck passing things. I'll ask what someone wants and hand it to them."

They beckoned. A few men came, then a few women. They began the process. Darren was keeping a careful check that there would be no repeats. A line formed. This went on for about half an hour. Then the queue got noisy. What can I say – from the description I was given chaos broke out! By now a large crowd had arrived. People came to get their items, but then others stole them before they could walk away. A lady jumped the queue. Another got angry. Then a young man elbowed an older man. The latter fell. When he did, another man castigated the youth. He got thumped for his efforts.

The queue disappeared. Instead, now there was a crush, hands stretched out, about fifty hands, Sam thought. People shouting. They could not understand what. Noise.

"Get in the truck," Wycliffe said. He and Darren scrambled to join Sam.

"Go, driver," Wycliffe shouted at the top of his voice.

Fortunately, the driver was in his seat and knew what to do. He started the engine and blew his horn full blast at the same time as he abruptly slipped the clutch, causing the truck to lurch forward like a pouncing lion while screaming like a bull elephant! Caught off guard, the crowd in front of the truck ran in fright. The driver took advantage and accelerated. By this time people were banging on the side of the truck. As they sped off, stones were thrown, some landing noisily on top of the truck, Darren later told me. The driver drove quickly. He knew exactly where was the only safe-spot in town – he drove straight into the police station, his passengers being violently thrown back and fore behind him as he made his way there.

At least Wycliffe thought quickly. "Adhula. Tell the other trucks straightaway to turn back. They must not come to Kosompa!" he shouted over the phone, even before we had come to a halt.

Then began a protracted conversation with the Kosompa police. One could say that they had the upper hand. "The three of you into remand right now," said the police officer, "and the truck we keep."

Those might have been scare tactics, but they worked. I won't pretend to explain all that happened because I'm not sure I know. Yet, $1,000 to the police officer in charge, Wycliffe told me later, to waive the case for disturbing the peace. Another $1,000 for a police escort that should have been free, and help in distributing the remaining aid on that truck. It was the $400 to Darren that surprised me most, which was offered to him not to report on the incident. Was it common to have to do that? I don't know. Did aid agencies regularly pay the media, to cover their tracks when things went wrong?

"Thank goodness the other two trucks turned back before they got into town," Wycliffe told me later.

* * *

Wycliffe might have thought that was the end of his troubles for a while. But then he was about to have another think coming! Later, back at the German mission, he was telling his story. We had not, up to then, realized just how astute was Noel, Iris's husband. While he might have seemed quiet and unassuming, we found that he did not suffer fools lightly.

"You did what!" Noel exclaimed when Wycliffe told him what had happened. Wycliffe's three colleagues, all experts in development, were with him at the time. They might have been experts in the comfort of their own universities. Here, on the ground in an African city, however, as the boxing match raged, they got a lot more punches to the head than I think they'd ever anticipated! Noel was amazing. I guess you could say brilliant! I sat in awe as the discussion progressed, and Noel systematically dismantled the theories that our flood-victim colleagues from the conference were presenting. Philo seemed similarly in awe. Western experts with fat budgets, wanting to displace people's own efforts at thriving with foreign aid, were that day knocked off their prestigious pedestal, at least within the confines of a sitting room in a German mission station in the city of Kosompa in Holima!

Sam sat quietly, but I suspect attentively, through Noel's demolition of Wycliffe and his colleagues' arguments for western intervention into Africa. Much that he heard were the kinds of things that we were glad for him to know. I, at least, was especially pleased that it was not coming from us, but from our host, an expatriate resident in Kosompa.

CHAPTER 44: AERIAL VIEW, TRANSFORMATION

"Will you join me tomorrow?" Sam said to Philo in due course. Sam had been maneuvring to find the right opportunity to pop an important question to Philo. He found it as Philo was using a laptop to catch up on correspondence. They were both outside the house in the German mission compound, enjoying the fresh air. Sam sat next to Philo. Philo gave him his attention, wondering what he was to be joining him for.

"We are to do a survey of the aid needs of the city," said Sam to Philo.

"Now," I thought, "how is Sam going to convince Philo to be involved in that?"

Philo didn't respond verbally. His eyes seemed to ask, "Just what are you inviting me to join you to do, Sam?"

"We have arranged for a balloon to fly over the city. We have photographic experts who want to improve the clarity of the digital imagery already available by satellite. We plan to make three trips over the city. We'll take advantage of the very regular westerly wind. There are two available 'pedestrian' places in the basket under the balloon. Will you join me there for a bird's-eye view of Kosompa?"

"If there's one thing that can make me nervous," Philo said, "then it is the prospect of being suspended in mid-air!" Yet, he told me later, he did not want to be quick to refuse an opportunity to spend time with Sam, whatever shape that was going to take. Up in a balloon, taking pictures of Msufa slums, was not an option he had even thought of! But – Philo had a few more days on 'white man's territory' before he reimmersed himself into African milieu. Sam had to come a long way, and a part, at least, of his intentions was to spend time with Philo.

"I'll come," said Philo. "What time tomorrow?"

"They'll pick us up at 8 a.m."

Philo tells me he did not sleep well. Instead, he kept dreaming about breaking through a hole in the basket of a balloon, and free falling through the air till he crashed through the roof of some old man in a slum! Philo tried to put on a brave face for breakfast. He probably needed some kind of pill to calm his nerves! I didn't have any of those pills.

Then at eight o'clock, a truck turned up outside the window. Off went Philo and Sam. The latter was relaxed and joking. Philo was a little paler than usual.

At the same time as having butterflies in his tummy, Philo said he was also excited at the prospect of having free balloon rides! That was a bonus he had not anticipated during his Kosompa stay.

As they drove, Sam told him various things, Philo shared with me later. "He even told me about his mom!" Philo said. It was not only us who had discovered that Sam and his mom had a very particular relationship. One had to pity Sam's wife when his mom kept elbowing her way into their activities. Sam had nothing contrary to say about his wife though, so we could only assume that he was happily married. Sam had spent some time the previous day talking with Rolly. Rolly and Sam went back a long way. Perhaps that conversation had done something to prepare Sam for what he was going to say today? Rolly had told Sam that they had been shadowing Philo without Philo's knowledge! I can only guess that this had intrigued and challenged Sam – that someone would go so much out of their way to avoid white company, said something about the reputation of Whites in Africa!

The truck arrived at the site of the balloon launch. Not unexpectedly, there was a considerable crowd of onlookers wanting to see what was going to happen. The research team had already done most of their preparation by the time Sam and Philo arrived. What remained was to inflate the balloon. As the hot air went in, like a miracle indeed, up went the balloon, till it towered above them, filling the sky. It was a fantastic sight – especially for someone who had not previously been to a balloon launch.

The first pass was to be to the south of the city. Wind speed was about 8 mph, perhaps a bit faster than they had hoped, but not problematic. The camera gear was evident in the base of the balloon. Two technicians, from the USA, were taking pictures. Up and to one side was a compartment for two additional people to enjoy the ride!

"All aboard," said the boss – identifiable by his orange overall. He was to fly the balloon. The two technicians, young men in their twenties who looked a bit like one would imagine computer geeks look like, climbed in. The man in the orange overall followed, then Sam and Philo occupied the 'spectators' balcony,' as Philo called it.

"We disconnected, and began to rise. The sensation was a strange one. Very different from that of a plane," Philo told me later. Whenever the burner was turned off things were incredibly quiet and tranquil. Once in the air, Philo's butterflies flew away, he told me. The men began talking about various things. Then it became evident, however, that this balloon trip was a strategy adopted by Sam to get a captive audience with Philo. As they talked, the African city and beyond it was visible clear as a bell (partly as the rain had reduced the dust). The African savannah stretched out for miles.

Sam wanted to make sure he started on a positive note. "We have reinstated Rolly," he said to Philo. We had told Philo that Rolly had been fired, as he could no longer track with the expressed vision of his bosses.

"Reinstated!" Philo said. That was good news! Philo was aware that Rolly had been very concerned as to what on earth he would do after the end of this trip. Now he was catered for! "What a relief," thought Philo. "But then," he thought, "does that mean Rolly has reverted to his previous 'unenlightened' way of thinking?"

Mostly the men paused their conversation whenever the burner was turned on. That gave ample opportunity to take in and enjoy the unique vista on display around them.

"We have reinstated him," Sam went on to explain, "as a result of the way that we have been convinced about the importance of the work you are doing. We have come to understand that we were foolish to ignore what you have been trying to do with such dedication."

At that point, Philo told me, he was concerned that he might float up and out of the basket into the sky! To hear a serious player in the whole field of international relations and charitable endeavor from the USA say that, was like an answer to thirty years of dreaming!

"Therefore, we have reinstated Rolly, with the mandate that he encourages the practice that you have been describing as vulnerable mission." Sam paused.

"It is strange that one can do something that seems obvious, even the only and logical thing to do. How we cannot see our own blind spot," Sam added. "Well. We have now seen one of our blind spots."

Philo did not say anything. He wanted Sam to carry on.

"We Westerners are determined to act as global policeman, and as global advocates for human rights, development, you name it. But – we have worked in the light of an enormous ignorance. That is, we have simply wanted everyone to become like us, and assumed that they will and must do as such. We have not considered ourselves to have any serious obligations to be-like-them."

"That's how Sam put it," Philo explained to me later.

"Now, we have nodded in that direction. I mean – we have said we want to listen to people in the majority world. But – only ever in English. We have even endeavored to recruit people from the majority world, notably Africa, into our structures. But – never the reverse. It has always been one-sided. It has always been 'you come to us,' never 'we come to you,' culturally speaking. You, Philo, have demonstrated how to do the latter."

"It was as if a load was lifted off my shoulders at that point," Philo told me later. "Tears came to my eyes."

"We have started to look carefully at what you have said and written. We agree with you – that it is far from adequate just to rely on what majority world nationals tell us for purposes of our evaluations regarding what to do and how. We must have Westerners immerse themselves into majority world cultures. That cannot be just for a year as do anthropologists. It must be for ten years or more. And it must be on a vulnerable basis, as you have often aptly described. This is more a role for Christian mission than for universities. Universities cannot do it! They are too loaded by other demands, especially by their budgets, given the way they operate. We need vulnerable people committed to serving God, Philo. People like you."

"Sam paused. We looked around. I was almost too choked up to speak," said Philo.

"We have a budget of $5 million to start this project. Rolly is to be the chief executive. We want you to be chief advisor. Another thing to mention straightaway," Sam added, "is that you need to understand. Although – I think you will be in favor anyway – is that some of this new orientation needs to kick in, while other mission and development activities continue. This is where we need your advice: how will vulnerable missionaries relate to others?"

A pause.

"With all the above we hope to be active, with immediate effect, against the fear of racism that has gripped our world today. We must learn to accept difference, and to relate with people who are different, other than just by trying to squeeze them into our shape! Not just by trying to squeeze other races into American shape, but also by squeezing Americans into the shape of other races."

"Somehow, hearing all that was thoroughly exhausting! By the time Sam had finished what he was saying, our balloon was on its way down on the far side of the city," Philo told me. Philo was still trying to process what Sam had said to him while they were flying high above the slums of Kosompa! The same crew that had launched them was waiting for them. They were an experienced outfit, and soon had the balloon packed into the truck, so that all could return to the West of the city. An hour later all were in the air again.

"This time, it being midday, the balloon shaded us from the sun. Our balloon was a rainbow – that is to say, it was multicolored. We could see our shadow below us. As we passed over the city, endless heads, of course, turned, looking up at us gliding over them. Just a day before, I was walking back and fore in one of those slums," Philo reminded me. "Being up in the sky seemed to be a conducive place for conversation," Philo said. "There was also the camera crew busy operating their instruments. Given the kind of equipment available these days, I wondered just how well they could see. For example – 'could they read a newspaper that someone laid on the ground'? I don't know the answer to that question!"

"I very much appreciated what you said during our last flight," Philo started saying to Sam. Then Philo told me what he went on to say. That is – Philo was not about promoting a methodology or a strategy but a person. That was the person of Jesus. Although he had appreciated what Sam had said, that must remain central. Jesus gave his life on the cross. That is the message he wanted to take to the people.

"By that time, I could see the city center looming in front of us," Philo told me.

Philo's issue was – how can we be sure that the activity of generous western donors in Africa was communicating faith in Jesus? Was it not talking about largesse? Was it not bamboozling people with technology and strength? How could that be compatible with Jesus, who had walked on the shores of Galilee? Sam had told Philo that they were ready to invest

$5 million into vulnerability by Westerners in mission. Philo was coming back to him, in a sense saying that was not enough.

Philo went on to say: "I am not trying to sound ungrateful. I am excited by your proposal, that you will be making a serious effort at promoting vulnerable mission. What I am saying is – that give an inch and you might lose a mile! Money is no substitute for people who are ready to give their lives."

"We will be looking into all these issues you are raising," said Sam. "We already have proposals that theologians should be engaged in the prayerful but critical evaluation of the role of vulnerability in mission."

"What kind of theologian?" Philo asked.

"What do you mean, Philo?" Sam responded.

"I mean, the theologians you are talking about will be western theologians?" Philo was feeling uneasy. He didn't like to 'clash' with people in this way. Sometimes it was like he had to.

"I see," said Sam. "Well yes, but we also have church leaders and theologians from all over the world we can draw on."

"Let's put it this way, Sam: what will be the language used in this theological engagement?"

"Well, English of course," Sam said. "What else do you expect?" he asked laughing.

"English-speaking theologians making decisions in English ways using English language and English culture. Then their decisions will be binding, and they will be deciding on the money to be used?" Philo asked.

"Well, yes," said Sam.

"So, what about other languages?"

"What about them?"

"What chance do other languages have, as long as English, the language of money, dominates? But how will it not dominate as long as English is associated with money?"

"I see," Sam said. "So what are you proposing, Philo?"

"That I can't be an official advisor on those issues," said Philo.

Sam was shocked. "Why not Philo? Don't you see – we need you!" Sam was going out of his way to 'include' Philo, and Philo was backing down!

"No, you don't need me," Philo said. "You need the Holy Spirit, not me! We need people to repent. You do not need a five-million-dollar project to park alongside other existing projects. What we need is repentance across the board."

"Repentance of what?" Sam asked.

"Repentance for sins of all sorts. Especially the sin of idolatry – taking the place of God, on the part of the West."

"How do we repent?" Sam asked.

Philo had to think about that for a while. "What you have proposed is good," Philo said. "Do it. As I said – don't expect me to be centrally involved. You can read what I have written. Hopefully, that will help you. I am not an important person for you though."

"I see," said Sam. He was looking blankly ahead of himself at that point. That wasn't a happy 'I see.'

"You know, Dave," Philo said to me later. "I did not intend to say all that. It just came out. I wanted to agree with Sam, and agree to be an advisor. I might have agreed to spend a month in America to share my wisdom. I think the Holy Spirit did not want me to go via that route. I have had to ask myself subsequently: 'why?' I think it is that – what is built on money won't survive. We needn't build on $5 million. Better speak to two people in their home, and that they be convinced, than to make all the impact that one wants with $5 million."

"Are you sure?" I asked Philo. "What about creating a badly needed language school?"

"I am not sure," he responded, "but that is what the Spirit seems to be saying to me." Philo paused. "I think I can see the reason for that," he added. "Once something is dependent on western donor money, then it will become captive to a certain logic. That is the logic to which I think we should not become captive. In other words, what I am saying is, that the promotion of vulnerable mission can't be a project. It must be a movement!"

"Yes, but projects are part of the substance of movements," I reminded him.

"Indeed, I am not against the project. It looks like decisions have been made. Good. That doesn't mean that I, or we, have to become part of them. When you think about it, Dave, that wasn't Jesus' way of doing things. If he had been more project-oriented, he might have postponed his crucifixion for ten years. Then he'd have had more time to 'do things.' Instead, he was crucified. Thus he was removed from 'the project.'"

It was probably at that point that I realized that Philo was a prophet!

What Philo did not say at that point, it seemed to me, was things that he had explained to me in the past. That is – from the West, vulnerable mission does not seem to make sense. It makes sense once one gets to be familiar with contexts of majority-world ministry. Hence, if Philo stands up to proclaim vulnerable mission in the West, he easily fights a losing battle. Hence, while Philo might be able to advise Sam's project, he wanted to avoid being their 'advisor'! As for his words, regarding repentance of the West, I thought that was interesting. Very interesting. A movement. Yes!

* * *

That evening, Wycliffe was set to make an announcement. The following day he and his colleagues were due to return to their accommodation at the conference center. The conference was to last for one more night. "Ladies and gentlemen," he said, "I hereby invite you …"

It was 7 p.m. when there was a banging on the door. Most of us started, as we were not expecting anyone else to arrive and join us.

Iris went to the door. A couple walked in. It was Gary and Gail! I remembered they had said that they might make it to Kosompa. Now we were merrier than ever! Introductions went on, and Gary and Gail joined our circle. They had become close to my heart very fast as a result of the amazing things we had been going through. We noticed Wycliffe phoning someone. "Two extra!" he said.

"Ladies and Gentlemen," Wycliffe started again, "I hereby invite you all, Gary and Gail included, to join our fellow conference-goers for the closing banquet at our esteemed Kosompa conference tomorrow evening. You are invited to reach the conference center at seven o'clock. The cost of your meal is covered. Just tell me please, if there is anyone here who will not be attending?" The response was silence.

The next night was to be our last night together. The following morning, Philo was to take the road again in his more 'lonely' travels. He had two more major stops to come before going back to his Holiman home. Our time was also up – we were done with our secret shadowing of Philo!

At about 6.45 p.m. we set off in convoy for the conference center. All our group was put around one large table. We were like the honored guests of the larger group. I guess there were about a hundred people there in all. The conference-goers put on some entertainment for us all as we began our meal.

Gary took the initiative to do the last thing that needed doing. While we were waiting for our cups of coffee and dessert, he whispered to Philo, "Philo. Follow me."

Philo seemed surprised but followed him. Gary found a space in the corner of the hall where there were three empty seats. He motioned to Philo to sit beside him. Philo obliged.

"Philo," Gary said, "have you been observing Mel at all?"

"Yes. What is going on?" Philo responded.

Gary had thought about how to engage this conversation. He had decided to be blunt. "Do you like her?"

Philo took a deep breath. "She is a beautiful girl and has a beautiful soul."

"She likes you too," Gary said. Philo was quiet. He really did like Mel's company! Philo was stroking his chin. "Do you have anything to say to her before you part company?" Gary asked Philo.

Philo then took the initiative. He walked to our table. He touched Mel's shoulder. "Mel, please come and join us," he said. Mel obliged. There were the three of them sat in a circle, or more like a huddle. By this point in the proceedings, a Holiman guitarist was sitting on the stage, singing to the accompaniment of a few traditional instruments. Mel had been unable to hear the words, but frequent repetition of the term '*Yesu*' made her realize that they were Christian songs. Some of the other people there at the banquet were talking in low voices. They were no doubt enjoying listening to the worship songs being performed, with or without a cup or dessert in their hands. The effect of the songs was powerful.

"Before we part ways, Mel, Gary suggested that we sit and talk," Philo said. Sweat was pouring from his brow as he spoke.

In that dim light, wearing the finest clothes Mel had brought with her, the dimmed lighting reflecting from her hair, Mel looked extremely glamorous.

"I want to thank you for coming, Mel," Philo said. His voice was clear, but his hands were shaking. He gathered his composure to continue. "Especially, for motivating the others to come and study mission in Africa. Your initiative has made a big difference. I want to add too, that I enjoyed our walk together in the slum looking for the victim-of-confusion, who we never found!" Philo paused, then he added quietly, "A missionary like me makes the sacrifice of his whole life to the work. When we spent our time together, I had to face what my life might have been. I thank you for that. I'll cherish the memory." Mel was breathing heavily. Philo's collar was wet with sweat.

Philo looked at Gary. Gary nodded. Philo and Gary walked back to our table. They whispered something to Rose. Rose went to put her arm around Mel. The two sat there alone like that for a long time. Philo was so choked up emotionally himself that that evening, he didn't say another word. He felt torn apart inside over what he had just done and said. He'd just rejected one who truly loved him. He felt he had had no choice.

As for me, I felt sad for Philo. I felt guilty yet also slightly hopeful. I needed to talk to Mel, at depth.

EPILOGUE

The following day, Philo continued with his journey. Gary and Gail stayed a little longer in Kosompa before returning to finish their notice-time in Michiki. In the USA, Rolly became the director of a new program, answerable to Sam and to Professor Nancy. The German missionaries stayed on in Kosompa. Darren, Mel, and I traveled back to Scotland. We were able to travel together. Mel eventually wrote her feature article. It started like this: "I had a friend in Africa. He loved God's work more than he loved himself. ..."

The following, mostly more academic books, have also been written by the author of this novel. Readers interested in the issues raised in this novel are encouraged to acquire copies to explore its key themes further:

Harries, Jim. 2011. *Vulnerable Mission: Insights into Christian Mission to Africa from a Position of Vulnerability.* Pasadena: William Carey Library.

Harries, Jim. 2011. *Three Days in the Life of an African Christian Villager.* Sandy, Bedfordshire; Authors online. (FICTION)

Harries, Jim. 2012. *From Theory to Practice in Vulnerable Mission: an academic appraisal.* Oregon: Wipf and Stock.

Harries, Jim. 2013. *Communication in Mission and Development; relating to the church in Africa.* Oregon: Wipf and Stock.

Harries, Jim. 2015, *Secularism and Africa: in the light of the Intercultural Christ.* Oregon: Wipf and Stock.

Harries, Jim, 2016, *New Foundations for Appreciating Africa: beyond religious and secular deceptions.* World of Theology Series 9, World Evangelical Alliance. Bonn: Verlag für Kultur und Wissenschaft.

Harries, Jim, 2017, *The Godless Delusion: Europe and Africa.* Oregon: Wipf and Stock.

Harries, Jim, 2018, *African Heartbeat and A Vulnerable Fool.* London: Apostolos Publishing Limited. (FICTION)

www.ingramcontent.com/pod-product-compliance
Lightning Source LLC
Chambersburg PA
CBHW071147100726
47908CB00002B/279